"Have yo[u] [...]
intense se[...]

Bailey didn't have to think long. "Not really. But I like the idea of that happening between Janice and Michael. It adds a whole new dimension to the plot."

"Oh, I'm not saying a strong reaction between them shouldn't happen," Parker said. "I'm just wondering how you plan to write such a powerfully emotional scene without any real experience of it yourself."

"Being able to create an atmosphere of romance just takes a little imagination. You don't expect me to go around kissing strange men."

"Why not? You had no qualms about following a strange man. Kissing me wouldn't be any different."

"Kissing you?"

"It'll add credibility to your writing."

"If I were writing a murder mystery would you suggest I go out and kill someone?"

"Don't be ridiculous! Murder would be out of the question, but a kiss is very much within your grasp. I suggest we go ahead with it, Bailey."

"All right," she agreed, barely recognizing her own voice.

No sooner had she spoken when Parker gently cupped her chin. "This is going to be good," she heard him whisper just before his lips settled over hers.

Debbie Macomber is a #1 *New York Times* bestselling author and a leading voice in women's fiction worldwide. Her work has appeared on every major bestseller list, with more than 170 million copies in print, and she is a multiple award winner. The Hallmark Channel based a television series on Debbie's popular Cedar Cove books. For more information, visit her website, debbiemacomber.com.

Lee Tobin McClain is the *New York Times* bestselling author of emotional small-town romances featuring flawed characters who find healing through friendship, faith and family. Lee grew up in Ohio and now lives in Western Pennsylvania, where she enjoys hiking with her goofy goldendoodle, visiting writer friends and admiring her daughter's mastery of the latest TikTok dances. Learn more about her books at leetobinmcclain.com.

MY HERO

#1 *NEW YORK TIMES* BESTSELLING AUTHOR
DEBBIE MACOMBER

H Harlequin

BESTSELLING AUTHOR COLLECTION

H Harlequin®
BESTSELLING
AUTHOR
COLLECTION

Recycling programs
for this product may
not exist in your area.

ISBN-13: 978-1-335-62977-7

My Hero
First published in 1992. This edition published in 2025.
Copyright © 1992 by Debbie Macomber

Engaged to the Single Mom
First published in 2015. This edition published in 2025.
Copyright © 2015 by Lee Tobin McClain

For questions and comments about the quality of this book, please contact
us at CustomerService@Harlequin.com.

TM and ® are trademarks of Harlequin Enterprises ULC.

Harlequin Enterprises ULC
22 Adelaide St. West, 41st Floor
Toronto, Ontario M5H 4E3, Canada
www.Harlequin.com

HarperCollins Publishers
Macken House, 39/40 Mayor Street Upper,
Dublin 1, D01 C9W8, Ireland
www.HarperCollins.com

Printed in U.S.A.

CONTENTS

Also by Debbie Macomber

MIRA

Blossom Street

Cedar Cove

Visit the Author Profile page
at Harlequin.com for more titles.

MY HERO

Debbie Macomber

For Virginia Myers, my mentor—
thanks for your friendship and encouragement!

One

The man was the source of all her problems, Bailey York decided. He just didn't cut it. The first time around he was too cold, too distant. Only a woman "who loved too much" could possibly fall for him.

The second time, the guy was a regular Milquetoast. A wimp. He didn't seem to have a single thought of his own. This man definitely needed to be whipped into shape, but Bailey wasn't sure she knew how to do it.

So she did the logical thing. She consulted a fellow romance writer. Jo Ann Davis and Bailey rode the subway together every day, and Jo Ann had far more experience in this. Three years of dealing with men like Michael.

"Well?" Bailey asked anxiously when they met on a gray, drizzly January morning before boarding San Francisco's Bay Area Rapid Transit system, or BART for short.

Jo Ann shook her head, her look as sympathetic as her words. "You're right—Michael's a wimp."

"But I've worked so hard." Bailey couldn't help feeling discouraged. She'd spent months on this, squeezing in every available moment. She'd sacrificed lunches, given up nighttime television and whole weekends. Even Christmas had seemed a mere distraction. Needless to say, her social life had come to a complete standstill.

"No one told me writing a romance novel would be so difficult," Bailey muttered, as the subway train finally shot into the station. It screeched to a halt and the doors slid open, disgorging a crowd of harried-looking passengers.

"What should I do next?" Bailey asked as she and Jo Ann made their way into one of the cars. She'd never been a quitter, and already she could feel her resolve stiffening.

"Go back to the beginning and start over again," Jo Ann advised.

"Again," Bailey groaned, casting her eyes about for a vacant seat and darting forward, Jo Ann close behind, when she located one. When they were settled, Jo Ann handed Bailey her battle-weary manuscript.

She thumbed through the top pages, glancing over the notes Jo Ann had made in the margins. Her first thought had been to throw the whole project in the garbage and put herself out of her misery, but she hated to admit defeat. She'd always been a determined person; once she set her mind to something, it took more than a little thing like characterization to put her off.

It was ironic, Bailey mused, that a woman who was such a failure at love was so interested in writing about it. Perhaps that was the reason she felt so strongly about selling her romance novel. True love had scurried past her twice, stepping on her toes both times. She'd learned her lesson the hard way. Men were wonderful to read about and to look at from afar, but when it came to involving herself in a serious relationship, Bailey simply wasn't interested. Not anymore.

"The plot is basically sound," Jo Ann assured her. "All you really need to do is rework Michael."

The poor man had been reworked so many times it was a wonder Janice, her heroine, even recognized him. And if *Bailey* wasn't in love with Michael, she couldn't very well expect Janice to be swept off her feet.

"The best advice I can give you is to re-read your favorite romances and look really carefully at how the author portrays her hero," Jo Ann went on.

Bailey heaved an expressive sigh. She shouldn't be complaining—not yet, anyway. After all, she'd only been at this a few months, unlike Jo Ann, who'd been writing and submitting manuscripts for more than three years. Personally, Bailey didn't think it would take *her* that long to sell a book. For one thing, she had more time to write than her friend. Jo Ann was married, the mother of two school-age children, plus she worked full-time. Another reason Bailey felt assured of success was that she had a romantic heart. Nearly everyone in their writers' group had said so. Not that it had done her any good when it came to finding a man of her own, but in the romance-writing business, a sensitive nature was clearly an asset.

Bailey prayed that all her creative whimsy, all her romantic perceptions, would be brilliantly conveyed on the pages of *Forever Yours*. They were, too—except for Michael, who seemed bent on giving her problems.

Men had always been an enigma to her, Bailey mused, so it was unreasonable to expect that to be any different now.

"Something else that might help you…" Jo Ann began thoughtfully.

"Yes?"

"Writers' Input recently published a book on characterization. I read a review of it, and as I recall, the author claims the best way to learn is to observe. It sounded rather abstract at the time, but I've had a chance to think about it, and you know? It makes sense."

"In other words," Bailey mused aloud, "what I really need is a model." She frowned. "I sometimes think I wouldn't recognize a hero if one hit me over the head."

No sooner had the words left her mouth than a dull object smacked the side of her head.

Bailey let out a sharp cry and rubbed the tender spot, twisting around to glare at the villain who was strolling casually past. She wasn't hurt so much as surprised.

"Hey, watch it!" she cried.

"I beg your pardon," a man said crisply, continuing down the crowded aisle. He carried a briefcase in one hand, with his umbrella tucked under his arm. As far as Bailey could determine, the umbrella handle had been the culprit. She scowled after him. The least he could've done was inquire if she'd been hurt.

"You're coming to the meeting tonight, aren't you?" Jo Ann asked. The subway came to a stop, which lowered the noise level enough for them to continue their conversation without raising their voices. "Libby McDonald's going to be there." Libby had published several popular romances and was in the San Francisco area visiting relatives. Their romance writers' group was honored that she'd agreed to speak.

Bailey nodded eagerly. Meeting Jo Ann couldn't have come at a better time. They'd found each other on the subway when Bailey noticed they were both reading the same romance, and began a conversation. She soon learned that they shared several interests; they began to meet regularly and struck up a friendship.

A week or so after their first meeting, Bailey sheepishly admitted how much she wanted to write a romance novel herself, not telling Jo Ann she'd already finished and submitted a manuscript. It was then that Jo Ann revealed that she'd written two complete manuscripts and was working on her third historical romance.

In the months since they'd met, Jo Ann's friendship had been invaluable to Bailey. Her mentor had introduced her to the local writers' group, and Bailey had discovered others all striving toward the same ultimate goal—publishing their stories. Since joining the group, Bailey had come to realize she'd made several mistakes, all typical of a novice writer, and had started the rewriting project. But unfortunately that hadn't gone well, at least not according to Jo Ann.

Bailey leafed through her manuscript, studying the notes her friend had made. What Jo Ann said made a lot of sense. "A romance hero is larger than life," Jo Ann had written in bold red ink along one margin. "Unfortunately, Michael isn't."

In the past few months, Bailey had been learning about classic romance heroes. They were supposed to be proud, passionate and impetuous. Strong, forceful men who were capable of tenderness. Men of excellent taste and impeccable style. That these qualities were too good to be true was something Bailey knew for a fact. A hero was supposed to have a burning need to find the one woman who would make his life complete.

That sounded just fine on paper, but Bailey knew darn well what men were *really* like.

She heaved an exasperated sigh and shook her head. "You'd think I'd know all this by now."

"Don't be so hard on yourself. You haven't been at this as long as I have. Don't make the mistake of thinking I have all the answers, either," Jo Ann warned. "You'll notice I haven't sold yet."

"But you will." Bailey was convinced of that. Jo Ann's historical romance was beautifully written. Twice her friend had been a finalist in a national writing competition, and everyone, including Bailey, strongly believed it was only a matter of time before a publishing company bought *Fire Dream*.

"I agree with everything you're saying," Bailey added. "I just don't know if I can do it. I put my heart and soul into this book. I can't do any better."

"Of course you can," Jo Ann insisted.

Bailey knew she'd feel differently in a few hours, when she'd had a chance to muster her resolve; by tonight she'd be revising her manuscript with renewed enthusiasm. But for now, she needed to sit back and recover her confidence. She was lucky, though, because she had Jo Ann, who'd taken the time to read *Forever Yours* and give much-needed suggestions.

Yet Bailey couldn't help thinking that if she had a model for Michael, her job would be much easier. Jo Ann used her husband, Dan. Half their writers' group was in love with him, and no one had even met the man.

Reading Jo Ann's words at the end of the first chapter, Bailey found herself agreeing once more. "Michael should be determined, cool and detached. A man of substance."

Her friend made it sound so easy. Again Bailey reflected on how disadvantaged she was. In all her life, she hadn't dated a single hero, only those who thought they were but then quickly proved otherwise.

Bailey was mulling over her dilemma when she noticed him. He was tall and impeccably dressed in a gray pin-striped suit. She wasn't an expert on men's clothing, but she knew quality when she saw it.

The stranger carried himself with an air of cool detachment. That was good. Excellent, in fact. Exactly what Jo Ann had written in the margin of *Forever Yours*.

Now that she was studying him, she realized he looked vaguely familiar, but she didn't know why. Then she got it. This was "a man of substance." The very person she was looking for...

Here she was, bemoaning her sorry fate, when lo and behold a handsome stranger strolled into her life. Not just any stranger. This man was Michael incarnate. The embodiment of everything she'd come to expect of a romantic hero. Only this version was living and breathing, and standing a few feet away.

For several minutes, Bailey couldn't keep her eyes off him. The subway cars were crowded to capacity in the early-morning rush, and while other people looked bored and uncomfortable, her hero couldn't have been more relaxed. He stood several spaces ahead of her, holding the overhead rail and reading the morning edition of the paper. His raincoat was folded over his arm and, unlike some of the passengers, he seemed undisturbed by the train's movement as it sped along.

The fact that he was engaged in reading gave Bailey the opportunity to analyze him without being detected.

His age was difficult to judge, but she guessed him to be in his mid-thirties. Perfect! Michael was thirty-four.

The man in the pin-striped suit was handsome, too. But it wasn't his classic features—the sculpted cheekbones, straight nose or high forehead—that seized her attention.

It was his jaw.

Bailey had never seen a more determined jaw in her life. Exactly the type that illustrated a touch of arrogance and a hint of audacity, both attributes Jo Ann had mentioned in her critique.

His rich chestnut-colored hair was short and neatly trimmed, his skin lightly tanned. His eyes were dark. As dark as her own were blue.

His very presence seemed to fill the subway car. Bailey was convinced everyone else sensed it, too. She couldn't understand why the other women weren't all staring at him just as raptly. The more she studied him, the better he looked. He was, without a doubt, the most masculine male Bailey had ever seen—exactly the way she'd always pictured her hero. Unfortunately she hadn't succeeded in transferring him from her imagination to the page.

Bailey was so excited she could barely contain herself. After months of writing and rewriting *Forever Yours*, shaping and reshaping the characters, she'd finally stumbled upon a real-life Michael. She could hardly believe her luck. Hadn't Jo Ann just mentioned this great new book that suggested learning through observing?

"Do you see the man in the gray pin-striped suit?" Bailey whispered, elbowing Jo Ann. "You know who he is, don't you?"

Jo Ann's eyes narrowed as she identified Bailey's hero and studied him for several seconds. She shook her head. "Isn't he the guy who clobbered you on the head with his umbrella a few minutes ago?"

"He is?"

"Who did you think he was?"

"You mean you don't know?" Bailey had been confident Jo Ann would recognize him as quickly as she had.

"*Should* I know him?"

"Of course you should." Jo Ann had read *Forever Yours*. Surely she'd recognize Michael in the flesh.

"Who do *you* think he is?" Jo Ann asked, growing impatient.

"That's Michael—my Michael," she added when Jo Ann frowned.

"Michael?" Jo Ann echoed without conviction.

"The way he was meant to be. The way Janice, my heroine, and I want him to be." Bailey had been trying to create him in her mind for weeks, and now here he was! "Can't you feel the sexual magnetism radiating from him?" she asked out of the corner of her mouth.

"Frankly, no."

Bailey decided to ignore that. "He's absolutely perfect. Can't you sense his proud determination? That commanding presence that makes him larger than life?"

Jo Ann's eyes narrowed again, the way they usually did when she was doing some serious contemplating.

"Do you see it now?" Bailey pressed.

Jo Ann's shoulders lifted in a regretful shrug. "I'm honestly trying, but I just don't. Give me a couple of minutes to work on it."

Bailey ignored her fellow writer's lack of insight. It didn't matter if Jo Ann agreed with her or not. The man in the gray suit was Michael. Her Michael. Naturally she'd be willing to step aside and give him to Janice, who'd been waiting all these weeks for Michael to straighten himself out.

"It hit me all of a sudden—what you were saying about observing in order to learn. I need a model for Michael, someone who can help me gain perspective," Bailey explained, her gaze momentarily leaving her hero.

"Ah…" Jo Ann sounded uncertain.

"If I'm ever going to sell *Forever Yours* I've got to employ those kinds of techniques." Bailey's eyes automatically returned to the man. Hmm, a little over six feet tall, she estimated. He really was a perfect specimen. All this time she'd been feeling melancholy, wondering how she could ever create an authentic hero, then, almost by magic, this one appeared in living color…

"Go on," Jo Ann prodded, urging Bailey to finish her thought.

"The way I figure it, I may never get this characterization down right if I don't have someone to pattern Michael after."

Bailey half expected Jo Ann to argue with her. She was pleasantly surprised when her friend agreed with a quick nod. "I think you're right. It's an excellent idea."

Grinning sheepishly, Bailey gave herself a mental pat on the back. "I thought so myself."

"What are you planning to do? Study this guy— research his life history, learn what you can about his family and upbringing? That sort of thing? I hope you understand that this may not be as easy as it seems."

"Nothing worthwhile ever is," Bailey intoned solemnly. Actually, how she was going to do any of this research was a mystery to her, as well. Eventually she'd come up with some way of learning what she needed to know without being obvious about it. The sooner the better, of course. "I should probably start by finding out his name."

"That sounds like a good idea," Jo Ann said as though she wasn't entirely sure this plan was such a brilliant one, after all.

The train came to a vibrating halt, and a group of people moved toward the doors. Even while they disembarked, more were crowding onto the train. Bailey kept her gaze on the man in the pin-striped suit for fear he'd step off the subway without her realizing it. When she was certain he wasn't leaving, she relaxed.

"You know," Jo Ann said thoughtfully once the train had started again. "My Logan's modeled after Dan, but in this case, I'm beginning to have—"

"Did you see that?" Bailey interrupted, grabbing her friend's arm in her enthusiasm. The longer she studied the stranger, the more impressed she became.

"What?" Jo Ann demanded, glancing around her.

"The elegant way he turned the page." Bailey was thinking of her own miserable attempts to read while standing in a moving train. Any endeavor to turn the unwieldy newspaper page resulted in frustration to her and anyone unfortunate enough to be standing nearby. Yet he did it as gracefully and easily as if he were sitting at his own desk, in his own office.

"You're really hung up on this guy, aren't you?"

"You still don't see it, do you?" Bailey couldn't help being disappointed. She would've expected Jo Ann, of all her friends, to understand that this stranger was everything she'd ever wanted in Michael, from the top of his perfect hair to the tip of his (probably) size-eleven shoe.

"I'm still trying," Jo Ann said squinting as she stared at Bailey's hero, "but I don't quite see it."

"That's what I thought." But Bailey felt convinced she was right. This tall, handsome man was Michael, and it didn't matter if Jo Ann saw it or not. She did, and that was all that mattered.

The subway train slowed as it neared the next stop. Once again, passengers immediately crowded the doorway. Her hero slipped the newspaper into his briefcase, removed the umbrella hooked around his forearm and stood back, politely waiting his turn.

"Oh, my," Bailey said, panic in her voice. This could get complicated. Her heart was already thundering like a Midwest storm gone berserk. She reached for her purse and vaulted to her feet.

Jo Ann looked at her as though she suspected Bailey had lost her wits. She tugged the sleeve of Bailey's coat. "This isn't our stop."

"Yes, I know," Bailey said, pulling an unwilling Jo Ann to her feet.

"Then what are you doing getting off here?"

Bailey frowned. "We're following him, what else?"

"We? But what about our jobs?"

"You don't expect me to do this alone, do you?"

Two

"You don't mean we're actually going to *follow* him?"

"Of course we are." They couldn't stand there arguing. "Are you coming or not?"

For the first time in recent history, Jo Ann seemed at a complete loss for words. Just when Bailey figured she'd have to do this on her own, Jo Ann nodded. The two dashed off the car just in time.

"I've never done anything so crazy in all my life," Jo Ann muttered.

Bailey ignored her. "He went that way," she said, pointing toward the escalator. Grabbing Jo Ann by the arm, she hurried after the man in the pin-striped suit, maintaining a safe distance.

"Listen, Bailey," Jo Ann said, jogging in order to keep up, but still two steps behind her. "I'm beginning to have second thoughts about this."

"Why? Not five minutes ago you agreed that modeling Michael on a real man was an excellent approach to characterization."

"I didn't know you planned to stalk the guy! Don't you think we should stay back a little farther?"

"No." Bailey was adamant. As it was, her hero's long, powerful strides were much faster than Bailey's normal walking pace. Jo Ann's short-legged stride was even slower.

By the time they reached the corner, Jo Ann was panting. She leaned against the street lamp and placed her hand over her heart, inhaling deeply. "Give me a minute, would you?"

"We might lose him." The look Jo Ann gave her suggested that might not be so bad. "Think of this as research," Bailey added, looping her arm through Jo Ann's again and dragging her forward.

Staying in the shadow of the buildings, the two trailed Bailey's hero for three more blocks. Fortunately he was walking in the direction of the area where Bailey and Jo Ann both worked.

When he paused for a red light, Bailey stayed several feet behind him, wandering aimlessly toward a widow display while glancing over her shoulder every few seconds. She didn't want to give him an opportunity to notice her.

"Do you think he's married?" Bailey demanded of her friend.

"How would I know?" Jo Ann snapped.

"Intuition."

The light changed and Bailey rushed forward. A reluctant Jo Ann followed on her heels. "I can't believe I'm doing this."

"You already said that."

"What am I going to tell my boss when I'm late?" Jo Ann groaned.

Bailey had to wait when Jo Ann came to a sudden

halt, leaned against a display window and removed her high heel. She shook it out, then hurriedly put it back on.

"Jo Ann," Bailey said in a heated whisper, urging her friend to hurry.

"There was something in my shoe," she said from between clenched teeth. "I can't race down the streets of San Francisco with a stone in my shoe."

"I don't want to lose him." Bailey stopped abruptly, causing Jo Ann to collide with her. "Look, he went into the Cascade Building."

"Oh, good," Jo Ann muttered on the tail end of a sigh that proclaimed relief. "Does that mean we can go to work now?"

"Of course not." It was clear to Bailey that Jo Ann knew next to nothing about detective work. She probably didn't read mysteries. "I have to find out what his name is."

"What?" Jo Ann sounded as though Bailey had suggested they climb to the top of Coit Tower and leap off. "How do you plan to do that?"

"I don't know. I'll figure it out later." Clutching her friend's arm, Bailey urged her forward. "Come on, we can't give up now."

"Sure we can," Jo Ann muttered as they entered the Cascade Building.

"Hurry," Bailey whispered, releasing Jo Ann's elbow. "He's getting into the elevator." Bailey slipped past several people, mumbling, "Excuse me, excuse me," as she struggled to catch the same elevator, Jo Ann stumbling behind her.

They managed to make it a split second before the doors closed. There were four or five others on board, and Jo Ann cast Bailey a frown that doubted her intelligence.

Bailey had other concerns. She tried to remain as unobtrusive as possible, not wanting to call attention to herself or Jo Ann. Her hero seemed oblivious to them, which served her purposes nicely. All she intended to do was find out his name and what he did for a living, a task that shouldn't require the FBI.

Jo Ann jerked Bailey's sleeve and nodded toward the stranger's left hand. It took Bailey a moment to realize her friend was pointing out the fact that he wasn't wearing a wedding ring. The realization cheered Bailey and she made a circle with thumb and finger, grinning broadly.

As the elevator sped upward, Bailey saw Jo Ann anxiously check her watch. Then the elevator came to a smooth halt. A few seconds passed before the doors slid open and two passengers stepped out.

Her hero glanced over his shoulder, then moved to one side. For half a second, his gaze rested on Bailey and Jo Ann.

Half a second! Bailey straightened, offended at the casual way in which he'd dismissed her. She didn't want him to notice her, but at the same time, she felt cheated that he hadn't recognized the heroine in her—the same way she'd seen the hero in him. She was, after all, heroine material. She was attractive and… Well, attractive might be too strong a word. Cute and charming had a more comfortable feel. Her best feature was her thick dark hair that fell straight as a stick across her shoulders. The ends curved under just a little, giving it shape and bounce. She was taller than average, and slender, with clear blue eyes and a turned-up nose. As for her personality, she had spunk enough not to turn away from a good argument and spirit enough to follow a stranger around San Francisco.

Bailey noted that once again his presence seemed to fill the cramped quarters. His briefcase was tucked under his arm, while his hand gripped the curved handle of his umbrella. For all the notice he gave those around him, he might have been alone.

When Bailey turned to her friend, she saw that Jo Ann's eyes were focused straight ahead, her teeth gritted as though she couldn't wait to tell Bailey exactly what she thought of this crazy scheme. It *was* crazy, Bailey would be the first to admit, but these were desperate times in the life of a budding romance writer. She would stop at nothing to achieve her goal.

Bailey grinned. She had to agree that traipsing after her hero was a bit unconventional, but *he* didn't need to know about it. He didn't need to ever know how she intended to use him.

Her gaze moved from Jo Ann, then to the man with the umbrella. The amusement drained out of her as she found herself staring into the darkest pair of eyes she'd ever seen. Bailey was the first to look away, her pulse thundering in her ears.

The elevator stopped several times until, finally, only the three of them were left. Jo Ann had squeezed into the corner. Behind the stranger's back she mouthed several words that Bailey couldn't hope to decipher, then tapped one finger against the face of her watch.

Bailey nodded and raised her hand, fingers spread, to plead for five more minutes.

When the elevator stopped again, her hero stepped out, and Bailey followed, with Jo Ann trailing behind her. He walked briskly down the wide hallway, then entered a set of double doors marked with the name of a well-known architectural firm.

"Are you satisfied now?" Jo Ann burst out. "Honestly, Bailey, have you gone completely nuts?"

"You told me I need a hero who's proud and determined and I'm going to find one."

"That doesn't answer my question. Has it occurred to you yet that you've gone off the deep end?"

"Because I want to find out his name?"

"And how do you plan to do that?"

"I don't know yet," Bailey admitted. "Why don't I just ask?" Having said that, she straightened her shoulders and walked toward the same doors through which the man had disappeared.

The pleasant-looking middle-aged woman who sat at the reception desk greeted her with a warm smile. "Good morning."

"Good morning," Bailey returned, hoping her smile was as serene and trusting as the older woman's. "This may seem a bit unusual, but I... I was on the subway this morning and I thought I recognized an old family friend. Naturally I didn't want to make a fool of myself in case I was wrong. He arrived in your office a few minutes ago and I was wondering... I know it's unusual, but would you mind telling me his name?"

"That would be Mr. Davidson. He's been taking BART the last few months because of the freeway renovation project."

"Mr. Davidson," Bailey repeated slowly. "His first name wouldn't be Michael, would it?"

"No." The receptionist frowned slightly. "It's Parker."

"Parker," Bailey repeated softly. "Parker Davidson."

She liked the way it sounded, and although it wasn't a name she would've chosen for a hero, she could see that it fit him perfectly.

"Is Mr. Davidson the man you thought?"

It took Bailey a second or two to realize the woman was speaking to her. "Yes," she answered with a bright smile. "I do believe he is."

"Why, that's wonderful." The woman was obviously delighted. "Would you like me to buzz him? I'm sure he'd want to talk to you himself. Mr. Davidson is such a nice man."

"Oh, no, please don't do that." Bailey hoped she was able to hide the panic she felt at the woman's suggestion. "I wouldn't want to disturb him and I really have to be getting to work. Thank you for your trouble."

"It was no trouble whatsoever." The receptionist glanced down at her appointment schedule and shook her head. "I was going to suggest you stop in at noon, but unfortunately Mr. Davidson's got a lunch engagement."

Bailey sighed as though with regret and turned away from the desk. "I'll guess I'll have to talk to him another time."

"That's really too bad. At least give me your name." The woman's soft brown eyes went from warm to sympathetic.

"Janice Hampton," Bailey said, mentioning the name of her heroine. "Thank you again for your help. You've been most kind."

Jo Ann was in the hallway pacing and muttering when Bailey stepped out of Parker's office. She stopped abruptly as Bailey appeared, her eyes filled with questions. "What happened?"

"Nothing. I asked the receptionist for his name and she told me. She even let it slip that he's got a lunch engagement..."

"Are you satisfied *now*?" Jo Ann sounded as though she'd passed from impatience to resignation. "In case you've forgotten, we're both working women."

Bailey glanced at her watch and groaned. "We won't be too late if we hurry." Jo Ann worked as an insurance specialist in a doctor's office and Bailey was a paralegal.

Luckily their office buildings were only a few blocks from the Cascade Building. They parted company on the next corner and Bailey half jogged the rest of the way.

No one commented when she slipped into the office ten minutes late. She hoped the same held true for Jo Ann, who'd probably never been late for work in her life.

Bailey settled down at her desk with her coffee and her files, then hesitated. Jo Ann was right. Discovering Parker's name was useless unless she could fill in the essential details about his life. She needed facts. Lots of facts. The kinds of people he associated with, his background, his likes and dislikes, everyday habits.

It wasn't until later in the morning that Bailey started wondering where someone like Parker Davidson would go for lunch. It might be important to learn that. The type of restaurant a man chose—casual? elegant? exotic?—said something about his personality. Details like that could make the difference between a sale and a rejection, and frankly, Bailey didn't know if Michael could tolerate another spurning.

At ten to twelve Bailey mumbled an excuse about having an appointment before she headed out the door.

Her boss gave her a funny look, but Bailey made sure she escaped before anyone could ask any questions. It wasn't like Bailey to take her duties lightly.

Luck was with her. She'd only been standing at the street corner for five minutes when Parker Davidson came out of the building. He was deeply involved in conversation with another man, yet when he raised his hand to summon a taxi, one appeared instantly, as if by magic. If she hadn't seen it with her own eyes, Bailey wouldn't have believed it. Surely this was the confidence, the command, others said a hero should possess. Not wanting to miss a single detail, Bailey took a pen and pad out of her purse and started jotting them down.

As Parker's cab slowly pulled away, she ventured into the street and flagged down a second cab. In order to manage that, however, she'd had to wave her arms above her head and leap up and down.

She yanked open the door and leapt inside. "Follow that cab," she cried, pointing toward Parker's taxi.

The stocky driver twisted around. "Are you serious? You want me to follow that cab?"

"That's right," she said anxiously, afraid Parker's taxi would soon be out of sight.

Her driver laughed outright. "I've been waiting fifteen years for someone to tell me that. You got yourself a deal, lady." He stepped on the accelerator and barreled down the street, going well above the speed limit.

"Any particular reason, lady?"

"I beg your pardon?" The man was doing fifty in a thirty-mile-an-hour zone.

"I want to know why you're following that cab." The car turned a corner at record speed, the wheels screeching, and Bailey slid from one end of the seat to the other.

If she'd hoped to avoid attention, it was a lost cause. Parker Davidson might not notice her, but nearly everyone else in San Francisco did.

"I'm doing some research for a romance novel," Bailey explained.

"You're doing *what?*"

"Research."

Apparently her answer didn't satisfy him, because he slowed to a sedate twenty miles an hour. "Research for a romance novel," he repeated, his voice flat. "I thought you were a private detective or something."

"I'm sorry to disappoint you. I write romance novels and— Oh, stop here, would you?" Parker's cab had pulled to the curb and the two men were climbing out.

"Sure, lady, don't get excited."

Bailey scrambled out of the cab and searched through her purse for her money. When she couldn't find it, she slapped the large bag onto the hood of the cab and sorted through its contents until she retrieved her wallet. "Here."

"Have a great day, lady," the cabbie said sardonically, setting his cap farther back on his head. Bailey offered him a vague smile.

She toyed with the idea of following the men into the restaurant and having lunch. She would have, too, if it weren't for the fact that she'd used all her cash to pay for the taxi.

But there was plenty to entertain her while she waited—although Bailey wasn't sure exactly what she was waiting for. The streets of Chinatown were crowded. She gazed about her at the colorful shops with their produce stands and souvenirs and rows of smoked ducks hanging in the windows. Street vendors

displayed their wares and tried to coax her to come examine their goods.

Bailey bought a fresh orange with some change she
scrounged from the bottom of her purse. Walking across
the street, she wondered how long her hero would daw-
dle over his lunch. Most likely he'd walk back to the
office. Michael would.

His lunch engagement didn't last nearly as long as
Bailey had expected. When he emerged from the restaurant, he took her by surprise. Bailey was in the process of using her debit card to buy a sweatshirt she'd
found at an incredibly low price and had to rush in an
effort to keep up with him.

He hadn't gone more than a couple of blocks when
she lost him. Stunned, she stood in the middle of the
sidewalk, wondering how he could possibly have disappeared.

One minute he was there, and the next he was gone.
Tailing a hero wasn't nearly as easy as she'd supposed.

Discouraged, Bailey clutched her bag with the sweatshirt and slung her purse over her shoulder, then started
back toward her office. Heaven only knew what she
was going to say to her boss once she arrived—half
an hour late.

She hadn't gone more than a few steps when someone grabbed her arm and jerked her into the alley. She
opened her mouth to scream, but the cry died a sudden death when she found herself staring up at Parker
Davidson.

"I want to know why the hell you're following me."

Three

"Ah... Ah..." For the life of her, Bailey couldn't string two words together.

"Janice Hampton, I presume?"

Bailey nodded, simply because it was easier than explaining herself.

Parker's eyes slowly raked her from head to foot. He obviously didn't see anything that pleased him. "You're not an old family friend, are you?"

Still silent, she answered him with a shake of her head.

"That's what I thought. What do you want?"

Bailey couldn't think of a single coherent remark.

"Well?" he demanded since she was clearly having a problem answering even the most basic questions. Bailey had no idea where to start or how much to say. The truth would never do, but she didn't know if she was capable of lying convincingly.

"Then you leave me no choice but to call the police," he said tightly.

"No...please." The thought of explaining everything to an officer of the law was too mortifying to consider.

"Then start talking." His eyes were narrow and as cold as the January wind off San Francisco Bay.

Bailey clasped her hands together, wishing she'd never given in to the whim to follow him on his lunch appointment. "It's a bit…complicated," she mumbled.

"Isn't it always?"

"Your attitude isn't helping any," she returned, straightening her shoulders. He might be a high-and-mighty architect—and her behavior might have been a little unusual—but that didn't give him the right to treat her as if she were some kind of criminal.

"*My* attitude?" he said incredulously.

"Listen, would you mind if we shorted this inquisition?" she asked, checking her watch. "I've got to be back at work in fifteen minutes."

"Not until you tell why you've been my constant shadow for the past hour. Not to mention this morning."

"You're exaggerating." Bailey half turned to leave when his hand flew out to grip her shoulder.

"You're not going anywhere until you've answered a few questions."

"If you must know," she said at the end of a protracted sigh, "I'm a novelist…"

"Published?"

"Not yet," she admitted reluctantly, "but I will be."

His mouth lifted at the corners and Bailey couldn't decide if the movement had a sardonic twist or he didn't believe a word she was saying. Neither alternative did anything to soothe her ego.

"It's true!" she said heatedly. "I am a novelist, only I've been having trouble capturing the true nature of a classic hero and, well, as I said earlier, it gets a bit involved."

"Start at the beginning."

"All right." Bailey was prepared now to do exactly that. He wanted details? She'd give him details. "It all began several months back when I was riding BART and I met Jo Ann—she's the woman I was with this morning. Over the course of the next few weeks I learned that she's a writer, too, and she's been kind enough to tutor me. I'd already mailed off my first manuscript when I met Jo Ann, but I quickly learned I'd made some basic mistakes. All beginning writers do. So I rewrote the story and—"

"Do you mind if we get to the part about this morning?" he asked, clearly impatient.

"All right, fine, I'll skip ahead, but it probably won't make much sense." She didn't understand why he was wearing that beleaguered look, since he was the one who'd insisted she start at the beginning. "Jo Ann and I were on the subway this morning and I was telling her I doubted I'd recognize a hero. You see, Michael's the hero in my book and I'm having terrible problems with him. The first time around he was too harsh, then I turned him into a wimp. I just can't seem to get him to walk the middle of the road. He's got to be tough, but tender. Strong and authoritative, but not so stubborn or arrogant the reader wants to throttle him. I need to find a way to make Michael larger than life, but at the same time the kind of man any woman would fall in love with and—"

"Excuse me for interrupting you again," Parker said, folding his arms across his chest and irritably tapping his foot, "but could we finish this sometime before the end of the year?"

"Oh, yes. Sorry." His sarcasm didn't escape her, but

she decided to be generous and overlook it. "I was telling Jo Ann I wouldn't recognize a hero if one hit me over the head, and no sooner had I said that than your umbrella whacked me." The instant the words were out, Bailey realized she should have passed over that part.

"I like the other version better," he said with undisguised contempt. He shook his head and stalked past her onto the busy sidewalk.

"What other version?" Bailey demanded, marching after him. She was only relaying the facts, the way *he'd* insisted!

"The one where you're an old family friend. This nonsense about being a novelist is—"

"The absolute truth," she finished with all the dignity she could muster. "You're the hero—well, not exactly the hero, don't get me wrong, but a lot like my hero, Michael. In fact, you could be his twin."

Parker stopped abruptly and just as abruptly turned around to face her. The contempt in his eyes was gone, replaced by some other emotion Bailey couldn't identify.

"Have you seen a doctor?" he asked gently.

"A doctor?"

"Have you discussed this problem with a professional?"

It took Bailey a moment to understand what he was saying. Once she did, she was so furious she couldn't formulate words fast enough to keep pace with her speeding mind.

"You think...mental patient...on the loose?"

He nodded solemnly.

"That's the most ridiculous thing I've ever heard in my life!" Bailey had never been more insulted. Parker

Davidson thought she was a crazy person! She waved her arms haphazardly as she struggled to compose her thoughts. "I'm willing to admit that following you is a bit eccentric, but…but I did it in the name of research!"

"Then kindly research someone else."

"Gladly." She stormed ahead several paces, then whirled suddenly around, her fists clenched. "You'll have to excuse me, I'm new to the writing game. There's a lot I don't know yet, but obviously I have more to learn than I realized. I was right the first time—you're no hero."

Not giving him the opportunity to respond, she rushed back to her office, thoroughly disgusted with the man she'd assumed to be a living, breathing hero.

Max, Bailey's cat, was waiting anxiously for her when she arrived home that evening, almost an hour later than usual since she'd stayed to make up for her lengthy lunch. Not that Max would actually deign to let her think he was pleased to see her. Max had one thing on his mind and one thing only.

Dinner.

The sooner she fed him, the sooner he could go back to ignoring her.

"I'm crazy about you, too," Bailey teased, bending over to playfully scratch his ears. She talked to her cat the way she did her characters, although Michael had been suspiciously quiet of late—which was fine with Bailey, since a little time apart was sure to do them both good. She wasn't particularly happy with her hero after the Parker Davidson fiasco that afternoon. Once again Michael had led her astray. The best thing to do was lock him in the desk drawer for a while.

Max wove his fat fluffy body between Bailey's legs while she sorted through her mail. She paused, staring into space as she reviewed her confrontation with Parker Davidson. Every time she thought about the things he'd said, she felt a flush of embarrassment. It was all she could do not to cringe at the pitying look he'd given her as he asked if she was seeking professional help. Never in her life had Bailey felt so mortified.

"Meow." Max seemed determined to remind her that he was still waiting for his meal.

"All right, all right," she muttered, heading for the refrigerator. "I don't have time to argue with you to-night. I'm going out to hear Libby McDonald speak." She removed the can of cat food from the bottom shelf and dumped the contents on the dry kibble. Max had to have his meal moistened before he'd eat it.

With a single husky purr, Max sauntered over to his dish and left Bailey to change clothes for the writers' meeting.

Once she was in her most comfortable sweater and an old pair of faded jeans, she grabbed a quick bite to eat and was out the door.

Jo Ann had already arrived at Parklane College, the site of their meeting, and was rearranging the class-room desks to form a large circle. Bailey automatically helped, grateful her friend didn't question her about Parker Davidson. Within minutes, the room started to fill with members of the romance writers' group.

Bailey didn't know if she should tell Jo Ann about the meeting with Parker. No, she decided, the whole sorry episode was best forgotten. Buried under the heading of Mistakes Not to Be Repeated.

If Jo Ann did happen to ask, Bailey mused, it would

be best to say nothing. She didn't make a habit of lying, but her encounter with that man had been too humiliating to describe, even to her friend.

The meeting went well, and although Bailey took copious notes, her thoughts persisted in drifting away from Libby's speech, straying to Parker. The man had his nerve suggesting she was a lunatic. Who did he think he was, anyway? Sigmund Freud? But then, to be fair, Parker had no way of knowing that Bailey didn't normally go around following strange men and claiming they were heroes straight out of her novel.

Again and again throughout the talk, Bailey had to stubbornly refocus her attention on Libby's speech. When Libby finished, the twenty or so writers who were gathered applauded enthusiastically. The sound startled Bailey, who'd been embroiled in yet another mental debate about the afternoon's encounter.

There was a series of questions, and then Libby had to leave in order to catch a plane. Bailey was disappointed that she couldn't stay for coffee. It had become tradition for a handful of the group's members to go across the street to the all-night diner after their monthly get-together.

As it turned out, everyone else had to rush home, too, except Jo Ann. Bailey was on the verge of making an excuse herself, but one glance told her Jo Ann was unlikely to believe it.

They walked across the street to the brightly lit and almost empty restaurant. As they sat down in their usual booth, the waitress approached them with menus. Jo Ann ordered just coffee, but Bailey, who'd eaten an orange for lunch and had a meager dinner of five pretzels, a banana and two hard green jelly beans left over from Christmas, was hungry, so she asked for a turkey sandwich.

"All right, tell me what happened," Jo Ann said the moment the waitress left their booth.

"About what?" Bailey tried to appear innocent as she toyed with the edges of the paper napkin. She carefully avoided meeting Jo Ann's eyes.

"I phoned your office at lunchtime," her friend said in a stern voice. "Do I need to go into the details?" She studied Bailey, who raised her eyes to give Jo Ann a brief look of wide-eyed incomprehension. "Beth told me you'd left before noon for a doctor's appointment and weren't back yet." She paused for effect. "We both know you didn't have a doctor's appointment, don't we?"

"Uh…" Bailey felt like a cornered rat.

"You don't need to tell me where you were," Jo Ann went on, raising her eyebrows. "I can guess. You couldn't leave it alone, could you? My guess is that you followed Parker Davidson to his lunch engagement."

Bailey nodded miserably. So much for keeping one of her most humiliating moments a secret. She hadn't even told Max! Her cat generally heard everything, but today's encounter was best forgotten.

If only she could stop thinking about it. For most of the afternoon she'd succeeded in pushing all thoughts of that man, that unreasonable insulting architect, out of her mind. Not so this evening.

"And?" Jo Ann prompted.

Bailey could see it was pointless to continue this charade with her friend. "And he confronted me, wanting to know why the hell I was following him."

Jo Ann closed her eyes, then slowly shook her head.

After a moment, she reached for her coffee. "I can just imagine what you told him."

"At first I had no idea what to say."

"That part I can believe, but knowing you, I'd guess you insisted on telling him the truth and nothing but the truth."

"You're right again." Not that it had done Bailey any good.

"And?" Jo Ann prompted again.

Bailey's sandwich arrived and for a minute or so she was distracted by that. Unfortunately she wasn't able to put off Jo Ann's questions for long.

"Don't you dare take another bite of that sandwich until you tell me what he said!"

"He didn't believe me." Which was putting it mildly.

"He didn't believe you?"

"All right, if you have to know, he thought I was an escaped mental patient."

Anger flashed in Jo Ann's eyes, and Bailey was so grateful she could have hugged her.

"Good grief, why'd you do anything so stupid as to tell him you're a writer?" Jo Ann demanded vehemently.

So much for having her friend champion her integrity, Bailey mused darkly.

"I can't understand why you'd do that," Jo Ann continued, raking her hand furiously through her hair. "You were making up stories all over the place when it came to discovering his name. You left me speechless with the way you walked into his office and spouted that nonsense about being an old family friend. Why in heaven's name didn't you make up something plausible when he confronted you?"

"I couldn't think." That, regrettably, was the truth.

Not that it would've made much difference even if she'd been able to invent a spur-of-the-moment excuse. She was convinced of that. The man would have known she was lying, and Bailey couldn't see the point of digging herself in any deeper than she already was. Of course she hadn't had time to reason that out until later. He'd hauled her into the alley and she'd simply followed her instincts, right or wrong.

"It wasn't like you didn't warn me," Bailey said, half her turkey sandwich poised in front of her mouth. "You tried to tell me from the moment we followed him off the subway how dumb the whole idea was. I should've listened to you then."

But she'd been so desperate to get a real hero down on paper. She'd been willing to do just about anything to straighten out this problem of Michael's. What she hadn't predicted was how foolish she'd end up feeling as a result. Well, no more—she'd learned her lesson. If any more handsome men hit her on the head, she'd hit them back!

"What are you going to do now?" Jo Ann asked.

"Absolutely nothing," Bailey answered without a second's hesitation.

"You mean you're going to let him go on thinking you're an escaped mental patient?"

"If that's what he wants to believe." Bailey tried to create the impression that it didn't matter to her one way or the other. She must have done a fairly good job because Jo Ann remained speechless, raising her coffee mug to her mouth three times without taking a single sip.

"What happens if you run into him on the subway again?" she finally asked.

"I don't think that'll be a problem," Bailey said blithely, trying hard to sound unconcerned. "What are the chances we'll be on the same car again at exactly the same time?"

"You're right," Jo Ann concurred. "Besides, after what happened today, he'll probably go back to driving, freeway renovation or not."

It would certainly be a blessing if he did, Bailey thought.

He didn't.

Jo Ann and Bailey were standing at the end of the crowded subway car, clutching the metal handrail when Jo Ann tugged hard at the sleeve of Bailey's bulky-knit cardigan.

"Don't turn around," Jo Ann murmured.

They were packed as tight as peas in a pod, and Bailey had no intention of moving in any direction.

"He's staring at you."

"Who?" Bailey whispered back.

She wasn't a complete fool. When she'd stepped onto the train earlier, she'd done a quick check and was thankful to note that Parker Davidson wasn't anywhere to be seen. She hadn't run into him in several days and there was no reason to think she would. He might have continued to take BART, but if that was the case their paths had yet to cross, which was fine with her. Their second encounter would likely prove as embarrassing as the first.

"He's here," Jo Ann hissed. "The architect you followed last week."

Bailey was convinced everyone in the subway car had turned to stare at her. "I'm sure you're mistaken," she muttered, furious with her friend for her lack of discretion.

"I'm not. Look." She motioned with her head.

Bailey did her best to be nonchalant about it. When she did slowly twist around, her heart sank all the way to her knees. Jo Ann was right. Parker stood no more than ten feet from her. Fortunately, they were separated by a number of people—which didn't disguise the fact that he was staring at Bailey as if he expected men in white coats to start descendingon her.

She glared back at him.

"Do you see him?" Jo Ann asked.

"Of course. Thank you so much for pointing him out to me."

"He's staring at you. What else was I supposed to do?"

"Ignore him," Bailey suggested sarcastically. "I certainly intend to." Still, no matter how hard she tried to concentrate on the advertising posted above the seats, she found Parker Davidson dominating her thoughts.

A nervous shaky feeling slithered down her spine. Bailey could *feel* his look as profoundly as a caress. This was exactly the sort of look she struggled to describe in *Forever Yours*.

Casually, as if by accident, she slowly turned her head and peeked in his direction once more, wondering if she'd imagined the whole thing. For an instant the entire train seemed to go still. Her blue eyes met his brown ones, and an electric jolt rocked Bailey, like nothing she'd ever felt before. A breathless panic filled her and she longed to drag her eyes away, pretend she didn't recognize him, anything to escape this fluttery sensation in the pit of her stomach.

This was exactly how Janice had felt the first time she met Michael. Bailey had spent days writing that scene, studying each word, each phrase, until she'd achieved the right effect. That was the moment Janice had fallen in love with Michael. Oh, she'd fought it, done everything but stand on her head in an effort to control her feelings, but Janice had truly fallen for him.

Bailey, however, was much too wise to be taken in by a mere look. She'd already been in love. Twice. Both times were disasters and she wasn't willing to try it again soon. Her heart was still bleeding from the last go-round.

Of course she was leaping to conclusions. She was the one with the fluttery stomach. Not Parker. He obviously hadn't been affected by their exchange. In fact, he seemed to be amused, as if running into Bailey again was an unexpected opportunity for entertainment.

She braced herself, and with a resolve that would've impressed Janice, she dropped her gaze. She inhaled sharply, then twisted her mouth into a sneer. Unfortunately, Jo Ann was staring at her in complete—and knowing—fascination.

"What's with you—and him?"

"Nothing," Bailey denied quickly.

"That's not what I saw."

"You're mistaken," Bailey replied in a voice that said the subject was closed.

"Whatever you did worked," Jo Ann whispered a couple of minutes later.

"I don't know what you're talking about."

"Fine, but in case you're interested, he's coming this way."

"I beg your pardon?" Bailey's forehead broke out in

a cold sweat at the mere prospect of being confronted by Parker Davidson again. Once in a lifetime was more than enough, but twice in the same week was well beyond her capabilities.

Sure enough, Parker Davidson boldly stepped forward and squeezed himself next to Bailey.

"Hello again," he said casually.

"Hello," she returned stiffly, refusing to look at him.

"You must be Jo Ann," he said, turning his attention to Bailey's friend.

Jo Anne's eyes narrowed. "You told him my name?" she asked Bailey in a loud distinct voice.

"I… Apparently so."

"Thank you very much," she muttered in a sarcastic voice. Then she turned toward Parker and her expression altered dramatically as she broke into a wide smile. "Yes, I'm Jo Ann."

"Have you been friends with Janice long?"

"Janice? Oh, you mean…" Bailey quickly nudged her friend in the ribs with her elbow. "Janice," Jo Ann repeated in a strained voice. "You mean *this* Janice?"

Parker frowned. "So that was a lie, as well?"

"As well," Bailey admitted coolly, deciding she had no alternative. "That was my problem in the first place. I told you the truth. Now, for the last time, I'm a writer and so is Jo Ann." She gestured toward her friend. "Tell him."

"We're both writers," Jo Ann confirmed with a sad lack of conviction. It wasn't something Jo Ann willingly broadcast, though Bailey had never really understood why. She supposed it was a kind of superstition, a fear of offending the fates by appearing too presumptuous— and thereby ruining her chances of selling a book.

Parker sighed, frowning more darkly. "That's what I thought."

The subway stopped at the next station, and he moved toward the door.

"Goodbye," Jo Ann said, raising her hand. "It was a pleasure to meet you."

"Me, too." He glanced from her to Bailey; she could have sworn his eyes hardened briefly before he stepped off the car.

"You told him your name was Janice?" Jo Ann cried the minute he was out of sight. "Why'd you do that?"

"I... I don't know. I panicked."

Jo Ann wiped her hand down her face. "Now he *really* thinks you're nuts."

"It might have helped if you hadn't acted like you'd never heard the word 'writer' before." Before Jo Ann could heap any more blame on her shoulders, Bailey had some guilt of her own to spread around.

"That isn't information I tell everyone, you know. I'd appreciate if you didn't pass it out to just anyone."

"Oh, dear," Bailey mumbled, feeling wretched. Not only was Jo Ann annoyed with her, Parker thought she was a fool. And there was little she could do to redeem herself in his eyes. The fact that it troubled her so much was something for the men with chaise longues in their offices to analyze. But trouble her it did.

If only Parker hadn't looked at her with those dark eyes of his—as if he was willing to reconsider his first assessment of her.

If only she hadn't looked back and felt that puzzling sensation come over her—the way a heroine does when she's met the man of her dreams.

* * *

The weekend passed, and although Bailey spent most of her time working on the rewrite of *Forever Yours*, she couldn't stop picturing the disgruntled look on Parker's face as he walked off the subway car. It hurt her pride that he assumed she was a liar. Granted, introducing herself as Janice Hampton had been a lie, but after that, she'd told only the truth. She was sure he didn't believe a single word she'd said. Still, he intrigued her so much she spent a couple of precious hours on Saturday afternoon on the Internet, learning everything she could about him, which unfortunately wasn't much.

When Monday's lunch hour arrived, she headed directly for Parker's building. Showing up at his door should merit her an award for courage—or one for sheer stupidity.

"May I help you?" the receptionist asked when Bailey walked into the architectural firm's outer office. It was the same woman who'd helped her the week before. The nameplate on her desk read Roseanne Snyder. Bailey hadn't noticed it during her first visit.

"Would it be possible to see Mr. Davidson for just a few minutes?" she asked in her most businesslike voice, hoping the woman didn't recognize her.

Roseanne glanced down at the appointment calendar. "You're the gal who was in to see Mr. Davidson the first part of last week, aren't you?"

So much for keeping her identity a secret. "Yes." It was embarrassing to admit that. Bailey prayed Parker hadn't divulged the details of their encounter to the firm's receptionist.

"When I mentioned your name to Mr. Davidson, he didn't seem to remember your family."

"Uh… I wasn't sure he would," Bailey answered vaguely.

"If you'll give me your name again, I'll tell him you're here."

"Bailey. Bailey York," she said with a silent sigh of relief. Parker didn't know her real name; surely he wouldn't refuse to see her.

"Bailey York," the friendly woman repeated. "But aren't you—?" She paused, staring at her for a moment before she pressed the intercom button. After a quick exchange, she nodded, smiling tentatively. "Mr. Davidson said to go right in. His office is the last one on the left," she said, pointing the way.

The door was open and Parker sat at his desk, apparently engrossed in studying a set of blueprints. His office was impressive, with a wide sweeping view of the Golden Gate Bridge and Alcatraz Island. As she stood in the doorway, Parker glanced up. His smile faded when he recognized her.

"What are you doing here?"

"Proving I'm not a liar." With that, she strode into his office and slapped a package on his desk.

"What's that?" he asked.

"Proof."

Four

Parker stared at the manuscript box as though he feared it was a time bomb set to explode at any moment.

"Go ahead and open it," Bailey said. When he didn't, she lifted the lid for him. Awkwardly she flipped through the first fifteen pages until she'd gathered up the first chapter, which she shoved into his hands. "Read it."

"Now?"

"Start with the header," she instructed, and then pointed to the printed line on the top right-hand side of each page.

"York... *Forever Yours*... Page one," he read aloud, slowly and hesitantly.

Bailey nodded. "Now move down to the text." She used her index finger to indicate where she wanted him to read.

"Chapter one. Janice Hampton had dreaded the business meeting for weeks. She was—"

"That's enough," Bailey muttered, ripping the pages out of his hands. "If you want to look through the rest of the manuscript, you're welcome to."

"Why would I want to do that?"

"So you no longer have the slightest doubt that I wrote it," she answered in a severe tone. "So you'll believe that I *am* a writer—and not a liar or a maniac. The purpose of this visit, though, why I find it necessary to prove I'm telling you the truth, isn't clear to me yet. It just seemed…important."

As she spoke, she scooped up the loose pages and stuffed them back into the manuscript box, closing it with enough force to crush the lid.

"I believed you before," Parker said casually, leaning back in his chair as if he'd never questioned her integrity. Or her sanity. "No one could've made up that story about being a romance writer and kept a straight face."

"But you—"

"What I didn't appreciate was the fact that you called yourself by a false name."

"You caught me off guard! I gave you the name of my heroine because…well, because I saw you as the hero."

"I see." He raised one eyebrow—definitely a hero-like mannerism, Bailey had to admit.

"I guess you didn't appreciate being followed around town, either," she said in a small voice.

"True enough," he agreed. "Take my advice, would you? The next time you want to research details about a man's life, hire a detective. You and your friend couldn't have been more obvious if you'd tried."

Bailey's ego had already taken one beating from this man, and she wasn't game for round two. "Don't worry, I've given up the chase. I've discovered there aren't any real heroes left in this world. I thought you might be one, but—" she shrugged elaborately "—alas, I was wrong."

"Ouch." Parker placed his hand over his heart as though her words had wounded him gravely. "I was just beginning to feel flattered. Then you had to go and ruin it."

"I know what I'm talking about when it comes to this hero business. They're extinct, except between the pages of women's fiction."

"Correct me if I'm wrong, but do I detect a note of bitterness?"

"I'm not bitter," Bailey denied vehemently. But she didn't mention the one slightly yellowed wedding dress hanging in her closet. She'd used her savings to pay for the elegant gown and been too mortified to return it unused. She tried to convince herself it was an investment, something that would gain value over the years, like gold. Or stocks. That was what she told herself, but deep down she knew better.

"I'm sorry to have intruded upon your busy day," she said, reaching for her manuscript. "I won't trouble you again."

"Do you object to my asking you a few questions before you go?" Parker asked, standing. He walked around to the front of his desk and leaned against it, crossing his ankles. "Writers have always fascinated me."

Bailey made a show of glancing at her watch. She had forty-five minutes left of her lunch hour; she supposed she could spare a few moments. "All right."

"How long did it take you to write *Forever and a Day*?"

"Forever Yours," Bailey corrected. She suspected he was making fun of her. "Nearly six months, but I worked on it every night after work and on weekends. I felt like I'd completed a marathon when I finished."

Bailey knew Janice and Michael were grateful, too. "Only I made a beginner's mistake."

"What's that?"

"I sent it off to a publisher."

"That's a mistake?"

Bailey nodded. "I should've had someone read it first, but I was too new to know that. It wasn't until later that I met Jo Ann and joined a writers' group."

Parker folded his arms across his broad chest. "I'm not sure I understand. Isn't having your work read by an editor the whole point? Why have someone else read it first?"

"Every manuscript needs a final polishing. It's important to put your best foot forward."

"I take it *Forever Yours* was rejected."

Bailey shook her head. "Not yet, but I'm fairly certain it will be. It's been about four months now, but meanwhile I've been working on revisions. And like Jo Ann says—no news is no news."

Parker arched his brows. "That's true."

"Well," she said, glancing at her watch again, but not because she was eager to leave. She felt foolish standing in the middle of Parker's plush office talking about her novel. Her guard was slipping and the desire to secure it firmly in place was growing stronger.

"I assume Jo Ann read the manuscript after you mailed it off?"

"Yes." Bailey punctuated her comment with a shrug. "She took it home and returned it the next morning with margin notes and a list of comments three pages long. When I read them over, I could see how right she was and, well, mainly the problem was with the hero."

"Michael?"

Bailey was surprised he remembered that. "Yes, with Michael. He's a terrific guy, but he needs a little help figuring out what women—in this case Janice Hampton—want."

"That's where I came in?"

"Right."

"How?"

Bailey made an effort to explain. "A hero, at least in romantic fiction, is determined, forceful and cool. When I saw you the first time, you gave the impression of being all three."

"Was that before or after I hit you in the head?"

"After."

Parker grinned. "Did you ever consider that my umbrella might have caused a temporary lack of, shall we say, good judgment? My guess is that you don't normally follow men around town, taking notes about their behavior, do you?"

"No, you were my first," she informed him coldly. This conversation was becoming downright irritating.

"I'm pleased to hear that," he said with a cocky grin.

"Perhaps you're right. Perhaps I *was* hit harder than I realized." Just when she was beginning to feel reasonably comfortable around Parker, he'd do or say something to remind her that he was indeed a mere mortal. Any effort to base Michael's personality on his would only be a waste of time.

Bailey clutched her manuscript to her chest. "I really have to go now. I apologize for the intrusion."

"It's fine. I found our discussion…interesting."

No doubt he had. But it didn't help Bailey's dignity to know she was a source of amusement to one of the city's most distinguished architects.

* * *

"What else did he say?" Jo Ann asked early the following morning as they sat side by side on the crowded subway car.

Even before Bailey could answer, Jo Ann asked another question. "Did you get a chance to tell him that little joke about your story having a beginning, a *muddle* and an end?"

Jo Ann's reaction had surprised her. When Bailey admitted confronting Parker with her completed manuscript, Jo Ann had been enthusiastic, even excited. Bailey had supposed that her friend wouldn't understand her need to see Parker and correct his opinion of her. Instead, Jo Ann had been approving—and full of questions.

"I didn't have time to tell Parker any jokes," Bailey answered. "Good grief, I was only in his office, I don't know, maybe ten minutes."

"Ten minutes! A lot can happen in ten minutes."

Bailey crossed her long legs and prayed silently for patience. "Believe me, nothing happened. I accomplished what I set out to prove. That's it."

"If you were in there a full ten minutes, surely the two of you talked."

"He had a few questions about the business of writing."

"I see." Jo Ann nodded slowly. "So what did you tell him?"

Bailey didn't want to think about her visit with Parker. Not again. She'd returned from work that afternoon and, as was her habit, went directly to her computer. Usually she couldn't wait to get home to write. But that afternoon, she'd sat there, her hands poised on the keys, and instead of composing witty sparkling dialogue for Michael and Janice, she'd reviewed every word of her conversation with Parker.

He'd been friendly, cordial. And he'd actually sounded interested—when he wasn't busy being amused. Bailey hadn't expected that. What she'd expected was outright rejection. She'd come prepared to talk to a stone wall.

Michael, the first time around, had been like that. Gruff and unyielding. Poor Janice had been in the dark about his feelings from page one. It was as though her hero feared that revealing emotion was a sign of weakness.

In the second version Michael was so...amiable, so pleasant, that any conflict in the story had been watered down almost to nonexistence.

"As you might have guessed," Jo Ann said, breaking into her thoughts, "I like Parker Davidson. You were right when you claimed he's hero material. You'll have to forgive me for doubting you. It's just that I've never followed a man around before."

"You like Parker?" Bailey's musing about Michael and his shifting personality came to a sudden halt. "You're married," Bailey felt obliged to remind her.

"I'm not interested in him for *me*, silly," Jo Ann said, playfully nudging Bailey with her elbow. "He's all yours."

"Mine!" Bailey couldn't believe what she was hearing. "You're nuts."

"No, I'm not. He's tall, dark and handsome, and we both know how perfect that makes him for a classic romance. And the way you zeroed in on Parker the instant you saw him proves he's got the compelling presence a hero needs."

"The only *presence* I noticed was his umbrella's! He nearly decapitated me with the thing."

"You know what I think?" Jo Ann murmured, nibbling on her bottom lip. "I think that something inside you, some innate sonar device, was in action. You're hungering to find Michael. Deep within your subconscious you're seeking love and romance."

"Wrong!" Bailey declared adamantly. "You couldn't be more off course. Writing and selling a romance are my top priorities right now. I'm not interested in love, not for myself."

"What about Janice?"

The question was unfair and Bailey knew it. So much of her own personality was invested in her heroine.

The train finally reached their station, and Bailey and Jo Ann stood up and made their way toward the exit.

"Well?" Jo Ann pressed, clearly unwilling to drop the subject.

"I'm not answering that and you know why," Bailey said, stepping onto the platform. "Now kindly get off this subject. I doubt I'll ever see Parker Davidson again, and if I do I'll ignore him just the way he'll ignore me."

"You're sure of that?"

"Absolutely positive."

"Then why do you suppose he's waiting for you? That *is* Parker Davidson, isn't it?"

Bailey closed her eyes and struggled to gather her wits. Part of her was hoping against hope that Parker would saunter past without giving either of them a second's notice. But another part of her, a deep womanly part, hoped he was doing exactly what Jo Ann suggested.

"Good morning, ladies," Parker said to them as he approached.

"Hello," Bailey returned, suspecting she sounded in need of a voice-box transplant.

"Good morning!" Jo Ann said with enough enthusiasm to make up for Bailey's sorry lack.

Parker bestowed a dazzling smile on them. Bailey felt the impact of it as profoundly as if he'd bent down and brushed his mouth over hers. She quickly shook her head to dispel the image.

"I considered our conversation," he said, directing his remark to Bailey. "Since you're having so many problems with your hero, I decided I might be able to help you, after all."

"Is that right?" Bailey knew she was coming across as defensive, but she couldn't seem to help it.

Parker nodded. "I assume you decided to follow me that day to learn pertinent details about my habits, personality and so on. How about if the two of us sit down over lunch and you just ask me what you want to know?"

Bailey recognized a gift horse when she saw one. Excitement welled up inside her; nevertheless she hesitated. This man was beginning to consume her thoughts already, and she'd be asking for trouble if she allowed it to continue.

"Would you have time this afternoon?"

"She's got time," Jo Ann said without missing a beat. "Bailey works as a paralegal and she can see you during her lunch hour. This afternoon would be perfect."

Bailey glared at her friend, resisting the urge to suggest *she* have lunch with Parker since she was so keen on the idea.

"Bailey?" Parker asked, turning his attention to her.

"I...suppose." She didn't sound very gracious, and the look Jo Ann flashed her told her as much. "This is, um, very generous of you, Mr. Davidson."

"Mr. Davidson?" Parker said. "I thought we were long past being formal with each other." He dazzled her with another smile. It had the same effect on Bailey as before, weakening her knees—and her resolve.

"Shall we say noon, then?" Parker asked. "I'll meet you on Fisherman's Wharf at the Sandpiper."

The Sandpiper was known for its wonderful seafood, along with its exorbitant prices. Parker might be able to afford to eat there, but it was far beyond Bailey's meager budget.

"The Sandpiper?" she repeated. "I... I was thinking we could pick up something quick and eat on the wharf. There are several park benches along Pier 39..."

Parker frowned. "I'd prefer the Sandpiper. I'm doing some work for them, and it's good business practice to return the favor."

"Don't worry, she'll meet you there," Jo Ann assured Parker.

Bailey couldn't allow her friend to continue speaking for her. "Jo Ann, if you don't mind, I'll answer for myself."

"Oh, sure. Sorry."

Parker returned his attention to Bailey, who inhaled sharply and nodded. "I can meet you there." Of course it would mean packing lunches for the next two weeks and cutting back on Max's expensive tastes in gourmet cat food, but she supposed that was a small sacrifice.

* * *

Parker was waiting for Bailey when she arrived at the Sandpiper at a few minutes after noon. He stood when the maitre d' ushered her to his table. The room's lighting, its thick dark red carpet and rich wood created a sense of intimacy and warmth that appealed to Bailey despite her nervousness.

She'd been inside the Sandpiper only once before, with her parents when they were visiting from Oregon. Her father had wanted to treat her to the best restaurant in town, and Bailey had chosen the Sandpiper, renowned for its elegance and its fresh seafood.

"We meet again," Parker said, raising one eyebrow— that hero quirk again—as he held out her chair.

"Yes. It's very nice of you to do this."

"No problem." The waiter appeared with menus. Bailey didn't need to look; she already knew what she wanted. The seafood Caesar salad, piled high with shrimp, crab and scallops. She'd had it on her last visit and thoroughly enjoyed every bite. Parker ordered sautéed scallops and a salad. He suggested a bottle of wine, but Bailey declined. She needed to remain completely alert for this interview, so she requested coffee instead. Parker asked for the same.

After they'd placed their order, Bailey took a pen and pad from her purse, along with her reading glasses. She had a list of questions prepared. "Do you mind if we get started?"

"Sure," Parker said, leaning forward. He propped his elbows on the table and stared at her intently. "How old are you, Bailey? Twenty-one, twenty-two?"

"Twenty-seven."

He nodded, but was obviously surprised. "According to Jo Ann you work as a paralegal."

"Yes." She paused. "You'll have to excuse Jo Ann. She's a romantic."

"That's what she said about *you*—that you're a romantic."

"Yes, well, I certainly hope it works to her advantage *and* to mine."

"Oh?" His eyebrows lifted.

"We're both striving to becoming published novelists. It takes a lot more than talent, you know."

Hot crisp sourdough rolls were delivered to the table and Bailey immediately reached for one.

"The writer has to have a feel for the genre," she continued. "For Jo Ann and me, that means writing from the heart. I've only been at this for a few months, but there are several women in our writers' group who've been submitting their work for five or six years without getting published. Most of them are pragmatic about it. There are plenty of small successes we learn to count along the way."

"Such as?"

Bailey swallowed before answering. "Finishing a manuscript. There's a real feeling of accomplishment in completing a story."

"I see."

"Some people come into the group thinking they're going to make a fast buck. They think anyone should be able to throw together a romance. Generally they attend a couple of meetings, then decide writing is too hard, too much effort."

"What about you?"

"I'm in this for the long haul. Eventually I will sell

because I won't stop submitting stories until I do. My dad claims I'm like a pit bull when I want something. I clamp on and refuse to let go. That's how I feel about writing. I'm going to succeed at this if it's the last thing I ever do."

"Have you always wanted to be a writer?" Parker helped himself to a roll.

"No. I wasn't even on my high-school newspaper, although now I wish I had been. I might not have so much trouble with sentence structure and punctuation if I'd paid more attention back then."

"Then what made you decide to write romances?"

"Because I read them. In fact, I've been reading romances from the time I was in college, but it's only been in the past year or so that I started creating my own. Meeting Jo Ann was a big boost for me. I might have gone on making the same mistakes for years if it wasn't for her. She encouraged me, introduced me to other writers and took me under her wing."

The waiter arrived with their meals and Bailey sheepishly realized that she'd been doing all the talking. She had yet to ask Parker a single question.

The seafood Caesar salad was as good as Bailey remembered. After one bite she decided to treat herself like this more often. An expensive lunch every month or so wouldn't sabotage her budget.

"You were telling me it only took you six months to write *Forever Yours*," Parker commented between forkfuls of his salad. "Doesn't it usually take much longer for a first book?"

"I'm sure it does, but I devoted every spare minute to the project."

"I see. What about your social life?"

It was all Bailey could do not to snicker. What social life? She'd lived in San Francisco for more than a year, and this lunch with Parker was as close as she'd gotten to a real date. Which was exactly how she wanted it, she reminded herself.

"Bailey?"

"Oh, I get out occasionally," but she didn't mention that it was always with women friends. Since her second broken engagement, Bailey had given up on the opposite sex. Twice she'd been painfully forced to accept that men were not to be trusted. After fifteen months, Tom's deception still hurt.

Getting over Tom might not have been so difficult if it hadn't been for Paul. She'd been in love with him, too, in her junior year at college. But like Tom, he'd found someone else he loved more than he did her. The pattern just kept repeating itself, so Bailey, in her own sensible way, had put an end to it. She no longer dated.

There were times she regretted her decision. This afternoon was an excellent example. She could easily find herself becoming romantically interested in Parker. She wouldn't, of course, but the temptation was there.

Parker with his coffee-dark eyes and his devastating smile. Fortunately Bailey was wise to the fickle hearts of men. Of one thing she was sure: Parker Davidson hadn't reached his mid-thirties, still single, without breaking a few hearts along the way.

There were other times she regretted her decision to give up on dating. No men equaled no marriage. And no children. It was the children part that troubled her most, especially when she was around babies. Her decision hit her hard then. Without a husband she wasn't likely to have a child of her own, since she wasn't interested in being a single mother. But so far, all she had to do was avoid places where she'd run into mothers and infants. Out of sight, out of mind...

"Bailey?"

"I'm sorry," she mumbled, suddenly aware that she'd allowed her thoughts to run unchecked for several minutes. "Did I miss something?"

"No. You had a...pained look and I was wondering if your salad was all right?"

"Yes. It's wonderful. As fantastic as I remember." She briefly relayed the story of her parents treating her to dinner at the Sandpiper. What she didn't explain was that their trip south had been made for the express purpose of checking up on Bailey. Her parents were worried about her. They insisted she worked too hard, didn't get out enough, didn't socialize.

Bailey had listened politely to their concerns and then hugged them both, thanked them for their love and sent them back to Oregon.

Spotting her pad and pen lying beside her plate, Bailey sighed. She hadn't questioned Parker once, which was the whole point of their meeting. Glancing at her watch, she groaned inwardly. She only had another fifteen minutes. It wasn't worth the effort of getting started. Not when she'd just have to stop.

"I need to get back to the office," she announced regretfully. She looked around for the waiter so she could ask for her check.

"It's been taken care of."

It took Bailey a moment to realize that Parker was talking about her meal. "I can't let you do that," she insisted, reaching for her purse.

"Please."

If he'd argued with her, shoveled out some chauvinistic challenge, Bailey would never have allowed him to pay. But that one word, that one softly spoken word, was her undoing.

"All right," she agreed, her own voice just as soft.

"You didn't get a chance to ask your questions."

"I know." She found that frustrating, but had no one to blame but herself. "I got caught up talking about romance fiction and writing and—"

"Shall we try again? Another time?"

"It looks like we'll have to." She needed to be careful that lunch with Parker didn't develop into a habit.

"I'm free tomorrow evening."

"Evening?" Somehow that seemed far more threatening than meeting for lunch. "Uh... I generally reserve the hours after work for writing."

"I see."

Her heart reacted to the hint of disappointment in his voice. "I might be able to make an exception." Bailey was horrified as soon as the words were out. She couldn't believe she'd said that. For the entire hour, she'd been lecturing herself about the dangers of getting close to Parker. "No," she said firmly. "It's crucial that I maintain my writing schedule."

"You're sure?"

"Positive."

Parker took a business card from his coat pocket. He scribbled on the back and handed it to her. "This is my home number in case you change your mind."

Bailey accepted the card and thrust it into her purse, together with her notepad and pen. "I really have to write... I mean, my writing schedule is important to me. I can't be running out to dinner just because someone asks me." She stood, scraping back her chair in her eagerness to escape.

"Consider it research."

Bailey responded by shaking her head. "Thank you for lunch."

"You're most welcome. But I hope you'll reconsider having dinner with me."

She backed away from the table, her purse held tightly in both hands. "Dinner?" she echoed, still undecided.

"For the purposes of research," he added.

"It wouldn't be a *date*." It was important to make that point clear. The only man she had time for was Michael. But Parker was supposed to help her with Michael, so maybe... "Not a date, just research," she repeated in a more determined voice. "Agreed?"

He grinned, his eyes lighting mischievously. "What do you think?"

Five

Max was waiting at the door when Bailey got home from work that evening. His striped yellow tail pointed straight toward the ceiling as he twisted and turned between her legs. His not-so-subtle message was designed to remind her it was mealtime.

"Just a minute, Maxie," she muttered. She leafed through the mail as she walked into the kitchen, pausing when she found a yellow slip.

"Meow."

"Max, look," she said, waving the note at him. "Mrs. Morgan's holding a package for us." The apartment manager was always kind enough to accept deliveries, saving Bailey more than one trip to the post office.

Leaving a disgruntled Max behind, Bailey hurried down the stairs to Mrs. Morgan's first-floor apartment, where she was greeted with a warm smile. Mrs. Morgan was an older woman, a matronly widow who seemed especially protective of her younger tenants.

"Here you go, dear," she said, handing Bailey a large manila envelope.

Bailey knew the instant she saw the package that this

wasn't an unexpected surprise from her parents. It was her manuscript—rejected.

"Thank you," she said, struggling to disguise her disappointment. From the moment Bailey had read Jo Ann's critique she'd realized *Forever Yours* would probably be rejected. What she hadn't foreseen was this stomach-churning sensation, this feeling of total discouragement. Koppen Publishing had kept the manuscript for nearly four months. Jo Ann had insisted no news was no news, and so Bailey had begun to believe that the editor had held on to her book for so long because she'd seriously considered buying it.

Bailey had fully expected that she'd have to revise her manuscript; nonetheless, she'd *hoped* to be doing it with a contract in her pocket, riding high on success.

Once again Max was waiting by the door, more impatient this time. Without thinking, Bailey walked into the kitchen, opened the refrigerator and dumped food into his bowl. It wasn't until she straightened that she realized she'd given her greedy cat the dinner she was planning to cook for herself.

No fool, Max dug into the ground turkey, edging his way between her legs in his eagerness. Bailey shrugged. The way she was feeling, she didn't have much of an appetite, anyway.

It took her another five minutes to find the courage to open the package. She carefully pried apart the seam. Why she was being so careful, she couldn't even guess. She had no intention of reusing the envelope. Once the padding was separated, she removed the manuscript box. Inside was a short letter that she quickly read, swallowing down the emotion that clogged her throat. The fact that the letter was personal, and not simply a standard rejection letter, did little to relieve the crushing disappointment.

Reaching for the phone, Bailey punched out Jo Ann's number. Her friend had experienced this more than once and was sure to have some words of wisdom to help Bailey through this moment. Jo Ann would understand how badly her confidence had been shaken.

After four rings, Bailey was connected to her friend's answering machine. She listened to the message, but didn't want to leave Jo Ann such a disheartening message, so she mumbled, "It's Bailey," and hung up.

Pacing the apartment in an effort to sort out her emotions didn't seem to help. She eyed her computer, which was set up in a corner of her compact living room, but the desire to sit down and start writing was nil. Vanished. Destroyed.

Jo Ann had warned her. So had others in their writers' group. Rejections hurt. She just hadn't expected it to hurt so much.

Searching in her purse for a mint, she felt her fingers close around a business card. *Parker's* business card. She slowly drew it out. He'd written down his phone number…

Should she call him? No, she decided, thrusting the card into her pocket. Why even entertain the notion? Talking to Parker now would be foolish. And risky. She was a big girl. She could take rejection. Anyone who became a writer had to learn how to handle rejection.

Rejections were rungs on the ladder of success. Someone had said that at a meeting once, and Bailey had written it down and kept it posted on the bottom edge of her computer screen. Now was the time to act on that belief. Since this was only the first rung, she had a long way to climb, but the darn ladder was much steeper than she'd anticipated.

With a fumbling resolve, she returned to the kitchen and reread the letter from Paula Albright, the editor, who wrote that she was returning the manuscript "with regret."

"Not as much regret as I feel," Bailey informed Max, who was busy enjoying *her* dinner.

"She says I show promise." But Bailey noted that she didn't say promise of what.

The major difficulty, according to the editor, was Michael. This wasn't exactly a surprise to Bailey. Ms. Albright had kindly mentioned several scenes that needed to be reworked with this problem in mind. She ended her letter by telling Bailey that if she revised the manuscript, the editorial department would be pleased to reevaluate it.

Funny, Bailey hadn't even noticed that the first time she'd read the letter. If she reworked Michael, there was still a chance.

With sudden enthusiasm, Bailey grabbed the phone. She'd changed her mind—calling Parker now seemed like a good idea. A great idea. He might well be her one and only chance to straighten out poor misguided Michael.

Parker answered on the second ring, sounding distracted and mildly irritated at being interrupted.

"Parker," Bailey said, desperately hoping she wasn't making a first-class fool of herself, "this is Bailey York."

"Hello." His tone was a little less disgruntled.

Her mouth had gone completely dry, but she rushed ahead with the reason for her call. "I want you to know

I've... I've been thinking about your dinner invitation. Could you possibly meet me tonight instead of tomorrow?" She wanted to start rehabilitating Michael as soon as possible.

"This is Bailey York?" He sounded as though he didn't remember who she was.

"The writer from the subway," she said pointedly, feeling like more of an idiot with every passing second. She should never have phoned him, but the impulse had been so powerful. She longed to put this rejection behind her and write a stronger romance, but she was going to need his help. Perhaps she should call him later. "Listen, if now is inconvenient, I could call another time." She was about to hang up when Parker spoke.

"Now is fine. I'm sorry if I seem rattled, but I was working and I tend to get absorbed in a project."

"I do that myself," she said, reassured by his explanation. Drawing a deep breath, she explained the reason for her unexpected call. "*Forever Yours* was rejected today."

"I'm sorry to hear that." His regret seemed genuine, and the soft fluttering sensation returned to her stomach at the sympathy he extended.

"I was sorry, too, but it didn't come as a big shock. I guess I let my hopes build when the manuscript wasn't immediately returned, which is something Jo Ann warned me about." She shifted the receiver to her other ear, surprised by how much better she felt having someone to talk to.

"What happens when a publisher turns down a manuscript? Do they critique the book?"

"Heavens, no. Generally manuscripts are returned with a standard rejection letter. The fact that the editor took the time to personally write me about revising is sort of a compliment. Actually, it's an excellent sign. Especially since she's willing to look at *Forever Yours* again." Bailey paused and inhaled shakily. "I was wondering if I could take you up on that offer for dinner. I realize this is rather sudden and I probably shouldn't have phoned, but tonight would be best for me since…since I inadvertently gave Max my ground turkey and there's really nothing else in the fridge, but if you can't I understand…" The words had tumbled out in a nervous rush; once she'd started, she couldn't seem to make herself stop.

"Do you want me to pick you up, or would you rather meet somewhere?"

"Ah…" Despite herself, Bailey was astounded. She hadn't really expected Parker to agree. "The restaurant where you had lunch a couple of weeks ago looked good. Only, please, I insist on paying for my own meal this time."

"In Chinatown?"

"Yes. Would you meet me there?"

"Sure. Does an hour give you enough time?"

"Oh, yes. An hour's plenty." Once again Bailey found herself nearly tongue-tied with surprise—and pleasure.

Their conversation was over so fast that she was left staring at the phone, half wondering if it had really happened at all. She took a couple of deep breaths, then dashed into her bedroom to change, renew her makeup and brush her hair.

Bailey loved Chinese food, especially the spicy Szechuan dishes, but she wasn't thinking about dinner as the taxi pulled up in front of the restaurant. She'd decided to indulge herself by taking a cab to Chinatown. It did mean she'd have to take the subway home, though.

Parker, who was standing outside the restaurant waiting for her, hurried forward to open the cab door. Bailey was terribly aware of his hand supporting her elbow as he helped her out.

"It's good of you to meet me like this on such short notice," she said, smiling up at Parker.

"No problem. Who's Max?"

"My cat."

Parker grinned and, clasping her elbow more firmly, led her into the restaurant. The first thing that caught Bailey's attention was a gigantic, intricately carved chandelier made of dark polished wood. She'd barely had a chance to examine it, however, when they were escorted down a long hallway to a narrow room filled with wooden booths, high-backed and private, each almost a little room of its own.

"Oh, my, this is nice," she breathed, sliding into their booth. She slipped the bag from her shoulder and withdrew the same pen and notepad she'd brought with her when they'd met for lunch.

The waiter appeared with a lovely ceramic teapot and a pair of tiny matching cups. The menus were tucked under his arm.

Bailey didn't have nearly as easy a time making her choice as she had at the Sandpiper. Parker suggested they each order whatever they wished and then share. There were so many dishes offered, most of them sounding delectable and exciting, that it took Bailey a good ten minutes to make her selection—spicy shrimp noodles. Parker chose the less adventurous almond chicken stir-fry.

"All right," Bailey said, pouring them each some tea. "Now let's get down to business."

"Sure." Parker relaxed against the back of the booth, crossing his arms and stretching out his legs. "Ask away," he said, motioning with his hand when she hesitated.

"Maybe I'd better start by giving you a brief outline of the story."

"However you'd like to do this."

"I want you to understand Michael," she explained. "He's a businessman, born on the wrong side of the tracks. He's a little bitter, but he's learned to forgive those who've hurt him through the years. Michael's in his mid-thirties, and he's never been married."

"Why not?"

"Well, for one thing he's been too busy building his career."

"As what?"

"He's in the exporting business."

"I see."

"You're frowning." Bailey hadn't asked a single one of her prepared questions yet, and already Parker was looking annoyed.

"It's just that a man doesn't generally reach the ripe old age of thirty-five without a relationship or two. If he's never had any, then there's a problem."

"You're thirty-something and you're not married," she felt obliged to point out. "What's your excuse?"

Parker shrugged. "My college schedule was very heavy, which didn't leave a lot of time for dating. Later I traveled extensively, which again didn't offer much opportunity. Oh, there were relationships along the way, but nothing ever worked out. I guess you could say I haven't found the right woman. But that doesn't mean I'm not interested in marrying and settling down some day."

"Exactly. That's how Michael feels, except he thinks getting married would only complicate his life. He's ready to fall in love with Janice, but he doesn't realize it."

"I see," Parker said with a nod, "go on. I shouldn't have interrupted you."

"Well, basically, Michael's life is going smoothly until he meets Janice Hampton. Her father has retired and she's taking over the operation of his manufacturing firm. A job she's well qualified for, I might add."

"What does she manufacture?"

"I was rather vague about that, but I let the reader assume it has something to do with computer parts. I tossed in a word here and there to give that suggestion."

Parker nodded. "Continue. I'll try not to butt in again."

"That's okay," she said briskly. "Anyway, Janice's father is a longtime admirer of Michael's, and the old coot would like to get his daughter and Michael together. Neither one of them's aware of it, of course. At least not right away."

Parker reached for the teapot and refilled their cups. "That sounds good."

Bailey smiled shyly. "Thanks. One of the first things that happens is Janice's father maneuvers Michael and Janice under the mistletoe at a Christmas party. Everyone's expecting them to kiss, but Michael is furious and he—"

"Just a minute." Parker held up one hand, stopping her. "Let me see if I've got this straight. This guy is standing under the mistletoe with a beautiful woman and he's furious. What's wrong with him?"

"What do you mean?"

"No man in his right mind is going to object to kissing a beautiful woman."

Bailey picked up her teacup and leaned against the hard back of the wooden booth, considering. Parker was right. And Janice hadn't been too happy about the situation herself. Was that any more believable? Imagine standing under the mistletoe with a man like Parker Davidson. Guiltily she shook off the thought and returned her attention to his words.

"Unless…" he was saying pensively.

"Yes?"

"Unless he recognizes that he was manipulated into kissing her and resents it. He may even think she's in cahoots with her father."

Brightening, Bailey nodded, making a note on her pad. "Yeah, that would work." Parker was as good at tossing ideas around as Jo Ann, which was a pleasant surprise.

"Still…" He hesitated, sighing. "A pretty woman is a pretty woman and he isn't going to object too strongly, regardless of the circumstances. What happens when he does kiss her?"

"Not too much. He does it grudgingly, but I've decided I'm going to change that part. You're right. He shouldn't make too much of a fuss. However, this happens early on in the book and neither of them's aware of her father's scheme. I don't want to tip the reader off so soon as to what's happening."

Bailey's mind was spinning as she reworked the scene. She could picture Michael and Janice standing under the mistletoe, both somewhat uneasy with the situation, but as Parker suggested, not objecting too strongly. Janice figures they'll kiss, and that'll be the end of it...until they actually do the kissing.

That was the part Bailey intended to build on. When Michael's and Janice's lips met it would be like...like throwing a match on dry tinder, so intense would be the reaction.

The idea began to gather momentum in her mind. Then, not only would Janice and Michael be fighting her father's outrageous plot, they'd be battling their feelings for each other.

"This is great," Bailey whispered, "really great." She started to tell Parker her plan when they were interrupted by the waiter, who brought their dinner, setting the steaming dishes before them.

By then, Bailey's appetite had fully recovered and she reached eagerly for the chopsticks. Parker picked up his own. They both reached for the shrimp noodles. Bailey withdrew her chopsticks.

"You first."

"No, you." He waved his hand, encouraging her.

She smiled and scooped up a portion of the noodles. The situation felt somehow intimate, comfortable, and yet they were still basically strangers.

They ate in silence for several minutes and Bailey watched Parker deftly manipulate the chopsticks. It was the first time she'd dated a man who was as skilled at handling them as she was herself.

Dated a man.

The words leapt out at her. Bright red warning signs seemed to be flashing in her mind. Her head shot up and she stared wide-eyed at the man across the table from her.

"Bailey? Are you all right?"

She nodded and hurriedly looked away.

"Did you bite into a hot pepper?"

"No," she assured him, quickly shaking her head. "I'm fine. Really, I'm all right." Only she wasn't, and she suspected he knew it.

The remainder of their meal passed with few comments.

Naturally Parker had no way of knowing about her experiences with Paul and Tom. Nor would he be aware that there was an unused wedding dress hanging in her closet, taunting her every morning when she got ready for work. The wedding gown was an ever-present reminder of why she couldn't put any faith in the male of the species.

The danger came when she allowed her guard to slip. Before she knew it, she'd be trusting a man once again, and that was a definite mistake. Parker made her feel somehow secure; she felt instinctively that he was a man of integrity, of candor—and therein lay the real risk. Maybe he *was* a real live breathing hero, but Bailey had been fooled twice before. She wasn't going to put her heart on the line again.

They split the tab. Parker clearly wasn't pleased about that, but Bailey insisted. They were about to leave the restaurant when Parker said, "You started to say something about rewriting that scene under the mistletoe."

"Yes," she answered, regaining some of her former enthusiasm. "I'm going to have that kiss make a dynamite impact on them both. Your suggestions were very helpful. I can't tell you how much I appreciate your willingness to meet with me like this."

It was as though Parker hadn't heard her. His forehead creased as he held open the door for her and they stepped onto the busy sidewalk.

"You're frowning again," Bailey noted aloud.

"Have you ever experienced that kind of intense sensation when a man kissed you?"

Bailey didn't have to think about it. "Not really."

"That's what I thought."

"But I like the idea of that happening between Janice and Michael," she argued. "It adds a whole new dimension to the plot. I can use that. Besides, there's a certain element of fantasy in a traditional romance novel, a larger-than-life perspective."

"Oh, I'm not saying a strong reaction between them shouldn't happen. I'm just wondering how you plan to write such a powerfully emotional scene without any real experience of it yourself."

"That's the mark of a good writer," Bailey explained, ignoring his less-than-flattering remark. She'd been kissed before! Plenty of times. "Being able to create an atmosphere of romance just takes imagination. You don't expect me to go around kissing strange men, do you?"

"Why not? You had no qualms about *following* a strange man. Kissing me wouldn't be any different. It's all research."

"Kissing you?"

"It'll add credibility to your writing. A confidence you might not otherwise have."

"If I were writing a murder mystery would you suggest I go out and kill someone?" Bailey had to argue with him before she found herself *agreeing* to this craziness!

"Don't be ridiculous! Murder would be out of the question, but a kiss…a kiss is very much within your grasp. It would lend authenticity to your story. I suggest we go ahead with it, Bailey."

They were strolling side by side. Bailey was deep in thought when Parker casually turned into a narrow alley. She guessed it was the same one he'd hauled her into the day she'd followed him.

"Well," he said, resting his hands on her shoulders and staring down at her. "Are you game?"

Was she? Bailey didn't know anymore. He was right; the scene would have far more impact if she were to experience the same sensations as Janice. Kissing Parker would be like Janice kissing Michael. The sale of her book could hinge on how well she developed the attraction between hero and heroine in that all-important first chapter.

"Okay," she said, barely recognizing her own voice.

No sooner had she spoken than Parker gently cupped her chin and directed her mouth toward his. "This is going to be good," she heard him whisper just before his lips settled over hers.

Bailey's eyes drifted shut. This *was* good. In fact, it was wonderful. So wonderful, she felt weak and dizzy—and yearned to feel even weaker and dizzier. Despite herself, she clung to Parker, literally hanging in his arms. Without his support, she feared she would have slumped to the street.

He tasted so warm and familiar, as if she'd spent a lifetime in his arms, as if she were *meant* to spend a lifetime there.

The fluttering sensation in her stomach changed to a warm heaviness. She felt strange and hot. Bailey was afraid that if this didn't end soon, she'd completely lose control.

"No more," she pleaded, breaking off the kiss. She buried her face in his shoulder and dragged in several deep breaths in an effort to stop her trembling.

It wasn't fair that Parker could make her feel this way. For Janice and Michael's sake, it was the best thing that could have happened, but for her own sake, it was the worst. She didn't *want* to feel any of this. The protective numbness around her heart was crumbling just when it was so important to keep it securely in place.

The hot touch of his lips against her temple caused her to jump away from him. "Well," she said, rubbing her palms briskly together once she found her voice. "That was certainly a step in the right direction."

"I beg your pardon?" Parker was staring at her as though he wasn't sure he'd heard her accurately.

"The kiss. It had pizzazz and a certain amount of charm, but I was looking for a little more...something. The kiss between Michael and Janice has got to have spark."

"Our kiss had spark." Parker's voice was deep, brooding.

"Charm," she corrected, then added brightly, "I will say one thing, though. You're good at this. Lots of practice, right?" Playfully she poked his ribs with her elbow. "Well, I've got to be going. Thanks again for meeting me on such short notice. I'll be seeing you around." Amazingly the smile on her lips didn't crack. Even more amazing was the fact that she managed to walk away from him on legs that felt like overcooked pasta.

She was about five blocks from the BART station, walking as fast as she could, mumbling to herself all the way. She behaved like an idiot every time she even came near Parker Davidson!

She continued mumbling, chastising herself, when he pulled up at the curb beside her in a white sports car. She didn't know much about cars, but she knew expensive when she saw it. The same way she knew his suit hadn't come from a department store.

"Get in," he said gruffly, slowing to a stop and leaning over to open the passenger door.

"Get in?" she repeated. "I was going to take BART."

"Not at this time of night you're not."

"Why shouldn't I?" she demanded.

"Don't press your luck, Bailey. Just get in."

She debated whether she should or not, but from the stubborn set of his jaw, she could see it would do no good to argue. She'd never seen a more obstinate-looking jaw in her life. As she recalled, it was one of the first things she'd noticed about Parker.

"What's your address?" he asked after she'd slipped inside.

Bailey gave it to him as she fiddled with the seat belt, then sat silently while he sped down the street, weaving his way in and out of traffic. He braked sharply at a red light and she glanced in his direction.

"Why are you so angry?" she demanded. "You look as if you're ready to bite my head off."

"I don't like it when a woman lies to me."

"When did I lie?" she asked indignantly.

"You lied a few minutes ago when you said our kiss was…lacking." He laughed humorlessly and shook his head. "We generated more electricity with that one kiss than the Hoover Dam does in a month. You want to kid yourself, then fine, but I'm not playing your game."

"I'm not playing any game," she informed him primly. "Nor do I appreciate having you come at me like King Kong because my assessment of a personal exchange between us doesn't meet yours."

"A personal exchange?" he scoffed. "It was a kiss, sweetheart."

"I only agreed to it for research purposes."

"If that's what you want to believe, fine, but we both know better."

"Whatever," she muttered. Parker could think what he wanted. She'd let him drive her home because he seemed to be insisting on it. But as far as having anything further to do with him—out of the question. He was obviously placing far more significance on their kiss than she'd ever intended.

Okay, so she *had* felt something. But to hear him tell it, that kiss rivaled the great screen kisses of all time.

Parker drove up in front of her apartment building and turned off the engine. "All right," he said coolly. "Let's go over this one last time. Do you still claim our kiss was merely a 'personal exchange'? Just research?"

"Yes," she stated emphatically, unwilling to budge an inch.

"Then prove it."

Bailey sighed. "How exactly am I supposed to do that?"

"Kiss me again."

Bailey could feel the color drain out of her face. "I'm not about to sit outside my apartment kissing you with half the building looking on."

"Fine, then invite me in."

"Uh…it's late."

"Since when is nine o'clock late?" he taunted.

Bailey was running out of excuses. "There's nothing that says a woman is obligated to invite a man into her home, is there?" she asked in formal tones. Her spine was Sunday-school straight and her eyes were focused on the street ahead of her.

Parker's laugh took her by surprise. She twisted around to stare at him and found him smiling roguishly. "You little coward," he murmured, pulling her toward him for a quick peck on the cheek. "Go on. Run home before I change my mind."

Six

"I like it," Jo Ann said. "The way you changed that first kissing scene under the mistletoe is a stroke of genius." She smiled happily. "This is exactly the kind of rewriting you'll need to turn that rejection into a sale. You've taken Michael and made him proud and passionate, but very real and spontaneous. He's caught off guard by his attraction to Janice and is reacting purely by instinct." Jo Ann tapped her fingers on the top page of the revised first chapter. "This is your most powerful writing yet."

Bailey was so pleased she could barely restrain herself from leaping up and dancing a jig down the center of the congested subway-car aisle. Through sheer determination, she managed to confine her response to a smile.

"It's interesting how coming at this scene from a slightly different angle puts everything in a new light, isn't it?"

"It sure is," Jo Ann concurred. "If the rest of the book reads as well as this chapter, I honestly think you might have a chance."

It was too much to hope for. Bailey had spent the entire weekend in front of her computer. She must have rewritten the mistletoe scene no less than ten times, strengthening emotions, exploring the heady response Michael and Janice had toward each other. She'd worked hard to capture the incredulity they'd experienced, the shock of their unexpected fascination. Naturally, neither one could allow the other to know what they were feeling yet—otherwise Bailey wouldn't have any plot.

Michael had been dark and brooding afterward. Janice had done emotional cartwheels in an effort to diminish the incident. But neither of them could forget it.

If the unable-to-forget part seemed particularly realistic, there was a reason. Bailey's reaction to Parker had been scandalously similar to Janice's feelings about Michael's kiss. The incredulity was there. The wonder. The shock. And it never should have happened.

Unfortunately Bailey had suspected that even before she'd agreed to the "research." Who did she think she was fooling? Certainly not herself. She'd wanted Parker to kiss her long before he'd offered her the excuse.

Halfway through their dinner, Bailey had experienced all the symptoms. She knew them well. The palpitating heart, the sweating palms, the sudden loss of appetite. She'd tried to ignore them, but as the meal had progressed she'd thought of little else.

Parker had gone suspiciously quiet, too. Then, later, he'd kissed her and everything became much, much worse. She'd felt warm and dizzy. A tingling sensation had slowly spread through her body. It seemed as though every cell in her body was aware of him. The sensations had been so overwhelming, she'd had to pretend nothing had happened. The truth was simply too risky.

"What made you decide to rework the scene that way?" Jo Ann asked, breaking into her thoughts.

Bailey stared at her friend and blinked rapidly.

"Bailey?" Jo Ann asked. "You look as if your mind's soaring through outer space."

"Uh… I was just thinking."

"A dangerous habit for a writer. We can't seem to get our characters out of our minds, can we? They insist on following us everywhere."

Characters, nothing! It was Parker Davidson she couldn't stop thinking about. As for the *following* part… Had her thoughts conjured him up? There he was, large as life, casually strolling toward them as though he'd sought her out. He hadn't, she told herself sternly. Nonetheless she searched for him every morning. She couldn't seem to help it. She'd never been so frighteningly aware of a man before, so eager—yet so reluctant to see him. Often she found herself scanning the faces around her, hoping to catch a glimpse of him.

Now here he was. Bailey quickly looked out the window into the tunnel's darkness, staring at the reflections in the glass.

"Good morning, ladies," Parker said jovially, standing directly in front of them, his feet braced slightly apart. The morning paper was tucked under his arm, and he looked very much as he had the first time she'd noticed him. Forceful. Appealing. Handsome.

"Morning," Bailey mumbled. She immediately turned back to the window.

"Hello again," Jo Ann replied warmly, smiling up at him.

For one wild second Bailey experienced a flash of resentment. Parker was *her* hero, not Jo Ann's! Her friend was greeting him like a long-lost brother or something. But what bothered Bailey even more was how delighted *she* felt. These were the very reactions she'd been combating all weekend.

"So," Parker said smoothly, directing his words to Bailey, "have you followed any strange men around town lately?"

She glared at him, annoyed at the way his words drew the attention of those sitting nearby. "Of course not," she snapped.

"I'm glad to hear it."

She'd just bet! She happened to glance at the man standing next to Parker. He was a distinguished-looking older gentleman who was peeking at her curiously over the morning paper.

"Did you rewrite the kissing scene?" Parker asked next.

The businessman gave up any pretense of reading, folded his paper and studied Bailey openly.

"She did a fabulous job of it," Jo Ann said with a mentor's pride.

"I was sure she would," Parker remarked. A hint of a smile raised the corners of his mouth and made his eyes sparkle. Bailey wanted to demand that he cease and desist that very instant. "I suspect it had a ring of sincerity to it," Parker added, his eyes meeting Bailey's. "A depth, perhaps, that was missing in the first account."

"It did," Jo Ann confirmed, looking mildly surprised. "The whole scene is beautifully written. Every emotion, every sensation, is right there, so vividly described it's difficult to believe the same writer is responsible for both versions."

Parker's expression reminded Bailey of Max when he'd discovered ground turkey in his dish instead of soggy cat food. His full sensuous mouth curved with satisfaction.

"I only hope Bailey can do as well with the dancing scene," Jo Ann said.

"The dancing scene?" Parker asked intently.

"That's several chapters later," Bailey explained, jerking the manuscript out of Jo Ann's lap. She shoved it inside a folder and slipped it into her spacious shoulder bag.

"It's romantic the way it's written, but there's something lacking," said Jo Ann. "Unfortunately I haven't been able to put my finger on what's wrong."

"The problem is and always has been Michael," Bailey inserted, not wanting the conversation to continue in this vein. She hoped her hero would forgive her for blaming her shortcomings as a writer on him.

"You can't fault Michael for the dancing scene," Jo Ann disagreed. "Correct me if I'm wrong, but as I recall, Michael and Janice were manipulated—by Janice's father—into attending a Pops concert. The only reason they went was that they couldn't think of a plausible excuse."

"Yes," she admitted grudgingly. "A sixties rock group was performing."

"Right. Then, as the evening went on, several couples from the audience started to dance. The young man sitting next to Janice asked her—"

"The problem is with Michael," Bailey insisted

again. She glanced hopefully at the older gentleman, but he just shrugged, eyes twinkling.

"What did Michael do that was so wrong?" Jo Ann asked with a puzzled frown.

"He...he should never have let Janice dance with another man," Bailey said in a desperate voice.

"Michael couldn't have done anything else," Jo Ann argued, "otherwise he would've looked like a jealous fool." She turned to Parker for confirmation.

"I may be new to this hero business, but I can't help agreeing."

Bailey was irritated with both of them. This was *her* story and she'd write it as she saw fit. However, she refrained from saying so—just in case they were right. She needed time to mull over their opinions.

The train screeched to a halt and people surged toward the door. Bailey noted, gratefully, that this was Parker's stop.

"I'll give you a call later," he said, looking directly into Bailey's eyes. He didn't wait for a response.

He knew she didn't want to hear from him. She was frightened. Defensive. Guarded. With good reason. Only he didn't fully understand what that reason was. But a man like Parker wouldn't let her attitude go unchallenged.

"He's going to call you." Jo Ann sighed enviously. "Isn't that thrilling? Doesn't that excite you?"

Bailey shook her head, contradicting everything she was feeling inside. "Excite me? Not really."

Jo Ann frowned at her suspiciously. "What's the matter?"

"Nothing," Bailey answered with calm determination. She'd strolled down the path of romantic delusion twice before, but this time her eyes were wide open. Romance was wonderful, exciting, inspiring—and it was best limited to the pages of a well-crafted novel. Men, at least the men in her experience, inevitably proved to be terrible disappointments. Painful disappointments.

"Don't you like Parker?" Jo Ann demanded. "I mean, who wouldn't? He's hero material. You recognized it immediately, even before I did. Remember?"

Bailey wasn't likely to forget. "Yes, but that was in the name of research."

"Research?" Jo Ann cocked her eyebrows in flagrant disbelief. "Be honest, Bailey. You saw a whole lot more than Michael in Parker Davidson. You're not the type of woman who dashes off subways to follow a man. Some deep inner part of your being was reaching out to him."

Bailey forced a short laugh. "I hate to say it, Jo Ann, but I think you've been reading too many romances lately."

Jo Ann shrugged in a lie-to-yourself-if-you-insist manner. "Maybe, but I doubt it."

Nevertheless, her friend had given Bailey something to ponder.

The writing didn't go well that evening. Bailey, dressed in warm gray sweats, sans makeup and shoes, sat in front of her computer, staring blankly at the screen. "Inspiration is on vacation," she muttered, and that bit of doggerel seemed the best she could manage at the moment. Her usual warmth and humor escaped her. Every word she wrote sounded flat. She was tempted to erase the entire chapter.

Max, who had appointed himself the guardian of her printer, was curled up fast asleep on top of it. Bailey had long ago given up trying to keep him off. She'd quickly surrendered and taken to folding a towel over the printer to protect its internal workings from cat hair. Whenever she needed to print out a chapter, she nudged him awake; Max was always put out by the inconvenience and let her know it.

"Something's wrong," she announced to her feline companion. "The words just aren't flowing."

Max didn't reveal the slightest concern. He stretched out one yellow striped leg and examined it carefully, then settled down for another lengthy nap. He was fed and content and that was all that mattered.

Crossing her ankles, Bailey leaned back and clasped her hands behind her head. Chapter two of *Forever Yours* was just as vibrant and fast-paced as chapter one. But chapter three... She groaned and reread Paula Albright's letter for the umpteenth time, wanting desperately to capture the feelings and emotions the editor had suggested.

The phone rang in the kitchen, startling her. Bailey sighed irritably, then got up and rushed into the other room.

"Hello," she said curtly, realizing two important things at the same time. The first was how unfriendly and unwelcoming she sounded, and the second...the second was that she'd been unconsciously anticipating this call the entire evening.

"Hello," Parker returned in an affable tone. He didn't seem at all perturbed by her disagreeable mood. "I take it you're working, but from the sound of your voice I'd guess the rewrite isn't going well."

"It's coming along nicely." Bailey didn't know why she felt the need to lie. She was immediately consumed by guilt, then tried to disguise that by being even less friendly. "In fact, you interrupted a critical scene. I have so little time to write as it is, and my evenings are important to me."

There was an awkward silence. "Then I won't keep you," Parker said with cool politeness.

"It's just that it would be better if you didn't phone me." Her explaining didn't seem to improve the situation.

"I see," he said slowly.

And Bailey could tell that he *did* understand. She'd half expected him to argue, or at least attempt to cajole her into a more responsive mood. He didn't.

"Why don't you call me when you have a free moment," was all he said.

"I will," she answered, terribly disappointed and not sure why. It *was* better this way, with no further contact between them, she reminded herself firmly. "Goodbye, Parker."

"Goodbye," he said after another uncertain silence.

Bailey was still gripping the receiver when she heard a soft click followed by the drone of the disconnected line. She'd been needlessly abrupt and standoffish—as if she was trying to prove something. Trying to convince herself that she wanted nothing more to do with Parker.

Play it safe, Bailey. Don't involve your heart. You've learned your lesson. Her mind was constructing excuses for her tactless behavior, but her heart would accept none of it.

Bailey felt wretched. She went back to her chair and stared at the computer screen for a full five minutes, unable to concentrate.

He's only trying to help, her heart told her.

Men aren't to be trusted, her mind said. *Haven't you learned that yet? How many times does it take to teach you something?*

Parker isn't like the others, her heart insisted.

Her mind, however, refused to listen. *All men are alike.*

But if she'd done the right thing, why did she feel so rotten? Yet she knew that if she gave in to him now, she'd regret it. She was treading on thin ice with this relationship; she remembered how she'd felt when he kissed her. Was she willing to risk the pain, the heartache, all over again?

Bailey closed her eyes and shook her head. Her thoughts were hopelessly tangled. She'd done what she knew was necessary, but she didn't feel good about it. In fact, she was miserable. Parker had gone out of his way to help her with this project, offering her his time and his advice. He'd given her valuable insights into the male point of view. And when he kissed her, he'd reminded her how it felt to be a desirable woman...

Bailey barely slept that night. On Tuesday morning she decided to look for Parker, even if it meant moving from one subway car to the next, something she rarely did. When she did run into him, she intended to apologize, crediting her ill mood to creative temperament.

"Morning," Jo Ann said, meeting her on the station platform the way she did every morning.

"Hello," Bailey murmured absently, scanning the windows of the train as it slowed to a stop, hoping to spot Parker. If Jo Ann noticed anything odd, she didn't comment.

"I heard back from the agent I wrote to a couple of months back," Jo Ann said, grinning broadly. Her eyes fairly sparkled.

"Irene Ingram?" Bailey momentarily forgot about Parker as she stared at her friend. Her sagging spirits lifted with the news. For weeks Jo Ann had been poring over the agent list, trying to decide whom to approach first. After much deliberation and thought, Jo Ann had decided to aim high. Many of the major publishers were no longer accepting non-agented material, and finding one willing to represent a beginner had been a serious concern. Irene was listed as one of the top romance-fiction agents in the industry. She represented a number of prominent names.

"And?" Bailey prompted, although she was fairly sure the news was positive.

"She's read my book and—" Jo Ann tossed her hands in the air "—she's crazy about it!"

"Does that mean she's going to represent you?" They were both aware how unusual it was for an established New York agent to represent an unpublished author. It wasn't unheard of, but it didn't happen all that often.

"You know, we never got around to discussing that— I assume she is. I mean, she talked to me about doing some minor revisions, which shouldn't take more than a week. Then we discussed possible markets. There's an editor she knows who's interested in historicals set in this time period. Irene wants to send it to her first, just as soon as I've finished with the revisions."

"Jo Ann," Bailey said, clasping her friend's hands tightly, "this is fabulous news!"

"I'm still having trouble believing it. Apparently Irene phoned while I was still at work and my eight-year-old answered. When I got home there was this scribbled message that didn't make any sense. All it said was that a lady with a weird name had phoned."

"Leave it to Bobby."

"He wasn't even home for me to question."

"He didn't write down the phone number?" Bailey asked.

"No, but he told Irene I was at work and she phoned me at five-thirty, our time."

"Weren't you the one who told me that being a writer means always knowing what time it is in New York?"

"The very one," Jo Ann teased. "Anyway, we spoke for almost an hour. It was crazy. Thank goodness Dan was home. I was standing in the kitchen with this stunned look on my face, frantically taking down notes. I didn't have to explain anything. Dan started dinner and then raced over to the park to pick up Bobby from Little League practice. Sarah set the table, and by the time I was off the phone, dinner was ready."

"I'm impressed." Several of the women in their writers' group had complained about their husbands' attitudes toward their creative efforts. But Jo Ann was fortunate in that department. Dan believed in her talent as strongly as Jo Ann did herself.

Jo Ann's dream was so close to being realized that Bailey could feel her own excitement rise. After three years of continuous effort, Jo Ann deserved a sale more than anyone she knew. She squeezed her writing in between dental appointments and Little League practices, between a full-time job and the demands of being a wife and mother. In addition, she was the driving force behind their writers' group. Jo Ann Webster had paid her dues, and Bailey sincerely hoped that landing Irene Ingram as her agent would be the catalyst to her first sale.

"I refuse to get excited," Jo Ann said matter-of-factly.

Bailey stared at her incredulously. "You're kidding, aren't you?"

"I suppose I am. It's impossible not to be thrilled, but there's a saying in the industry we both need to remember. Agents don't sell books, good writing does. Plotting and characterization are what interest an editor. Agents negotiate contracts, but they don't sell books."

"You should've phoned and told me she called," Bailey chastised.

"I meant to. Honest, I did, but when I'd finished the dinner dishes, put the kids to bed and reviewed my revision notes, it was too late. By the way, before I forget, did Parker call you?"

He was the last person Bailey wanted to discuss. If she admitted he had indeed phoned her, Jo Ann was bound to ask all kinds of questions Bailey preferred not to answer. Nor did she want to lie about it.

So she compromised. "He did, but I was writing at the time and he suggested I call him back later."

"Did you?" Jo Ann asked expectantly.

"No," Bailey said in a small miserable voice. "I should have, but... I didn't."

"He's marvelous, you know."

"Would it be okay if we didn't discuss Parker?" Bailey asked. She'd intended to seek him out, but she decided against it, at least for now. "I've got so much on my mind and I... I need to clear away a few cobwebs."

"Of course." Jo Ann's look was sympathetic. "Take your time, but don't take too long. Men like Parker Davidson don't come along often. Maybe once in a lifetime, if you're lucky."

This wasn't what Bailey wanted to hear.

Max was curled up on Bailey's printer later that same evening. She'd worked for an hour on the rewrite and wasn't entirely pleased with the results. Her lack of satisfaction could be linked, however, to the number of times she'd inadvertently typed Parker's name instead of Michael's.

That mistake was simple enough to understand. She was tired. Parker had been in her thoughts most of the day. Good grief, when *wasn't* he in her thoughts?

Then, when she decided to take a break and scan the evening paper, Parker's name seemed to leap right off the page. For a couple of seconds, Bailey was convinced the typesetter had made a mistake, just as she herself had a few minutes earlier. Peering at the local-affairs page, she realized that yes, indeed, Parker was in the news.

She sat down on the kitchen stool and carefully read the brief article. Construction crews were breaking ground for a high-rise bank in the financial district. Parker Davidson was the project's architect.

Bailey read the item twice and experienced a swelling sense of pride and accomplishment.

She had to phone Parker. She owed him an explanation, an apology; she owed him her gratitude. She'd known it the moment she'd abruptly ended their conversation the night before. She'd known it that morning when she spoke with Jo Ann. She'd known it the first time she'd substituted Parker's name for Michael's.

Even the afternoon paper was telling her what she already knew.

Something so necessary shouldn't be so difficult, Bailey told herself, standing in front of her telephone. Her hand still on the receiver, she hesitated. What could she possibly say to him? Other than to apologize for her behavior and congratulate him on the project she'd read about, which amounted to about thirty seconds of conversation.

Max sauntered into the kitchen, no doubt expecting to be fed again.

"You know better," she muttered, glaring down at him.

Pacing the kitchen didn't lend her courage. Nor did examining the contents of her refrigerator. The only thing that did was excite Max, who seemed to think she'd changed her mind, after all.

"Oh, for heaven's sake," she muttered, furious with herself. She picked up the phone, punched out Parker's home number—and waited. The phone rang once, twice, three times.

Parker was apparently out for the evening. Probably with some tall blond bombshell, celebrating his success. Every woman's basic nightmare. Four rings. Well, what did she expect? He was handsome, appealing, generous, kind—

"Hello?"

He caught her completely off guard. "Parker?"

"Bailey?"

"Yes, it's me," she said brightly. "Hello." The things she'd intended to say had unexpectedly disintegrated.

"Hello." His voice softened a little.

"Am I calling at a bad time?" she asked, wrapping

the telephone cord around her index finger, then her wrist and finally her elbow. "I could call back later if that's more convenient."

"Now is fine."

"I saw your name in the paper and wanted to congratulate you. This project sounds impressive."

He shrugged it off, as she knew he would. Silence fell between them, the kind of silence that needed to be filled or explained or quickly extinguished.

"I also wanted to apologize for the way I acted last night, when you phoned," Bailey said, the cord so tightly drawn around her hand that her fingers had gone numb. She loosened it now, her movements almost frantic. "I was rude and tactless and you didn't deserve it."

"So you ran into a snag with your writing?"

"I beg your pardon?"

"You're having a problem with your novel."

Bailey wondered how he knew that. "Uh…"

"I suggest it's time to check out the male point of view again. Get my insights. Am I right or wrong?"

"Right or wrong? Neither. I called to apologize."

"How's the rewrite coming?"

"Not too well." She sighed.

"Which tells me everything I need to know."

Bailey was mystified. "If you're implying that the only reason I'm calling is to ask for help with *Forever Yours* you couldn't be more mistaken."

"Then why *did* you call?"

"If you must know, it was to explain."

"Go on, I'm listening."

Now that she had his full attention, Bailey was beginning to feel foolish. "My mother always told me there's no excuse for rudeness, so I wanted to tell you something—something that might help you understand." Suddenly she couldn't utter another word.

"I'm listening," Parker repeated softly.

Bailey took a deep breath and closed her eyes. "Uh, maybe you *won't* understand, but you should know there's...there's a slightly used wedding dress hanging in my closet."

Seven

Of all the explanations Bailey could have given, all the excuses she could have made to Parker, she had no idea why she'd mentioned the wedding dress. Sheer embarrassment dictated her next action.

She hung up the phone.

Immediately afterward it started ringing and she stared at it in stupefied horror. Placing her hands over her ears, she walked into the living room, sank into the overstuffed chair and tucked her knees under her chin.

Seventeen rings.

Parker let the phone ring so many times Bailey was convinced he was never going to give up. The silence that followed the last peal seemed to reverberate loudly through the small apartment.

She was just beginning to gather her thoughts when there was an impatient pounding on her door.

Max imperiously raised his head from his position on her printer as though to demand she do something. Obviously all the disruptions this evening were annoying him.

"Bailey, open this door," Parker ordered in a tone even she couldn't ignore.

Reluctantly she got up and pulled open the door, knowing intuitively that he would've gotten in one way or another. If she'd resisted, Parker would probably have had Mrs. Morgan outside her door with a key.

He stormed into her living room as though there was a raging fire inside that had to be extinguished. He stood in the center of the room and glanced around, running his hand through his hair. "What was that you said about a wedding dress?"

Bailey, who still clutched the doorknob, looked up at him and casually shrugged. "You forgot the slightly used part."

"Slightly used?"

"That's what I tried to explain earlier," she returned, fighting the tendency to be flippant.

"Are you married?" he asked harshly.

The question surprised her, although she supposed it shouldn't have. After all, they were talking about wedding dresses. "Heavens, no!"

"Then what the hell did you mean when you said it was slightly used?"

"I tried it on several times, paid for it, walked around in it. I even had my picture taken in it, but that dress has never, to the best of my knowledge, been inside a church." She closed the door and briefly leaned against it.

"Do you want to tell me what happened?"

"Not particularly," she said, joining him in the middle of the room. "I really don't understand why I even brought it up. But now that you're here, do you want a cup of coffee?" She didn't wait for his response, but went into her kitchen and automatically took down a blue ceramic mug.

"What was his name?"

"Which time? The first time around it was Paul. Tom followed a few years later," Bailey said with matter-of-fact sarcasm as she filled the mug and handed it to him. She poured a cup for herself.

"I take it you've had to cancel two weddings, then?"

"Yes," she said leading the way back into her living area. She curled up on the couch, her feet tucked beneath her, leaving the large overstuffed chair for Parker. "This isn't something I choose to broadcast, but I seem to have problems holding on to a man. To be accurate, I should explain I bought the dress for Tom's and my wedding. He was the second fiancé. Paul and I hadn't gotten around to the particulars before he...left." The last word was barely audible.

"Why'd you keep the dress?" Parker asked, his dark eyes puzzled.

Bailey looked away. She didn't want his pity any more than she needed his tenderness, she told herself. But if that was the case, why did she feel so cold and alone?

"Bailey?"

"It's such a beautiful dress." Chantilly lace over luxurious white silk. Pearls along the full length of the sleeves. A gently tapered bodice; a gracefully draped skirt. It was the kind of dress every woman dreamed she'd wear once in a lifetime. The kind of dress that signified love and romance...

Instead of leaving the wedding gown with her parents, Bailey had packed it up and transported it to San Francisco. Now Parker was asking her why. Bailey supposed there was some psychological reason behind her actions. Some hidden motive buried in her subconscious. A reminder, perhaps, that men were not to be trusted?

"You loved them?" Parker asked carefully.

"I thought I did," she whispered, staring into her coffee. "To be honest, I… I don't know anymore."

"Tell me about Paul."

"Paul," she repeated in a daze. "We met our junior year of college." That seemed like a lifetime ago now.

"And you fell in love," he finished for her.

"Fairly quickly. He intended to go into law. He was bright and fun and opinionated. I could listen to him for hours. Paul seemed to know exactly what he wanted and how to get it."

"He wanted you," Parker inserted.

"At first." Bailey hesitated, struggling against the pain before it could tighten around her heart the way it once had. "Then he met Valerie. I don't think he intended to fall in love with her." Bailey had to believe that. She knew Paul had tried to hold on to his love for her, but in the end it was Valerie he chose. "I dropped out of college afterward," she added, her voice low and trembling. "I couldn't bear to be there, on campus, seeing the two of them together." It sounded cowardly now. Her parents had been disappointed, but she'd continued her studies at a business college, graduating as a paralegal a year later.

"I should've known Paul wasn't a hero," she said, glancing up at Parker and risking a smile.

"How's that?"

"He drank blush wine."

Parker stared at her a moment without blinking. "I beg your pardon?"

"You prefer straight Scotch, right?"

"Yes." Parker was staring at her. "How'd you know?"

"You also get your hair cut by a real barber and not a hairdresser."

He nodded.

"You wear well-made conservative clothes and prefer socks with your shoes."

"That's all true," Parker agreed, as though he'd missed the punch line in a joke. "But how'd you know?" he asked again.

"You like your coffee in a mug instead of a cup."

"Yes." His voice was even more incredulous.

"You're a hero, remember?" She sent him another smile, pleased with how accurately she'd assessed his habits. "At least I've learned one thing in all of this, and that's how to recognize a real man."

"Paul and Tom weren't real men?"

"No, they were costly imitations. Costly to my pride, that is." She altered her position and pulled her knees beneath her chin, wrapping her arms around her legs. She'd consciously assumed a defensive position—just in case he felt the need to comfort her. "Before you leap to conclusions, I think you should know that the only reason I need a hero is for the sake of *Forever Yours*. You're perfect as a model for Michael."

"But you don't want to become personally involved with me."

"Exactly." Now that everything was out in the open, Bailey felt an immediate sense of relief. Now that Parker understood, the pressure would be gone. There would be no unrealistic expectations. "I write romances and you're a hero type. Our relationship is strictly business. Though of course I'm grateful for your...friendship," she added politely.

Parker seemed to mull over her words for several seconds before shaking his head. "I could accept that—except there's one complication."

"Oh?" Bailey's gaze sought Parker's.

"The kiss."

Abruptly she dropped her gaze as a chill raced up her spine. "Foul!" she wanted to yell. "Unfair!" Instead, she muttered, "Uh, I don't think we should discuss that."

"Why not?"

"It was research," she said forcefully. "That's all." She was working hard to convince herself. Harder still at smiling blandly in his direction, hoping all the while he'd leave her comment untouched.

He didn't.

"Well, then it wouldn't hurt to experiment a second time, would it?" he argued. Unfortunately she had to acknowledge the logic of that—but she wouldn't admit it.

"No, please, there isn't any need," she told him, neatly destroying her own argument with her impassioned plea.

"I disagree," Parker said, standing up and striding toward her.

"Ah…" She clasped her bent legs even more tightly.

"There's nothing to worry about," Parker assured her.

"Isn't there? I mean…of course, there isn't. It's just that kissing makes me uncomfortable."

"Why's that?"

Couldn't the man accept a simple explanation? Just once?

Bailey sighed. "All right, you can kiss me if you insist," she said ungraciously, dropping her feet to the floor. She straightened her sweatshirt, dutifully squeezed her eyes shut, puckered her lips and waited.

And waited.

Finally she grew impatient and opened her eyes to discover Parker sitting next to her, staring. His face was inches from her own. A smile nipped at the corners of his mouth, making his lips quiver slightly.

"I amuse you?" she asked, offended. He was the one who'd requested this demonstration in the first place. He was the one who'd demanded proof.

"Not exactly *amuse*," Parker said, but from the gleam in his eyes she suspected he was fighting the urge to laugh out loud.

"I think we should forget the whole thing." She spoke with as much dignity as possible then got up to carry her cup into the kitchen. Turning to collect Parker's mug from the living room, she walked headlong into his arms.

His hands rested on her shoulders. "Both of those men were fools," he whispered, his gaze warm, his words soft.

Trapped between his body and the kitchen counter, Bailey felt the flutterings of panic. Her heart soared to her throat, beating wildly. He'd had his chance to kiss her, to prove his point. He should've done it then. Not now. Not when she wasn't steeled and ready. Not when his words made her feel so helpless and vulnerable.

Gently his mouth claimed hers. The kiss was straightforward, uncomplicated by need or desire. A tender kiss. A kiss to erase the pain of rejection and the grief of loss.

Bailey didn't respond. Not at first. Then her lips trembled to life in a slow awakening.

Like the first time Parker had kissed her, Bailey felt besieged by confusion and a sense of shock. She wasn't ready for this! She jerked herself free of his arms and twisted around. "There!" she said, her voice quavering. "Are you happy?"

"No," he answered starkly. "You can try to fool yourself if you want, but we both know the truth. You've been burned."

"Since I can't stand the heat," she said in a reasonable tone, "I got out of the kitchen." The fact that she'd just been kissed by him *in* the kitchen only made her situation more farcical. She brushed the hair back from her forehead, managed a false smile and turned around to face him. "I should never have said anything about the wedding dress. I don't know why I did. I'm not even sure what prompted that display of hysteria."

"I'm glad you did. And, Bailey, don't feel you have to apologize to me."

"Thank you," she mumbled, leading the way to her door.

Parker stopped to pat Max, who didn't so much as open his eyes to investigate. "Does he always sleep on your printer?"

"No, he sometimes insists on taking up a large portion of my pillow, generally when I'm using it myself."

Parker grinned. Bailey swore she'd never met a man with a more engaging smile. It was like watching the sun break through the clouds after a heavy downpour. It warmed her spirit, and only with the full strength of her will was she able to look away.

"I'll be seeing you," he said, pausing at the door.

"Yes," she whispered, yearning to see him again, yet in the same heartbeat hoping it wouldn't be soon.

"Bailey," Parker said, pressing his hand to her cheek, "just remember you haven't been the only one betrayed by love. It happens to all of us."

Perhaps, Bailey thought, but Parker was a living, breathing hero. The type of man women bought millions of books a year to read about, to dream about. She doubted he knew what it was like to have love humiliate him and break his heart.

"You look like you don't believe me."

Bailey stared at him, surprised he'd read her reaction so clearly.

"You're wrong," he said quietly. "I lost someone I loved, too." With that he dropped his hand and walked out, closing the door behind him.

By the time Bailey had recovered her wits enough to race after him, question him, the hallway was empty. Parker had lost at love, too? No woman in her right mind would walk away from Parker Davidson.

He was a hero.

"I'm afraid I did it again," Bailey announced to Jo Ann as they walked briskly toward their respective office buildings. The noise on the subway that morning had made private conversation impossible.

"Did what?"

"Put my foot in my mouth with Parker Davidson. He—"

"Did you see his name in the paper last night?" Jo Ann asked excitedly, cutting her off. "It was a small piece in the local section. I would've phoned you, but I knew I'd see you this morning and I didn't want to interrupt your writing time."

"I saw it."

"Dan was impressed that we even knew Parker. Apparently he's made quite a name for himself in the past few years. I never pay attention to that sort of thing. If it doesn't have to do with medical insurance or novel-writing, it's lost on me. But Dan's heard of him. He would, being in construction and all. Did you know Parker won a major national award for an innovative house he designed last year?"

"N-no."

"I'm sorry, I interrupted you, didn't I?" Jo Ann said, stopping midstride. "What were you about to say?"

Bailey wasn't sure how much she should tell her. "He stopped by my apartment—"

"Parker came to your place?" Jo Ann sounded awe-struck, as though Bailey had experienced a heavenly visitation.

Bailey didn't know what was wrong with Jo Ann. She wasn't letting her get a word in edgewise. "I made the mistake of telling him about the wedding dress in my closet. And at first I think he assumed I was mar-ried."

Jo Ann came to an abrupt halt. Her eyes narrowed. "There's a wedding dress in your closet?"

Bailey had forgotten she'd never told Jo Ann about Paul and Tom. She felt neither the inclination nor the desire to explain now, especially on a cold February day in the middle of a busy San Francisco sidewalk.

"My, my, will you look at the time?" Bailey mut-tered, staring down at her watch. It was half-past frus-tration and thirty minutes to despair. The only way she could easily extricate herself from this mess was to leave—now.

"Oh, no, you don't, Bailey York," Jo Ann cried, grasp-ing her forearm. "You're not walking away from me yet. Not without filling me in first."

"It's nothing. I was engaged."

"When? Recently?"

"Yes and no," Bailey responded cryptically with a longing glance at her office building two blocks south.

"What does that mean?" Jo Ann demanded.

"I was engaged to be married twice, and both times the man walked out on me. All right? Are you satisfied now?"

Her explanation didn't seem to appease Jo Ann. "Twice? But what's any of this got to do with Parker? It wasn't his fault those other guys dumped you, was it?"

"Of course not," Bailey snapped, completely exasperated. She'd lost her patience. It had been a mistake to ever mention the man's name. Jo Ann had become Parker's greatest advocate. Never mind that she was also *her* good friend and if she was going to champion anyone, it should be Bailey. However, in Jo Ann's starry-eyed view, Parker apparently could do no wrong.

"He assumed you were married?"

"Don't worry, I explained everything," she said calmly. "Listen, we're going to be late for work. I'll talk to you later."

"You bet you will. You've got a lot more explaining to do." She took a couple of steps, walking backward, staring at Bailey. "You were engaged? To different men each time?" she repeated. "Two different men?"

Bailey nodded and held up two fingers as they continued to back away from each other. "Two times, two different men."

Unexpectedly Jo Ann's face broke into a wide smile. "You know what they say, don't you? Third time's the charm, and if Parker Davidson is anything, it's charming. Talk to you this evening." With a quick wave, her friend turned and hurried down the street.

* * *

By lunchtime, Bailey decided the day was going to be a disaster. She'd misfiled an important folder, accidentally disconnected a client on the phone and worst of all spent two hours typing up a brief, then pressed the wrong key and lost the entire document. Following the fiasco with the computer, she took an early lunch and decided to walk off her frustration.

Either by accident or unconscious design—she couldn't decide which—Bailey found herself outside Parker's office building. She gazed at it for several minutes, wavering with indecision. She wanted to ask him what he'd meant about losing someone he loved. It was either that or spend the second half of the day infuriating her boss and annoying important clients. She was disappointed in Parker, she decided. He shouldn't have walked away without explaining. It wasn't fair. He'd been willing enough to listen to the humiliating details of *her* love life, but hadn't shared his own pain.

Roseanne Snyder, the firm's receptionist, brightened when Bailey walked into the office. "Oh, Ms. York, it's good to see you again."

"Thank you," Bailey answered, responding naturally to the warm welcome.

"Is Mr. Davidson expecting you?" The receptionist was flipping through the pages of the engagement calendar. "I'm terribly sorry if I—"

"No, no," Bailey said, stepping close to the older woman's desk. "I wasn't even sure Parker would be in."

"He is, and I know he'd be pleased to see you. Just go on back and I'll tell him you're coming. You know the way, don't you?" She turned in her chair and pointed down the hallway. "Mr. Davidson's office is the last door on your left."

Bailey hesitated, more doubtful than ever that showing up like this was the right thing to do. She would have left, crept quietly away, if Roseanne hadn't spoken into the intercom just then and gleefully announced her presence.

Before Bailey could react, Parker's office door opened. He waited there, hands in his pockets, leaning indolently against the frame.

Fortifying her resolve, she hurried toward him. He moved aside and closed the door when she entered. Once again she was struck by the dramatically beautiful view of the bay, but she couldn't allow that to deter her from her purpose.

"This is an unexpected surprise," Parker said.

Her nerves were on edge, and her words were more forceful than she intended. "That was a rotten thing you did."

"What? Kissing you? Honestly, Bailey are we going to go through all that again? You've got to stop lying to yourself."

"My day's a complete waste," she said, clenching her hands, "and this has nothing to do with our kiss."

"It doesn't?"

She sank down in a chair. "I dragged my pride through the mud of despair for you," she said dramatically.

He blinked as though she'd completely lost him.

"All right," she admitted with a flip of her hand, "that may be a little on the purple side."

"Purple?"

"Purple prose." Oh, it was so irritating having to explain everything to him. "Do you think I enjoy sharing my disgrace? It isn't every woman who'd willingly dig up the most painful episodes in her past and confess them to you. It wasn't easy, you know."

Parker walked around to his side of the desk, sat down and rubbed the side of his jaw. "Does this conversation have anything to do with the slightly used wedding dress?"

"Yes," she returned indignantly. "Oh, it was perfectly acceptable for me to describe how two—not one, mind you, but two—different men dumped me practically at the altar steps."

The amusement faded from Parker's eyes. "I realize that."

"No, you don't," she said, "otherwise you'd never have left on that parting shot."

"Parting shot?"

She shut her eyes for a moment and prayed for patience. "As you were leaving, you oh-so-casually mentioned something about losing someone you loved. Why was it fine for me to share my humiliation but not for you? I'm disappointed and—" Her throat closed before she could finish.

Parker was strangely quiet. His eyes held hers, his look somber. "You're right. That was rude of me, and I don't have any excuse."

"Oh, but you do," she said dryly. She should have known. He was a hero, wasn't he? She shook her head, angry with herself as much as with him.

"I do?" Parker countered.

"Yes, I should've figured it out sooner. Heroes often have a difficult time exposing their vulnerabilities. Obviously this…woman you loved wounded your pride.

She unmasked your vulnerability. Believe me, I know about that from experience. You don't have to explain it to me." She stood up to go, guiltily aware that she'd judged Parker too harshly.

"But you're right," he argued. "You shared a deep part of yourself and I should have been willing to do the same. It was unfair of me to leave the way I did."

"Perhaps, but it was true to character." She would have said a quick goodbye and walked out the door if not for the pain that suddenly entered his eyes.

"I'll tell you. It's only fair that you know. Sit down."

Bailey did as he requested, watching him carefully.

Parker smiled, but this wasn't the winsome smile she was accustomed to seeing. This was a strained smile, almost a grimace.

"Her name was Maria. I met her while I was traveling in Spain about fifteen years ago. We were both so young and in love. I wanted to marry her, bring her back with me to the States, but her family...well, suffice it to say her family didn't want their daughter marrying a foreigner. Several hundred years of tradition and pride stood between us, and when Maria was forced to choose between her family and me, she chose to remain in Madrid." He paused, shrugging one shoulder. "She did the right thing, I realize that now, much as it hurt at the time. I also realize how difficult her decision must have been. I learned a few months later that she'd married someone far more acceptable to her family than an American student."

"I'm sorry."

He shook his head as though to dispel the memories. "There's no reason you should be. Although I loved her a great deal, the relationship would never have lasted.

Maria would've been miserable in this country. I understand now how perceptive she was."

"She loved you."

"Yes," he said. "She loved me as much as she dared, but in the end duty and family were more important to her than love."

Bailey didn't know what to say. Her heart ached for the young man who had lost his love, and yet she couldn't help admiring the brave woman who had sacrificed her heart for her family and her deepest beliefs.

"I think what hurt the most was that she married someone else so soon afterward," Parker added.

"Paul and Tom got married, too… I think." Bailey understood his pain well.

The office was quiet for a moment, until Parker broke the silence. "Are we going to sit around and mope all afternoon? Or are you going to let me take you to lunch?"

Bailey smiled. "I think you might be able to talk me into it." Her morning had been miserable, but the afternoon looked much brighter now. She got to her feet, still smiling at Parker. "One thing I've learned over the years is that you can't allow misery to interfere with mealtimes."

Parker laughed and the robust sound of it was contagious. "I have a small surprise for you," he told her, reaching inside his suit pocket. "I was going to save it for later, but now seems more fitting." He handed her two tickets.

Bailey stared at them, speechless.

"The Pops concert," Parker said. "They're having a rock group from the sixties perform. It seems only fitting that Janice and Michael attend."

Eight

It wasn't until they'd finished lunch that Bailey noticed what a good time she was having with Parker. They'd sat across the table from each other and chatted like old friends. Bailey had never felt more at ease with him, nor had she ever allowed herself to be more open. Her emotions had undergone a gradual but profound change.

Fear and caution had been replaced by genuine contentment. And by hope.

After lunch they strolled through Union Square tossing breadcrumbs to the greedy pigeons. The early-morning fog had burned away and the sun was out in a rare display of brilliance. The square was filled with tourists, groups of old men and office workers taking an outdoor lunch. Bailey loved Union Square. Being there now, with Parker, seemed especially…fitting. And not just because Janice and Michael did the same thing in chapter six!

He was more relaxed with her, as well. He talked freely about himself, something he'd never done before. He was the oldest of three boys and the only one still unmarried.

"I'm the baby of the family," Bailey explained. "Pampered and spoiled. Overprotected, I'm afraid. My parents tried hard to dissuade me from moving to California." She paused.

"What made you leave Oregon?"

Bailey waited for the tightness that always gripped her heart when she thought of Tom, but it didn't come. It simply wasn't there anymore.

"Tom," she admitted, glancing down at the squawking birds, fighting over crumbs.

"He was fiancé number two?" Parker's hands were locked behind his back as they strolled along the paved pathway.

Bailey couldn't resist wondering if he'd hidden his hands to keep from touching her. "I met Tom a couple of years after…Paul. He was, is, a junior partner in the law firm where I worked as a paralegal. We'd been dating off and on for several months, nothing serious for either of us. Then we got involved in a case together and ended up spending a lot of time in each other's company. Within three months we were engaged."

Parker placed his hand lightly on her shoulder as though to lend her support. She smiled up at him in appreciation. "Actually it doesn't hurt as much to talk about it now." Time did heal all wounds, or as she preferred to think, time wounds all heels.

"I'm not sure when he met Sandra," she continued. "For all I know, they might have been childhood sweethearts. What I do remember is that we were only a few weeks away from the wedding. The invitations were all finished and waiting to be picked up at the printer's when Tom told me there was someone else."

"Were you surprised?"

"Shocked. In retrospect, I suppose I should have recognized the signs, but I'd been completely wrapped up in preparing for the wedding—shopping with my bridesmaids for their dresses, arranging for the flowers, things like that. In fact, I was so busy picking out china patterns I didn't even notice that my fiancé had fallen out of love with me."

"You make it sound as though it was your fault."

Bailey shrugged. "In some ways I think it was. I'm willing to admit that now, to see my own faults. But that doesn't make up for the fact that he was engaged to me and seeing another woman on the sly."

"No, it doesn't," Parker agreed. "What did you say when he told you?" By now, his hand was clasping her shoulder and she was leaning into him. The weight of her humiliation no longer seemed as crushing, but it was still there, and talking about it produced a flood of emotions she hadn't wanted to face. It was ironic that she could do so now, after all this time, and with another man.

"Have you forgiven him?"

Bailey paused and nudged a fallen leaf with the toe of her shoe. "Yes. Hating him, even disliking him, takes too much energy. He was truly sorry. By the time he talked to me, I think poor Tom was completely and utterly miserable. He tried so hard to avoid doing or saying anything to hurt me. I swear it took him fifteen minutes to get around to telling me he wanted to call off the wedding and another thirty to confess that there was someone else. I remember the sick feeling in my stomach. It was like coming down with a bad case of the flu, having all the symptoms hit me at once." Her mind returned to that dreadful day and how she'd sat and stared at Tom in shocked disbelief. He'd been so uncomfortable, gazing at his hands, guilt and confusion muffling his voice.

"I didn't cry," Bailey recalled. "I wasn't even angry, at least not at first. I don't think I felt any emotion." She gave Parker a chagrined smile. "In retrospect I realize my pride wouldn't allow it. What I do remember is that I said the most nonsensical things."

"Like what?"

Bailey's gaze wandered down the pathway. "I told him I expected him to pay for the invitations. We'd had them embossed with gold, which had been considerably more expensive. Besides, I was already out the money for the wedding dress."

"Ah, the infamous slightly used wedding dress."

"It was expensive!"

"I know," Parker said, his eyes tender. "Actually you were just being practical."

"I don't know what I was being. It's crazy the way the mind works in situations like that. I remember thinking that Paul and Tom must have been acquainted with each other. I was convinced the two of them had plotted together, which was utterly ridiculous."

"I take it you decided to move to San Francisco after Tom broke the engagement."

She nodded. "Within a matter of hours I'd given my notice at the law firm and was making plans to move."

"Why San Francisco?"

"You know," she said, laughing lightly, "I'm not really sure. I'd visited the area several times over the years and the weather was always rotten. Mark Twain wrote somewhere that the worst winter he ever spent was a summer in San Francisco. I guess the city, with its overcast skies and foggy mornings, suited my mood. I couldn't have tolerated bright sunny days and moonlit nights in the weeks after I left Oregon."

"What happened to Tom?"

"What do you mean?" Bailey cocked her head to look up at him, taken aback by the question.

"Did he marry Sandra?"

"Heavens, I don't know."

"Weren't you curious?"

Frankly she hadn't been. He obviously hadn't wanted *her*, and that was the only thing that mattered to Bailey. She'd felt betrayed, humiliated and abandoned. If Tom ever regretted his decision or if things hadn't worked out between him and Sandra, she didn't know. She hadn't stuck around to find out. Furthermore, she wouldn't have cared, not then, anyway.

She'd wanted out. Out of her job. Out of Oregon. Out of her dull life. If she was going to fall in love, why did it have to be with weak men? Men who couldn't make up their minds. Men who fell in and out of love, men who were never sure of what they wanted.

Perhaps it was some flaw in her own character that caused her to choose such men. That was the very reason she'd given up on relationships and dating and the opposite sex in general. And she knew it was also why she enjoyed reading romances, why she enjoyed writing them. Romance fiction offered her the happy ending that had been so absent in her own life.

The novels she read and wrote were about men who were *real* men—strong, traditional, confident men— and everyday women not unlike herself.

She'd been looking for a hero when she stumbled on Parker Davidson. Yes, she could truly say her heart was warming toward him. Warming, nothing! It was *on fire* and had been for weeks, although she'd refused to acknowledge that until now.

Parker's dark eyes caressed hers. "I'm glad you moved to the Bay area."

"So am I."

"You won't change your mind, will you?" he asked as they began to walk back. He must have read the confusion in her eyes because he added, "The concert tonight? It's in honor of Valentine's Day."

"No, I'm looking forward to going." She hadn't even realized what day this was. Bailey suddenly felt a thrill of excitement at the thought of spending the most romantic evening of the year with Parker Davidson. Although of course it would mean no time to work on *Forever Yours*...

"Think of the concert as research," Parker said, grinning down at her.

"I will." A woman could be blinded by eyes as radiant as Parker's. They were alight with the sensitivity and strength of his nature.

"Goodbye," she said reluctantly, lifting her hand in a small wave.

"Until tonight," Parker said, sounding equally reluctant to part.

"Tonight," she repeated softly. She'd seen her pain reflected in his eyes when she told him about Tom. He understood what it was to lose someone you loved, regardless of the circumstances. She sensed that in many ways the two of them were alike. During that short walk around Union Square, Bailey had felt a closeness to Parker, a comfortable and open honesty she'd rarely felt with anyone before.

"I'll pick you up at seven," he said.

"Perfect." Bailey was convinced he would have kissed her if they hadn't been standing in such a public place. And she would have let him.

The afternoon flew by. Whereas the morning had been excruciatingly slow, filled with one blunder after another, the hours after her lunch with Parker were trouble free. No sooner had she returned to the office than it seemed time to pack up her things and head for the subway.

True to form, Max was there to greet her when she walked in the door. She set her mail, two bills and an ad for the local supermarket, on the kitchen counter, and quickly fed him. Max seemed mildly surprised at her promptness and stared at his food for several minutes, as though he was hesitant about eating it.

Grumbling that it was impossible to please the dratted cat, Bailey stalked into her bedroom, throwing open the closet door.

For some time she did nothing but stare at the contents. She finally made her decision, a printed dress she'd worn when she was in college. The paisley print was bright and cheerful, the skirt widely pleated. The style was slightly dated, but it was the best she could do. If Parker had given her even a day's notice she would have gone out and bought something new. Something red in honor of Valentine's Day.

The seats Parker had purchased for the concert at Civic Center were among the best in the house. They were situated in the middle about fifteen rows from the front.

The music was fabulous. Delightful. Romantic. There were classical pieces she recognized, interspersed with soft rock, and a number of popular tunes and "golden oldies."

The orchestra was spectacular, and being this close to the stage afforded Bailey an opportunity so special she felt tears of appreciation gather in her eyes more than once. Nothing could ever duplicate a live performance.

The warm generous man in her company made everything perfect. At some point, early in the program, Parker reached for her hand. When Bailey's heartbeat finally settled down to a normal rate, she felt an emotion she hadn't experienced in more than a year, not since the day Tom had called off their wedding.

Contentment. Complete and utter contentment.

She closed her eyes to savor the music and when she opened them again, she saw Parker studying her. She smiled shyly and he smiled back. And at that moment, cymbals clanged. Bailey jumped in her seat as though caught doing something illegal. Parker chuckled and raised her hand to his lips, gently brushing her knuckles with a kiss.

The second group, Hairspray, performed after the intermission. Bailey found their music unfamiliar with the exception of two or three classic rock numbers. But the audience responded enthusiastically to the group's energy and sense of fun. Several people got to their feet, swaying to the music. After a while some couples edged into the aisles and started dancing. Bailey would have liked to join them, but Parker seemed to prefer staying where they were. She couldn't very well leave him sitting there while she sought out a partner. Especially when the only partner she wanted was right beside her.

Eventually nearly everyone around them rose and moved into the aisle, which meant a lot of awkward shifting for Parker and Bailey. She was convinced they were the only couple in the section not on their feet.

She glanced at Parker, but he seemed oblivious to what was happening around them. At one point she thought she heard him grumble about not being able to see the band because of all those people standing.

"Miss?" An older balding man moved into their nearly empty row and tapped Bailey on the shoulder in an effort to get her attention. He wore his shirt open to the navel and had no less than five pounds of gold draped around his neck. Clearly he'd never left the early seventies. "Would you care to dance?"

"Uh…" Bailey certainly hadn't been expecting an invitation. She wasn't entirely confident of the protocol. She'd come with Parker and he might object.

"Go ahead," Parker said, reassuring her. He actually seemed relieved someone else had asked her. Perhaps he was feeling guilty about not having done so himself, Bailey mused.

She shrugged and stood, glancing his way once more to be sure he didn't mind. He urged her forward with a wave of his hand.

Bailey was disappointed. She wished with all her heart that it was Parker taking her in his arms. Parker, not some stranger.

"Matt Cooper," the man with the gold chains said, holding out his hand.

"Bailey York."

He grinned as he slipped his arm around her waist.

"There must be something wrong with your date to leave you sitting there."

"I don't think Parker dances."

It had been a long while since Bailey had danced, and she wasn't positive she'd even remember how. She needn't have worried. The space was so limited that she couldn't move more than a few inches in any direction.

The next song Hairspray performed was an old rock song from the sixties. Matt surprised her by placing two fingers in his mouth and whistling loudly. The piercing sound cut through music, crowd noises and applause. Despite herself, Bailey laughed.

The song was fast-paced and Bailey began swaying her hips and moving to the beat. Before she was sure how it had happened, she was quite a distance from her friend. She found herself standing next to a tall good-looking man about Parker's age, who was obviously enjoying the group's performance.

He smiled at Bailey and she smiled shyly back. The next song was another oldie, one written with young lovers in mind and perfect for slow dancing.

Bailey tried to make it down the aisle to Parker's seat, but the row was empty. Although she glanced all around she couldn't locate him.

"We might as well," the good-looking man said, holding out his hands to her. "My partner has taken off for parts unknown."

"Mine seems to have disappeared, too." Scanning the crowd, she still couldn't find Parker but then, the area was so congested it was impossible to see anyone clearly. A little worried, she wondered how they'd ever find each other when the concert was over.

She and her new partner danced two or three dances

without ever exchanging names. He twirled her about with an expertise that masterfully disguised her own less-inspired movements. They finished a particularly fast dance, and Bailey fanned her face, flushed from the exertion, with one hand.

When Hairspray introduced another love ballad, it seemed only natural for Bailey to slip into her temporary partner's arms. He said something and laughed. Bailey hadn't been able to make out his words, but she grinned back at him. She was about to say something herself when she saw Parker edging toward them, scowling.

"My date's here," she said, breaking away from the man who held her. She gave him an apologetic look and he released her with a decided lack of enthusiasm.

"I thought I'd lost you," she said when Parker made it to her side.

"I think it's time we left," he announced in clipped tones.

Bailey blinked, surprised by his irritation. "But the concert isn't over yet." Cutting a path through the horde of dancers would be difficult, perhaps impossible. "Shouldn't we at least stay until Hairspray is finished?"

"No."

"What's wrong?"

Parker shoved his hands in his pockets. "I didn't mind you dancing with that Barry Gibb look-alike, but the next thing I know, you've taken off with someone else."

"I didn't *take off* with anyone," she said, disliking his tone as much as his implication. "We were separated by the crowds."

"Then you should've come back to me."

"You didn't honestly expect me to fight my way through this mass of humanity, did you? Can't you see how crowded the aisles are?"

"I made it to you."

Bailey sighed, fighting the urge to be sarcastic. And lost. "Do you want a Boy Scout award? I didn't know they issued them for pushing and shoving."

Parker's eyes flashed with resentment. "I didn't push anyone. I think it would be best if we sat down," he said, gripping her by the elbow and leading her back into a row, "before you make an even greater spectacle of yourself."

"A spectacle of myself," Bailey muttered furiously. "If anyone was a spectacle, it was you! You were the only person in ten rows who wasn't dancing."

"I certainly didn't expect my date to take off with another man." He sank down in a seat and crossed his arms as though he had no intention of continuing this discussion.

"Your date," she repeated, struggling to hold on to her temper by clenching her fists. "May I remind you this entire evening was for the purposes of research and nothing more?"

Parker gave a disbelieving snort. "That's not how I remember it. At the time, you seemed eager enough." He laughed, a cynical, unpleasant sound. "I'm not the one who chased after you."

Standing there arguing with him was attracting more attention than Bailey wanted. Reluctantly she sat down, primly folding her hands in her lap, and stared directly ahead. "I didn't chase after you," she informed him through gritted teeth. "I have *never* chased after any man."

"Oh, forgive me, then. I could have sworn it was you who followed me off the subway. Were you aware that someone who closely resembles you stalked me all the way into Chinatown?"

"Oh-h-h," Bailey moaned, throwing up her hands, "you're impossible."

"What I am is correct."

Bailey didn't deign to reply. She crossed her legs and swung her ankle ferociously until the concert finally ended.

Parker didn't say a word as he escorted her to his car, which was fine with Bailey. She'd never met a more unreasonable person in her life. Less than an hour earlier, they'd practically been drowning in each other's eyes. She'd allowed herself to get caught up in the magic of the moment, that was all. Some Valentine's Day!

They parted with little more than a polite goodnight. Bailey informed him there was no need to see her to her door. Naturally he claimed otherwise, just to be obstinate. She wanted to argue, but knew it would be a waste of breath.

Max was at the door to greet her, his tail waving in the air. He stayed close to her, rubbing against her legs, and Bailey nearly tripped over him as she hurriedly undressed. She started to tell him about her evening, changed her mind and got into bed. She pulled the covers up to her chin, forcing the cantankerous Parker Davidson from her mind.

Jo Ann was waiting for her outside the BART station the following morning. "Well?" she said, racing to Bailey's side. "How was your date?"

"What date? You couldn't possibly call that outing with Parker a date."

"I couldn't?" Jo Ann was clearly puzzled.

"We attended the Pops Concert—"

"For research," Jo Ann finished for her. "I gather the evening didn't go well?" They filed through the turnstile and rode the escalator down to the platform where they'd board the train.

"The whole night was a disaster."

"Tell Mama everything," Jo Ann urged.

Bailey wasn't in the mood to talk, but she made the effort to explain what had happened and how unreasonable Parker had been. She hadn't slept well, convinced she'd made the same mistake with Parker as she had with the other men in her life. All along she'd assumed he was different. Not so. Parker was pompous, irrational and arrogant. She told Jo Ann that. "I was wrong about him being a hero," she said bleakly.

Jo Ann frowned. "Let me see if I've got this straight. People started dancing. One man asked you to dance, then you got separated and danced with another guy and Parker acted like a jealous fool."

"Exactly." It infuriated Bailey every time she thought about it, which she'd been doing all morning.

"Of course he did," Jo Ann said enthusiastically, as though she'd just made an important discovery. "Don't you see? He was being true to character. Didn't more or less the same thing happen between Janice and Michael when they went to the concert?"

Bailey had completely forgotten. "Now that you mention it, yes," she admitted slowly.

The train arrived. When the screeching came to a

halt, Jo Ann said, "I told Parker all about that scene myself, remember?"

Bailey did, vaguely.

"When you sit down to rewrite it, you'll know from experience exactly what Janice was feeling and thinking because those were the very thoughts you experienced yourself. How can you be angry with him?"

Bailey wasn't finding it difficult.

"You should be grateful."

"I should?"

"Oh, yes," Jo Ann insisted. "Parker Davidson is more of a hero than either of us realized."

Nine

"Don't you understand what Parker did?" Jo Ann asked when they met for lunch later that same day. The topic was one she refused to drop.

"You bet I understand. He's a... Neanderthal, only he tried to be polite about it. As if that makes any difference."

"Wrong," Jo Ann argued, looking downright mysterious. "He's given you some genuine insight into your character's thoughts and actions."

"What he did," Bailey said, waving her spoon above her cream-of-broccoli soup, "was pretty well ruin what started out as a perfect evening."

"You said he acted like a jealous fool, but you've got to remember that's exactly how Michael reacted when Janice danced with another man."

"Then he went above and beyond the call of duty, and I'm not about to reward that conduct in a man, hero or not." She crumbled her soda crackers into her soup, then brushed her palms free of crumbs.

Until Bailey accepted the invitation to dance, her evening with Parker had been wonderfully romantic.

They'd sat together holding hands, while the music swirled and floated around them. Then the dancing began and her knight in shining armor turned into a fire-breathing dragon.

"You haven't forgotten the critique group is meeting tonight, have you?" Jo Ann asked, abruptly changing the subject.

Bailey's head was so full of Parker that she had, indeed, forgotten. She'd been absentminded lately. "Tonight?"

"Seven, at Darlene's house. You'll be there, won't you?"

"Of course." Bailey didn't need to think twice. Every other week, women from their writing group took turns hosting a session in which they evaluated one another's work.

"Oh, good. For a moment I wondered whether you'd be able to come."

"Why wouldn't I?" Bailey demanded. She was as dedicated as the other writers. She hadn't missed a single meeting since the group was formed two months ago.

"Oh, I thought you might be spending the evening with Parker. You two need to work out your differences. You're going to be miserable until this is resolved."

Bailey slowly lowered her spoon. "Miserable?" she repeated, giving a brief, slightly hysterical laugh. "Do I look like I'm the least bit heartbroken? Honestly, Jo Ann, you're making a mountain out of a molehill. The two of us had a falling out. I don't want to see him, and I'm sure he feels the same way. I won't have any problem making the group tonight."

Jo Ann calmly drank her coffee, then just as calmly

stated, "You're miserable, only you're too proud to admit it."

"I am *not* miserable," Bailey asserted, doing her utmost to smile serenely.

"How much sleep did you get last night?"

"Why? Have I got circles under my eyes?"

"No. Just answer the question."

Bailey swallowed uncomfortably. "Enough. What's with you? Have you taken up writing mystery novels? Parker Davidson and I had a parting of the ways. It would have happened eventually. Besides, it's better to learn these sorts of things in the beginning of a... relationship." She shrugged comically. "A bit ironic to have it end on Valentine's Day."

"So you won't be seeing him again?" Jo Ann made that sound like the most desolate of prospects.

"We probably won't be able to avoid a certain amount of contact, especially while he's taking the subway, but for the record, no. I don't intend to ever go out with him again. He can save his caveman tactics for someone else."

"Someone else?" Jo Ann filled the two words with tearful sadness. Until Parker, Bailey had seen only the tip of the iceberg when it came to her friend's romantic nature.

Bailey finished her soup and, glancing at her watch, realized she had less than five minutes to get back to the office.

"About tonight—I'll give you a ride," Jo Ann promised. "I'll be by to pick you up as close to six-thirty as I can. It depends on how fast I can get home and get everyone fed."

"Thanks," Bailey said. "I'll see you then."

They parted and Bailey hurried back to her office. The large vase of red roses on the reception desk was the first thing she noticed when she walked in.

"Is it your birthday, Martha?" she asked as she removed her coat and hung it on the rack.

"I thought it must be yours," the secretary replied absently.

"Mine?"

"The card has your name on it."

Bailey's heart went completely still. Had Parker sent her flowers? It seemed too much to hope for, yet... "My name's on the card?"

"A tall good-looking man in a suit delivered them not more than ten minutes ago. He seemed disappointed when I said you'd taken an early lunch. Who is that guy, anyway? He looks vaguely familiar."

Bailey didn't answer. Instead she removed the envelope and slipped out the card. It read, "Forgive me, Parker."

She felt the tightness around her heart suddenly ease.

"Oh, I nearly forgot," Martha said, reaching for a folded slip of paper next to the crystal vase. "Since you weren't here, he left a message for you."

Carrying the vase with its brilliant red roses in one hand and her message in the other, Bailey walked slowly to her desk. With eager fingers, she unfolded the note.

"Bailey," it said. "I'm sorry I missed you. We need to talk. Can you have dinner with me tonight? If so, I'll pick you up at seven. Since I'll be tied up most of the afternoon, leave a message with Roseanne."

He'd written down his office number. Bailey reached for the phone with barely a thought. The friendly—

and obviously efficient—receptionist answered on the first ring.

"Hello, Roseanne, this is Bailey York."

"Oh, Bailey, yes. It's good to hear from you. Mr. Davidson said you'd be phoning."

"I missed him by only a few minutes."

"How frustrating for you both. I've been concerned about him this morning."

"You have?"

"Why, yes. Mr. Davidson came into the office and he couldn't seem to sit still. He got himself a cup of coffee, then two minutes later came out again and poured a second cup. When I pointed out that he already had coffee, he seemed surprised. That was when he started muttering under his breath. I've worked with Mr. Davidson for several years now and I've never known him to mutter."

"He was probably thinking about something important regarding his work." Bailey was willing to offer a face-saving excuse for Parker's unprecedented behavior.

"That's not it," the woman insisted. "He went into his office again and came right back out, asking me if I read romance novels. I have on occasion, and that seemed to satisfy him. He pulled up a chair and began asking me questions about a hero's personality. I answered him as best I could."

"I'm sure you did very well."

"I must have, because he cheered right up and asked me what kind of flowers a woman enjoys most. I told him roses, and a minute later, he's looking through my phone book for a florist. Unfortunately no florist could promise a delivery this morning, so he said he'd drop them off personally. He phoned a few minutes ago to tell me you'd be calling in sometime today and that I should take a message."

"I just got back from lunch."

So Parker's morning hadn't gone any better than her own, Bailey mused, feeling almost jubilant. She'd managed to put on a good front for Jo Ann, but Bailey had felt terrible. Worse than terrible. She hadn't wanted to discuss her misery, either. It was much easier to pretend that Parker meant nothing to her.

But Jo Ann had been right. She *was* miserable.

"Could you tell Mr. Davidson I'll be ready at seven?" She'd call Jo Ann later and tell her she wouldn't be able to make the critique group, after all.

"Oh, my, that *is* good news," Roseanne said, sounding absolutely delighted. "I'll pass the message along as soon as he checks in. I'm so pleased. Mr. Davidson is such a dear man, but he works too hard. I've been thinking he needed to meet a nice girl like you. Isn't it incredible that the two of you have known each other for so long?"

"We have?"

"Oh, yes, don't you remember? You came into the office that morning and explained how Mr. Davidson is a friend of your family's. You must have forgotten you'd told me that."

"Oh. Oh, yes," Bailey mumbled, embarrassed by the silly lie. "Well, if you'd give him the message, I'd be most grateful."

"I'll let Mr. Davidson know," Roseanne said. She hesitated, as though she wanted to add something else and wasn't sure she should. Then, decision apparently made, the words rushed out. "As I said before, I've been with Mr. Davidson for several years and I think you should know that to the best of my knowledge, this is the first time he's ever sent a woman roses."

For the rest of the afternoon, Bailey was walking on air. At five o'clock, she raced into the department store closest to her office, carrying one long-stemmed rose. Within minutes she found a lovely purple-and-gold silk dress. Expensive, but it looked wonderful. Then she hurried to the shoe department and bought a pair of pumps. In accessories, she chose earrings and a matching gold necklace.

From the department store she raced to the subway, clutching her purchases and the single red rose. She'd spent a fortune but didn't bother to calculate how many "easy monthly installments" it would take to pay everything off. Looking nice for Parker was worth the cost. No man had ever sent her roses, and every time she thought about it, her heart positively melted. It was such a *romantic* thing to do. And to think he'd conferred with Roseanne Snyder.

By six-thirty she was almost ready. She needed to brush her hair and freshen her makeup, but that wouldn't take long. She stood in front of the mirror in a model's pose, one hand on her hip, one shoulder thrust forward, studying the overall effect, when there was a knock at the door.

Oh, no! Parker was early. Much too early. It was either shout at him from this side of the door to come back later, or make the best of it. Running her fingers through her hair, she shook her head for the breezy effect and opted to make the best of it.

"Are you ready?" Jo Ann asked, walking inside, her book bag in one hand and her purse in the other. She gaped openly at Bailey's appearance. "Nice," she said, nodding, "but you might be a touch overdressed for the critique group."

"Oh, no, I forgot to call you." How could she have let it slip her mind?

"Call me?"

Bailey felt guilty—an emotion she was becoming increasingly familiar with—for not remembering tonight's arrangement. It was because of Parker. He'd occupied her thoughts from the moment he'd first kissed her.

There had been no kiss last night. The desire—no, more than desire, the *need*—for his kiss, his touch had flared into urgent life. Since the breakup with Tom she'd felt frozen, her emotions lying dormant. But under the warmth of Parker's humor and generosity, she thawed a little more each time she saw him.

"Someone sent you a red rose," Jo Ann said matter-of-factly. She walked farther into the room, lifting the flower to her nose and sniffing appreciatively. "Parker?"

Bailey nodded. "There were a dozen waiting for me when I got back to the office."

Jo Ann's smile was annoyingly smug.

"He stopped by while I was at lunch—we'd missed each other..." Bailey mumbled in explanation.

Jo Ann circled her, openly admiring the dress. "He's taking you to dinner?" Her gaze fell to the purple suede pumps that perfectly matched the dress.

"Dinner? What gives you that idea?"

"The dress is new."

"This old thing?" Bailey gave a nervous giggle.

Jo Ann tugged at the price tag dangling from Bailey's sleeve and pulled it free.

"Very funny!" Bailey groaned. She glanced at her watch, hoping Jo Ann would take the hint.

Jo Ann was obviously pleased about Parker's reappearance. "So, you're willing to let bygones be bygones?" she asked in a bracing tone.

"Jo Ann, he's due here any minute."

Her friend disregarded her pleas. "You're really falling for this guy, aren't you?"

If it was any more obvious, Bailey thought, she'd be wearing a sandwich board and parading in front of his office building. "Yes."

"Big time?"

"Big time," Bailey admitted.

"How do you feel about that?"

Bailey was sorely tempted to throw up her arms in abject frustration. "How do you think it makes me feel? I've been jilted twice. I'm scared to death. Now, isn't it time you left?" She coaxed Jo Ann toward the door, but when her friend ignored that broad hint, Bailey gripped her elbow. "Sorry you had to leave so soon, but I'll give your regards to Parker."

"All right, all right," Jo Ann said, sighing, "I can take a hint when I hear one."

Bailey doubted it. "Tell the others that...something came up, but I'll be there next time for sure." Her hands were at the small of Jo Ann's back, urging her forward. "Goodbye, Jo Ann."

"I'm going, I'm going," her friend said from the other side of the threshold. Suddenly earnest, she turned to face Bailey. "Promise me you'll have a good time."

"I'm sure we will." *If* she could finish getting ready before Parker arrived. *If* she could subdue her nerves. *If*...

Once Jo Ann was gone, Bailey slammed the door

and rushed back to her bathroom. She was dabbing cologne on her wrists when there was a second knock. Inhaling a calming breath, Bailey opened the door, half expecting to find Jo Ann on the other side, ready with more advice.

"Parker," she whispered unsteadily, as though he was the last person she expected to see.

He frowned. "I did get the message correctly, didn't I? You were expecting me?"

"Oh, yes, of course. Come inside, please."

"Good." His face relaxed.

He stepped into the room, but his eyes never left hers. "I hope I'm not too early."

"Oh, no." She twisted her hands, staring down at her shoes like a shy schoolgirl.

"You got the roses?"

"Oh, yes," she said breathlessly, glancing at the one she'd brought home from her office. "They're beautiful. I left the others on my desk at work. It was so sweet of you."

"It was the only way I could think to apologize. I didn't know if a hero did that sort of thing or not."

"He...does."

"So once again, I stayed in character."

"Yes. Very much so."

"Good." His mouth slanted charmingly with the slight smile he gave her. "I realize this dinner is short notice."

"I didn't mind changing my plans," she told him. The critique group was important, but everyone missed occasionally.

"I suppose I should explain we'll be eating at my parents' home. Do you mind?"

His parents? Bailey's stomach tightened instantly. "I'd enjoy meeting your family," she answered, doing her best to reassure him. She managed a fleeting smile.

"Mom and Dad are anxious to meet you."

"They are?" Bailey would have preferred not to know that. The fact that Parker had even mentioned her to his family came as a surprise.

"So, how was your day?" he asked, walking casually over to the window.

Bailey lowered her gaze. "The morning was difficult, but the afternoon...the afternoon was wonderful."

"I behaved like a jealous fool last night, didn't I?" He didn't wait for her to respond. "The minute I saw you in that other man's arms, I wanted to get you away from him. I'm not proud of how I acted." He shoved his fingers through his hair, revealing more than a little agitation. "As I'm sure you've already guessed, I'm not much of a dancer. When that throwback from the seventies asked you to dance with him, I had no objections. If you want the truth, I was relieved. I guess men are supposed to be able to acquit themselves on the dance floor, but I've got two left feet. No doubt I've blown this whole hero business, but quite honestly that's the least of my worries. I know it matters to you, but I can't change who I am."

"I wouldn't expect you to."

He nodded. "The worst part of the whole evening was the way I cheated myself out of what I was looking forward to the most."

"Which was?"

"Kissing you again."

"Oh, Parker..."

He was going to kiss her. She realized that at about

the same time she knew she'd cry with disappointment if he didn't. Bailey wasn't sure who reached out first. What she instantly recognized was the perfect harmony between them, how comfortable she felt in his arms—as though they belonged together.

His mouth found hers with unerring ease. A moan of welcome and release spilled from her throat as she began to tremble. An awakening, slow and sure, unfolded within her like the petals of a hothouse rose.

That sensation was followed by confusion. She pulled away from Parker and buried her face in his strong neck. The trembling became stronger, more pronounced.

"I frighten you?"

If only he knew. "Not in the way you think," she said slowly. "It's been so long since a man's held me like this. I tried to convince myself I didn't want to feel this way ever again. I didn't entirely succeed."

"Are you saying you *wanted* me to kiss you?"

"Yes." His finger under her chin raised her eyes to his. Bailey thought they would have gone on gazing at each other forever if Max hadn't chosen that moment to walk across the back of the sofa, protesting loudly. This was his territory and he didn't take kindly to invasions.

"We'd better leave," Parker said reluctantly.

"Oh, sure…" Bailey said. She was nervous about meeting Parker's family. More nervous than she cared to admit. The last set of parents she'd been introduced to had been Tom's. She'd met them a few days before they'd announced their engagement. As she recalled, the circumstances were somewhat similar. Tom had unexpectedly declared that it was time to meet his family. That was when Bailey had realized how serious their relationship had grown. Tom's family was very nice, but Bailey had felt all too aware of being judged and, she'd always suspected, found wanting.

Bailey doubted she said more than two words as Parker drove out to Daley City. His family's home was an elegant two-story white stone house with a huge front garden.

"Here we are," Parker said needlessly, placing his hand on her shoulder when he'd helped her out of the car.

"Did you design it?"

"No, but I love this house. It gave birth to a good many of my ideas."

The front door opened and an older couple stepped outside to greet them. Parker's mother was tall and regal, her white hair beautifully waved. His father's full head of hair was a distinguished shade of gray. He stood only an inch or so taller than his wife.

"Mom, Dad, this is Bailey York." Parker introduced her, his arm around her waist. "Bailey, Yvonne and Bradley Davidson, my parents."

"Welcome, Bailey," Bradley Davidson said with a warm smile.

"It's a pleasure to meet you," Yvonne said, walking forward. Her eyes briefly connected with Parker's before she added, "At last."

"Come inside," Parker's father urged, leading the way. He stood at the door and waited for them all to walk into the large formal entry. The floor was made of black-and-white squares of polished marble, and there was a long circular stairway on the left.

"How about something to drink?" Bradley suggested. "Scotch? A mixed drink? Wine?" Bailey and

Parker's mother both chose white wine, Parker and his father, Scotch.

"I'll help you, Dad," Parker offered, leaving the two women alone.

Yvonne took Bailey into the living room, which was strikingly decorated in white leather and brilliant red.

Bailey sat on the leather couch. "Your home is lovely."

"Thank you," Yvonne murmured. A smile trembled at the edges of her mouth, and Bailey wondered what she found so amusing. Perhaps there was a huge run in her panty hose she knew nothing about, or another price tag dangling from her dress.

"Forgive me," the older woman said. "Roseanne Snyder and I are dear friends, and she mentioned your name to me several weeks back."

Bailey experienced a moment of panic as she recalled telling Parker's receptionist that she was an old family friend. "I…guess you're wondering why I claimed to know Parker."

"No, although it did give me a moment's pause. I couldn't recall knowing any Yorks."

"You probably don't." Bailey folded her hands in her lap, uncertain what to say next.

"Roseanne's right. You really are a charming young lady."

"Thank you."

"I was beginning to wonder if Parker was ever going to fall in love again. He was so terribly hurt by Maria, and he was so young at the time. He took it very hard…" She hesitated, then spoke briskly. "But I suppose that's neither here nor there."

Bailey decided to ignore the implication that Parker had fallen in love with her. Right now there were other concerns to face. "Did Parker tell you how we met?" She said a silent prayer that he'd casually mentioned something about the two of them bumping into each other on the subway.

"Of course I did," Parker answered for his mother, as he walked into the room. He sat on the arm of the sofa and draped his arm around Bailey's shoulders. His laughing eyes held hers. "I did mention Bailey's a budding romance writer, didn't I, Mom?"

"Yes, you did," his mother answered. "I hope you told her I'm an avid reader."

"No, I hadn't gotten around to that."

Bailey shifted uncomfortably in her chair. No wonder Yvonne Davidson had trouble disguising her amusement if Parker had blabbed about the way she'd followed him off the subway.

Parker's father entered the room carrying a tray of drinks, which he promptly dispensed.

Then he joined his wife, and for some time, the foursome chatted amicably.

"I'll just go and check on the roast," Yvonne said eventually.

"Can I help, dear?"

"Go ahead, Dad," Parker said, smiling. "I'll entertain Bailey with old family photos."

"Parker," Bailey said once his parents were out of earshot. "How *could* you?"

"How could I what?"

"Tell your mother how we met? She must think I'm crazy!"

Instead of revealing any concern, Parker grinned widely. "Honesty is the best policy."

"In principle I agree, but our meeting was a bit... unconventional."

"True, but I have to admit that being described as classic hero material was flattering to my ego."

"I take everything back," she muttered, crossing her legs.

Parker chuckled and was about to say something else when his father came into the room carrying a bottle of champagne.

"Champagne, Dad?" Parker asked when his father held out the bottle for Parker to examine. "This is good stuff."

"You're darn right," Bradley Davidson said. "It isn't every day our son announces he's found the woman he wants to marry."

Ten

Bailey's gaze flew to Parker's in shocked disbelief. She found herself standing, but couldn't remember rising from the chair. The air in the room seemed too thin and she had difficulty catching her breath.

"Did I say something I shouldn't have?" Bradley Davidson asked his son, distress evident on his face.

"It might be best if you gave the two of us a few minutes alone," Parker said, frowning at his father.

"I'm sorry, son, I didn't mean to speak out of turn."

"It's fine, Dad."

His father left the room.

Bailey walked over to the massive stone fireplace and stared into the grate at the stacked logs and kindling.

"Bailey?" Parker spoke softly from behind her.

She whirled around to face him, completely speechless, able only to shake her head in bemused fury.

"I know this must come as...something of a surprise."

"Something of a surprise?" she shrieked.

"All right, a shock."

"We…we met barely a month ago."

"True, but we know each other better than some couples who've been dating for months."

The fact that he wasn't arguing with her didn't comfort Bailey at all. "I… Isn't it a bit presumptuous of you…to be thinking in terms of an engagement?" She'd made it plain from the moment they met that she had no intention of getting involved with a man. Who could blame her after the experiences she'd had with the opposite sex? Another engagement, even with someone as wonderful as Parker, was out of the question.

"Yes, it was presumptuous."

"Then how could you suggest such a thing? Engagements are disastrous for me! I won't go through that again. I won't!"

He scowled. "I agree I made a mistake."

"Obviously." Bailey stalked to the opposite side of the room to stand behind a leather-upholstered chair, one hand clutching its back. "Twice, Parker, twice." She held up two fingers. "And both times, *both* times, they fell out of love with me. I couldn't go through that again. I just couldn't."

"Let me explain," Parker said, walking slowly toward her. "For a long time now, my parents have wanted me to marry."

"So in other words, you used me. I was a decoy. You made up this story? How courageous of you."

She could tell from the hard set of his jaw that Parker was having difficulty maintaining his composure. "You're wrong, Bailey."

"Suddenly everything is clear to me." She made a sweeping gesture with her hand.

"It's obvious that nothing is clear to you," he countered angrily.

"I suppose I'm just so naive it was easy for me to fall in with your...your fiendish plans."

"*Fiendish* plans? Don't you think you're being a bit melodramatic?"

"Me? You're talking to a woman who's been jilted. Twice. Almost every man I've ever known has turned into a fiend."

"Bailey, I'm not using you." He crossed the room, stood directly in front of her and rested his hands on her shoulders. "Think what you want of me, but you should know the truth. Yes, my parents are eager for me to marry, and although I love my family, I would never use you or anyone else to satisfy their desires."

Bailey frowned uncertainly. His eyes were so sincere, so compelling... "Then what possible reason could you have for telling them you'd found the woman you want to marry?"

"Because I have." His beautiful dark eyes brightened. "I'm falling in love with you. I have been almost from the moment we met."

Bailey blinked back hot tears. "You may believe you're in love with me now," she whispered, "but it won't last. It never does. Before you know it, you'll meet someone else, and you'll fall in love with her and not want me anymore."

"Bailey, that's not going to happen. You're going to wear that slightly used wedding dress and you're going to wear it for me."

Bailey continued to stare up at him, doubtful she could trust what she was hearing.

"The mistake I made was in telling my mother about

you. Actually Roseanne Snyder couldn't wait to mention you to Mom. Next thing I knew, my mother was after me to bring you over to the house so she and Dad could meet you. To complicate matters, my father got involved and over a couple of glasses of good Scotch I admitted that my intentions toward you were serious. Naturally both my parents were delighted."

"Naturally." The sinking feeling in her stomach refused to go away.

"I didn't want to rush you, but since Dad's brought everything out into the open, maybe it's best to clear the air now. My intentions are honorable."

"Maybe they are now," she argued, "but it'll never last."

Parker squared his shoulders and took a deep breath. "It will last. I realize you haven't had nearly enough time to figure out your feelings for me. I'd hoped—" he hesitated, his brow furrowed "—that we could have this discussion several months down the road when our feelings for each other had matured."

"I'll say it one more time—engagements don't work, at least not with me."

"It'll be different this time."

"If I was ever going to fall in love with anyone, it would be you. But Parker, it just isn't going to work. I'm sorry, really I am, but I can't go through with this." Her hands were trembling and she bit her lower lip. She was in love with Parker, but she was too frightened to acknowledge it outside the privacy of her own heart.

"Bailey, would you listen to me?"

"No," she said. "I'm sorry, but everything's been blown out of proportion here. I'm writing a romance

novel and you…you're the man I'm using for the model."
She gave a resigned shrug. "That's all."

Parker frowned. "In other words, everything between
us is a farce. The only person guilty of using anyone
is you."

Bailey clasped her hands tightly in front of her,
so tightly that her nails cut deep indentations in her
palms. A cold sweat broke out on her forehead. "I never
claimed anything else."

"I see." The muscles in his jaw tightened again.
"Then all I can do is beg your forgiveness for being so
presumptuous."

"There's no need to apologize." Bailey felt terrible,
but she had to let him believe their relationship *was*
a farce, otherwise everything became too risky. Too
painful.

A noise, the muffled steps of Parker's mother enter-
ing the room, distracted them. "My dears," she said,
"dinner's ready. I'm afraid if we wait much longer, it'll
be ruined."

"We'll be right in," Parker said.

Bailey couldn't remember a more uncomfortable dinner in her life. The tension was so thick, she thought
wryly, it could have been sliced and buttered.

Parker barely spoke during the entire meal. His
mother, ever gracious, carried the burden of conversation. Bailey did her part to keep matters civilized, but
the atmosphere was so strained it was a virtually impossible chore.

The minute they were finished with the meal, Parker
announced it was time to leave. Bailey nodded and
thanked his parents profusely for the meal. It was an

honor to have met them, she went on, and this had been an exceptionally pleasant evening.

"Don't you think you overdid that a little?" Parker muttered once they were in the car.

"I had to say something," she snapped. "Especially since you were so rude."

"I wasn't rude."

"All right, you weren't rude, you were completely tactless. Couldn't you see how uncomfortable your father was? He felt bad enough about mentioning your plans. You certainly didn't need to complicate everything with such a rotten attitude."

"He deserved it."

"That's a terrible thing to say."

Parker didn't answer. For someone who, only hours before, had declared tender feelings for her, he seemed in an almighty hurry to get her home, careering around corners as though he were in training for the Indianapolis 500.

To Bailey's surprise he insisted on walking her to the door. The night before, he'd also escorted her to the door, and after a stilted good-night, he'd left. This evening, however, he wasn't content to leave it at that.

"Invite me in," he said when she'd unlatched the lock.

"Invite you in," Bailey echoed, listening to Max meowing plaintively on the other side.

"I'm coming in whether you invite me or not." His face was devoid of expression, and Bailey realized he would do exactly as he said. Her stomach tightened with apprehension.

"All right," she said, opening the door. She flipped on the light and removed her coat. Max, obviously sensing her state of mind, immediately headed for the bedroom. "I'd make some coffee, but I don't imagine you'll be staying that long."

"Make the coffee."

Bailey was grateful to have something to do. She concentrated on preparing the coffee and setting out mugs.

"Whatever you have to say isn't going to change my mind," Bailey told him. She didn't sound as calm and controlled as she'd hoped.

Parker ignored her. He couldn't seem to stand still, but rapidly paced her kitchen floor, pausing only when Bailey handed him a steaming mug of coffee. She'd seen Parker when he was angry and frustrated, even when he was jealous and unreasonable, but she'd never seen him quite like this.

"Say what you want to say," she prompted, resting her hip against the kitchen counter. She held her cup carefully in both hands.

"All right." Parker's eyes searched hers. "I resent having to deal with your irrational emotions."

"My irrational emotions!"

"Admit it, you're behaving illogically because some other man broke off his engagement to you."

"Other *men*," Bailey corrected sarcastically. "Notice the plural, meaning more than one. Before you judge me too harshly, *Mr.* Davidson, let me remind you that every person is the sum of his or her experiences. If you stick your hand in the fire and get burned, you're not as likely to play around the campfire again, are you? It's as simple as that. I was fool enough to risk the fire twice, but I'm not willing to do it a third time."

"Has it ever occurred to you that you weren't in love with either Paul or Tom?"

Bailey blinked at the unexpectedness of the question. "That's ridiculous. I agreed to marry them. No woman does that without being in love."

"They both fell for someone else."

"How kind of you to remind me."

"Yet when they told you, you did nothing but wallow in your pain. If you'd been in love, deeply in love, you would've done everything within your power to keep them. Instead you did nothing. Absolutely nothing. What else am I to think?"

"Frankly I don't care what you think. I know what was in my heart and I was in love with both of them. Is it any wonder I refuse to fall in love again? An engagement is out of the question!"

"Then marry me now."

Bailey's heart leapt in her chest, then sank like a dead weight. "I—I'm not sure I heard you correctly."

"You heard. Engagements terrify you. I'm willing to accept that you've got a valid reason, but you shouldn't let it dictate how you live the rest of your life."

"In other words, bypassing the engagement and rushing to the altar is going to calm my fears?"

"You keep repeating that you refuse to go through another engagement. I can understand your hesitancy," he stated calmly. "Reno is only a couple of hours away." He glanced at his watch. "We could be married by this time tomorrow."

"Ah…" Words twisted and turned in her mind, but no coherent thought emerged.

"Well?" Parker regarded her expectantly.

"I…we…elope? I don't think so, Parker. It's rather… heroic of you to suggest it, actually, but it's an impossible idea."

"Why? It sounds like the logical solution to me."

"Have you stopped to consider that there are other factors involved in this? Did it occur to you that I might not be in love with you?"

"You're so much in love with me you can't think straight," he said with ego-crushing certainty.

"How do you know that?"

"Easy. It's the way you react, trying too hard to convince yourself you don't care. And the way you kiss me. At first there's resistance, then gradually you warm to it, letting your guard slip just a little, enough for me to realize you're enjoying the kissing as much as I am. It's when you start to moan that I know everything I need to know."

A ferocious blush exploded in Bailey's cheeks. "I do not moan," she protested heatedly.

"Do you want me to prove it to you?"

"No," Bailey cried, backing away.

A smug smile moved over his mouth, settling in his eyes.

Bailey's heart felt heavy. "I'm sorry to disappoint you, Parker, but I'd be doing us both a terrible disservice if I agreed to this."

Parker looked grim. She stared at him and knew, even as she rejected his marriage proposal, that if ever there was a man who could restore peace to her heart, that man was Parker. But she wasn't ready yet; she still had healing and growing to do on her own. But soon… Taking her courage in both hands, she whispered, "Couldn't we take some time to decide about this?"

Parker had asked her to be his wife. Parker Davidson, who was twice the man Paul was and three times the man Tom could ever hope to be. And she was so frightened all she could do was stutter and tremble and plead for time.

"Time," he repeated. Parker set his mug down on the kitchen counter, then stepped forward and framed her face in his large hands. His thumbs gently stroked her cheeks. Bailey gazed up at him, barely breathing. Warm anticipation filled her as he lowered his mouth.

She gasped sharply as his lips touched hers, moving over them slowly, masterfully. A moan rose deep in her throat, one so soft it was barely audible. A small cry of longing and need.

Parker heard it and responded, easing her closer and wrapping her in his arms. He kissed her a second time, then abruptly released her and turned away.

Bailey clutched the counter behind her to keep from falling. "What was that for?"

A slow easy grin spread across his face. "To help you decide."

"The worst part of this whole thing is that I haven't written a word in an entire week," Bailey complained as she sat on her living-room carpet, her legs pulled up under her chin. Pages of Jo Ann's manuscript littered the floor. Max, who revealed little or no interest in their writing efforts, was asleep as usual atop her printer.

"In an entire week?" Jo Ann sounded horrified. Even at Christmas neither of them had taken more than a three-day break from writing.

"I've tried. Each and every night I turn on my computer and then I sit there and stare at the screen. This is the worst case of writer's block I've ever experienced. I can't seem to make myself work."

"Hmm," Jo Ann said, leaning against the side of

the couch. "Isn't it also an entire week since you saw Parker? Seems to me the two must be connected."

She nodded miserably. Jo Ann wasn't telling her anything she didn't already know. She'd relived that night in her memory at least a dozen times a day.

"You've never told me what happened," Jo Ann said, studying Bailey closely.

Bailey swallowed. "Parker is just a friend."

"And pigs have wings."

"My only interest in Parker is as a role model for Michael," she tried again, but she didn't know who she was trying to convince, Jo Ann or herself.

She hadn't heard from him all week. He'd left, promising to give her the time she'd requested. He'd told her the kiss was meant to help her decide if she wanted him. Wanted him? Bailey didn't know if she'd ever *stop* wanting him, but she was desperately afraid that his love for her wouldn't last. It hadn't with Paul or Tom, and it wouldn't with Parker. And with Parker, the pain of rejection would be far worse.

Presumably Parker had thought he was reassuring her by suggesting they skip the engagement part and rush into a Nevada marriage. What he didn't seem to understand, what she couldn't seem to explain, was that it wouldn't make any difference. A wedding ring wasn't a guarantee. Someday, somehow, Parker would have a change of heart; he'd fall out of love with her.

"Are you all right?" Jo Ann asked.

"Of course I am." Bailey managed to keep her voice steady and pretend a calm she wasn't close to feeling. "I'm just upset about this writer's block. But it isn't the end of the world. I imagine everything will return to

normal soon and I'll be back to writing three or four
pages a night."

"You're sure about that?"

Bailey wasn't sure about anything. "No," she admitted.

"Just remember I'm here any time you want to talk."

A trembling smile touched the edges of Bailey's
mouth and she nodded.

Bailey saw Parker three days later. She was waiting
at the BART station by herself—Jo Ann had a day off—
when she happened to glance up and see him walking
in her direction. At first she tried to ignore the quak-
ing of her heart and focus her attention away from him.
But it was impossible.

She knew he saw her, too, although he gave no out-
ward indication of it. His eyes met hers as though challenging her to ignore him. When she took a hesitant
step toward him, his mouth quirked in a mocking smile.

"Hello, Parker."

"Bailey."

"How have you been?"

He hesitated a split second before he answered,
which made Bailey hold her breath in anticipation.

"I've been terrific. How about you?"

"Wonderful," she lied, astonished that they could
stand so close and pretend so well. His gaze lingered
on her lips and she felt the throb of tension in the air.
Parker must have rushed to get to the subway—his hair
was slightly mussed and he was breathing hard.

He said something but his words were drowned out
by the clatter of the approaching train. It pulled up and

dozens of people crowded out. Neither Parker nor Bailey spoke as they waited to board.

He followed her inside, but sat several spaces away. She looked at him, oddly shocked and disappointed that he'd refused to sit beside her.

There were so many things she longed to tell him. Until now she hadn't dared admit to herself how much she'd missed his company. How she hungered to talk to him. They'd known each other for such a short while and yet he seemed to fill every corner of her life.

That, apparently, wasn't the case with Parker. Not if he could so casually, so willingly, sit apart from her. She raised her chin and forced herself to stare at the advertising panels that ran the length of the car.

Bailey felt Parker's eyes on her. The sensation was so strong his hand might as well have touched her cheek, held her face the way he had when he'd last left her. When she could bear it no longer, she turned and glanced at him. Their eyes met and the hungry desire in his tore at her heart.

With every ounce of strength she possessed, Bailey looked away. Eventually he would find someone else, someone he loved more than he would ever love her. Bailey was as certain of that as she was of her own name.

She kept her gaze on anything or anyone except Parker. But she felt the pull between them so strongly that she had to turn her head and look at him. He was staring at her, and the disturbing darkness of his eyes seemed to disrupt the very beat of her heart. A rush of longing jolted her body.

The train was slowing and Bailey was so grateful it was her station she jumped up and hurried to the exit.

"I'm still waiting," Parker whispered from directly behind her. She was conscious as she'd never been before of the long muscled legs so close to her own, of his strength and masculinity. "Have you decided yet?"

Bailey shut her eyes and prayed for the courage to do what was right for both of them. She shook her head silently; she couldn't talk to him now. She couldn't make a rational decision while the yearning in her heart was so great, while her body was so weak with need for him.

The crowd rushed forward and Bailey rushed with them, leaving him behind.

The writers' group met the following evening, for which Bailey was thankful. At least she wouldn't have to stare at a blank computer screen for several hours while she tried to convince herself she was a writer. Jo Ann had been making headway on her rewrite, whereas Bailey's had come to a complete standstill.

The speaker, an established historical-romance writer who lived in the San Francisco area, had agreed to address their group. Her talk was filled with good advice and Bailey tried to take notes. Instead, she drew meaningless doodles. Precise three-dimensional boxes and neat round circles in geometric patterns.

It wasn't until she was closing her spiral notebook at the end of the speech that Bailey realized all the circles on her page resembled interlocking wedding bands. About fifteen pairs of them. Was her subconscious sending her a message? Bailey had given up guessing.

"Are you going over to the diner for coffee?" Jo Ann asked as the group dispersed. Her eyes didn't meet Bailey's.

"Sure." She studied her friend and knew instinctively

that something was wrong. Jo Ann had been avoiding her most of the evening. At first she'd thought it was her imagination, but there was a definite strain between them.

"All right," Bailey said, once they were outside. "What is it? What's wrong?"

Jo Ann sighed deeply. "I saw Parker this afternoon. I know it's probably nothing and I'm a fool for saying anything but, Bailey, he was with a woman and they were definitely more than friends."

"Oh?" Bailey's legs were shaky as she moved down the steps to the street. Her heart felt like a stone in the center of her chest.

"I'm sure it doesn't mean anything. For all I know, the woman could be his sister. I... I hadn't intended on saying a word, but then I thought you'd want to know."

"Of course I do," Bailey said, swallowing past the tightness in her throat. Her voice was firm and steady, revealing none of the chaos in her thoughts.

"I think Parker saw me. In fact, I'm sure he did. It was almost as if he *wanted* me to see him. He certainly didn't go out of his way to disguise who he was with—which leads me to believe it was all very innocent."

"I'm sure it was," Bailey lied. Her mouth twisted in a wry smile. She made a pretense of looking at her watch. "My goodness, I didn't realize it was so late. I think I'll skip coffee tonight and head on home."

Jo Ann grabbed her arm. "Are you all right?"

"Of course." But she was careful not to look directly at her friend. "It really doesn't matter, you know—about Parker."

"Doesn't matter?" Jo Ann echoed.

"I'm not the jealous type."

Her stomach was churning, her head spinning, her hands trembling. Fifteen minutes later, Bailey let herself into her apartment. She didn't stop to remove her coat, but walked directly into the kitchen and picked up the phone.

Parker answered on the third ring. His greeting sounded distracted. "Bailey," he said, "it's good to hear from you. I've been trying to call you most of the evening."

"I was at a writers' meeting. You wanted to tell me something?"

"As a matter of fact, yes. You obviously aren't going to change your mind about the two of us."

"I…"

"Let's forget the whole marriage thing. There's no need to rush into this. What do you think?"

Eleven

"Oh, I agree one hundred percent," Bailey answered. It didn't surprise her that Parker had experienced a change of heart. She'd been expecting it to happen sooner or later. It was a blessing that he'd recognized his feelings so early on.

"No hard feelings then?"

"None," she assured him, raising her voice to a bright confident level. "I've gotten used to it. Honestly, you don't have a thing to worry about."

"You seem…cheerful."

"I am," Bailey answered, doing her best to sound as though she'd just won the lottery and was only waiting until she'd finished with this phone call to celebrate.

"How's the writing going?"

"Couldn't be better." Couldn't be worse actually, but she wasn't about to admit that. Not to Parker, at any rate.

"I'll be seeing you around then," he said.

"I'm sure you will." Maintaining this false enthusiasm was killing her. "One question."

"Sure."

"Where'd you meet her?"

"Her?" Parker hesitated. "You must mean Lisa. We've known each other for ages."

"I see." Bailey had to get off the phone before her facade cracked. But her voice broke as she continued, "I wish you well, Parker."

He paused as though he were debating whether or not to say something else. "You, too, Bailey."

Bailey replaced the receiver, her legs shaking so badly she stumbled toward the chair and literally fell into it. She covered her face with her hands, dragging deep gulps of air into her lungs. The burning ache in her stomach seemed to ripple out in hot waves, spreading to the tips of her fingers, to the bottoms of her feet.

By sheer force of will, Bailey lifted her head, squared her shoulders and stood up. She'd been through this before. Twice. Once more wouldn't be any more difficult than the first two times. Or so she insisted to herself.

After all, this time there was no ring to return, no wedding arrangements to cancel, no embossed announcements to burn.

No one, with the exception of Jo Ann, even knew about Parker, so the embarrassment would be kept to a minimum.

Getting over Parker should be quick and easy.

It wasn't.

A hellishly slow week passed and Bailey felt as if she were living on another planet. Outwardly nothing had changed, and yet the world seemed to be spinning off its axis. She went to work every morning, discussed character and plot with Jo Ann, worked an eight-hour day, took the subway home and plunked herself down in front of her computer, working on her rewrite with demonic persistence.

She appeared to have everything under control. Yet her life was unfolding in slow motion around her, as though she was a bystander and not a participant.

It must have shown in her writing because Jo Ann phoned two days after Bailey had given her the complete rewrite.

"You finished reading it?" Bailey couldn't hide her excitement. If Jo Ann liked it, then Bailey could mail it right off to Paula Albright, the editor who'd asked to see the revised manuscript.

"I'd like to come over and discuss a few points. Have you got time?"

Time was the one thing Bailey had in abundance. She hadn't realized how large a role Parker had come to play in her life or how quickly he'd chased away the emptiness. The gap he'd left behind seemed impossible to fill. Most nights she wrote until she was exhausted. But because she couldn't sleep anyway, she usually just sat in the living room holding Max.

Her cat didn't really care for the extra attention she was lavishing on him. He grudgingly endured her stroking his fur and scratching his ears. An extra serving of canned cat food and a fluffed-up pillow were appreciated, but being picked up and carted across the room to sit in her lap wasn't. To his credit, Max had submitted to two or three sessions in which she talked out her troubles, but his patience with such behavior had exhausted itself.

"Put on a pot of coffee and I'll be over in a few minutes," Jo Ann said, disturbing Bailey's musings.

"Fine. I'll see you when I see you," Bailey responded, then frowned. My goodness, *that* was an original statement. If she was reduced to such a glaring lack of originality one week after saying farewell to Parker, she hated to consider how banal her conversation would be a month from now.

Jo Ann arrived fifteen minutes later, Bailey's manuscript tucked under her arm.

"You didn't like it," Bailey said in a flat voice. Her friend's expression couldn't have made it any plainer.

"It wasn't that, exactly," Jo Ann told her, setting the manuscript on the coffee table and curling up in the overstuffed chair.

"What seems to be the problem this time?"

"Janice."

"Janice?" Bailey cried, restraining the urge to argue. She'd worked so hard to make the rewrite of *Forever Yours* work. "I thought *Michael* was the source of all the trouble."

"He was in the original version. You've rewritten him just beautifully, but Janice seemed so—I hate to say this—weak."

"Weak?" Bailey shouted. "Janice isn't weak! She's strong and independent and—"

"Foolish and weak-willed," Jo Ann finished. "The reader loses sympathy for her halfway through the book. She acts like a robot with Michael."

Bailey was having a difficult time not protesting. She knew Jo Ann's was only one opinion, but she'd always trusted her views. Jo Ann's evaluation of the manuscript's earlier versions had certainly been accurate.

"Give me an example," Bailey said, making an effort to keep her voice as even and unemotional as possible.

"Everything changed after the scene at the Pops concert."

"Parker was a real jerk," Bailey argued. "He deserved everything she said and did."

"Parker?" Jo Ann's brows arched at her slip of the tongue.

"Michael," Bailey corrected. "You know who I meant!"

"Indeed I did."

During the past week, Jo Ann had made several awkward attempts to drop Parker's name into conversation, but Bailey refused to discuss him.

"Michael did act a bit high-handed," Jo Ann continued, "but the reader's willing to forgive him, knowing he's discovering his true feelings for Janice. The fact that he felt jealous when she danced with another man hit him like an expected blow. True, he did behave like a jerk, but I understood his motivation and was willing to forgive him."

"In other words, the reader will accept such actions from the hero but not the heroine?" Bailey asked aggressively.

"That's not it at all," Jo Ann responded, sounding surprised. "In the original version Janice comes off as witty and warm and independent. The reader can't help liking her and sympathize with her situation."

"Then what changed?" Bailey demanded, raising her voice. Her inclination was to defend Janice as she would her own child.

Jo Ann shrugged. "I wish I knew what happened to Janice. All I can tell you is that it started after the scene at the Pops concert. From that point on I had problems identifying with her. I couldn't understand why she was so willing to accept everything Michael said and did. It was as if she'd lost her spirit. By the end of the book, I actively disliked her. I wanted to take her by the shoulders and shake her."

Bailey felt like weeping. "So I guess it's back to the drawing board," she said, putting on a cheerful front. "I suppose I should be getting used to that."

"My best advice is to put the manuscript aside for a few weeks," Jo Ann said in a gentle tone. "Didn't you tell me you had another plot idea you wanted to develop?"

Bailey nodded. But that was before. Before almost all her energy was spent just surviving from day to day. Before she'd begun pretending her life was perfectly normal although the pain left her barely able to function. Before she'd lost hope...

"What will putting it aside accomplish?" she asked.

"It will give you perspective," Jo Ann advised. "Look at Janice. Really look at her. Does she deserve a man as terrific as Michael? You've done such a superb job writing him."

It went without saying that Parker had been the source of her inspiration.

"In other words Janice is unsympathetic?"

Jo Ann's nod was regretful. "I'm afraid so. But remember that this is strictly my opinion. Someone else may read *Forever Yours* and feel Janice is a fabulous heroine. You might want to have some of the other writers in the group read it. I don't mean to be discouraging, Bailey, really I don't."

"I know that."

"It's only because you're my friend that I can be so honest."

"That's what I wanted," Bailey admitted slowly. Who was she kidding? She was as likely to become a published writer as she was a wife. The odds were so bad it would be a sucker's bet.

"I don't want to discourage you," Jo Ann repeated in a worried voice.

"If I'd been looking for someone to tell me how talented I am, I would've given the manuscript to my mother."

Jo Ann laughed, then glanced at her watch. "I've got to scoot. I'm supposed to pick up Dan at the muffler shop. The station wagon's beginning to sound like an army tank. If you have any questions give me a call later."

"I will." Bailey led the way to the door and held it open as Jo Ann gathered up her purse and coat. Her friend paused, looking concerned. "You're not too depressed about this, are you?"

"A little," Bailey said. "All right, a lot. But it's all part of the learning process, and if I have to rewrite this manuscript a hundred times, then I'll do it. Writing isn't for the faint of heart."

"You've got that right."

Jo Ann had advised her to set the story aside but the instant she was gone, Bailey tore into the manuscript, leafing carefully through the pages.

Jo Ann's notes in the margins were valuable—and painful. Bailey paid particular attention to the comments following Michael and Janice's fateful evening at the concert. It didn't take her long to connect this scene in her novel with its real-life equivalent, her evening with Parker.

She acts like a robot with Michael, Jo Ann had said. As Bailey read through the subsequent chapters, she couldn't help but agree. It was as though her feisty, spirited heroine had lost the will to exert her own personality. For all intents and purposes, she'd lain down and died.

Isn't that what you've done? her heart asked.

But Bailey ignored it. She'd given up listening to the deep inner part of herself. She'd learned how painful that could be.

"By the end of the book I actively disliked her." Jo Ann's words resounded like a clap of thunder in her mind. Janice's and Bailey's personalities were so intimately entwined that she no longer knew where one stopped and the other began.

"Janice seemed so...so weak."

Bailey resisted the urge to cover her ears to block out Jo Ann's words. It was all she could do not to shout, "You'd be spineless too if you had a slightly used wedding dress hanging in your closet!"

When Bailey couldn't tolerate the voices any longer, she reached for her jacket and purse and escaped. Anything was better than listening to the accusations echoing in her mind. The apartment felt unfriendly and confining. Even Max's narrowed green eyes seemed to reflect her heart's questions.

The sky was overcast—a perfect accompaniment to Bailey's mood. She walked without any real destination until she found herself at the BART station and her heart suddenly started to hammer. She chided herself for the small surge of hope she felt. What were the chances of running into Parker on a Saturday afternoon? Virtually none. She hadn't seen him in over a week. More than likely he'd been driving to work to avoid her.

Parker.

The pain she'd managed to hold at bay for several

days bobbed to the surface. Tears spilled from her eyes. She kept on walking, her pace brisk as though she was in a hurry to get somewhere. Bailey's destination was peace and she had yet to find it. Sometimes she wondered if she ever would.

Men fell in love with her easily enough, but they seemed to fall out of love just as effortlessly. Worst of all, most demeaning of all, was the knowledge that there was always another woman involved. A woman they loved more than Bailey. Paul, Tom and now Parker.

Bailey walked for what felt like miles. Somehow, she wasn't altogether shocked when she found herself on Parker's street. He'd mentioned it in passing the evening they'd gone to the concert. The condominiums were a newer addition to the neighborhood, ultramodern, ultra-expensive, ultra-appealing to the eye. It wouldn't surprise her to learn that Parker had been responsible for their design. Although the dinner conversation with his parents had been stilted and uncomfortable, Parker's mother had taken delight in highlighting her son's many accomplishments. Parker obviously wasn't enthusiastic about his mother's bragging, but Bailey had felt a sense of pride in the man she loved.

The man she loved.

Abruptly Bailey stopped walking. She closed her eyes and clenched her hands into tight fists. She did *not* love Parker. If she did happen to fall in love again, it wouldn't be with a man as fickle or as untrustworthy as Parker Davidson, who apparently fell in and out of love at the drop of a—

You love him, you fool. Now what are you going to do about it?

Bailey just wanted these questions, these revelations,

to stop, to leave her alone. Alone in her misery. Alone in her pain and denial.

An anger grew in Bailey. One born of so much strong emotion she could barely contain it. Without sparing a thought for the consequences, she stormed into the central lobby of the condominium complex. The doorman stepped forward.

"Good afternoon," he said politely.

Bailey managed to smile at him. "Hello." Then, when she noticed that he was waiting for her to continue, she added, "Mr. Parker Davidson's home, please," her voice remarkably calm and impassive. They were going to settle this once and for all, and no one, not a doorman, not even a security guard, was going to stand in her way.

"May I ask who's calling?"

"Bailey York," she answered confidently.

"If you'll kindly wait here." He was gone only a moment. "Mr. Parker says to send you right up. He's in unit 204."

"Thank you." Bailey's determination hadn't dwindled by the time her elevator reached the second floor.

It took Parker a couple of minutes to answer his door. When he did, Bailey didn't wait for an invitation. She marched into his apartment, ignoring the spectacular view and the lush traditional furnishings of polished wood and rich fabric.

"Bailey." He seemed surprised to see her.

Standing in the middle of the room, hands on her hips, she glared at him with a week's worth of indignation flashing from her eyes. "Don't Bailey me," she raged. "I want to know who Lisa is and I want to know *now.*"

Parker gaped at her as though she'd taken leave of her senses.

"Don't give me that look." She walked a complete circle around him; he swiveled slowly, still staring. "There's no need to stand there with your mouth hanging open. It's a simple question."

"What are you doing here?"

"What does it look like?"

"Frankly I'm not sure."

"I've come to find out exactly what kind of man you are." That sounded good, and she said it in a mocking challenging way bound to get a response.

"What kind of man I am? Does this mean I have to run through a line of warriors waiting to flog me?"

Bailey was in no mood for jesting. "It just might." She removed one hand from her hip and waved it under his nose. "I'll have you know Janice has been ruined and I blame you."

"Who?"

"My character Janice," she explained with exaggerated patience. "The one in my novel, *Forever Yours*. She's wishy-washy, submissive and docile. Reading about her is like…like vanilla pudding instead of chocolate."

"I happen to be partial to vanilla pudding."

Bailey sent him a furious look. "I'll do the talking here."

Parker raised both hands. "Sorry."

"You should be. So…exactly what kind of man *are* you?"

"I believe you've already asked that question." Bailey spun around to scowl at him. "Sorry," he muttered, his mouth twisting oddly. "I forgot you're doing the talking here."

"One minute you claim you're in love with me. So much in love you want me to marry you." Her voice faltered slightly. "And the next you're involved with some woman named Lisa and you want to put our relationship on hold. Well, I've got news for you, Mr. Unreliable. I refuse to allow you to play with my heart. You asked me to marry you…" Bailey paused at the smile that lifted the corners of his mouth. "Is this discussion amusing you?" she demanded.

"A little."

"Feel free to share the joke," she said, motioning with her hand.

"Lisa's my sister-in-law."

The words didn't immediately sink in. "Your what?"

"She's my brother's wife."

Bailey slumped into a chair. A confused moment passed while she tried to collect her scattered thoughts. "You're in love with your brother's wife?"

"No." He sounded shocked that she'd even suggest such a thing. "I'm in love with you."

"You're not making a lot of sense."

"I figured as much, otherwise—"

"Otherwise what?"

"Otherwise you'd either be in my arms or finding ways to inflict physical damage on my person."

"You'd better explain yourself," she said, frowning, hardly daring to hope.

"I love you, Bailey, but I didn't know how long it would take you to discover you love me, too. You were so caught up in the past—"

"With reason," she reminded him.

"With reason," he agreed. "Anyway I asked you to marry me."

"To be accurate, your father's the one who did the actual speaking," Bailey muttered.

"True, he spoke out of turn, but it was a question I was ready to ask..."

"But..." she supplied for him. There was always a "but" when it came to men and love.

"But I didn't know if your feelings for me were genuine."

"I beg your pardon?"

"Was it me you fell for or Michael?" he asked quietly.

"I don't think I understand."

"The way I figure it, if you truly loved me you'd do everything in your power to win me back."

"Win you back? I'm sorry, Parker, but I still don't get it."

"All right, let's backtrack a bit. When Paul announced he'd found another woman and wanted to break your engagement, what did you do?"

"I dropped out of university and signed up for paralegal classes at the business college."

"What about Tom?"

"I moved to San Francisco."

"My point exactly."

Bailey lost him somewhere between Paul and Tom. "*What* is your point exactly?"

Parker hesitated, then looked straight into her eyes. "I wanted you to love me enough to fight for me," he told her simply. "Don't worry. Lisa and I are not, repeat not, in love."

"You just wanted me to think so?"

"Yes," he said with obvious embarrassment. "She

reads romances, too. Quite a few women do apparently. I was telling her about our relationship, and she came up with the idea of using the 'other woman' the way some romance novels do."

"That's the most underhand unscrupulous thing I've ever heard."

"Indulge me for a few more minutes, all right?"

"All right," she agreed.

"When Paul and Tom broke off their engagements to you, you didn't say or do anything to convince them of your love. You calmly accepted that they'd met someone else and conveniently got out of their lives."

"So?"

"So I needed you to want me so much, love me so much, that you wouldn't give me up. You'd put aside that damnable pride of yours and confront me."

"Were you planning to arrange a mud-wrestling match between Lisa and me?" she asked wryly.

"No!" He looked horrified at the mere thought. "I wanted to provoke you—just enough to come to me. What took you so long?" He shook his head. "I was beginning to lose heart."

"You're going to lose a whole lot more than your heart if you ever pull that stunt again, Parker Davidson."

His face lit up with a smile potent enough to dissolve her pain and her doubts. He opened his arms then, and Bailey walked into his embrace.

"I should be furious with you," she mumbled.

"Kiss me first, then be mad."

His mouth captured hers in hungry exultation. In a single kiss Parker managed to make up for the long cheerless days, the long lonely nights. She was breathless when he finally released her.

"You really love me?" she whispered, needing to hear him say it. Her lower lip trembled and her hands tightened convulsively.

"I really love you," he whispered back, smiling down at her. "Enough to last us two lifetimes."

"Only two?"

His hand cradled the back of her head. "At least four." His mouth claimed hers again, then he abruptly broke off the kiss. "Now, what was it you were saying about Janice? What's wrong with her?"

A slow thoughtful smile spread across Bailey's face. "Nothing that a wedding and a month-long honeymoon won't cure."

Epilogue

Bailey paused to read the sign in the bookstore window, announcing the autographing session for two local authors that afternoon.

"How does it feel to see your name in lights?" Jo Ann asked.

"You may be used to this, but I feel... I feel—" Bailey hesitated and flattened her palms on the smooth roundness of her stomach "—I feel almost the same as I did when I found out I was pregnant."

"It does funny things to the nervous system, doesn't it?" Jo Ann teased. "And what's this comment about me being used to all this? I've only got two books published to your one."

The bookseller, Caroline Dryer, recognized them when they entered the store and hurried forward to greet them, her smile welcoming. "I'm so pleased you could both come. We've had lots of interest." She steered them toward the front where a table, draped in lace, and two chairs were waiting. Several women were already lined up patiently, looking forward to meeting Jo Ann and Bailey.

They did a brisk business for the next hour. Family, friends and other writers joined the romance readers who stopped by to wish them well.

Bailey was talking to an older woman, a retired schoolteacher, when Parker and Jo Ann's husband, Dan, casually strolled past the table. The four were going out for dinner following the autograph session. There was a lot to celebrate. Jo Ann had recently signed a two-book contract with her publisher and Bailey had just sold her second romance. After weeks of work, Parker had finished the plans for their new home. Construction was scheduled to begin the following month and with luck would be completed by the time the baby arrived.

"What I loved best about *Forever Yours* was Michael," the older woman was saying to Bailey. "The scene where he takes her in his arms right in the middle of the merry-go-round and tells her he's tired of playing childish games and that he loves her was enough to steal my heart."

"He stole mine, too," Bailey said, her eyes linking with her husband's.

"Do you think there are any men like that left in this world?" the woman asked. "I've been divorced for years, and now that I'm retired, well, I wouldn't mind meeting someone."

"You'd be surprised how many heroes there are all around us," Bailey said, her gaze still holding Parker's. "They take the subway and eat peanut-butter sandwiches and fall in love—like you and me."

"Well, there's hope for me, then," the teacher said jauntily. "And I plan to have a good time looking." She smiled. "That's why I enjoy romance novels so much. They give me encouragement, they're fun—and they tell me it's okay to believe in love," she confided. "Even for the second time."

"Or the third," Parker inserted quietly.

Bailey grinned. She couldn't argue with that!

* * * * *

Also by Lee Tobin McClain

Love Inspired

Rescue Haven

The Secret Christmas Child
Child on His Doorstep
Finding a Christmas Home

Rescue River

Engaged to the Single Mom
His Secret Child
Small-Town Nanny
The Soldier and the Single Mom
The Soldier's Secret Child
A Family for Easter

Canary Street Press

The Off Season

Cottage at the Beach
Reunion at the Shore
Christmas on the Coast
Home to the Harbor
First Kiss at Christmas
Forever on the Bay

Visit the Author Profile page
at Harlequin.com for more titles.

ENGAGED TO
THE SINGLE MOM

Lee Tobin McClain

I owe much appreciation to my Wednesday-morning critique group—Sally Alexander, Jonathan Auxier, Kathy Ayres, Colleen McKenna and Jackie Robb—for being patient through genre shifts while gently insisting on excellence. Thanks also to my colleagues at Seton Hill University, especially Michael Arnzen, Nicole Peeler and Albert Wendland, whose support and encouragement keep me happily writing. Ben Wernsman helped me brainstorm story ideas, and Carrie Turansky read an early draft of the proposal and critiqued it most helpfully. I'm grateful to be working with my agent, Karen Solem, and my editor, Shana Asaro—dog lovers both—who saw the potential of the story and helped me make it better. Most of all, thanks belong to my daughter, Grace, for being patient with her creative mom's absentmindedness and for offering inspiration, recreation and eye-rolling, teenage-style love every step of the way.

And we know that all things work together for good
to them that love God, to them who are
the called according to His purpose.
—*Romans* 8:28

One

"You can let me off here." Angelica Camden practically shouted the words over the roar of her grandfather's mufflerless truck. The hot July air, blowing in through the pickup's open windows, did nothing to dispel the sweat that dampened her neck and face.

She rubbed her hands down the legs of the full-length jeans she preferred to wear despite the heat, took a deep breath and blew it out yoga-style between pursed lips. She could do this. Had to do it.

Gramps raised bushy white eyebrows as he braked at the top of a long driveway. "I'm taking you right up to that arrogant something-or-other's door. You're a lady and should be treated as one."

No chance of that. Angelica's stomach churned at the thought of the man she was about to face. She'd fight lions for her kid, had done the equivalent plenty of times, but this particular lion terrified her, brought back feelings of longing and shame and sadness that made her feel about two inches tall.

This particular lion had every right to eat her alive. Her heart fluttered hard against her ribs, and when she took a deep breath, trying to calm herself, the truck's exhaust fumes made her feel light-headed.

I can't do this, Lord.

Immediately the verse from this morning's devotional, read hastily while she'd stirred oatmeal on Gramps's old gas stove, swam before her eyes: *I can do all things through Him who gives me strength.*

She believed it. She'd recited it to herself many times in the past couple of difficult years. She could do all things through Christ.

But this, Lord? Are You sure?

She knew Gramps would gladly go on the warpath for her, but using an eighty-year-old man to fight her battles wasn't an option. The problem was hers. She'd brought it on herself, mostly, and she was the one who had to solve it. "I'd rather do it my own way, Gramps. Please."

Ignoring her—of course—he started to turn into the driveway.

She yanked the handle, shoved the truck door open and put a booted foot on the running board, ready to jump.

"Hey, careful!" Gramps screeched to a stop just in front of a wooden sign: A Dog's Last Chance: No-Cage Canine Rescue. Troy Hinton, DVM, Proprietor. "DVM, eh? Well, he's still a—"

"Shhh." She swung back around to face him, hands braced on the door guards, and nodded sideways toward the focus of her entire life.

Gramps grunted and, thankfully, lapsed into silence.

"Mama, can I go in with you?" Xavier shot her a pleading look—one he'd perfected and used at will, the rascal—from the truck's backseat. "I want to see the dogs."

If she played this right, he'd be able to do more than just see the dogs during a short visit. He'd fulfill a dream, and right now Angelica's life pretty much revolved around helping Xavier fulfill his dreams.

"It's a job interview, honey. You go for a little drive with Gramps." At his disappointed expression, she reached back to pat his too-skinny leg. "Maybe you can see the dogs later, if I get the job."

"You'll get it, Mama."

His brilliant smile and total confidence warmed her heart at the same time that tension attacked her stomach. She shot a glance at Gramps and clung harder to the truck, which suddenly felt like security in a storm.

He must have read her expression, because his gnarled hands gripped the steering wheel hard. "You don't have to do this. We can try to get by for another couple of weeks at the Towers."

Seeing the concern in his eyes took Angelica out of herself and her fears. Gramps wasn't as healthy as he used to be, and he didn't need any extra stress on account of her. Two weeks at the Senior Towers was the maximum visit from relatives with kids, and even though she'd tried to keep Xavier quiet and neat, he'd bumped into a resident who used a walker, spilled red punch in the hallway and generally made too much noise. In other words, he was a kid. And the Senior Towers was no place to raise a kid.

They'd already outstayed their welcome, and she knew Gramps was concerned about it. She leaned back in to rub his shoulder. "I know what I'm doing. I'll be fine."

"You're sure?"

She nodded. "Don't worry about me."

But once the truck pulled away, bearing with it the only two males in North America she trusted, Angelica's strength failed her. She put a hand on one of the wooden fence posts and closed her eyes, shooting up a desperate prayer for courage.

As the truck sounds faded, the Ohio farmland came to life around her. A tiny creek rippled its way along the driveway. Two fence posts down, a red-winged blackbird landed, trilling the *oka-oka-LEE* she hadn't heard in years. She inhaled the pungent scent of new-mown hay.

This was where she'd come from. Surely the Lord had a reason for bringing her home.

Taking another deep breath, she straightened her spine. She was of farm stock. She could do this. She reached into her pocket, clutched the key chain holding a cross and a photo of her son in better days, and headed toward the faint sound of barking dogs. Toward the home of the man who had every reason to hate her.

As the sound of the pickup faded, Troy Hinton used his arms to lift himself halfway out of the porch rocker. In front of him, his cast-clad leg rested on a wicker table, stiff and useless.

"A real man plays ball, even if he's hurt. Get back up and into the game, son." His dad's words echoed in his head, even though his logical side knew he couldn't risk worsening his compound fracture just so he could stride down the porch steps and impress the raven-haired beauty slowly approaching his home.

Not that he had any chance of impressing Angelica

Camden. Nor any interest in doing so. She was one mistake he wouldn't make again.

His dog, Bull, scrabbled against the floorboards beside him, trying to stand despite his arthritic hips. Troy sank back down and put a hand on the dog's back. "It's okay, boy. Relax."

He watched Angelica's slow, reluctant walk toward his house. Why she'd applied to be his assistant, he didn't know. And why he'd agreed to talk to her was an even bigger puzzle.

She'd avoided him for the past seven years, ever since she'd jilted him with a handwritten letter and disappeared not only from his life, but from the state. A surge of the old bitterness rose in him, and he clenched his fists. Humiliation. Embarrassment. And worse, a broken heart and shattered faith that had never fully recovered.

She'd arrived in her grandfather's truck, but the old man had no use for him or any of his family, so why had he brought her out here for her interview? And why wasn't he standing guard with a shotgun? In fact, given the old man's reputation for thrift, he'd probably use the very same shotgun with which he'd ordered Troy off his hardscrabble farm seven years ago.

Troy had come looking for explanations about why Angelica had left town. Where she was. What her letter had meant. How she was surviving; whether she was okay.

The old man had raved at him, gone back into the past feud between their families over the miserable acre of land he called a farm. That acre had rapidly gone to seed, as had Angelica's grandfather, and a short while later he'd moved into the Senior Towers.

In a way, the old man had been abandoned, too, by

the granddaughter he'd helped to raise. Fair warning. No matter how sweet she seemed, no matter what promises she made, she was a runner. Disloyal. Not to be counted on.

As Angelica approached, Troy studied her. She was way thinner than the curvy little thing she'd been at twenty-one. Her black hair, once shiny and flowing down her back in waves, was now captured in a careless bun. She wore baggy jeans and a loose, dusty-red T-shirt.

But with her full lips and almond-shaped eyes and coppery bronze skin, she still glowed like an exotic flower in the middle of a plain midwestern cornfield. And doggone it if his heart didn't leap out of his chest to see her.

"Down, boy," Troy ordered Bull—or maybe himself—as he pushed up into a standing position and hopped over to get his crutches.

His movements must have caught the attention of Lou Ann Miller, and now she hobbled out the front screen door.

She pointed a spatula at him. "You get back in that chair."

"You get back in that kitchen." He narrowed his eyes at the woman who'd practically raised him. "This is something I have to do alone. And standing up."

"If you fall down those steps, you'll have to hire yet another helper, and you've barely got the charm to keep me." She put her hands on bony hips. "I expect you to treat that girl decent. What I hear, she's been through a lot."

Curiosity tugged at him. People in town were too kind

to tell him the latest gossip about Angelica. They danced around the subject, sparing his ego and his feelings.

What had Angelica been through? How had it affected her?

The idea that she'd suffered or been hurt plucked at the chords of his heart, remnants of a time he'd have moved mountains to protect her and care for her. She'd had such a hard time growing up, and it had made him feel ten feet tall that she'd chosen him to help her escape her rough past.

Women weren't the only ones who liked stories of knights in shining armor. Lots of men wanted to be heroes as well, and Angelica was the kind of woman who could bring out the heroic side of a guy.

At least for a while. He swallowed down his questions and the bad taste in his mouth and forced a lightness he didn't feel into his tone. "Who says I won't treat her well? She's the only person who's applied for the job. I'd better." Looking at his cast, he could only shake his head. What an idiot he'd been to try to fix the barn roof by himself, all because he didn't want to ask anyone for help.

"I'll leave you alone, but I'll know if you raise your voice," Lou Ann warned, pointing the spatula at him again.

He hopped to the door and held it for her. Partly to urge her inside, and partly to catch her if she stumbled. She was seventy-five if she was a day, and despite her high energy and general bossiness, he felt protective.

Not that he'd be much help if she fell, with this broken leg.

She rolled her eyes and walked inside, shaking her head. When he turned back, Angelica was about ten feet away from the front porch. She'd stopped and was watching him. Eyes huge, wide, wary. From here, he could see the dark circles under them.

Unwanted concern nudged at him. She looked as though she hadn't slept, hadn't been eating right. Her clothes were worn, suggesting poverty. And the flirty sparkle in her eyes, the one that had kept all the farm boys buying gallons of lemonade from her concession stand at the county fair...that was completely gone.

She looked defeated. At the end of her rope.

What had happened to her?

Their mutual sizing-up stare-fest lasted way too long, and then he beckoned her forward. "Come on up. I'm afraid I can't greet you properly with this bum leg."

She trotted up the stairs, belying his impression that she was beaten down. "Was that Lou Ann Miller?"

"It was." He felt an illogical urge to step closer to her, which he ascribed to the fact that he didn't get out much and didn't meet many women. "She runs my life."

"Miss Lou Ann!" Angelica called through the screen door, seemingly determined to ignore Troy. "Haven't seen you in ages!"

Lou Ann, who must have been directly inside, hurried back out.

Angelica's face broke into a smile as she pulled the older woman into a gentle hug. "It's so nice to see you! How's Caleb?"

Troy drummed his fingers on the handle of his crutch. Caleb was Lou Ann's grandson, who'd been in Angelica's grade in school, and whom Angelica had dated before the two of them had gotten together. He was just one of the many members of Angelica's fan club back then, and Troy, with his young-guy pride and testosterone, had been crazy jealous of all of them.

Maybe with good reason.

"He's fine, fine. Got two young boys." Lou Ann held Angelica's shoulders and studied her. "You're way too thin. I'll bring out some cookies." She glared at Troy. "They're not for you, so don't you go eating all of them."

And then she was gone and it was just the two of them.

Angelica studied the man she'd been so madly in love with seven years ago.

He was as handsome as ever, despite the cast on his leg and the two-day ragged beard on his chin. His shoulders were still impossibly broad, but now there were tiny wrinkles beside his eyes, and his short haircut didn't conceal the fact that his hairline was a little higher than it used to be. The hand he held out to her was huge.

Angelica's stomach knotted, but she forced herself to reach out and put her hand into his.

The hard-calloused palm engulfed hers and she yanked her hand back, feeling trapped. She squatted down to pet the grizzled bulldog at Troy's side. "Who's this?"

"That's Bull."

She blinked. Was he calling her on her skittishness?

That impression increased as he cocked his head to one side. "You're not afraid of me, are you?"

"No!" She gulped air. "I'm not afraid of you. Like I said when we texted, I'm here to apply for the job you advertised in the *Tribune*."

He gestured toward one of the rockers. "Have a seat.

Let's talk about that. I'm curious about why you're interested."

Of course he was. And she'd spent much of last night sleepless, wondering how much she'd have to tell him to get the job she desperately needed, the job that would make things as good as they could be, at least for a while.

Once she sat down, he made his way back to his own rocker and sat, grimacing as he propped his leg on the low table in front of him.

She didn't like the rush of sympathy she felt. "What happened?"

"Fell off a roof. My own stupid fault."

That was new in him, the willingness to admit his own culpability. She wondered how far it went.

"That's why I need an assistant with the dogs," he explained. "Lou Ann helps me around the house, but she's not strong enough to take care of the kennels. I can't get everything done, and we've got a lot of dogs right now, so this is kind of urgent."

His words were perfectly cordial, but questions and undercurrents rustled beneath them.

Angelica forced herself to stay in the present, in sales mode. "You saw my résumé online, right? I worked as a vet assistant back in Boston. And I've done hospital, um, volunteer work, and you know I grew up in the country. I'm strong, a lot stronger than I look."

He nodded. "I've no doubt you could do the work if you wanted to," he said, "but why would you want to?"

"Let's just say I need a job."

He studied her, his blue eyes troubled. "You haven't shown your face in town for seven years. Even when you visit your grandfather, you hide out at the Senior

Towers. If I'm giving you access to my dogs and my computer files and my whole business, especially if you're able to live here on the grounds, I need to know a little more about what you've been up to."

He hadn't mentioned his main reason for mistrusting her, and she appreciated that. She pulled her mind out of the past and focused on the living arrangement, one of the main reasons this job was perfect for her. "I'm very interested in living in. Your ad said that's part of the job?"

"That's right, in the old bunkhouse." He gestured toward a trim white building off to the east. "I figured the offer of housing might sweeten the deal, given that this is just a temporary job."

"Is it big enough for two?"

"Ye-es." He leaned back in the rocker and studied her, his eyes hooded. "Why? Are you married? I thought your name was still Camden."

"I'm not married." She swallowed. "But I do have a son."

His eyebrows lifted. "How old is your son?"

"Is that important?" She really, really didn't want to tell him.

"Yes, it's important," he said with a slight sigh. "I can't have a baby or toddler here. It wouldn't be safe, not with some of the dogs I care for."

She drew in a breath. Now or never. "My son's six, almost seven." She reached a hand out to the bulldog, who'd settled between them, rubbed it along his wrinkled head, let him sloppily lick her fingers.

"Six! Then…"

She forced herself to look at Troy steadily while he did the math. Saw his eyes harden as he realized her son must have been conceived right around the time she'd left town.

Heat rose in her cheeks as the familiar feeling of shame twisted her insides. But she couldn't let herself go there. "Xavier is a well-behaved kid." At least most of the time. "He loves animals and he's gentle with them."

Troy was still frowning.

He was going to refuse her, angry about the way she'd left him, and then what would she do? How would she achieve the goal she'd set for herself, to fulfill as many of Xavier's wishes as she could? This was such a perfect arrangement.

"I really need this job, Troy." She hated to beg, but for Xavier, she'd do it.

He looked away, out at the fields, and she did, too. Sun on late-summer corn tassels, puffy clouds in a blue sky. Xavier would love it so.

"If you ever felt anything for me…" Her throat tightened and she had to force out the words. "If any of your memories about me are good, please give me the job."

He turned back toward her, eyes narrowing. "Why do you need it so badly?"

She clenched her hands in her lap. "Because my son wants to be close to Gramps. And because he loves animals."

"Most people don't organize their careers around their kids' hankerings."

She drew in a breath. "Well, I do."

His expression softened a little. "This job…it might not be what you want. It's just until my leg heals. The doc says it could be three, four months before I'm fully back on my feet. Once that happens, I won't need an assistant anymore."

She swallowed and squeezed her hands together. *Lord, I know I'm supposed to let You lead, but this seems so right. Not for me, but for Xavier, and that's what matters. It is of You, isn't it?*

No answer from above, but the roar of a truck engine pierced the country quiet.

Oh no. Gramps was back too soon. He'd never gotten along with Troy, never trusted him on account of his conflicts with Troy's dad. But she didn't want the two men's animosity to get in the way of what both she and her son wanted and needed.

The truck stopped again at the end of the driveway. Gramps got out, walked around to the passenger door.

She surged from her chair. "No, don't!" she called, but the old man didn't hear her. She started down the porch steps.

Troy called her back. "It's okay, they can come up. Regardless of what we decide about the job, maybe your son would like to see the dogs, look around the place."

"There's nothing he'd like better," she said, "but I don't want to get his hopes up if this isn't going to work out."

Troy's forehead wrinkled as he stared out toward the truck, watching as Gramps helped Xavier climb out.

Angelica rarely saw her son from this distance, and now, watching Gramps steady him, her hand rose to her throat. He looked as thin as a scarecrow. His baseball cap couldn't conceal the fact that he had almost no hair.

Her eyes stung and her breathing quickened as if she were hyperventilating. She pinched the skin on the back of her hand, hard, and pressed her lips together.

Gramps held Xavier's arm as they made slow progress down the driveway. The older supporting the younger, opposite of how it should be.

Troy cleared his throat. "Like I said, the job won't be long-term. I…it looks like you and your son have some…issues. You might want to find something more permanent."

His kind tone made her want to curl up and cry for a couple of weeks, but she couldn't go there. She clenched her fists. "I know the job is short-term." Swallowing the lump that rose in her throat, she added, "That's okay with us. We take things a day at a time."

"Why's that?" His gaze remained on the pair making their slow way up the driveway.

He was going to make her say it. She took a shuddering breath and forced out the words. "Because the doctors aren't sure how long his remission will last."

Troy stared at Xavier, forgetting to breathe. Remission? "Remission from what?"

Angelica cleared her throat. "Leukemia. He has…a kind that's hard to beat."

Every parent's nightmare. Instinctively he reached out to pat her shoulder, the way he'd done so many times with pet owners worried about seriously ill pets.

She flinched and sidled away.

Fine! Anger flared up at the rejection and he gripped the porch railing and tamped it down. Her response was crystal clear. She didn't want any physical contact between them.

But no matter his own feelings, no matter what Angelica had done to him, the past was the past. This pain, the pain of a mother who might lose her child, was in the present, and Angelica's worn-down appearance suddenly made sense.

And no matter whose kid Xavier was…no matter who she'd cheated on him with…the boy was an innocent, and the thought of a child seriously, maybe terminally, ill made Troy's heart hurt.

Again he suppressed his emotions as his medical instincts went into overdrive. "What kind of doctors has he seen? Have you gotten good treatments, second opinions?"

She took a step back and crossed her arms over her chest. "I can't begin to tell you how many doctors and opinions."

"But are they the best ones? Have you tried the Cleveland—"

"Troy!" She blew out a jagged breath. "Look, I don't need medical interference right now. I need a job."

"But—"

"Don't you think I've done everything in my power to help him?" She turned away and walked down the steps toward her son. Her back was stiff, her shoulders rigid.

He lifted a hand to stop her and then let it fall. *Way to go, Hinton. Great social skills.*

He'd find out more, would try to do something to help. Obviously Angelica hadn't done well financially since she left him and left town. Xavier's father must have bolted. And without financial resources, getting good medical care wasn't easy.

"Mom! Did you get the job?"

Angelica shot Troy a quick glance. "It's still being decided."

The boy's face fell. Then he nodded and bit his lip. "It's okay, Mama. But can we at least see the dogs?"

"Absolutely," Troy answered before Angelica could deny the boy. Then he hobbled down the porch stairs and sank onto the bottom one, putting him on a level with the six-year-old. "I'm Troy," he said, and reached out to shake the boy's hand.

The boy smiled—wow, what a smile—and reached out to grasp Troy's hand, looking up at his mother for reassurance.

She nodded at him. "You know what to say."

Frowning with thought, the boy shook his head.

"Pleased to…" Angelica prompted.

The smile broke out again like sunshine. "Oh yeah. Pleased to meet you, sir. I'm Xavier." He dropped Troy's hand and waved an arm upward, grinning. "And this is my grandpa. My *great*-grandpa."

"I've already had the pleasure." Troy looked up and met the old man's hostile eyes.

Camden glared down at him, not speaking.

Oh man. Out of the gazillion reasons not to hire Angelica, here was a major one. Obviously her grandfather was an important part of her life, one of her only living relatives. If she and Xavier came to live here, Troy would see a lot of Homer Camden, something they'd managed to avoid for the years Angelica was out of town.

Of course, he'd been working like crazy himself. Setting up his private practice, opening the rescue, paying off debt from vet school, which was astronomical even though his family had helped.

Troy pushed himself to his feet and got his crutches

underneath him. "Dogs are out this way, if you'd like to see them." He nodded toward the barn.

"Yes!" Xavier pumped his arm. "I asked God to get me a bunch of dogs."

"Zavey Davey..." Angelica's voice was uneasy. "Remember, I don't have the job yet. And God doesn't always—"

"I know." Xavier sighed, his smile fading a little. "He doesn't always answer prayers the way we want Him to."

Ouch. Kids were supposed to be all about Jesus Loves Me and complete confidence in God's—and their parents'—ability to fix anything. But from the looks of things, young Xavier had already run up against some of life's hard truths.

"Come on, Gramps." When the old man didn't move, Xavier tugged at his arm. "You promised you'd be nice. Please?"

The old man's face reddened. After a slight pause that gave Troy and Angelica the chance to glance at each other, he turned in the direction Troy had indicated and started walking, slowly, with Xavier.

Angelica touched Troy's arm, more like hit him, actually. "Don't let him go back there if you don't want to give me the job," she growled.

Even angry, her voice brushed at his nerve endings like rich, soft velvet. Her rough touch plucked at some wildness in him he'd never given way to.

Troy looked off over the cornfields, thinking, trying to get control of himself. He didn't trust Angelica, but that sweet-eyed kid...how could he disappoint a sick kid?

Homer Camden and the boy were making tracks toward the barn, and Troy started after them. He didn't want them to reach the dogs before he'd had a chance to lay some ground rules about safety. He turned to make sure Angelica was following.

She wasn't. "Well?" Her arms were crossed, eyes narrowed, head cocked to one side.

"You expect me to make an instant decision?"

"Since my kid's feelings are on the line…yeah. Yeah, I do."

Their eyes locked. Some kind of stormy electrical current ran between them.

This was bad. Working with her would be difficult enough, since feelings he thought he'd resolved years ago were resurfacing. He'd thought he was over her dumping him, but the knowledge that she'd conceived a child with someone else after seeming so sincere about their decision to wait until marriage… His neck felt as tight as granite. Yeah. It was going to take a while to process that.

Having her live here on the grounds with that very child, someone else's child, the product of her unfaithfulness…he clenched his jaw against all the things he wanted to say to her.

Fools vent their anger, but the wise hold it back. It was a proverb he'd recently taught the boys in his Kennel Kids group, little dreaming how soon and how badly he'd need it himself.

"Mom! Come on! I wanna see the dogs!" Xavier was tugging at his grandfather's arm, jumping around like a kid who wasn't at all sick, but Troy knew that was deceptive. Even terminally ill animals went through energetic periods.

Could he deprive Xavier of being with dogs and of

having a decent home to live in? Even if having Angelica here on the farm was going to be difficult?

When he met her eyes again, he saw that hers shone with unshed tears.

"Okay," he said around a sigh. "You're hired."

Her face broke into a sunshiny smile that reminded him of the girl she'd been. "Thank you, Troy," she said softly. She walked toward him, and for a minute he thought she was going to hug him, as she'd been so quick to do in the past.

But she walked right by him to catch up with her son and grandfather. She bent over, embraced Xavier from behind and spoke into his ear.

The boy let out a cheer. "Way to go, Mama! Come on!"

They hurried ahead, leaving Troy to hop along on his crutches, matching Angelica's grandfather's slower pace.

"Guess you hired her," the old man said.

"I did."

"Now you listen here." Camden stopped walking, narrowed his eyes, and pointed a finger at Troy. "If you do anything to hurt that girl, you'll have me to contend with."

Troy took a deep breath and let it out slowly. He was doing this family a favor, but he couldn't expect gratitude, not with the history that stood between them. "I have no plans to hurt her. Hoping she'll be a help to me until I'm back on my feet." He glanced down. "Foot."

"Humph." Camden turned and started making his way toward the barn again. "Heard you fell off a roof. Fool thing to do."

Troy gritted his teeth and swung into step beside

Camden. "According to my brother and dad, you've done a few fool things in your day." This was a man who'd repeatedly refused a massive financial package that would have turned his family's lives around, all in favor of keeping his single-acre farm that stood in the middle of the Hinton holdings.

Not that Troy blamed the old man, particularly. Troy's father was an arrogant, unstable man with plenty of enemies. Including Troy himself, most of the time.

Even after Homer Camden's health had declined, forcing him to move into the Senior Towers, he clung stubbornly to the land. Rumor had it that his house had fallen into disrepair and the surrounding fields were nothing but weeds.

Not wanting to say something he'd regret, Troy motored ahead on his crutches until he reached Xavier and Angelica, who'd stopped at the gate.

"If you wait there," he said to them, "I'll let the dogs out into the runs." The breeze kicked up just as he passed Angelica, and the strawberry scent of her hair took him back seven years, to a time when that smell and her gentle, affectionate kisses had made him light-headed on a regular basis.

"Wait. Mr. Hinton." Xavier was breathing hard. "Thank you...for giving Mama...the job." He smiled up at Troy.

Troy's throat constricted. "Thank you for talking her into doing it," he managed to say, and then swung toward the barn.

He was going to do everything in his power to make that boy well.

Inside, joyful barks and slobbery kisses grounded him. His dogs ranged in age and size but tended toward the large, dark-coated bully breeds. The dogs no one else wanted to take a risk with: pit bulls, aggressive Dobermans and Rotties, large mutts. They were mixed in with older, sicker dogs whose owners couldn't or wouldn't pay the vet bills to treat them.

He moved among them, grateful that he'd found his calling in life.

Yes, he was lonely. Yes, he regretted not having a family around him, people to love. But he had his work, and it would always be there. Unlike people, dogs were loyal and trustworthy. They wouldn't let you down.

He opened the kennel doors to let them run free.

When he got back outside, he heard the end of Homer Camden's speech. "There's a job might open up at the café," he was saying. "And Jeannette Haroldson needs a caregiver."

For some reason that went beyond his own need for a temporary assistant, Troy didn't want the old man to talk her out of working for him. "Look, I know you've got a beef with the Hintons. But it's my dad and my brother who manage the land holdings. My sister's not involved, and I just run my rescue."

"That's as may be, but blood runs true. Angie's got other choices, and I don't see why—"

"That's why, Grandpa." Angelica pointed to Xavier. He'd knelt down beside the fence, letting the dogs lick him through it. On his face was an expression of the purest ecstasy Troy had ever seen.

All three adults looked at each other. They were three people at odds. But in that moment, in complete silence, a pact arose between them: whatever it takes, we'll put this child first and help him be happy.

Two

Angelica watched her son reach thin, bluish fingers in to touch the dogs. Listened to Troy lecture them all about the rules for safety: don't enter the pens without a trained person there, don't let the dogs out, don't feed one dog in the presence of others. Her half-broken heart sang with gratitude.

Thanks to God, and Troy, Xavier would have his heartfelt wish. He'd have dogs—multiple dogs—to spend his days with. He'd have a place to call home. He'd have everything she could provide for him to make his time on this earth happy.

And if Xavier was happy, she could handle anything: Troy's intensity, the questions in his eyes, the leap in her own heart that came from being near this too-handsome man who had never been far from her thoughts in all these years.

"Do you want to see the inside of the barn?" Troy asked Xavier.

"Sure!" He sounded livelier than he had in weeks.

Troy led the way, his shoulders working the crutches.

He was such a big man; he'd probably had to get the extra-tall size.

Gramps patted her back, stopping her. "I don't like it," he said, "but I understand what you're doing."

She draped an arm around his shoulders. "Thanks. That means a lot."

"Think I'll wait in the truck, though," he said. "Being around a Hinton sticks in my craw."

"Okay, sure." Truthfully, she was glad to see Gramps go. She doubted that he and Troy could be civil much longer.

She held Xavier's hand as they walked into the barn and over to the dog pens. The place was pretty clean, considering. Troy must have been wearing himself out to keep it that way.

As Xavier and Troy played with the dogs, she looked around, trying to get a clue into the man. She wandered over to a desk in the corner, obviously a place where he did the kennel business, or some of it.

And there, among a jumble of nails and paper clips, was a leather-studded bracelet she hadn't seen in seven years. She sucked in a breath as her heart dove down, down, down.

She closed her eyes hard, trying to shut out the memories, but a slide show of them raced through her mind. First date, whirlwind courtship and the most romantic marriage proposal a girl from her background could have imagined. For a few months, she'd felt like a princess in a fairy tale.

Back then, as an engaged couple, they'd helped with the youth group and had gotten the kids True Love Waits bracelets—leather and studs for the guys, more delicate chains for the girls. There had been a couple of extra ones, and one night when the waiting had been difficult, she and Troy had decided to each wear one as a reminder.

Carefully, she picked up the leather band. Her eyes filled with tears as she remembered stroking it on his arm, sometimes jokingly tugging at it when their kisses had gotten too passionate. Back in those innocent, happy days.

She'd ripped hers off and thrown it away on the most awful night of her life. The night she'd turned twenty-one and stupidly gone out with a bunch of friends to celebrate. The night she'd had too much to drink, realized it and accepted the offer of an older acquaintance to walk her home.

The night her purity and innocence and dreams of waiting for marriage had been torn forcibly away.

The next day, when Troy had noticed her bracelet was missing, she'd lied to him, telling him it must have fallen off.

But he'd continued to wear his, joking that he probably needed the reminder more than she did.

"Hey." He came up behind her now. When he noticed what she was holding, his eyebrows shot up and he took a step back.

She dropped it as if it were made of hot metal. "I'm sorry. That's not my business. I just happened to see it and…got carried away with the memories."

He nodded, pressed his lips together. Turned away.

That set face had to be judging her, didn't it? Feeling disgust at her lack of purity.

She'd been right to leave him. He could never have accepted her after what happened, although knowing him, he'd have tried to pretend. He'd have felt obligated to marry her anyway.

"Mom! Come see!" Xavier cried.

"Xavier!" He'd gone into a section of the barn Troy had warned them was off-limits. "I'm sorry," she said to Troy, and hurried over to her son. "You have to follow the rules! You could get hurt!"

"But look, Mama!" He knelt in front of a small heap of puppies, mostly gray and white, all squirming around a mother who lay on her side. Her head was lifted, her teeth bared.

"Careful of a mama dog," Troy said behind her. "Pull him back a foot or two, will you, Angelica? These little guys are only two weeks old, and the mom's still pretty protective."

She did, hating the crestfallen expression on Xavier's face. This ideal situation might have its own risks.

And then Troy reached down, patted the mother dog and carefully lifted a tiny, squirming puppy into Xavier's lap.

Xavier froze, then put his face down to nuzzle the puppy's pink-and-white snout. It nudged and licked him back, and then two more puppies crawled into his lap, tumbling over each other. Yips and squeals came from the mass of warm puppy bodies.

"Mom," Xavier said reverently. "This is *so* cool."

Angelica's heart did a funny little twist. She reached out and squeezed Troy's arm before she could stop herself.

"Do we really get to live here? Can we sleep in the barn with the puppies?"

Troy laughed. "No, son. You'll stay in a bunkhouse. Kind of like an Old West cowboy. Want to see?"

"Sure!" His eyes were on Troy with something like

hero worship, and worry pricked at Angelica's chest. Was Xavier going to get too attached to Troy?

Then again, if it would make him happy... Angelica swallowed hard and shut out thoughts of the future. "Let's go!" she said with a voice that was only slightly shaky.

When they reached the bunkhouse and walked inside, Angelica felt her face break out into a smile. "It's wonderful, Troy! When did you do all this work on it?" She remembered the place as an old, run-down outbuilding, but now modern paneling and new windows made it bright with sunshine on wood. It needed curtains, maybe blue-and-white gingham. The rough-hewn pine furniture was sparse, but with a few throw pillows and afghans, the place would be downright homey.

A home. She'd wanted one forever, and even more after she'd become a mom.

Troy's watchful eyes snapped her out of her happy fantasies. "You like it?"

"It's fantastic." She realized he'd never answered her question about when he'd done the work.

"You're easy to please." His voice was gruff.

She smiled and squatted down beside Xavier. "We both are. Pretty near perfect, isn't it, Zavey Davey?"

"Yes. Sure, Mama."

Her ear was so attuned to his needs that she heard the slight hesitation in his voice. "What's wrong?" she asked, keeping her voice low to make the conversation private, just between her and her son. "Isn't this everything you've always wanted?"

"Yes. Except..." He wrinkled his freckled nose as though he was trying to decide something.

"What? What is it, honey?"

He pressed his lips together and then lost the battle

with himself, shrugged and grinned winningly at her. "It's the last thing on my list, Mama."

The last thing. Her heart twisted tight. "What? What do you need?"

He leaned over and whispered into her ear, "A dad."

When Angelica emerged from the bunkhouse the next Saturday, every nerve in Troy's body snapped to attention. Was this the same woman who'd been working like a ranch hand this week, wearing jeans and T-shirts and boots, learning the ropes in the kennel?

It was the first time he'd seen her in a top that wasn't as loose as a sack. And was that makeup on her eyes, making them look even bigger?

"What?" she asked as she walked up beside him. She seemed taller. He looked down and saw that she was wearing sandals with a little heel, too.

Angelica had always been cute and appealing. But now she was model-thin, and with her hair braided back, her cheekbones stood out in a heart-shaped face set off by long silver earrings. A pale pink shirt edged with lace made her copper-colored skin glow. With depth and wisdom in her brown eyes, and a wry smile turning up the edges of her mouth, she was a knockout.

And one he needed to steer clear of. Beauty didn't equate to morality or good values, and one whirl with this little enchantress had just about done him in.

Though to be fair, he didn't know the rest of her story. And he shouldn't judge. "Nothing. You look nice."

"Do you have the keys?"

"What?"

"Keys." She held out her hand.

He had to stop staring. The keys. He pulled them out of his pocket and handed them over.

She wasn't here for him. She was here because she needed something, and when she got it, she'd leave. He knew that from experience.

"Bye, Mama!" Xavier's voice was thin, reedy, but for all that, cheerful.

When he turned, he saw Xavier and Lou Ann standing on the porch, waving.

"You be good for Miss Lou Ann." Angelica shook her finger at Xavier, giving him a mock-stern look.

"I will, Mama."

Lou Ann put an arm around the boy. "We'll have fun. He's going to help me do some baking."

"Thank you!" Angelica shot a beaming smile toward the porch, and Troy's heart melted a little more.

With him, though, she was all business. "Let's get going. If we're to get there by nine, we don't have time to stand around."

She walked toward the truck, and he couldn't help noticing how well her jeans fit her slender frame.

Then she opened the passenger door and held it for him.

He gritted his teeth. Out of all the indignities of being injured, this had to be the worst. He liked to drive, liked to be in control, liked to open the door for a lady. Not have the door held for him. That was a man's proper role, pounded into him from childhood. No weakness; no vulnerability. Men should be in charge.

While his years in college and vet school, surrounded by capable and brilliant professional women, had knocked some feminist sense into his head, his alpha-male instincts were as strong as ever.

"You need help getting in?" she asked.

Grrrr. "I have a broken leg. I'm not paralyzed." He swung himself into the truck, grunting with the awkward effort.

"Sor-ry." She shrugged and walked back around to the driver's side.

When they headed down the driveway, he said, "Take a right up there at the stop sign."

She did, rolling down her window at the same time. Hot, dusty July air blew tendrils of her hair loose, but she put her head back and breathed it in deeply, a tiny smile curving her full lips.

He liked that she'd stayed a farm girl, not all prissy and citified. Maybe liked it a little too much. "Slow down, this is a blind curve. Then go left after that barn."

"Troy." She shifted gears with complete competence. "I grew up here, remember? I know how to get to town."

Of course she did. She was a capable assistant…and no more. He needed to focus on his weekly vet clinic and how he was going to manage it on crutches. Forget about Angelica.

Easier said than done.

Angelica turned down the lane that led into town, trying to pay attention to the country air blowing through the truck's open windows rather than on the man beside her. He'd been staring at her nonstop since she came outside today. She already felt self-conscious, all dolled up, and Troy's attitude made it worse. She wasn't sure if he was judging her or…something else, but his gaze made her feel overheated, uncomfortable.

Or maybe the problem was that she'd dressed up on purpose, with the notion of finding a dad—or a temporary stand-in for one—to fulfill Xavier's wish. The thought of putting herself out there for men to approach made her feel slightly ill; dating was the last thing she wanted to do. And it wasn't likely that anyone would want damaged goods like her, not likely she'd attract interest, but she had to try. She'd promised herself to make her son's days happy, since she couldn't be sure how many he had left, and she was going to do her best.

Once they reached the residential area that surrounded Rescue River's downtown, Angelica's stomach knotted. Everyone in town knew about what she'd done to Troy, their beloved high school quarterback and brilliant veterinarian and all-around good guy. No doubt her own reputation was in the gutter.

There was the town's famous sign, dating back to Civil War years when the tiny farm community had been home to several safe houses on the Underground Railroad:

Rescue River, Ohio.

All Are Welcome, All Are Safe.

Funny, she didn't feel so safe now. She cruised past the bank and the feed store, and then thoughts of herself vanished when she saw the line of people snaking around the building that housed Troy's veterinary practice. "Wow. Looks like your clinic is a success."

"Lots of people struggling these days."

"It's free?"

He nodded, pointed. "Park right in front. They always save me a place."

She noticed a few familiar faces turning toward their truck. Someone ran to take a lawn chair out of the single remaining parking spot and she pulled in, stopped and went around to see if Troy needed help getting out. But he'd already hopped down, so she grabbed his crutches out of the back and took them to him.

"Here." She handed him the crutches, and his large, calloused hand brushed hers.

Something fluttered inside her chest. She yanked her hand back, dropping a crutch in the process.

"Hey, that you, Angie? Little Angie?"

She turned to see a tall, skinny man, his thin hair pulled back in a ponytail, his face stubbly. She cocked her head to one side. "Derek? Derek Moseley?"

"It *is* you!" He flung an easy arm around her and she shrugged away, and then suddenly Troy was there, stepping between them. "Whoa, my friend," he said. "Easy on my assistant."

"I'm fine!" She took another sidestep away.

Derek lifted his hands like stop signs. "Just saying hi to my old buddy's little sister, Doc." He turned to Angelica. "Girl, I ain't seen you in ages. How's your brother?"

She shook her head. "I don't see him much myself. He's overseas, doing mission work."

"Carlo? A missionary?"

"Well, something like that." In reality, her brother, Carlo, was halfway between a missionary and a mercenary, taking the word of God to people in remote areas where he was as likely to be met with a machete as a welcome.

"Carlo's a great guy. Tell him I said hello."

"I will." That evaluation was spot-on—her brother was a great guy. Carlo was the one who'd gone to Gramps and told him he had to take her in when their parents' behavior had gone way out of control. He'd been sixteen; she'd been nine. He'd gone out on his own then, had his dark and dangerous times, but now he'd found Jesus and reformed. He wrote often, sent money even though she told him not to, probably more than he could afford. But she didn't see him enough and she wished he'd come home. Especially now, with Xavier's health so bad.

A shuffling sound broke into her consciousness. She looked around for Troy and saw him working his way toward the clinic on his crutches, large medical bag clutched awkwardly at his side.

She hurried to him. "Here, let me carry that."

"I can get it."

Stepping in front of him, she took hold of the bag. "Probably, but not very well. This is what you're paying me for."

He held on to the bag a second longer and then let it go. "Fine."

As they walked toward the clinic, people greeted Troy, thanked him for being there, asked about his leg. The line seemed endless. Most people held dogs on leads, but a few had cat carriers. One man sat on a bench beside an open-topped cardboard box holding a chicken.

How would Troy ever take care of all these people? "The clinic's only until noon, right? Do you have help?"

"A vet tech, whenever he gets here. And I stay until I've seen everyone. We work hard. You up for this?"

She was and they did work hard; he wasn't lying. The morning flew by with pet after pet. She held leashes for Pomeranians and pit bulls, got scratched by a frightened tomcat with a ripped ear and comforted a twenty-something girl who cried when her two fluffy fur-ball puppies, one black and one white, had to get shots. She wrote down the particulars of rescue situations people told Troy about. Dogs needed rabies shots and ear medicine, X-rays and spaying. If it was something he couldn't do right at the moment, he made a plan to do it later in the week.

She asked once, "Can you even do surgery, with your leg?"

"My leg doesn't hurt as much as that guy's hurting," he said, scratching the droopy ears of a basset-beagle mix with a swollen stomach. The owner was pretty sure he'd swallowed a baby's Binky. "Feed him canned pumpkin to help things along," he told the owner. "If he doesn't pass it within three days, or if he's in more pain, call me."

A fiftysomething lady came in with a small, scruffy white dog wrapped in a towel. "Afraid he's got to be put to sleep, Doc." Her voice broke as she lifted the skinny animal to the metal exam table.

Angelica moved closer and patted the woman's back, feeling completely ineffectual. She wanted to help, but sometimes there wasn't anything you could do.

"Let's not jump to that conclusion." Troy picked up the whimpering little creature, ignoring its feeble effort to bite at him. He felt carefully around the dog's abdomen and examined its eyes and ears. "I'm guessing pancreatitis," he said finally, "but we'll need to do some blood work to be sure."

"What's that mean, Doc?" the woman asked. "I don't have much extra money...and I don't want him to suffer." She buried her face in her hands.

Angelica's throat ached. She could identify. She found a box of tissues and brought it over.

"Hey." Troy put a hand on the woman's shoulder. "Let's give treatment a try. If you can't afford the medicine, we'll work something out."

"Is he even likely to live?"

"Fifty-fifty," Troy admitted. "But I'm not a quitter. We can bring the dog to the farm if you don't have time to do the treatments. Aren't you a night waitress out at the truck stop?"

She nodded. "That's the other thing. I can't stick around home to care for him. I gotta work to pay my rent."

"Let me take him to the farm, then," Troy said. "It's worth it. He may have years of running around left. Don't you want me to try?"

"You'd really do that for him?" Hope lit the woman's face as she carefully picked up the little dog and cradled him to her chest. When she looked up, her eyes shone. "You don't know how much this means to me, Doc. He's been with me through two divorces and losing my day job and a bout with cancer. I want to be able to give back to him. I'll donate all my tips when I get them."

"Give what you can. That's all I ask." He told Angelica what to do next and took the dog away.

A man in jeans and a scrub top strode into the clinic then, and Angelica studied him as he greeted Troy. He must be the vet tech they'd been waiting for.

"Buck," Troy said. "How goes it?"

Buck. So that was why he looked so familiar—he was an old classmate, one of the nicer boys. "Hey," she greeted him. "Remember me?"

"Is that you, Angie?" A smile lit his eyes. "Haven't seen you in forever. How's your grandpa?"

They chatted for a few minutes while Troy entered data into a computer, preparing for the next appointment. Buck kept smiling and stepped a little closer, and Angelica recognized what was happening: he *like* liked her, as her girlfriends back in Boston would say. She took a step away.

And then it dawned on her: Buck would be a perfect guy to help fulfill Xavier's dream. Oh, not to marry, she couldn't go that far, but if she could find a nice, harmless man to hang out with some in the evenings, watch some family shows with, play board games with...that didn't sound half-bad. Xavier would be thrilled.

Come on, flirt with the man. You used to be good at it.

But she barely remembered how to talk to a man that way. And anyway, it felt like lying. How could she pretend to have an interest in a nice guy like Buck just to make her son happy? Maybe this wasn't such a good plan after all.

When Troy came back, ready for the next patient, Buck cocked his head to one side. "Are you two together? I remember you used to—"

"No!" they both said at the same time.

"Whoa, okay! I just thought you were engaged, back in the day."

Angelica felt her face heat. "I'm just his assistant while he gets back on his feet," she explained as the next patient came in.

"Glad to hear you've come to your senses about him," Buck joked.

Troy's lips tightened and he turned away, limping over to greet a couple with a cat carrier who'd just walked in.

"You back in town for a while?" Buck looked at Angelica with sharpened interest.

"Yes. For a...a little while."

"Long enough to have dinner with an old friend?"

He was asking her out. To dinner, and really, what would be the harm? This was what she wanted.

"Sure," she said. "I'll have dinner with you."

"Saturday night? Where are you staying?" He touched her shoulder to usher her over to the side of the exam area, and she forced herself not to pull away.

They agreed on a time and exchanged phones to punch in numbers.

When she looked up, Troy was watching them, eyes narrowed, jaw set.

She shook her hair back. There was no reason for him to feel possessive. What had been between them was long gone.

So why did she feel so guilty?

Three

By the time they'd gotten back to the farm, it was suppertime and Troy's blood was boiling as hot as the pot of pasta on the stove.

Did Angelica have to make her date plans right in front of him? And with Buck Armstrong?

But it wasn't his business, and he had no reason to care. He just needed some time to himself.

Which apparently he wasn't going to get, because the minute they set down their things, Xavier was pulling at his hand. "Mr. Troy, Mr. Troy, we're all going to have dinner together!"

Great. He smiled down at the boy. How was he going to get out of this?

"Xavier, honey." Angelica knelt down beside her son. "We'll have dinner at the bunkhouse. We can't impose."

She tugged the ponytail holder out of her hair, and the shiny locks flowed down her back. Her hand kneaded Xavier's shoulder. She was all loving mother.

And all woman.

"But, Mama! Wait till you see what Miss Lou Ann and me cooked!"

Lou Ann rubbed Xavier's bald head. "I'm sorry, Angelica. I told him we could probably all eat together. We picked zucchini and tomatoes from the garden and cooked up some of that ratatouille."

"And we made a meat loaf, and I got to mix it up with my hands!"

The boy sounded so happy. Troy's throat tightened as he thought about how Angelica must feel, cherishing every moment with him and wondering at the same time whether he'd ever make meat loaf again, whether this was the last chance for this particular activity.

Angelica glanced up at him, eyebrows raised. "Maybe we'll get together another time. Mr. Troy's been working all day and he's tired. Let's let him rest."

What was he supposed to do now, squash down all of this joy? And he had to admit that the thought of having company for dinner in the farmhouse kitchen didn't sound half-bad, except that the pretty woman opposite him was hankering after another man.

At the thought of Angelica dating Buck Armstrong, something dark twisted his insides. With everything he knew about Buck, he should warn her off, and yet it would serve her right to go out with him and find out what he was really like.

"Can we stay, Mr. Troy?"

He looked at the boy's hopeful eyes. "Of course." His words sounded so grudging that he added, "Sounds like a good meal you fixed."

"It is good, and wait till you see dessert!"

By the time Xavier helped Lou Ann serve dessert—sliced pound cake, topped with berries and whipped cream—he looked beat. But his smile was joyous. "I had so much fun this afternoon, Mama!"

Troy praised the food, which was really good, thanks he was sure to Lou Ann's guidance. But his stomach was turning, wouldn't let him really enjoy it.

Angelica looked beautiful at the other end of the table, her black hair tumbling down past her shoulders and her cheeks pink as apples. And now, with Xavier so happy, she didn't seem as worried as usual; the little line that tended to live between her eyebrows was gone, and her smile flashed frequently as Xavier described all that he and Lou Ann had done that day.

Troy had always wanted this. He wanted a warm, beautiful woman and cute, enthusiastic children at his table, wanted to be the man of the family. And this sweet, feisty pair seemed to fit right into his home and his heart. But he had to keep reminding himself that this wasn't his and it wouldn't last.

Looking at Xavier, he couldn't believe the child had been so sick and might relapse at any moment. Yeah, he was drooping, getting tired, but he was so full of life that it made no sense that God might take him away.

Any more than it made sense that God would put him and his siblings in a loveless family, let alone give Angelica all the heartaches she'd endured growing up, but that was God for you—making sense wasn't what He was about. That was why Troy had stopped trusting Him, starting taking most things into his own hands. He believed, sure; he just didn't trust. And he sure didn't want to join the men's Bible study his friend Dion was always bugging him about.

"This little one needs to get to bed," Lou Ann said. "Troy, I know you can't carry much with those crutches, but why don't you at least help her with the doors and such?"

"Oh, you don't have to—" Angelica stood, looking suddenly uncomfortable. "We've already taken too much of your time. We can make it."

But Troy moved to intercept her protest. "Come on, pal. Let's get you out to bed."

Angelica started gathering Xavier's pills and toys and snacks together, stuffing them into a Spider-Man backpack. Before she could bend to pick Xavier up, Troy leaned on one crutch, steadied himself with a hip against the table and picked up the boy himself. He was amazingly light. He nestled right against Troy's chest and Troy felt his heart break a little. He glanced over at Angelica and saw that she had tears in her eyes. "Ready?" he asked. Then, gently, he put her son in her arms, taking the boy's backpack to carry himself.

She bit her lip, turned and headed off, and he grabbed his crutches and followed her. They walked out to the bunkhouse together and Troy helped Angelica lay Xavier in his bed, noticing the homey touches Angelica had put around—a teddy bear, a poster of a baseball player, a hand-knitted afghan in shades of blue and brown. It was a boy's room, and it should be filling up with trophies from Little League games. They said every kid got a trophy these days, and wasn't that awful? But not Xavier. This kid hadn't had the opportunity to play baseball.

Not yet.

Angelica knelt beside the bed. "Let's thank God for today."

"Thank You, God, for letting me cook dinner. And for Lou Ann. And the dogs."

Angelica was holding Xavier's hand. "Thank You for giving us food and love and each other."

"Bless all the people who don't have so much," they said together.

"And, God, please get me a daddy before..." Xavier trailed off, turned over.

Whoa. Troy's throat tightened.

"Night, sweetie, sleep tight." Angelica's voice sounded choked.

"Don't let the bedbugs... Love you, Mama." The words were fading off and the boy was asleep.

They both stood looking down at him, Troy on one side of the bed and Angelica on the other.

"Did he say he wants a...dad?" Troy ventured finally.

Angelica nodded.

"Does his dad ever spend time with him?"

She looked up at him. "No. Never."

"Does he even know him?"

Her lips tightened. "I... Look, Troy, I don't want to talk about that."

"Sure." But he'd like to strangle the guy who'd loved and left her, and not just because he remembered how difficult it had been to keep his hands off Angelica back when they were engaged. He took a deep breath and loosened his tightly clasped fists. She'd gotten pregnant with Xavier right around the time she left town, so was Xavier's dad—the jerk—from here or from elsewhere? She hadn't married him, apparently, but... "If the guy knew Xavier, knew what he was like and what he's facing, surely he'd be willing—"

"No."

"No?"

"Just...no, okay?" She stood and stalked out to the living room, and Troy wondered whether he'd ever stop putting his plaster-covered foot in his mouth around her.

* * *

The next Saturday, Angelica touched up her hair with a curling wand and applied blush and mascara. And tried not to throw up.

She didn't want to go out on a date. But there was no other way to get Xavier off her case.

In fact, he was beside her now, hugging her leg. "You never had a date before, Mama."

She laughed. "Yes, I did. Back in the day. Before you."

"Did you go on dates with my dad?"

All Xavier knew was that his father had died. He hadn't ever asked whether Angelica and his father had been married, and Angelica hoped he didn't go there any time soon. For now, she would stick as close to the truth as possible. "No, not with him, but with a few other guys." She tried to deflect his attention. "Just like I'm doing now. Do I look all right?"

"You're beautiful, Mama."

She hugged him. "Thanks, Zavey Davey. You're kinda cute yourself."

"Do I get to meet him? Because I want to see, you know, if he's the right kind of guy for us."

"My little protector. You can meet him sometime, but not now. Miss Lou Ann is going to come over and play with you. And I think I hear her now."

Sure enough, there was a knock on the bunkhouse door. Xavier ran over to get it while Angelica fussed with herself a little more. She'd much rather just stay home with Xavier tonight. What if Buck tried something? She knew him to be a nice guy, but still...

"Well, how's my little friend for the evening?" Lou Ann asked, pinching Xavier's cheek. "You set up for a

Candy Land marathon, or are we building a fort out of sheets and chairs?"

"You'll build a fort with me?" Xavier's eyes turned worshipful. "Mom always says it's too messy."

"It's only too messy if we don't clean up later. And we will, right?"

"Right. I'll get the extra sheets."

As soon as he was out of the room, Lou Ann turned to Angelica. "You look pretty," she said. "Somebody's already cranky, and when he sees you looking like that…" She smacked her lips. "Sparks are gonna fly."

That was the last thing she needed. Her face heated and she changed the subject. "Xavier can stay up until eight thirty. He gets his meds and a snack half an hour before bed." She showed Lou Ann the pills and the basket of approved snacks.

"That's easy. Don't worry about us." Lou Ann leaned back and looked out the window. "I think your friend just pulled in."

"I wanna see him!" Xavier rushed toward the window, dropping the stack of sheets he'd been carrying.

"Well," Lou Ann said, "that's just fine, because I want to claim the best spot in the fort."

Xavier spun back to Lou Ann. "I'm king of the fort!"

"You'd better get over here and help me, then."

Thank you, Angelica mouthed to Lou Ann, and slipped out the door.

Buck emerged from his black pickup, looking good from his long jean-clad legs to his slightly shaggy brown curls. Any girl would feel fortunate to be dating such a cute guy, Angelica told herself, trying to lighten the lead weight in her stomach.

He's a nice guy. And it's for Xavier. "Hi there!"

"Well, don't you look pretty!" He walked toward her, loose limbed.

To her right, the front door of the main house opened. Troy. He came out on the porch and stood, arms crossed. For all the world as if he were her father.

She narrowed her eyes at him, trying to ignore his rougher style of handsome, the way his broad shoulders, leaning on his crutches, strained the seams of his shirt. She was through with Troy Hinton, and he was most certainly through with her, wouldn't want anything to do with her if he knew the truth.

She deliberately returned her attention to Buck. He reached her and opened his arms.

Really? Was a big hug normal on a first date? It had been so long…and she'd been so young… She took a deep breath and allowed him to hug her, at the same time wrinkling her nose. Something was wrong…

"Baby, it's great to see you. Man, feels good to hug a woman." Buck's words were slurred. And yes, that smell was alcohol, covered with a whole lot of peppermint.

She tried to pull back, but he didn't let go.

Panic rose in her. She stepped hard onto his foot. "Let go," she said, loud, right in his ear.

From the corner of her eye, the sight of Troy made her feel secure.

"Sorry!" Buck stepped back. "I didn't mean… I was just glad…oh man, you look so good." He moved as though he was going to hug her again.

She sidestepped. "Buck. How much have you had to drink?"

"What?" He put an arm around her and started guiding her toward his truck. "I had a drink before I came over. One drink. Don't get uptight."

Could that be true? Without a doubt, she was up-tight around men. But this felt wrong in a different way. "Wait a minute. I... I think we should talk a little bit before we go."

"Sure!" He shifted direction, guiding her toward a bench and plopping down too hard, knocking into her so that she sat down hard, too.

She drew in a breath and let it out in a sigh. He was drunk, all right. It wasn't just her being paranoid. But now, how did she get rid of him?

"I really like you, Angelica," he said, putting an arm around her. He pulled her closer.

She scooted away. "Look, Buck, I can't... I don't think I can go out with you. You've had too much to drink."

"One drink!" He sounded irritated.

Angelica stood and backed away. Couldn't some-thing, just once, be easy? "Sorry, friend, but I can't get in the truck with you. And you shouldn't be driv-ing, either."

There was a sound of booted feet, and then Troy was beside her. "She's right, Buck."

"What you doing here, Hinton?"

"I live here, as you very well know."

"Well, I'm taking this little lady out for a meal, once—"

"You're not going anywhere except home. As soon as your sister gets here to pick you up."

"Oh man, you didn't call Lacey!" Buck staggered to his feet, his hand going to his pocket. He pulled out truck keys. "This has been a bust."

Angelica glanced at Troy, willing him to let her han-dle it. She had plenty of experience with drunk people, starting with her own parents. "Can I see the car keys a minute?"

He held them out, hope lighting up his face. "You gonna come after all? I'll let you drive."

She took the keys. "I'm not going, and sorry, but you're not fit to drive yourself, either."

He lunged to get them back and Troy stuck out a crutch to trip him. "You're not welcome on this property until you're sober."

Angelica kept backing off while, in the distance, a Jeep made clouds on the dusty road. That must be Buck's sister.

So she could go home now. Back inside. Face Xavier and tell him the date was off.

Except she couldn't, because tears were filling her eyes and blurring her vision. She blinked hard and backed up as far as the porch steps while Troy greeted the woman who'd squealed up in the Jeep.

The woman pushed past Troy, poked a finger in Buck's chest and proceeded to chew him out. Then she and Troy helped him into the passenger seat. They stood beside the Jeep for a minute, talking.

When Angelica turned away, she realized that Xavier could see her here if he looked out the window. Hopefully he was too deep into fort-building to notice, but she wasn't ready to see him and she couldn't take the risk. She headed out to the kennels at a jog. Grabbed one of the pit bulls she'd been working with, a black-and-white beauty named Sheena, attached a leash to her and started walking down the field road as unwanted, annoying tears came faster and faster.

She sank to her knees beside a wooden fence post,

willing the tears to stop, hugging the dog that licked her cheek with canine concern.

"Get yourself together, girlie. Nobody said life's a tea party."

Gramps's words, harsh but kindly meant, had guided her through the storms of adolescence and often echoed in her mind.

Today, for some reason, they didn't help. She squeezed her eyes shut and tried to pray, but the tears kept coming.

After long moments, one of the verses she'd memorized during Xavier's treatment came into her mind.

Fear not, for I am with you; be not dismayed, for I am your God; I will strengthen you, I will help you, I will uphold you with My righteous right hand.

Slowly, peace, or at least resignation, started to return. But every time she thought about Xavier and how disappointed he'd be, the tears overflowed again.

A hand gripped her shoulder, making her start violently. "You that upset about Buck?" Troy asked.

She shook her head, fighting for control. It wasn't about Buck, not really. He was a small disappointment in the midst of a lot of big ones, but it was enough to push her over the edge. She couldn't handle the possibility of losing Xavier, the only good thing in her life, and yet she had to handle it. And she had to stay strong and positive for him.

It was pretty much her mantra. She breathed in, breathed out. *Stay strong*, she told herself. *Stay strong.*

A couple of minutes later she was able to accept Troy's outstretched hand and climb to her feet. He took the dog leash from her and handed her an ancient-looking, soft bandanna. "It's not pretty, but it's clean."

She nodded and wiped her eyes and nose and came

back into herself enough to be embarrassed at how she must look. She wasn't one of those pretty, leak-a-few-tears criers; she knew her eyes must be red and puffy, and she honked when she blew her nose. "Sorry," she said to him.

"For what?"

She shook her head, and by unspoken agreement they started walking. "Sorry to break down."

"You're entitled."

The sun was setting now, sending pink streaks across the sky, and a slight breeze cooled the air. Crickets harmonized with bullfrogs in a gentle rise and fall. Angelica breathed in air so pungent with hay and summer flowers that she could almost taste it, and slowly the familiar landscape brought her calm.

"You know," Troy ventured after a few minutes, "Buck Armstrong's not really worth all that emotion. Not these days. If I'd known you were this into dating him, I might have warned you he has a drinking problem."

She laughed, and that made her cry a little more, and she wiped her eyes. "It's not really about Buck."

He didn't say anything for a minute. Then he gave her shoulder a gentle squeeze. "You've got a lot on your plate."

"I've got a plan, is what I've got," she said, "and I was hoping Buck could be a part of it." Briefly, she explained her intention of finding a stand-in dad for Xavier.

Troy shook his head. "That's not going to work."

"What do you mean?"

"He's a smart kid. He'll know. You can't just pretend you're dating someone so that he'll think he's getting a dad."

"I can if I want to." They came to a crossroads and she glanced around. "I'm not ready to go back home and admit defeat yet, and I don't want him looking out the window and seeing me cry."

"Come the back way, by the kennel."

Sheena, the dog she'd brought with her, jumped at a squirrel, and Troy let her off the lead to chase it. She romped happily, ears flopping.

"So you think getting a dad will make Xavier happy? Even if it's a fake dad?"

"It's not fake! Or, well, it is, but for a good reason." She reached into her pocket and pulled out the picture she always carried, Xavier in happier times. "Look at that face! For all I know, he'll never be really healthy again." She cleared her throat. "If I can make his life happy, I'm going to do it."

He studied the picture. "He played Little League?"

She swallowed hard around the lump in her throat. "T-ball. He'd just started when he was diagnosed. He had one season."

"He started young."

She nodded. "They let him start a few weeks before his birthday, even though officially they aren't supposed to start until they turn four."

"Because he was sick?"

She shook her head. "Because he was so good. He loved it." Tears rushed to her eyes again and she put her hands to her face.

"Hey." He took the sloppy bandanna from her hand, wiped her eyes and nose as if she were a child, and pulled her to his chest. And for just a minute, after a reflexive flinch, Angelica let herself enjoy the feeling. His chest was broad and strong, and she heard the slow beating of his heart. She aligned her breath with his and it steadied her, calmed her.

In just a minute, she'd back away. Because this was dangerous and it wasn't going anywhere. Troy wouldn't want a woman like Angelica, not really, so letting an attraction build between them was a huge mistake.

Troy patted Angelica's back and breathed in the strawberry scent of her hair, trying to remind himself why he needed to be careful.

He wanted to help Angelica and Xavier in the worst way. His heart was all in with this little family. But that heart was broken, wounded, not whole.

He felt her stiffen in his arms, as though she was just realizing how close he was. For the thousandth time since he'd reencountered her, he wondered about her skittishness around men. Or was it just around him? No, he'd seen her tense up when Armstrong had hugged her, too.

Carefully, he held her upper arms and stepped away. Her face was blotched and wet, but she still looked beautiful. Her Western-style shirt was unbuttoned down to a modest V, sleeves rolled up to reveal tanned forearms. Her jeans clung to her slim figure. Intricate silver earrings hung from her ears, sparkling against her wavy black hair.

"Come on," he said gruffly, "let's go in the house. We'll get you something to drink."

"Okay." She looked up at him, her eyes vulnerable, and he wanted nothing more than to protect her.

Don't go there, fool.

They walked back along the country road as the last bit of sun set in a golden haze. A few dogs barked out their farewell to the day. At the kennel, they put Sheena back inside, and then he led Angelica up to the house.

He loved his farm, his dogs, his life. He had so much. But what right did he have to be happy when Angelica's problems were so big?

How could he help her?

An idea slammed into him, almost an audible voice. *You could marry her.*

Immediately he squelched the notion. Ridiculous. No way. He wouldn't go down that path. Not again, not after what she'd done to him.

And even outside of the way she'd dumped him, he'd never seen a good marriage. He didn't know how to be married; didn't know how to relate to people that way; didn't know how to keep a woman happy or make it last. He didn't want to be like his dad, the person who failed his wife. He didn't want to let Xavier down.

But the point was, he thought as he held the door for her, Xavier might not have the time to be let down. Xavier needed and wanted a dad now, and Troy already knew the boy liked him.

As they walked into the kitchen, he remembered proposing to Angelica the last time. Then he'd been all about wanting to impress her, to sweep her away. He'd hired Samantha Weston, who usually used her small plane for crop dusting, to sky-write his proposal at sunset during an all-town Memorial Day picnic. Angelica had laughed, and cried, and joyously accepted. Her friends had clustered around them, and he'd presented her with a diamond way too big for a new vet with school loans to pay off.

He still had that ring, come to think of it. He'd stuffed it in his sock drawer when she mailed it back to him, and he'd never looked at it again.

It was upstairs right now. He could go and get it. Help her handle this massive challenge life had given her. And Xavier... Boy, did he want to help that kid!

Angelica perched on a kitchen stool and rested her chin in her hands. "I guess the idea of Buck as a pretend husband does seem kinda crazy, when I think about it," she admitted. "Anyway, enough about me. How long has Buck had a drinking problem?"

"Since he lost his wife and child," Troy said. "Not only that, but he served a couple of tours in Afghanistan. Which is why I cut the guy a break and let him work at my weekend clinic. I've offered him a full-time job, too, but only if he'll stay sober for six months first. So far, he hasn't been able to do that."

"That's so sad." She bit her lip. "I hope he's going to be okay tonight. I felt bad, but there was no way I was getting into a truck with him."

"And no way he could be Xavier's pseudodad."

"No."

He cracked open a Pepsi and handed it to her. "Here. Sugar and caffeine. It'll make you feel better."

"Always. Thanks." She swung her feet. "Remember buying me a Coke at the drugstore, that very first time we went out?"

He nodded. "And I remember how you sat there drinking it and explaining to me your dating rules. No kissing until the third date. No parking. No staying out past eleven."

"I know, and it wasn't even Gramps making those rules, it was me. I was so scared of getting myself into the same bad situations that landed my folks in trouble. Plus, my brother told me I should be careful about you. Since you were an older man and all." She smiled up at him through her lashes.

His heart rate shot through the ceiling. "Your brother was protective," he said, trying to keep his voice—and his thoughts—on something other than how pretty she was. One question still nagged at him: if she'd had all those rules, then how had she ended up unmarried and pregnant?

"Xavier really misses my brother. Carlo lived near us in Boston for a while, and he's the one who got Xavier involved in T-ball. He did the whole male influence thing, until he got the call to go overseas." She flashed Troy a smile. "If I keep thinking about Carlo I'll get sad again. Save me, Bull!" She slid off the stool and sat cross-legged on the floor. The old bulldog climbed into her lap, and she leaned down and let him lick her face.

"Whoa, Bull, be a gentleman! She'll pass out from your breath!" But he couldn't help enjoying Angelica's affectionate attitude toward his dog. A lot of women didn't want a smelly old dog anywhere around their stockings and fancy dresses, but Angelica was a blue-jeans girl from way back.

He sank down beside her, petting Bull. "So, what are you going to do now? About your plan, I mean?"

She shook her head. "I don't know. I guess I'll have to disappoint him. I mean, I'm not the most outgoing person when it comes to dating, and I don't want to mislead any guys about where it's all headed." She forced a smile. "Know any eligible bachelors I could snare?"

"Me," he heard himself saying. "You could marry me."

Four

As he watched the color drain from Angelica's face, Troy's chest tightened and he wished he could take back his words. What had he just said? What had he been thinking?

Cynical doubts kicked at the crazy adrenaline rush coursing through his body. Why would he want to propose to Angelica again when she'd dumped him without explanation before? He'd already done what he could to help her and her son. He'd given her a job and provided a place to live, but this was way beyond the call of duty.

He opened his mouth to say so, but she held up a hand.

"Look, it's amazingly kind of you to offer that, especially after...after everything. You've already done so much for us. But I could never expect anything like that. And I couldn't marry someone without..."

He crossed his arms over his chest. "Without loving him?"

"I was going to say..." She lowered her head and let out a sigh. "Never mind."

Suddenly warm, he stood, grabbed a crutch

and limped across the room. He flicked on the air-conditioning and fiddled with the thermostat on the wall.

She'd brought up all the very same objections he'd had himself. She'd given him a way to back out.

So why did he feel so let down?

She scrambled to her feet, watching him as if he were a wild animal she had to protect herself from. All comfort, all closeness between them was gone. "Um, I should go." Her hand on the screen door handle, she stilled. "Uh-oh."

"What's wrong?" He came up behind her and looked over her shoulder out the door as the scent of her hair tickled his nose.

In the outdoor floodlight he saw Xavier was running toward the house, his face furrowed. Teary hiccups became more audible as he got closer. Behind him, Lou Ann followed at a dangerously fast pace, huffing and puffing and calling the boy.

Angelica opened the screen door just as Xavier got to the top of the porch steps. She knelt, and Xavier ran into her arms, causing her to reel backward.

Troy balanced on his crutch and reached out to steady the pair. "Whoa there, partner, slow down!"

"Is it true?" Xavier demanded. "What Miss Lou Ann said?"

At that moment the lady in question arrived at the top of the front porch steps. "Xavier!" She paused for breath. "You come…when I call you. I'm sorry," she added, turning to Angelica. "I said something I shouldn't have. It upset him."

"She said it wasn't going to work out for that man to be my daddy, and I might not get a daddy!"

"Come on in, baby." Angelica scooped her son into her arms and struggled to her feet, shrugging off Troy's attempt to help her. She carried Xavier inside. "Is it okay if we talk a minute in here?"

"Sure."

And then he watched her focus entirely on her son. She sat down on the couch and pulled the boy, all angular arms and long legs, in her lap. "So tell me more about those tears, mister."

"I want a daddy!" he sulked. "I thought you were gonna get me one."

She rubbed his hairless head. "I know how much you want a dad. You want to be like other kids."

"I want somebody to play T-ball with me and take me fishing." Behind the words, Troy heard a poignant yearning for all Xavier wanted and might not get, all he'd missed during the long months of treatment.

"I know," Angelica said, rocking a little. "I know, honey."

"So why did you send that man away?"

She shot a glance at Troy. "He wasn't feeling well."

"So he might come back when he's better?"

Slowly, Angelica shook her head. "No, honey. Turns out he's not right for us."

Tears welled in the boy's eyes again, but she pulled his head against her chest. "Shh. I know it's hard, but we have to let God do His work. He takes care of us, remember?"

"Sometimes He does a bad job!"

Angelica chuckled, a low vibration that brushed along Troy's nerve endings. "He never does a bad job, sweetie. Sometimes you and I can't understand His ways, but He's always taking care of us. We can relax because of that."

Her voice sounded totally confident, totally sure, and Troy wished for some of that certainty for himself.

She was such a good mother. She knew exactly how to reach her son, even when he was upset. She could listen, handle his bratty moments and get him to laugh. She was meant to mother this boy, and most of the resentment Troy felt about her pregnancy fell away. Whatever had happened, whatever mistakes she'd made, she'd paid for them. And as she said, God was always taking care of things. He'd given one sick young boy the perfect mother.

Who, when she met his eyes over the child's head and gave him a little smile, looked like the perfect wife, as well.

A week later, Angelica was chopping vegetables for stew and marveling at how quickly they'd settled into a routine. Lou Ann took an online class every Tuesday and Thursday, so those days, Angelica started dinner for all of them while Xavier rested.

As she chopped the last carrot, though, Xavier burst into the kitchen. "Can I go outside and see Mr. Troy and the dogs?"

Thrilled to see this sign of improved energy, she nonetheless narrowed her eyes at him. "What are you doing off the couch? You're supposed to rest from two to four every afternoon. Doctor's orders."

"I don't want to rest anymore. Besides, it's almost four."

"Is it really?" She looked at the clock. "Three thirty isn't four, buster." But it was close. Where had the time gone? Troy had been wonderful about letting her set up a flexible schedule around Xavier, but she needed to get back out to the kennels at four. She bit the inside of her cheek.

"I want to go outside." Xavier's lower lip pushed out.

"That's not going to work, honey. After you rest, you need to stay in here with Miss Lou Ann so I can work."

"But I wanna go outside!" Xavier yelled.

Angelica dried her hands on a dishcloth and shot up a prayer for patience. Then she knelt in front of Xavier. "Inside voice and respect, please."

"Sorry." He didn't sound it, but she stood up anyway. With a sick kid, you had to choose your battles.

"I see someone's feeling better." Troy limped into the kitchen, wearing jeans and a collared shirt. His shoulder muscles flexed as he hopped nimbly over on his crutches.

He looks good! was her first thought, and it made her cheeks heat up. "I didn't know you were here today. Thought you had vet patients in town."

"I come home early on Thursdays. Snagged a ride with our receptionist." He was looking at her steadily, eyebrows raised a little, as if he could read her mind. How embarrassing!

Xavier tugged at his leg. "Can I come outside with you, Mr. Troy? Please?"

"It's okay with me, buddy." Troy reached down to pat Xavier's shoulder. "But what does your mom say? She's the boss."

"I can't let him follow you around and bother you."

"I think you and Xavier were at the doctor's last week, so you wouldn't know that Thursdays are special. I do some other stuff."

"Stuff I can do with you?" Xavier was staring up at Troy, eyes wide and pleading.

Angelica bit back a smile. Her son, the master manipulator. "Honey, we have to respect—"

"Actually," Troy interrupted, "this might be a really good activity for Xavier. If you're willing."

"What is it?" She covered the stew pot and lowered the gas heat.

"Dog training. Takes a lot of patience." He winked at her. "Some kid training, too. Let him come with me, and then you come out, too, in a little while. I may need some help."

"Please, Mom?"

She threw up her hands. "I give up. Go ahead."

She watched out the window as Xavier and Troy walked off together. Troy was getting more and more agile with his crutches, and she suspected he'd be off them soon. His head was inclined to hear what Xavier was saying, and as for her son, he was chattering away so joyously that she was glad she'd let him go with Troy.

She wanted him to be happy, and right now, somehow, that happiness was all tied up in Troy. Troy and the dogs. Pray God it would last.

"They look more like father and son than most father and sons," Lou Ann said, walking into the room with an armload of books and paperwork. "That's good for Troy. He didn't have a great relationship with his own dad. Still doesn't, for that matter."

"I remember, but I never knew why." Angelica reached down to scratch Bull's head. "Go back to your bed, buddy. I'm done cooking, and Daddy says no table scraps for you."

"That doesn't keep him from begging, though." Lou

Ann put her laptop and books on the built-in desk in the corner of the kitchen. "Clyde Hinton is a hard man, especially with his boys. His older son fought back, and that's why the two of them can work together now. Troy, though, wasn't having any of it. He shut the door on his dad a long time ago. They hardly ever see each other."

"Interesting." During their engagement, she and Troy hadn't visited much with his father, and the little time they'd spent at Troy's family home was stiff and uncomfortable.

Settling into a chair at the kitchen table, Lou Ann put her feet up on one of the other chairs and stretched. "Where's Xavier going, anyway? I'm ready to play some *Extreme Flight Simulator* with him. Clear my brain from all that psychology."

"Troy's taking him out to the kennels." Angelica turned to the woman who was rapidly becoming a good friend. "I'm so impressed you're working on your degree online."

"Never had the chance before," Lou Ann said, "and it's a kick. I always did like school, just never had time to really pursue it. And Troy insists on paying for it. Says it's the least he can do since I agreed to come back to work for him."

"Wow, I didn't know that."

"There's a lot of things you don't know about that man," Lou Ann said. "He's not one to toot his own horn."

Angelica tucked that away for consideration. "He's sure being good to Xavier. Though he doesn't know what he's getting into, taking him out to the kennels. He'll have to watch him like a hawk, and he won't get any of his own work done."

"It's Thursday, isn't it?" Lou Ann glanced up at the calendar on the wall. "Thursdays, he has the rascals over. Maybe he's going to get Xavier involved with them."

"The rascals, huh?" Just what Xavier needed. "Who are they?"

One side of Lou Ann's mouth quirked up. "They're some kids I wouldn't work with to save my life, but somehow Troy has them helping at the kennel, training dogs and cleaning cages. He's a rescuer, always has been."

"Dangerous kids?" Angelica paused in the act of handing Lou Ann a cup of coffee.

"No, not dangerous. Just full of beans. Relax!" Lou Ann reached for the coffee, took a sip and put it down on the table. "Thanks, hon. There are some real poor folks in this county. Kids who live on hardscrabble farms, hill people just up from down South, migrants who've set up their trailers at the edge of some field."

"Sounds like the way I grew up," Angelica said wryly.

"That's right." Lou Ann looked thoughtful for a minute. "Anyway, when Troy was...well, when he went through a rough spot a while back, Pastor Ricky approached him about setting up a program for those kids. Troy went along, because a lot of them hadn't a notion of the right way to take care of a dog. It's grown, and now he's got ten or twelve coming every week to help out."

"That's amazing, with everything else he does."

"He'd help anyone in the world. What doesn't come so easy to him is taking help himself."

"I'm going to go out." Angelica rinsed the cutting board and stood it in the drainer. "Just as soon as I get those bathrooms clean."

"You go ahead now," Lou Ann said. "I can tell you're a little worried about your boy. I think you'll like what you see."

"Thanks." Impulsively, she gave the older woman a hug.

Five minutes later, Angelica was leaning on the fence outside the kennel, watching Xavier run and play with dogs and boys of all sizes, shapes and colors. He looked so happy that it took Angelica's breath away. She didn't know she was crying until Troy came up beside her and ran a light finger under each eye.

She jerked back, not comfortable with the soft, tender touch.

"You okay?"

She drew in a breath and let it out in a happy sigh. "I'm fine. And I'm so grateful to you for letting Xavier have some normal kid moments."

Troy frowned. "He doesn't get to do stuff like this often?"

She shook her head. "He's been in treatment so much that he hasn't had the chance to play with other boys. Let alone a bunch of dogs."

"It's good for the kids. They need to get their energy out in an accepting environment. And I need someone to play with the dogs. Easy there, Enrique!" he called to a boy who was roughhousing with a small white mutt a little too vigorously.

"Sorry, Señor Troy." The boy in question backed off immediately, then knelt and petted the dog.

"Hey, that's the little dog from the clinic! The owner thought he was going to die!"

Troy nodded, looking satisfied. "He's responding to the medication. He should be able to go back home within a week. I know Darlene will be glad. She calls every couple of days."

She studied Troy's profile. He helped dogs who needed it, owners who couldn't pay, kids who'd grown up without advantages. And of course, he was helping her and Xavier.

"Anyway, thanks for giving my son this opportunity."

When he looked down at her, arms propped on the fence beside hers, she realized how close together they were.

The thought she'd been squelching for the past week, the topic she'd been dodging the couple of times Troy had brought it up, burst into the front of her mind: he'd asked her to marry him just a week ago. He was a man of his word. She could have this. She could have a home, a farm, a man who liked to help others. Most of all, a father for Xavier.

But she'd struggled so long alone that being here, in this perfect life, felt scary, almost wrong. She didn't deserve it.

The other thing she'd been trying not to think about made its way to the surface. She was tainted, dirty. In his heart, Troy would want someone pure. He'd said it enough times when they were engaged—how important it was to him that she'd never been with anyone, that she'd saved herself for marriage. *"I'm a jealous guy,"* he'd said. *"I want you all for my own."*

She tore her eyes away from him, cleared her throat and focused on Xavier, who was rolling on the grass while a couple of the pit bull puppies, already bigger and steadier than they'd been a week ago, licked his face.

She had to live in the moment and focus on all the

benefits this lifestyle was bringing her son. And stay as far as possible away from this man who'd proposed marriage.

Troy was a good person, even a great one, but she wasn't a rescue dog. She needed to be with a man who loved her and could accept her mistakes and her past.

"Mom!" Xavier came over, panting, two high red spots on his cheeks. "This is so much fun. Did you see how I was throwing the Frisbee with the guys?"

When he said "the guys," his tone rang with amazed, self-conscious pride. He'd never been one of the guys, but it was high time he started. And Troy was helping make that happen. "I missed your Frisbee throwing, buddy," she said, "but I'll watch it the next time, okay?"

When she glanced up at Troy to thank him again, she found him staring down at her with a look in his dark eyes that was impossible to read. Impossible to look away from, too. She caught her breath, licked her lips.

As if from a great distance, she heard Xavier calling her name, felt him tugging at her hand. "Hey, Mom, I had a great idea," he was saying.

She shook her head a little, blinked and turned to look at her son. "What's the idea, honey?"

"Do you think Mr. Troy could be my dad?"

Five

Xavier's words were still echoing in Troy's mind the next day. He was riding shotgun—man, he hated that, but the doctor hadn't yet cleared him to drive—while his friend Dion Grant drove his van. They were taking a group from their church, including Angelica and Xavier, to weed the garden at the Senior Towers.

"Do you think Mr. Troy could be my dad?"

He listened to the group's chatter as they climbed out of the van and pulled garden tools from the back. *Could* he become Xavier's dad? Angelica's husband?

It seemed as if those questions hovered in the air every time he was around Angelica. She'd never responded to his proposal, and yesterday she'd brushed aside Xavier's words and scolded the child.

But was the thought so repugnant to her? Once, she'd wanted to marry him.

Sure, she'd left him, apparently for someone else, since she immediately became pregnant. Knowing her now, he didn't think she'd cheated on him while they were together; she wouldn't have had that in her.

But if she'd fallen in love with someone else and been

too embarrassed to admit it…maybe when she'd gone to visit her aunt that summer…

The moment he emerged from the driver's seat, a small hand tugged at his. "Dad! Dad!"

"Xavier!" Angelica hurried up behind Xavier and put her hands on his shoulders. "Honey, you can't call Mr. Troy 'Dad.'" Her face was bright red, and she wouldn't meet Troy's eyes.

"It's okay." Troy patted her shoulder.

"No, it's really not." Angelica kept her voice low and nodded sideways toward the row of ladies sitting on the porch of the Senior Towers. "Let's just hope nobody heard. Come on, Zavey Davey," she said, "you have a playdate with your new friend Becka from church."

"A girl?" Xavier groaned.

"Yes, and she's a lot of fun. Her mom said you two were going to hunt for bugs in the park. She has a magnifying glass."

Xavier screwed up his face and looked thoughtful.

"And she's into soccer, so maybe you two can kick around a soccer ball."

"Okay. That's cool."

Troy watched as Angelica led her son toward a one-story house set between the Senior Towers and the town park. Her long hair was caught up in a high ponytail, and she wore old jeans and a T-shirt emblazoned with a Run for Shelter/Stop Domestic Violence logo. When had she gotten time to do a charity run, with all she had on her plate? And how did she manage to put zero time into her appearance and still look absolutely gorgeous?

"Breathe, buddy." His friend Dion gave him a light punch in the arm. "Didn't know she was your baby mama, but half the town will pretty soon."

"What? She's not my baby mama," Troy said automatically, and then met his friend's eyes. "Uh-oh. Who all heard what Xavier just said?"

"Miss Minnie Falcon, for one." Dion nodded toward the front porch of the Senior Towers.

Troy shrugged and lifted his hands, palms up. "Xavier's not my kid, but he wants me to be his dad. Guess he's decided to pretend it's so."

"You could do a lot worse than those two."

"Yeah. Except she dumped me once before, and she doesn't want anything but a professional relationship with me."

"You sure about that, my friend?"

He wasn't sure of anything and he felt too confused to discuss the subject. "Come on, we'd better start weeding or the ladies are going to outshine us."

He'd brought a low lawn chair so he could weed without bending his injured leg. Working the earth, just slightly damp from a recent rain, felt soothing to Troy, and he realized he'd been spending too much time indoors, doing paperwork and staying late at his office in town. The dirt was warm and pungent with an oniony scent. Nearby, he could hear the shouts of kids at the park and the occasional car or truck driving by.

Even after Angelica returned and started weeding across the gardens from him, he didn't sweat it. The jokes and chatter of the group, most of whom knew each other well from years of adult Sunday school class together, made for an easy feeling. He was glad they'd come.

"Hey, beautiful, when did you get back to town?"

The voice, from a passerby, sounded pleasant enough, but he turned to see who was calling a member of the group "beautiful" with the tiniest bit of snarkiness in his tone. It took a minute, but he recognized the guy from a few classes behind him in high school, dressed in a scrub shirt and jeans. Logan Filmore. Brother of a friend of his. Guy must be in some kind of medical field now.

And of course, he was speaking to Angelica.

Troy's eyes flashed to her and read her concern, even distaste.

He pushed to his feet, grabbed a crutch and limped across the garden to stand beside her. "How's it going?"

"Okay." She looked uneasily at Logan, who'd stopped in front of them.

The guy looked at Troy and seemed to read something in his eyes, because he took a step back. He gave Angelica a head-to-toes once-over, then waved and walked on, calling, "Nice to see you" over his shoulder.

Angelica squatted back down and Troy eased himself down beside her.

"Someone you know?"

She yanked a thistle out of the ground. "Sort of."

"Is there anything I can do?"

Another weed hit the heap in the center of the garden. "Stop talking about it?"

He lifted his hands, palms up. "Okay. Just trying to help."

For several minutes they pulled weeds in silence. Troy was totally aware of her, though: the glow of her skin, the fine sheen of sweat on her face, the vigorous, almost angry way she tugged weeds.

Finally she turned her face partway toward him. "I'm sorry. I... I used to know him and I really dislike him. Thanks for coming over."

"Sure." A few more weeds hit the pile. "I like helping you, you know."

"Thanks."

"I like it a lot." He wanted to protect her from people like the guy who'd just passed by. He wanted to protect her full-time. Of course, he mainly wanted to marry her for Xavier's sake. That was all.

He reached across her to tug on a vine. Their hands brushed.

He was expecting her to jerk away, but she didn't; she just went a little still.

That gave him the hope he needed. "You still haven't answered my question," he said quietly.

"What question was that?"

"About whether you'd marry me."

She laughed a little. "Oh, that."

"Yes, that. Have you thought about it?"

She shut her eyes for a moment. "I've hardly thought of anything else."

"And?"

"And... I don't know."

"Fair enough," he said. "But is there anything I could do to help you decide?"

She gave him a narrow-eyed look and for a moment, he thought she was going to scold him. "Yes," she said finally. "You could tell me why you want to do it."

"That's easy. I want to do it because Xavier wants a dad. And because I like helping you."

Her mouth got a pinched look. If he hadn't known better, he'd have thought she felt hurt. "Those aren't... those aren't the reasons people get married."

"Are they bad reasons, though?"

She shook her head, staring at the ground. "They're not bad, no. They're fine. Kind. Good."

"Then what's standing in the way?"

She shrugged, looked away. There was a fine film of tears over her eyes. "Nothing. I don't know."

"Look," he said, touching her under the chin with one finger, lifting her face toward his. "Let's do it. Let's surprise Xavier." He didn't know what was making him force the issue.

Maybe something he saw in her eyes. Some part of her wanted to. And maybe it was for Xavier, or mostly so; but he had a funny feeling that she saw him as a man and was drawn to him.

"We'd be doing it for Xavier." She stared at him, her eyes huge.

"Yes, for Xavier. So, are you saying yes?"

"I think I am."

He nodded. "Then…let's seal it with a kiss." He leaned over and ever so gently brushed her lips with his.

It was meant to be just a friendly peck on the lips, but he lingered a couple of seconds, feeling the tingle of awareness he'd felt before but something else, too, something deeper.

She gasped and jerked away. "We'll…have to figure out…what kind of boundaries…" She trailed off, still staring at him. "You know."

She looked so appealing that he wanted to kiss her again, a real kiss. But the defenseless look on her face got to him and he pulled her into his arms, as slow and light and careful as if she were a wounded animal. "We'll figure it out," he whispered into her soft, dark hair.

* * *

"Mom! Can I? Can I?"

Angelica turned away from the church group and from Troy, standing just a little too close for comfort, to greet her son. It was late afternoon, and they were all saying their goodbyes in front of the weeded, re-mulched Senior Towers gardens.

Running ahead of Becka and her mom, Xavier looked so...normal. His striped shirt was mud-stained, his legs pumping sturdily beneath thrift-store gym shorts. Joy flooded her to see how healthy he looked. And what a relief to get out of the sticky, messy, impossibly emotional situation with Troy and back to what grounded her.

"Can you what, honey?" She knelt to catch Xavier as he ran into her arms, relishing the sweaty, little-boy smell of him.

"Can I play soccer with Becka? Her mom is the coach of the team!"

She hugged him close. "We'll see."

"You say that when you mean no!" Xavier pulled away. "Please, Mom?"

Becka and her mom arrived and Angelica stood up. "Thanks so much for watching him," she said.

"Well, I may have done something wrong." Becka's mom wore shorts and a T-shirt, her hair back in a no-nonsense ponytail under a baseball cap. "Becka and I were talking about soccer practice tonight, and when Xavier was interested, I told him he could join the team."

Angelica felt her eyebrows draw together. "Hmm. I'm not sure."

"Mom!"

"We'll have to see." Angelica bit her lip. She wanted

him to be able to do it, to do everything a normal, healthy boy could do, but... "Soccer's pretty strenuous, isn't it?"

"At this age? No more so than normal play." Linda Mason gave her trademark grin. "The kids run around a lot, yeah. And I try to teach them some skills. But it's not competitive. It's just for fun."

"Practice is tonight, Mom!"

"Tonight?" Xavier hadn't had his usual afternoon rest. "I don't think so, sweetie. That's just too much."

A light touch warmed her shoulder. Troy. Her heart skittered as she looked back at him.

He raised an eyebrow, squeezed her shoulder once and then reached out to shake Linda's hand. "Hey, Linda. He'd need a sports physical anyway, wouldn't he?"

"Exactly." Linda nodded. "What we could do, if you don't think it's too much, is to have him come over to the park for a half-hour practice session I do with some of the kids, before the official practice. But you're right, Troy, he couldn't actually be on the team until getting a physical."

Angelica flashed Troy a grateful smile. She hadn't known that kids needed physicals for team sports, and it made the perfect delay tactic.

Xavier's face fell, and tears came to his eyes. "I just wanna play!"

"Then you have to get a physical, buddy!" Angelica gave him a one-armed hug. "All the kids have to get physicals. I'm sure Becka did, right?"

"Yeah, and I had to get a shot."

Xavier grimaced. "Yuck."

As the kids started comparing horror stories about

doctors and needles, the three adults sat down on the bench outside the Senior Towers. "I'm really sorry," Linda said. "I didn't mean to get him all excited. But he seems like a great kid, and he had so much fun kicking around a ball with Becka. I'm sure he'd be good at soccer."

"We'll see what the doctor says," Troy said.

Angelica stared at him. "Excuse me?"

"Um, I'm going to go check on the kids." Linda looked from one to the other, frank curiosity in her eyes. "If that half-hour practice is okay, I'll walk them over to the park. Come on over and watch."

"Okay," Angelica said distractedly as Linda herded the kids toward the park. What did Troy mean, acting as if he had some say in Xavier's life? "Look, I'm sure you didn't mean it this way, but it sounded like you thought we'd all go to the doctor together."

"That's what I was thinking." Troy raised his eyebrows and met her eyes. "Is that a problem?"

"I don't want you to think you're the authority on Xavier after knowing him for, what, three weeks?"

"I can tell," Troy said mildly. "But after all, I'm going to be his father."

Angelica stared at him, momentarily speechless. Adrenaline flooded her body, and her breathing quickened.

She'd have to set some boundaries. She was so used to having full say about Xavier and what he did, how he lived—whether he could play soccer, for instance—and now Troy was wanting to get all high-handed.

In most matters, she'd be fine collaborating with Troy. But where Xavier was concerned, not so much.

"Some people say a two-parent family is good for

this very reason." Troy sounded maddeningly calm. "A lot of moms are a little more protective. Dads help kids get out there and see the world."

"Look, you have no experience being a parent, and you don't know what Xavier's been through."

"Come on, let's walk. You want to see him play, don't you?"

"Um...yes! Of course!" Angelica stood, feeling a stiffness in her neck that bespoke a headache to come. "But we're not done talking about this."

How had Troy so smoothly taken control? She had to admit, looking up at him as he strode by her side, ushering her around a broken spot in the sidewalk, nodding to people he knew, that something about his confidence felt good. That it attracted her. She had to admit it, but... "Listen, this is making me a little uncomfortable," she said. "I'm used to having control of Xavier, and I'm not sure I'm willing to give that up."

He nodded. "I understand. I feel like I should have some say, but of course, you're his mom."

"And I make the decisions."

He slanted his eyes down at her. "Right. Okay. You make...the final decisions. Right."

She had to laugh. "Boy, that was pretty hard for you to say. Control much, do you?"

"You know me."

She did. She'd known him for a long time. But this new, older version, a little less driven, a little more humble... Wow. Despite all the craziness in her life, a core of excitement and hope was building inside her.

They approached the park together. Large oaks and maples provided shade against the late-afternoon sun, shining bright in a sky spotted with a few puffy white clouds. Kids shouted and ran around the old-fashioned swings and slide. Ragweed and earth scents mingled with the savory smell of someone's grilled burgers.

On the other side of town, a train on its late afternoon run made a forlorn whistle.

A family sprawled on a blanket together: Mom, Dad, a boy about Xavier's age and a toddler girl with curly red hair and an old-fashioned pink romper. The little girl put her arms around the boy and hugged him, and the father and mother exchanged a smile. Angelica's heart caught. That was what she'd always longed for: a loving man who could share in the raising of the children. A little sister for Xavier.

But that wasn't in the cards for her. What Troy was proposing was purely a marriage of convenience. She had to remember the limits, the reason he'd proposed at all: he wanted to help her, and especially to help Xavier. It wasn't romantic, it wasn't love. Nothing of the kind. Troy was a rescuer, and she and Xavier just so happened to be in need of some rescuing.

They walked over to the area where Linda was leading Xavier, Becka and three other kids through some soccer drills. "He seems to be doing okay," Troy said. "What do you think?"

Tugging her thoughts away from what couldn't be changed, she studied her son, noticing the high spots of color in his cheeks. "He's getting tired. But I'll let him stay for the half hour. I'll make sure he gets some extra rest tomorrow."

They sat down on the bleachers by the soccer field. Troy took her hand and squeezed it, and warmth and impossible hope flooded through her.

"We should talk about those other boundaries," Troy said.

"What...oh." When she saw the meaningful look in his eyes she knew exactly what he was talking about. The physical stuff.

"I'm attracted to you. You can probably tell."

Angelica looked down. She was attracted to him, too, or she thought she was. What else would her breathless, excited feeling be about? But she was too afraid to say so. Too afraid to tell him about all her issues. She pulled her hand away and pressed her lips together to keep herself from blurting out this shameful part of her past.

After a minute, he let out a sigh. "We don't have to hold hands or kiss or anything like that. I know you're doing this for Xavier, not for love. I want the same thing. I want to take care of you and Xavier, but I won't put pressure on you."

"Right." Her heart felt as if it were shrinking in her chest.

"Now, what about our...personal lives?" He looked at her sideways, raising an eyebrow.

Did he have any idea how handsome he was? "What?"

"I mean your...social life."

What was he talking about?

"Other men, Angelica."

"Other...ooooh." She shook her head. "It's not an issue. I don't date." In fact, she'd never really been in love with anyone but Troy.

"You sure?" He looked skeptical.

"I'm sure!" She looked away. This was the best someone like her could hope for.

Other families were arriving for the soccer game. Mothers in pretty clothes with designer handbags, kids with proper soccer garb. In her garden-stained jeans and T-shirt, carrying her discount-store purse, Angelica wondered if she could ever fit in. If the other families would look askance at Xavier for his murky background, his lack of a father, his mismatched, thrift-shop clothes.

Being with Troy was a chance to be a real part of the community. She wouldn't impose on him to buy her fancy things, but she'd happily accept decent clothing and soccer duds for Xavier. Would happily accept Troy's good name in the town, too, paving the way for her son to be accepted and have friends.

Troy was giving her a lot, and he was even saying he wouldn't expect the physical side of marriage in return.

She should be grateful instead of wanting more.

Six

Two days later, on a rainy Monday, Angelica was cleaning out kennels when the door burst open and two women stalked in, slamming it behind them.

"Where is he?" one of them asked loudly over the dogs' barking.

She started to put down her shovel and then paused, wondering if she should keep it for self-defense. "Where's who?"

"The boy. Xavier."

Angelica's fingers tightened on the handle of the shovel. "Why do you want to see Xavier?"

As the dogs' barking subsided, one of the women stepped forward into the light, and Angelica recognized her. "Daisy! I haven't seen you in—"

Troy's sister, Daisy, held out one hand like a stop sign. "Don't try to be nice."

Angelica studied the woman she'd once called a friend. Just a couple of years older than Angelica, she wore purple harem pants and a gold shirt. Her hair flowed down her shoulders in red curls, and rings glittered on every finger. Short, adorably chubby and always full of life, she'd been Angelica's main ally in Troy's family back when she and Troy were engaged. Angelica had hoped they'd be friends again one day.

But Daisy pointed a finger at Angelica. "I want to see my nephew, and I want to see him now."

"Your nephew? Wait a minute. What's going on? What's got you mad?"

"What's got me mad is that I have a nephew who's six years old and I've never even met him. I may not ever be going to have children of my own, but I've always wanted to be an aunt. And now I hear I've been one for years and the boy's been kept from me!"

"Oh, Daisy." Things were starting to fall into place. "Xavier isn't your nephew."

The other woman, whom Angelica didn't recognize, stepped forward—tall and thin, with streaked hair and Asian features. "We heard it on good faith from Miss Minnie Falcon."

Of course. The day of weeding at the Senior Towers. News traveled fast. Angelica shook her head. "Come on, you guys. Sit down. Miss Minnie's got it wrong, but I can explain."

"You've got some explaining to do, all right." Daisy made her way over to Troy's office area and pulled out the desk chair, clearly at home here. "I was already mad at you for what you did to Troy, but this beats all. And I'm sorry, but you were engaged to Troy, and then you left, and now you have a kid. How can he not be my nephew?"

Angelica perched on a crate and gestured to the other woman to do the same.

The woman held out a hand to Angelica. "I'm Susan,

Daisy's best friend," she said, "and I'm here to keep her from becoming violent."

"It's nothing to joke about!" Daisy glared at her friend.

Angelica leaned forward. "Daisy, I can tell you for sure that Troy isn't Xavier's father." She explained Xavier's desire for a father and how he'd wishfully called Troy Dad.

"But word was you and Troy were all over each other," Daisy said skeptically.

"All over each other." Angelica rubbed her chin. She was tempted to tell the ladies what was really going on, except she hated to do that without Troy. They hadn't had the chance to discuss what they'd tell the world about their so-called engagement; Xavier didn't even know, because once Xavier knew, everyone in town would know.

She needed time to prepare, but there wasn't any. "Listen," she said, "I'm gonna go get Troy."

"Don't you try to hide behind him. He's a sucker where you're concerned."

"Daisy," the other woman said in a low voice. "We shouldn't judge. Especially considering we came straight from Bible group."

"Even Jesus got righteously angry." Daisy sulked, but then she nodded at her friend. "You're right. I'm not giving you much of a chance, Angelica, am I? But the truth is, I always really liked you, and when you dumped Troy, you dumped me, too. And now to hear that you've actually had a baby... That pretty much beats all."

"Let me get Troy."

"No, I'll text him."

Before Angelica could stop her, Daisy was on her phone, and a couple of minutes of awkward small talk later, Troy walked in. "What's going on?"

Angelica's mind raced through the possible outcomes of this confrontation. They weren't great. If they didn't reveal their marriage of convenience now, it would make Daisy mad, and as Daisy went, so went the family. On the other hand, if they did explain that it wasn't a real marriage, that would get out, too. And that was exactly what she didn't want Xavier to find out.

Without thinking it through, she walked over to Troy and put an arm around him. "Honey," she said. "Can we spill the beans a tiny bit early and tell Daisy and Susan our news?"

When Angelica put her arm around him, Troy almost fell off his crutches. She was so resistant to getting physically close that her act of affection stunned him. It took another moment for him to realize what she'd said.

Really? She wanted to tell his sister, who knew everyone in town and loved to talk, about their pseudoengagement?

Troy blinked in the dark kennel. Automatically, he hobbled over—his leg was bad today—toward one of the barking dogs in the front, a fellow named Crater for the ugly scar in the middle of his back, and opened the gate of his kennel. Crater leaped with joy and Troy knelt awkwardly to rub and pet him.

Then he looked back at Angelica.

She cocked her head to one side and raised her eyebrows. She must have had a reason for what she'd done; she wasn't one to playact for no reason. And if he was going to marry her, maybe even to make it a good marriage, he needed to show her his trust. "Are you sure about this?"

"I think we should tell them." She was communicating with her eyes, willing him to say something, and he only hoped he'd get it right.

"Okay," he said, pushing himself to his feet and limping over to drape an arm around Angelica's shoulders. "Guys... Angelica and I have decided to get married."

There were no happy hugs, no shouts of joy. Daisy's lips pressed together. "Are you sure that's a good idea?"

"Of course," he said. "We've...settled our differences." He tightened his arm around Angelica for emphasis and noticed that she was shaking. "Hey, it's okay. It's Daisy. She'll be happy for us!" He glared at his sister. "Won't you?"

"Are you kidding?" Daisy was nothing if not blunt. "I can't be happy to watch you setting yourself up for another fall."

He felt Angelica cringe.

"Daisy!" Susan put a hand on her hip. "Be nice."

Troy rubbed Angelica's shoulder a little, still feeling her tension. "Look, the past is water under the bridge. We've started over, and we'd appreciate it if you would be supportive." He frowned at Daisy. "For all of us, especially Xavier."

He watched as his opinionated sister struggled with herself. Finally she nodded. "All right," she said. "I'll do my best."

Angelica chimed in. "You said you'd always wanted to be an aunt. Well, now you'll be one. Xavier will be thrilled to have a bigger family. We've been pretty much..." She cleared her throat. "Pretty much on our own, since my aunt passed away."

For the millionth time, he wondered what had happened to make her leave him and leave town. And what had happened to Xavier's father.

Apparently he wasn't the only one. "One thing I've got to know," Daisy said. "Who's Xavier's father if it's not Troy?"

The question hung in the air. It was what Troy had wanted to ask but hadn't had the guts to. Trust Daisy to get the difficult topics out into the open.

Angelica didn't speak. She was staring at the ground as if the concrete floor held the answer to Daisy's question.

"Well?" Daisy prompted. "If we're all starting fresh, what better basis than honesty?"

Angelica looked up, shot a glance at Troy and then lifted her chin and met Daisy's eyes. "I'm not at liberty to share that information," she said. "It's Xavier's story, and when he's old enough, he'll decide who he wants to share it with. Until then, it's private."

"Does he even know?" Daisy blurted.

"No!" Angelica stood, crossed her arms and paced back and forth. "And I'd appreciate all of you avoiding the topic with him. He's not old enough to understand, and I don't want him to start questioning. Not yet."

Something ugly twisted in Troy's chest. He wanted to know, if only so he could watch out for the guy, keep him away from her in the future, know his enemy. To have that unknown rival out there made the hairs on the back of his neck stand up.

"I guess that makes sense," Daisy said doubtfully.

"Thank you for respecting my son's right to privacy." As he accepted the forced hugs of his sister and pretended to be an excited, normal fiancé to Angelica, Troy had to wonder whether they were doing the right thing.

"I don't know, man." Troy's friend Dion, the police chief of Rescue River, sat across from him at the table of the Chatterbox Café later that afternoon. They were drinking coffee and Troy had confided the truth about the marriage of convenience, knowing Dion could keep a secret. "I just don't know. You say you're doing it for Xavier, but Father God has His plans for that boy. What if He takes him young, him being so sick with leukemia? You going to divorce Angelica then?"

"No!" Troy's coffee cup clattered into the saucer, liquid sloshing over the sides. "I wouldn't leave her, not in her time of need, not ever."

"Think she'll stay with you?"

Troy drew in a breath and let it out in a sigh. "I hope so, but I can't know for sure. She left me before."

"And she won't tell you who the daddy is?"

Troy shook his head. "Says it's between her and Xavier, and she doesn't want the whole town to know before he does. Says it's his story to tell."

Dion shook his head. "That's a nice theory. But a man and his wife shouldn't have secrets." He rubbed a hand over his nearly shaved head. "Secrets destroy a marriage. I'm living proof of that."

Troy nodded. Dion didn't talk much about his marriage, but Troy knew there had been rough patches. Then they'd straightened things out, and then Dion's wife had passed away. Dion had turned to God and he had a deeper faith than anyone else Troy knew, which was why he'd come to his friend with his own issue.

"Do I try to force it out of her, though?" he asked. "Is it even my right to know?"

"All kinds of reasons to know about paternity," Dion pointed out. He paused while the waitress, a little too interested in their conversation, poured them some more coffee. "Thanks, Felicity," he said to her. "We won't be needing anything else."

After she left, Troy chuckled. "She's curious what we're talking about, and she's even more curious what you're doing Friday night."

Dion shook his head. "Got a date with the baseball game on TV, just like usual. Anyway, what if something happened to Angelica? You'd need to know Xavier's story. For his health, if nothing else, it's important to know who his daddy is."

"I guess."

"Something else. Everybody in town gonna think you're the daddy. Some already do. You okay with that?"

"What people say doesn't matter."

Dion looked out the window, a little smile on his face. "Maybe not," he said finally. "But you won't look like the good guy anymore. People might think you've been neglecting your duties."

"What the gossips say doesn't matter. Period."

"Okay." Dion studied him. "I believe you. Still, you gotta know."

"You've convinced me of that."

"Talk to her, man. But pray first. Because it's not easy to be calm about the guy who got your girl pregnant, but in this situation, calm is what you'll have to be."

Troy nodded thoughtfully. How was he going to

bring this up? One thing Dion was sure right about—
he needed every bit of help the good Lord could offer
him. Only thing was, he hated asking for help of any
kind. Even from God.

Seven

Angelica was in the kitchen washing breakfast dishes when she heard the screeching of brakes out on the road.

"Zavey?"

No answer.

She grabbed a dish towel on her way out the door, drying her hands as she climbed the slight rise to where she could see the road.

Her heart seemed to stop. Xavier was on his knees beside the road, screaming.

She practically flew over the ground until she reached him and saw the situation.

In front of Xavier, a couple of feet from the edge of the road, Bull lay in the gravel, his sturdy body twisted at an odd angle. A car was pulled halfway into the ditch across the road, and in front of it, a middle-aged woman pressed her hand to her mouth.

Heart pounding, Angelica knelt by her son, patting his arms and legs, examining him. "Are you okay?"

Xavier gulped and nodded and pointed toward Bull. "I'm… It's my fault… I let him off his lead. I wanted him to play fetch." His voice rose to a wail. "I think he's dead."

"I'm sorry, I'm so sorry!" The driver came over and sank to her knees beside them, her voice shaking, tears streaking her face. "I didn't see the dog, he came running out so fast..."

And suddenly Troy was there, kneeling awkwardly beside Bull.

"Oh, honey." Angelica scooped Xavier up into her arms, reached out a hand to pat the stranger's shoulder and leaned toward Troy and Bull, her heart aching at the sight of the still, twisted dog. "Is...is he alive?"

Busy examining Bull, Troy didn't answer, so she set Xavier down and instructed him to stay out of Troy's way. She took information from the distraught driver and walked her back to her vehicle, promising to call and let her know how the dog was, making sure the woman was calm enough to drive and able to back her car out of the ditch.

And then she knelt beside Troy and Xavier, putting her arm around her son.

"I'm sorry I let him off his lead! It's my fault!" Xavier buried his face in her shoulder, weeping.

"Shh. It was an accident. You didn't know." She bit her lip and touched Troy's arm. "Is he breathing?"

Troy took one quick glance toward them and then went back to examining the dog. "Yes, but he's pretty badly injured. I'd like to do surgery right away. Here. No time to get to town." He scanned the area. "Can you grab me a big board out of the shed? There's a stack beside the door."

"Of course. Xavier, stay here." She ran to the shed and came back with a piece of plywood.

"Give me your hoodie." Troy was saying to Xavier. "I'm going to wrap Bull up in it. T-shirt, too, buddy."

Xavier shucked his hoodie and started pulling off his T-shirt, shivering in the chilly morning air.

Her son was so vulnerable to colds. "But, Troy, he shouldn't—"

"I can do it, Mom!" Xavier's trembly voice firmed up and he sniffed loudly and wiped his face on the T-shirt before handing it over to Troy.

"We need to keep Bull warm," Troy explained in a calm voice, slipping out of his own much larger T-shirt and kneeling to cover the old bulldog. "And," he said, lowering his voice so only Angelica could hear, "Xavier needs to help."

Gratitude spread through Angelica's chest. "Thank you." She knelt and helped him ease the dog onto the wide wooden plank she'd found.

Bull yelped once and his old eyes opened, then closed again. His breathing came in hard bursts.

Together, Angelica and Troy lifted the makeshift stretcher. Once, Troy lurched hard to one side, and it took both Xavier and Angelica to steady Bull. Angelica's heart twisted when she saw that a smear of blood had gotten on Xavier's hand. With his medical history, he was oversensitive to blood.

But he just wiped his hand on his jeans. "Where are your crutches, Mr. Troy?"

"Dumped 'em. Come on."

Worry pinged Angelica's heart. Troy had been to the doctor just yesterday and had gotten another full cast and a warning that he was putting too much weight on his leg.

"Can you fix him?" Xavier asked as they walked toward the kennel building.

Troy glanced down at Xavier. "They say I'm good," he tried to joke, but his voice cracked. He was limping badly now.

Angelica gulped in a breath. "Who can I call to help?"

"Buck's my only trained surgical assistant, but I'm not having him on the property. I'll manage."

"I'll help as best I can." But how would she do that? she wondered; Lou Ann wasn't here and Xavier needed her. He couldn't watch the surgery.

They got Bull to the kennel and onto the small examining table Troy had for emergencies.

"You've gotta fix him, Mr. Troy! I love him!"

"I know, son." Troy turned to Xavier. "Watch him, and if he starts to move, hold him while I wash up and prep. Angelica, you help him."

"Okay. But I don't think Xavier should stick around."

By the time Troy had assembled his instruments and gotten back to the dog, he had to lean hard on the operating table, and Angelica saw his face twist with pain.

How would he stand, possibly for several hours, and do delicate surgery without help?

Angelica hurried Xavier outside and pulled out her phone. Buck had given her his number when they were going to go out, and hopefully… Good, she'd never deleted it. She hit the call button.

"Hey, Angie," he said, sounding sleepy.

"I've got an emergency," she said, not bothering to greet him. "Listen, are you sober?"

"Yeah. Just woke up."

"Can you come out to the farm and help Troy with a surgery? Bull is hurt."

"Be right there."

She went back in and helped Troy hold Bull still and administer something with a needle. As he ran careful hands over the dog's leg, his face was set, jaw clenched.

"Is he gonna be okay, Mr. Troy?" Xavier asked from the doorway.

Angelica and Troy met each other's eyes over the table.

"I don't know," Troy said, his voice husky. "I'm going to do my very best. You've been a big help."

The dog's laceration looked bad, but as Troy continued to examine it, his face relaxed a little. "I don't think any internal organs are affected, though we can't be sure about that. It's the leg I'm worried about. I'll try to pin it, but I'm not sure it'll work."

"You can fix him. Right?" Xavier's voice was hopeful.

Troy turned to her son. "It's hard to tell," he said. "He's an older guy, and I had to give him strong medicine to make him sleep. That's hard on him. And his leg might be the more serious injury. We just don't know, buddy."

The anesthetic had set in and Troy was just starting to clean the wound when a car sounded. "Can you see who that is?" Troy said without looking up.

She went out, opened the door and let Buck in. "He's just getting started," she said. "Let me walk back with you. He doesn't know you're here."

Buck, already dressed in scrubs, followed her in.

"Troy, I have Buck here to help you."

Troy's shoulders stiffened. "How'd you manage that?"

"I have his number from before."

No answer.

"Stone-cold sober, man, and ready to help." Buck pulled on some gloves. He glanced up at Troy's face. "Whoa, chill. I'm here by invitation. And truth is, you look like you could use the help. Sure you didn't get hit, too?"

Troy's glance at Angelica was as cold as ice.

She swallowed hard. "I'm going to tend to Xavier. He needs to get inside, get cleaned up and rest."

"Fine." He turned away.

Letting her know things were anything but fine.

The surgery took longer than Troy expected, and operating on his own pet threw professional objectivity right out the window. Armstrong's help was crucial, but even with it, the outcome was touch and go.

Discouraged, his leg on fire with the pain of standing without support for several hours, Troy cleaned up while Buck finished bandaging Bull. Troy watched the younger man easily manage the heavy dog in one arm while he opened the crate door with the other, and the anger he'd shoved aside during the delicate surgery rushed back in.

Since when was Angelica in touch with Buck? How often did they talk, get together? Why hadn't she mentioned the friendship if, in fact, it was innocent?

He could barely manage to thank Buck, and the other man's cheerful "Anytime, my man" rang as guilty in Troy's ears. When they walked out together, Buck held the door for him and then checked his phone and jogged off toward his Jeep and swung in. Leaving Troy to hobble toward the house on both crutches, wanting nothing more than some pain medication and a place to put his leg up.

Angelica greeted him at the door. "How is he?"

Just looking at her made his stomach roil. "The dog or your boyfriend?"

She paled. "What?"

He clenched his jaw. "Bull is resting peacefully, but it'll be a few days before we know how well he does. He did come out of the anesthesia, so he's at least survived that."

"Oh, that's wonderful." She backed away from the door to let him by. "But, Troy, what did you mean by that other crack?"

He spun, faced her down. "Why did you keep Armstrong's phone number? How long have you had something going on with him?"

Her forehead wrinkled. "I don't have anything going on with anybody."

To Troy's ears, her denial sounded forced. He squeezed his eyes shut and turned away from her. "I'm beat. I'm going to get some rest."

"I'll take care of the dogs," she said, her voice hesitant. "But I don't want to have this stand between us. I had Buck's phone number because I never deleted it from before. Not because I'm seeing him."

"Yeah, right." Troy had heard so many denials all his life. He remembered his mother's lies to his father, remembered the first time he'd seen her driving by with another man and realized that she wasn't telling the truth about her whereabouts.

Angelica herself had left him to sleep with another man.

It crushed him that Angelica was seeing Buck. He'd

half expected something like this to happen, but not so soon. He'd never thought she would cheat on him even before the wedding.

In fact, he'd even thought she had feelings for him. He felt his shoulders slump, as if the bones that held up his body had turned to jelly. Women were treacherous and his own meter of awareness was obviously broken.

Fool that he was.

"Listen," she said now, stepping in front of him as he tried to leave the room. A high flush had risen to her cheeks, and her eyes sparked fire. "I don't appreciate what you're accusing me of. I have no feelings for Buck. I barely know the man."

He leaned against the wall as exhaustion set in. "You were all set to date him. The only obstacle was his drinking. Well, he's sober today, so go for him."

"I. Don't. Want. Him. I never did. And anyway, I'm getting married to you."

"Yeah, well, we both know how real that marriage is," he said bitterly. "It's a sham, for your convenience and Xavier's. You said you never dated, but obviously that wasn't true."

"You're not listening."

"I don't listen to lies."

She shook her head, staring at him, her brown eyes gone almost black. "You're insulting my integrity and I don't appreciate that. I'm committed to you until we decide different. Which it looks like you're doing right now."

"It's not me who made the decision to seek comfort elsewhere." He rubbed the back of his neck. "Tell me, when you act all scared about being touched, is that fake? Or are you just repulsed by me?"

"Is it... Oh man." Her hands went to her hips. "You are making me so mad, Troy Hinton. Just because your parents had their problems—and yeah, I know about that, I heard it from your sister—it doesn't mean you get free rein to accuse me of whatever other women have done to you."

"I'm not..." He paused. Maybe he was. He didn't know. "Look, I'm too tired to think. Can we just put this whole conversation on hold for now?"

"What, so you can build up even more of a case against me? No way." She was small but she was determined and she obviously wasn't budging. "I'm not letting you do this, Troy. I'm not letting you fall in hate with me."

"Why not? Wouldn't it be easier for you?"

She heaved out a sigh and looked up at the ceiling. "No, it wouldn't be easier and it wouldn't be right. Stop judging me!"

"I wasn't—"

"Yes, you were," she pressed on, stepping in closer. "To think I'm dating Buck in all my spare time—which if you haven't noticed, is nonexistent—is totally insulting. As well as ridiculous. So can it and apologize before I whack you one."

That unexpected image made him smile. "You're scaring me, Angelica."

"Mom will do it, too. What do you mean, Mom's dating Buck? And how's Bull?"

They both froze. In the doorway stood Xavier, in sweats and a T-shirt, his hair sticking up in all directions. He swayed a little and grabbed on to the door frame.

Angelica knelt before him, steadying him with a hand on his shoulder. "Honey! I didn't know you were up from your rest."

"I heard you guys fighting. Is Bull okay?" He looked plaintively up at Troy.

Hard as it was to kneel on one leg with his casted leg stuck awkwardly out beside him, he got himself down to Xavier's level. "Bull is sleeping. The drugs we gave him during the surgery made him tired. But he's looking pretty good for an old guy."

Xavier wasn't to be placated with that. "Is he gonna die?"

Troy's heart clenched in his chest. This was a kid too familiar with death. "I can't promise you that he won't, because he's an old dog. The accident was hard on him, and surgery is, too. But I did my best, and we're going to take good care of him. Okay?"

"Can I see him?"

Troy glanced at Angelica. "How about we bring him inside in a couple of hours, once he's gotten some rest? Okay?"

Angelica and Xavier nodded, both looking serious, and Troy's chest clenched painfully. He cared for both of them way too much. He wanted to protect them, wanted to answer Xavier's questions, wanted to help him heal.

Wanted to trust Angelica.

Now that he'd come down from his angry high, now that he was looking at the sunshine on her black hair as she leaned forward to hug her son, he thought he must have been crazy to accuse her.

But at the same time, there was that nagging doubt.

"You better get some rest, Troy." Angelica's tone was guarded. "And we'll do the same, right, Zavey? We'll have a quiet day. Because tomorrow, we get to go meet your teacher and see your classroom. Just a couple of weeks until school starts."

Troy nudged Xavier with his crutch. "That's a big deal, buddy. You're going to have a blast."

Concern darkened Angelica's eyes and she was biting her lip. He knew she wanted Xavier to go to school, wanted him to have as normal a life as possible for as long as possible.

He headed toward the stairs but turned back to look at Angelica. She was ushering Xavier toward the door, but he was dawdling over a handheld video game. Angelica stopped, looking half patient and half exasperated, and then she squeezed her eyes shut. He saw her lips moving.

He felt like an utter cad. She was dealing with the worst thing a mother could face, the possible death of her child, and doing it beautifully, focusing on Xavier and his needs. Given his health issues, educating him at home would have been easier, but Xavier was a social kid and needed friends, so she'd called umpteen social workers and school administrators and the school nurse to figure out a way he could attend as much as possible and make up his work when he had to be out. She was super stressed out, and how had he supported her?

By calling her out for cheating, when she'd just been trying to help him. At least he thought so.

He scrubbed a hand over his face and headed up the stairs. Reopening their discussion would likely just result in more misunderstanding. He had to get a little rest.

And then he'd get up and be a better man. With God's help.

Eight

As soon as the school secretary buzzed them in, Angelica marched into Xavier's new elementary school—her own alma mater—holding Xavier by one hand.

Immediately memories assailed her, brought on by the smell of strong cleaning chemicals and the sight of cheerful, bright alphabet letters hanging from the ceiling. She could almost feel the long patchwork skirt brushing her first-grade legs and taste the peanut-butter-and-sprouts sandwiches that had marked her as just a little different from the other kids.

Behind her, Gramps was breathing hard, and she paused to hold the office door open for him. Gramps had driven them there because he knew how important this was. They all wanted to see Xavier have a real childhood, and a big part of that was a regular school.

The other reason Gramps had driven her was that Troy had taken the truck to drive himself and Bull into town today for a consultation with another vet. He wasn't supposed to drive with his cast, but he'd insisted that they keep this appointment for Xavier, that he could manage driving with his left foot.

She knew the real reason he didn't want her to drive him: he was still a little mad at her. Well, fine. She was mad at him, too. Things hadn't been the same since he had accused her of dating Buck on the sly, an idea that would be laughable except he so obviously took it seriously.

It made her feel hopeless about their relationship. If he was that quick to suspect her morals when she'd called Buck in to help him, how would he react to finding out about her assault?

And underneath her anger, a dark thread of shame twisted through her gut. She *had* gone out drinking. She'd even flirted. If she hadn't, if she'd stayed safely at home by herself, she wouldn't have been assaulted.

But she couldn't think about that now; she had to gear up to fight yet another battle for Xavier. Had to get the right teacher and the best classroom situation for him. "Hello, I'm here to see Dr. Kapp," she said to the plump, middle-aged secretary who was working the desk in the front office.

"Okay, and this must be Xavier," the woman said, smiling down at him. "Welcome to your new school! Dr. Kapp will be right out."

Xavier's grin was so wide it made his eyes crinkle and his cheeks go round as red apples.

Meanwhile, Angelica took deep breaths, trying not to be nervous. Dr. Kapp had always been strict, and she must be ancient now, probably even more set in her ways. How would she respond to Angelica, who'd been notorious in the town for having parents who bummed around in their ancient Volkswagen minivan, spent too much time in bars and sold weed?

While Gramps and Xavier looked at a low showcase

of children's art, Angelica tried to forget about Troy and prepare for the battle ahead.

Please, Lord, help me remember. I'm not that mixed-up little hippie girl anymore. I'm Your child and You're here with me.

"Well, Angelica Camden! It's been a long time." Dr. Kapp's tone was dry. "So you have a son now."

Was that accusation in her voice? Angelica couldn't be sure, but she felt it. "Hello," she said, extending her hand to the woman whose close-cropped hair and dark slacks and jacket still made her look like an army general. *God's child. God's child.* "It *has* been a long time."

"I know you're here to talk about your son, but I think we have all the necessary information." Dr. Kapp's eyebrows went up, suggesting Angelica was wasting her time. "Was there something else before you meet Xavier's teacher and see the classroom?"

Angelica glanced back at Gramps for support, but he'd sat down heavily in one of the chairs in the waiting section of the office. Xavier had come over to press against her leg in an uncharacteristic display of neediness. So he was scared, too.

Angelica swallowed. "I'd like to talk to you about Xavier's placement in first grade." She'd rehearsed these words, but her voice still wobbled like the little girl she'd been. She drew in a deep breath. "I understand one of the first-grade teachers is a man, and I'd like for him to be in that class."

Dr. Kapp nodded. "A lot of parents want to choose their child's teacher, but we don't do things that way. I've placed Xavier in Ms. Hayashi's classroom. I think you'll like her."

"Go see if Gramps wants to play tic-tac-toe," Angelica said to Xavier, who was staring up at Dr. Kapp with a sort of awe.

Once he'd gotten out of earshot, she spoke quickly. "I'm a single mother, and that's why I'd like for him to have a male influence."

Dr. Kapp nodded. "That's understandable, but from what you said on the phone, Xavier may have some special needs. That's why we've placed him in Ms. Hayashi's class. She's dual-certified in special education, and I think she's the best choice for Xavier."

So Dr. Kapp wasn't just being autocratic. Angelica bit her lip. "Yes, the doctors said his chemo might have caused some cognitive delays, so a teacher who gets that makes a difference, for sure. I just…don't have many men in his life, and I think that's important for him."

Dr. Kapp nodded toward Gramps and Xavier, heads bent over Gramps's cell phone. "Looks like he has one good male influence, at least."

"Yes, and I'm so thankful. But—"

"Tell you what," Dr. Kapp interrupted. "Why don't I take you down to see Ms. Hayashi? She's here now, setting up her classroom. I'm sure she'll be glad to talk to you about Xavier, and then if you're still feeling dissatisfied, we can talk. I know it's a special situation, but I just have a hunch that Ms. Hayashi is going to be the right placement for Xavier."

Troy parked the truck in the elementary school parking lot. Man, it felt good to be in the driver's seat again, but the doctor had been right about how he shouldn't drive. He could tell he was overdoing it. He used his crutches to make his way to the school's front door.

As he waited to be buzzed in, feelings from his past

flooded him. The fun of going to school, the escape from the tension in his family, the relief of making new friends who didn't know anything about his big fancy home. He started to walk into the office when he saw Angelica, her grandfather and Xavier following—could that be Kapp the cop, still running this place?—around a corner in the brightly painted hallway ahead, and he followed them. "Hey, sorry to be late."

"He's gonna be my dad!" Xavier said proudly to the school principal.

Troy's heart constricted at the boy's trusting comment. What had he, Troy, done to deserve that affection and trust? Nothing, but there it was, and it got to him. Made him want to earn it by being a really good dad to Xavier.

"Some say he always was the boy's dad," Gramps muttered, frowning at Troy.

Troy's fist clenched. Homer Camden was even older than Dr. Kapp, but someday he was going to get Troy put in jail for assault on a senior citizen.

"Gramps!" Angelica hissed, nodding sideways at Xavier, who fortunately had darted over to the wall to examine a fire alarm.

As the principal walked over to explain the fire alarm and caution Xavier never to pull it unless there was a fire, Camden glared at Troy. "Just saying what I've heard around town," he said in a lower voice.

Troy glared back. What an idiot. "If you want to talk to me about something, we'll talk later where the boy won't hear."

"Let's do that." He muttered, "Sorry" to Angelica as he walked over to study the fire alarm with Xavier and the principal.

"How's Bull?" Angelica asked. "Is he going to be okay?"

"Yeah, did you bring him with you?" Back at Angelica's side, Xavier wrapped his arms around his mom's legs and looked worriedly up at Troy.

Troy hesitated. "He's...he's not doing that well. He might need another operation. He's staying at the office in town for now."

"Oh no!" Xavier's eyes filled with tears. "He's gonna have to get his leg cut off and it's my fault!"

Immediately Troy squatted down, barely stabilizing himself on one crutch, his bad leg awkwardly out in front. "If Bull's leg has to be amputated, we'll do everything we can to help him do okay with it. Most dogs are just fine with three legs. There's even a special name for three-legged dogs."

"What is it?"

"Tripod," he said, tapping his palm with three fingers of his other hand. "See? One, two, three."

"I have to talk to Ms. Hayashi," Angelica said. "Do you think—"

Troy got it. "Hey, buddy," he said to Xavier as he shoved himself painfully to his feet. "What do you think about seeing the gym and the lunchroom first? Let Mom talk to your new teacher, and then we'll come back and look around the classroom. Okay?"

"Sure!" Xavier reached up and gripped Troy's hand where it rested on the handle of his crutch.

Troy looked at Homer Camden, red-faced and frowning, and for a split second, he got the image of a man who didn't know what to do with his feelings, who was jealous of a new man in Xavier's and Angelica's life, and who wanted only the best for them. He sighed. "Want to come along?"

Thank you, Angelica mouthed to him before disappearing into the classroom.

"Guess I can," Homer Camden groused. "If you can't handle the boy alone."

It was going to be a long half hour. But he'd do it for Angelica. He'd do almost anything for her, if she'd let him, even though he wasn't at all sure that was wise.

"Where's the lunchroom?" Xavier asked as the three of them headed down the hall.

"Straight down thataway," Camden said, pointing, before Troy could answer.

"Wait a minute," Troy said, "did you go to this school, too?"

Camden nodded. "I was a member of the first graduating class. Back then, it was the new K-eight building, and I was here for seventh and eighth grade."

"That's cool, Gramps!" Xavier grabbed the older man's hand and swung his arms between the two of them, practically pulling Troy off his crutches.

"Back in those days," Camden said, "a lot of farm kids only finished eighth grade, so it truly was a graduation."

"What about you?" Troy had never thought about the old man's schooling, or lack thereof.

"Oh, I finished high school," Gramps said, a note of pride in his voice. "I was always good at math and science. English, not so much."

"Me, too," Troy said as they entered the school lunchroom, where a summer of cleaning couldn't quite erase the smell of sour milk and peanut butter. "That's why vet school had more appeal than, say, lawyering."

"But don't get too friendly," Gramps said as Xavier ran around looking at the colorful posters and sitting in various chairs. "I want to know why you're taking such an interest in Angelica and her son. Is there something you want to tell me?"

"Well, you know about our engagement." He felt duplicitous still, talking about something that might not happen. But it might. He was willing to marry Angelica and be a father to Xavier; he'd meant it when he'd offered, and he would stick with it.

"Is that because you're Xavier's dad?" Camden asked bluntly.

Troy stopped, turned and faced the other man. "No. I don't know who Xavier's father is. I'd like to, but so far, Angelica hasn't been willing to tell me."

Camden studied him. "I'm supposed to believe that? When you were engaged and spending practically every evening together?"

"It's not up to me what you believe," Troy said, "but it's the truth. Angelica and I had decided to wait until marriage." He couldn't keep the bitterness out of his voice. "Why she decided to change that plan, and with whom, I have no idea. But it wasn't me."

Camden crossed his arms over his chest and shook his head. "Guessin' that don't sit right," he said finally. "I always thought it was you. Thought you'd gotten her pregnant and then sent her away. But when you said you were marrying her now, you really threw me off."

Troy drew in a breath. "So you don't know what happened, who the father is?" He knew he shouldn't probe, should only discuss this with Angelica, but it felt like important information, and she wouldn't tell him. Maybe if he knew…

Camden shook his head. "Can't help you there."

"Come see this, Gramps!" Xavier was calling, and the two of them headed over just in time to stop him from squirting an entire container of ketchup into the sink. Plenty had gotten onto his shirt and shorts as well, and the two of them looked at each other with guilty expressions, obviously thinking the same thing: *we're going to be in trouble with Angelica.* A few paper towels later, they headed toward the gym.

"Do you know how to play basketball, Mr. Troy?"

"I sure do. I used to play at this school."

"Were you that tall then?"

Troy laughed. "No, son. I wasn't very tall at all."

"He was a pip-squeak. A lot smaller than you. I remember him in those days."

That hadn't occurred to Troy before, that Homer Camden had known him as a kid. On a whim, Troy put down his crutches. Camden grabbed a basketball, and they took turns lifting Xavier up to shoot baskets.

When they headed back toward the classroom, Xavier rested his hand on Troy's crutch again.

Which made Troy feel that all was right with the world. When had this boy put such a hold on his heart, enough to make him even see the good in Homer Camden?

When Xavier walked into the classroom between Troy and Gramps, tears sprang to Angelica's eyes. It felt as if all of her dreams were coming true.

She'd always wished her son could have a real father. And she'd hoped he could go to a regular school. It hadn't happened for kindergarten, because of all of his treatments, so this was his first opportunity.

"Hey, cool!" Xavier ran into the room and sat down at one of the desks. "I'm ready!"

"And is your name Sammy?" asked Ms. Hayashi.

Angelica was pretty sure she liked this teacher, who turned out to be the friend who'd come to the kennel with Daisy. She seemed very knowledgeable about children with medical issues, and her educational background was impeccable.

Her tight jeans, Harley-Davidson T-shirt and biker boots weren't everyone's idea of a first-grade teacher, even one who was at the school early to move books and set up her classroom. From Gramps's raised eyebrows, she could tell he thought the same. Angelica hoped the woman wouldn't intimidate Xavier.

But her son put his hands on his hips and spoke right up. "I'm not Sammy, I'm Xavier!"

"Aha. And do you know what letter your name starts with?" The woman squatted effortlessly in front of Xavier.

Xavier nodded eagerly. "An *X*, and I can write it, too!"

His enthusiasm made Angelica smile. They'd been practicing letters for months, and she'd taught him to write his name, but it had taken quite a while. His treatment had caused some cognitive issues that might or might not go away, according to the various nurses and social workers they'd dealt with.

"That's good. Can you find your desk?"

"How can I…"

The woman put a hand to her lips, took Xavier's hand and pointed to the sign on the front of the desk where he'd been sitting. "See? It's Ssssammy," she said, emphasizing the *S*. "What we need to do is to find your desk, the one that says 'Xavier.'"

He frowned and nodded. "With an *X*."

"Yes, like this." She held her fingers crossed.

Xavier did the same with his hands. "I remember. Your nails are cool. I like purple."

"Me, too. Let's find that *X*."

So far, the woman hadn't even said hello to Troy or Gramps, but Angelica didn't care. She was impressed by Ms. Hayashi's educational focus and by how much learning was already taking place.

If only her son would remain healthy enough to benefit from it.

He'd woken up with a fever several mornings this week, which filled her with the starkest terror. Fear of relapse stalked every parent of a cancer kid. But, according to Dr. Lewis, all they could do was wait and see.

"Come see my new desk, Mr. Troy!"

Troy limped over, and Angelica followed, her arm around Gramps. Who didn't look as disgruntled as he had looked before. As Xavier showed with pride how the desk opened and closed, and Troy pretended amazement over the schoolbooks inside, Angelica snapped pictures and pondered.

She'd wanted Xavier to have a male role model. And maybe he already did.

Nine

Angelica was paying bills the next Saturday morning—thanking God for the job that allowed her to—when she heard a tapping on the door. Her heart did a double thump. Since she hadn't heard a car drive up, it had to be Troy.

They hadn't talked since their visit to Xavier's classroom and the closeness that had come out of that. She didn't know what to think of their up-and-down relationship. One minute he was mad at her about Buck, and then the next day he was acting like the sweetest father Xavier could possibly have, making her fall hard for him.

"Hey." Outlined in the early morning sunlight, his well-worn jeans and faded T-shirt made him look as young as when they'd been engaged. But now his shoulders bulged with the muscles of someone who ran a farm and lifted heavy animals and equipment. Running her hands up those arms, over his shoulders, as she'd done back then…it would feel totally different now.

"Hey yourself." When her words came out low, husky, she looked away and cleared her throat. "What's up? Everything okay at the kennels?"

He blinked. "The kennels are fine, but I wondered if you could help me with Bull." He nodded downward, and for the first time she realized that the bulldog was sitting patiently beside him, his wrinkly face framed by his recovery collar.

"Hey, big guy!" Feeling strangely warm, she knelt down to pet Bull, and he obligingly pushed up into a crooked standing position and wagged his stub of a tail.

"Is he okay?" She looked up at Troy. Man, was he handsome!

"He's doing pretty well. I can't tell for sure until the stitches are out, and it's time to do that. Then we'll see how he gets around."

He was saying it all without taking his eyes off her, and the intensity in his gaze seemed to be about more than the dog.

She looked down, focusing on Bull, feeling confused. Between her own feelings and the way Troy was looking at her, she was starting to feel as though they had an actual relationship.

Except they didn't. It was all about business and Xavier. Because if Troy knew the truth about her and her past and why she'd left, he'd never have anything to do with her. And what kind of relationship could you build on secrets and shame?

Back to business. "I need to get Xavier up and give him some breakfast," she said. "When were you thinking?"

He shrugged. "Whenever."

Something about the way he said it made her think of him rattling around his big house. Weekends could be so lonely when you were single. She knew it well, but at least she'd always had Xavier. "Would you...would you want to have breakfast with us first? I can make us something."

His face lit up. "Sure would. I'm strictly a cold cereal guy when I'm trusting my own cooking, but I do like breakfast food."

"Pancakes are my specialty." She didn't add that there'd been many nights when pancakes were all they could afford for dinner. "You go wake up Xavier. He'll love the surprise of it."

"Even better, how about if Bull and I wake him up together? We could probably even take the stitches out right here, if you don't mind my using your front porch as an exam room."

"Perfect." They smiled at each other as the sunlight came in the windows, their gazes connecting just a little too long. And then Angelica spun away and walked toward the kitchen, weak-kneed, her smile widening to where it almost hurt.

Half an hour later, she looked around the kitchen table and joy rose in her. Xavier was just starting to sprout a few patches of hair and his grin stretched wide. Troy sniffed appreciatively at the steaming platter of pancakes. Beneath the table, Bull sighed and flopped onto his side.

"Let's pray," she suggested, and they all took hands while Xavier recited a short blessing. Then she dished up pancakes and warm syrup to all of them.

"Delicious," Troy said around a mouthful.

"Mom's a good cook."

He swallowed. "Obviously." Then, a few bites later: "I'm impressed that you sit down at the table for meals and start them with prayer."

Angelica chuckled. "I could let you go on thinking we do that at every meal, but the truth is, there are plenty of nights when we eat off the coffee table and watch *Fresh Prince* reruns."

"Yeah, that's fun!" Xavier shoved another bite into his mouth.

"And we don't always remember to pray, either. I'm not a perfect mom *or* a perfect Christian."

Troy put a hand over hers. "Perfectly imperfect."

Yeah, if only you knew.

Later, Troy went and got his exam bag and then called Bull out to the porch, putting his crutches aside and lifting the dog down the hard-to-maneuver step. In every painstaking move, she saw his care for the old bulldog.

She got Xavier involved in a new video game, then went outside and petted Bull while Troy gathered his materials for removing stitches. "Hey, buddy, you gonna get your fancy collar off, huh?"

As if answering her, Bull pawed at the recovery collar that formed a huge bell around his neck.

"I'm going to try him without it," Troy said. "It's been driving him crazy, and he can't get around that well with it on. Depends on whether he'll leave the leg alone."

He put his hand on the dog and turned to her. "Angelica, I have to apologize."

She tipped her head to the side. "For what?"

"For going off on you that day. You were right. This guy wouldn't have survived without my having Buck to help me. I owe you."

She lifted an eyebrow. "You *were* quick to judge."

"I know. And I'm sorry. I'm kind of a Neanderthal

where you're concerned." He looked at her with a possessive intensity that flooded her with warmth.

Troy had grown, for sure. He could see when he was wrong and apologize. And he definitely had a softer heart these days. It looked as if he was blinking back tears when he gazed down at his old dog.

She didn't dare focus on what else his words evoked in her.

Troy removed Bull's stitches with skilled hands while she held the dog's head still and murmured soothing words. But as Troy examined the dog's leg more carefully, moving it back and forth, he frowned. "The range of movement isn't good," he said. "This is what my buddy the specialist warned me about. Once he starts to walk on it, I'm worried what will happen."

"Is there anything we can do?"

"Not right now," he said, still moving Bull's leg, intensely focused. "We'll have to watch him for a few more days, see how he does when he's free to move around."

After the stitches were removed, Angelica insisted on carrying Bull back to Troy's house. She'd noticed how badly Troy was limping, and it wouldn't do for him to ditch his crutches and carry Bull himself.

As she knelt beside Bull's crate, helping the dog settle in and petting him, Troy came up behind her and put a hand on her shoulder. After an initial flinch, she relaxed into his touch. Which felt amazing.

"So you were right about getting Buck's help and I was wrong," he said. "But I'm right about something else. Will you listen to me?"

She kept petting Bull, superaware of Troy's hand on her shoulder. "Okay."

"I want to take Xavier to a new doctor for his physical tomorrow."

She let go of Bull and scooted around to look at Troy. "What?"

"I found a new doctor for Xavier," he repeated. "We scored big-time. Great cancer doctor, hard to get, but he's an old friend of mine from college so I called in a favor. He's at the Cleveland Clinic, just about an hour and fifteen minutes away."

Before she could analyze her own response, it was out of her mouth. "No."

"What?" He looked startled.

"He likes the doctor we've started seeing here. I'd rather go to him. Anyway, it's just a simple physical for school and sports." She stood. "And I have to get back to Xavier."

He grabbed his crutches and held the door for her. "I'll walk with you if you'll listen."

"I listened. And then I said no." She started walking back toward the bunkhouse.

He followed. "Angelica, this is a really good doctor. Someone who specializes in leukemia."

"No."

"Wait." He turned toward her, leaning on his crutches, and looked hard into her eyes. "Why not? Why really?"

She looked away from his intensity. Why didn't she want a great new cancer doctor for Xavier? She took in a deep breath and started walking again. "Because I'm scared."

He fell into step beside her. "Of what? It can only be good for Xavier."

She stared at the hard dirt beneath their feet. "What if this doesn't work out?"

"What are you talking about?"

She glanced over at him. The morning they'd spent together, the delight of Xavier's happiness, of Troy's appreciation for her cooking, all of it made this so hard to say. "Look, I know the chances of us—you and me, this so-called engagement—making it are fifty-fifty at best. So what if we don't? What if you decide you don't want to go through with the marriage, or even if we do go through with it, that you don't want to stay? What are Xavier and I supposed to do then?"

He stared at her and then, slowly, shook his head. "You don't trust me, do you?"

"It's not you necessarily." She shrugged. "But why would you stick with us? What's in it for you? People don't just do things out of the goodness of their hearts."

They'd reached the bunkhouse porch, and he waited while she climbed the steps, then hopped up behind her. "What world have you been living in? Around here, people do things to help others all the time."

"Sure, give them a ride or watch their dog when they go on vacation. But marry someone? Stand by a kid with serious health issues? That's way, way beyond the call of duty, Troy. I appreciate your willingness, and for Xavier's sake, I have to give it a try. But—"

He tugged her down onto the porch swing and then sat next to her, held out a hand to touch her chin, ran his thumb ever so lightly over her lips. "Really? It's just for Xavier's sake?"

She stared at him, willing herself to stay still and explore the mix of feelings that his touch evoked. But she couldn't handle it. She scooted away and stood, and at a safe distance, pacing, she switched back to a safer topic. "Xavier hates changing doctors. If our relationship doesn't work, I certainly can't afford a fancy specialist. So that's why I'd rather just stick with the doctor we've been going to since we moved here."

"So you'd rather go with safe and mediocre."

"Dr. Lewis comes highly recommended," she protested.

"By whom?"

"Gramps and his friends." At his expression, she flared up. "I know you don't like Gramps, but he's been in the area forever, and all of his friends have medical issues, as does he. They know doctors."

"Geriatric doctors, not pediatricians. Look, this is a great opportunity. He'll get the athletic physical times ten. We're really blessed to see this guy, Ange."

Ange. It was what he'd called her when they were engaged, and hearing it thrust her back to that time. His excitement did, too.

Back then, she would have joined in readily, would have shared his optimism; she'd have been eager to try something new and take a risk.

But now, given her life experiences since that time, her stomach clenched. "I think Dr. Lewis will be just fine."

"Not really." He was getting serious now, leaning in, crossing his arms. "I asked around about Dr. Lewis. He's been in practice forty years. He isn't likely to be up on the latest research."

Angelica's spine stiffened and she felt her face getting hot. "I researched all the CHIP-eligible doctors within fifty miles. He's by far the best of those."

"Of those." His tone had gone gentle. "I'm not questioning that you did the best you could—"

"He seems really experienced. And Xavier liked him when we went when we first arrived in town."

He sighed. "Look, I just don't understand why you're not excited about this. It's a chance for your son to have the very best care around. Don't you want that?"

"Of course I do," she said, forcing herself not to strangle the guy. "But listen, would you? It's hard for Xavier to handle a new doctor. He's suffered through a lot of them. I don't want to make a change when it might not be permanent."

He leaned over and clamped a hand on her forearm. "I'm not going to fall through. I'm here for you!"

She stared at him, meeting his eyes, trying to read them. But something about his expression took her breath away and she pulled free and turned to look out over the fields, biting her lip.

God, what do I do?

She wanted to trust Troy. She wanted to trust God, and hadn't she been praying for better medical treatment? Hadn't she had her own issues with Dr. Lewis's wait-and-see attitude?

Xavier banged out the front door, sporting a T-shirt Angelica hadn't seen before, and she pulled him toward her, hands on shoulders, to read it.

Rescue River Midget Soccer.

"Where'd you get this, buddy?"

He smiled winningly. "Becka gave it to me. It's her old one. But she said I can get a new one as soon as I'm 'ficial on the team."

Angelica's heart gave a little thump as she put her

arms around him, noticing he was warm and sweaty. He must have been running around inside.

He wanted this so badly, and she did, too. But she worried about whether it was the right thing to do.

Here Troy was offering her an opportunity to get the best medical opinion, even on something so minor as whether a six-year-old could play soccer. Shouldn't she be grateful, and thanking God, rather than trying to escape their good fortune?

Even if it poked at her pride?

She took a deep breath. "Guess what! Mr. Troy found us a new doctor for you, a really good one. We're going to get you a super soccer checkup, to make sure you're ready to do your best."

The next day at the clinic, watching his friend and expert cancer doctor, Ravi Verma, examine Xavier's records and latest test results, Troy heaved a sigh of relief.

He had to admire the way Angelica was handling this. He knew he'd gone beyond the boundaries when he pulled strings to make the appointment, but he just couldn't stand to think that they were making do with a small-town doctor when the best medical care in the world was just another hour's drive away.

Obviously Angelica hadn't loved his approach, but she wasn't taking it out on Xavier. She'd pep-talked him through today's blood tests and played what seemed like a million games of tic-tac-toe as a distraction. Now she had an arm around her son as he leaned against her side.

She was a great mom. She was also gorgeous, her hair curlier than she usually wore it and tumbling over her shoulders, her sleeveless dress revealing shapely bronzed arms and legs.

Troy swallowed and shifted in his plastic chair. Man, this consultation room was small. And warm.

The doctor cleared his throat and turned to them. "There's so much that looks good on his chart and in the testing," he said, "but I'm afraid his blasts are up just a little."

"No!" Angelica's hand flew to her mouth, her eyes suddenly wide and desperate.

Troy pounded his fist on his knee. Just when things had been going so well. "What does that mean, Ravi?"

His friend held up a hand. "Maybe nothing, and I can see why my colleague Dr. Lewis wanted to wait—"

"He didn't even tell us about it!" Angelica sounded anguished.

"And that's common. The impulse not to alarm the patient about what might be a normal fluctuation."

"Might be...or might be something else?" Angelica's throat was working, and he saw her taking breath after breath, obviously trying to calm herself down. She stroked Xavier's back with one hand; her other hand gripped the chair arm with white knuckles. "What can we do about it?"

Ravi nodded. "Let's talk about possibilities. The first, of course, is to wait and see."

"Let's do that." Xavier buried his head in Angelica's skirt. He sounded miserable.

"Other options?" Troy heard the brusqueness in his own voice, but he couldn't seem to control his tone. Hadn't had the practice Angelica had.

"There is an experimental treatment for this kind of...probable relapse."

Angelica's shoulders slumped. "Probable relapse?"

Ravi's dark eyes flashed sympathy. "I'm afraid so. You see, his numbers have crept up again since his last test. Not much at all, so not necessarily significant, but from what I have seen in these cases..." He reached out and put a hand on Angelica's. "I think it might be best to treat it aggressively."

"Treat it how?" Angelica's voice was hoarse, and Troy could hear the tears right at the edge of it.

Xavier looked up at his mother. "Mom?"

"We'll figure it out, buddy." She smiled down reassuringly and stroked his hair with one hand. The other dug into the chair's upholstery so hard it looked as if she was about to rip it.

"The traditional protocol is radiation and chemo, quite intensive and quite...challenging on the patient."

Angelica pressed her lips together.

Troy leaned forward. "Is there another option?"

"Yes, the experimental treatment I mentioned. Cell therapy. Using the body's own immunological cells. Now, most of the participants in the trial are adults, but there is one other child, a girl of about twelve. It's possible I could talk my colleagues into allowing Xavier in, if he passes the tests."

"Isn't that going to be really expensive? We don't have good insurance."

"In an experimental trial, the patient's medications are fully funded. However..." He looked up at Angelica. "There may be some expenses not covered by our grant or your insurance."

"That's not a problem," Troy said. "Is this new treatment what you'd recommend?" he pressed.

Ravi looked at Xavier's bent head with eyes full of

compassion. "If he were one of my own, this is the approach I would take."

Angelica opened her mouth and then closed it again. Shut her eyes briefly, and then turned back to Ravi. "How difficult is the treatment?"

"That is the wonder of it. It is noninvasive and not harmful as far as cancer treatments go because it uses the body's own cells. Of course, there are the usual tests and injections..." He reached down and patted Xavier's shoulder. "Nothing about cancer is easy for a child."

"I don't want a treatment." Xavier's head lifted to look at his mother. "I want to play soccer."

She lifted him into her lap and clasped him close. "I know, buddy. I want that, too."

Troy leaned toward the pair, not sure whether to touch Xavier or not. In the mysteries of sick children, he was a rank beginner. He had to bow to the expertise of Ravi, and especially of Angelica. At most, he was a mentor and a friend to the boy. "Buddy, this could make you well."

"It never did before." Xavier's expression held more discouragement than looked right on that sweet face. "Mom, I don't want a treatment."

"We'll talk about it and think about it. And pray about it." She straightened her back and squared her shoulders and Troy watched, impressed, as she took control of the situation. "Listen, I think Mr. Troy is feeling worried. And I also think I have a bag of chocolate candy in my purse. Could you get him some?"

Xavier sniffed and nodded and reached for her purse. She let him dig in it, watching him with the most intense expression of love and fierce care that he'd ever seen on a woman's face.

"Here it is!"

"Give Mr. Troy the first choice." She took back the purse and reached in herself, pulling out a creased sheet of paper. While Xavier fumbled through the bag of candy, patently ignoring her instruction to let Troy go first, Angelica skimmed down a list and started pelting Ravi with questions.

Troy imagined he could see the sweat and tears of their history with cancer on that well-worn paper. He didn't pray often enough, but now he thanked God for allowing him the honor of helping Angelica cope.

He focused on Xavier for a few minutes while the other two talked, bandying about terms and phrases he'd not heard even with his vet school history. Finally Angelica folded the paper back up, glanced over at Xavier and frowned. "Is there time for me to think about this?"

"Of course," Ravi said, "but it's best to get started early, before his numbers go up too high. If there is any chance you'll be interested in participating, we should start the paperwork now."

She closed her eyes for a moment, drew in a slow breath and then opened her eyes and nodded. "Let's do it."

During the little flurry of activity that followed—forms to fill out, a visit from the office manager to pin down times and details, some protests from Xavier—Troy kept noticing Angelica's strength, her fierceness and her decision-making power. She'd grown so much since he knew her last, and while he'd been aware of it before, he was even more so now. She had his total respect.

And she deserved a break. When Xavier's protests turned into crying and the office manager started talking about initial tests that would be costly but not covered by the trial's grant, he nudged the boy toward her. "Why don't you two go out and get some fresh air, maybe hit the park across the street? I need to talk to my friend here for a minute. And I'll settle up some of the financial details with the office manager and then come on out."

"Can we go, Mom?"

She pressed her lips together and then nodded. "I'll be in touch," she said to Ravi. She mouthed a thank-you to Troy, and then the two of them left.

Troy stood, too, knowing his friend's time was valuable, but Ravi gestured him back into the chair. "You cannot escape without telling me about her."

"She's...pretty special. And so is the boy."

"I see that." Ravi nodded. "They've not had an easy road, I can tell from the charts. Lots of free clinics, lots of delays."

"Has it affected the outcome?"

"No, I think not. It has just been hard on both of them."

"What are his chances of getting into the trial?"

"Honestly? Fifty-fifty. We have to look more deeply into all his previous treatments and his other options. But I will do my best."

"Thank you." And Troy made a promise to himself: he *would* make sure they got in. And, God willing, the treatment would make Xavier well.

That night, Angelica was helping Lou Ann clean up the kitchen—they'd all eaten together again—while Troy and Xavier sat in the den building something complicated out of LEGO blocks. The sound of the two of them laughing was a pleasant, quiet backdrop to the clattering of pots and dishes, and Angelica didn't know she was sighing until Lou Ann called her on it. "What's going on in your mind, kiddo?"

Angelica smiled at the older woman. "I'm just... wishing this could go on forever."

"Which part? With Xavier, or with Troy?"

"Both."

"Xavier we pray about. Is there a problem with your engagement we should take to the Lord, too?"

Lou Ann didn't know that the engagement was for show, and normally Angelica felt that was right and would have continued the deception. But something in the older woman's sharp eyes told her that she'd guessed the truth. "Yes," she said slowly, "we could use some prayer. I just don't know that it will work, not really."

"Why's that?" Lou Ann carried the roaster over to the sink and started scrubbing it.

Angelica wiped at the counter aimlessly. "Well, because I... I don't know, I just don't believe it can happen."

Lou Ann shook her head. "Why the two of you can't see what's under your noses, that you love each other, I don't know."

"We don't love each other!" And then Angelica's hand flew to her mouth. If the fact that their engagement was a sham hadn't been out before, it was now.

"I think you have more feelings than you realize," the older woman said. "So what's holding you back, really?"

Angelica leaned against the counter, abandoning all pretense of working. "I... I just don't believe he'll love me. Don't believe I'm able to keep him."

"The man's crazy about you!"

Lou Ann's automatic, obviously sincere response made Angelica's breath catch. "You really think so?"

"Yep."

Lou Ann's certainty felt amazing, but Angelica couldn't let herself trust it. "That's because he doesn't know much about me. If he did, he'd feel differently."

Lou Ann pointed at her with the scrubber stick. "What did you do that's so all-fired awful?"

Angelica shook her head. "Nothing. I... I can't talk about it."

"If it's about Xavier's daddy," Lou Ann said with her usual shrewdness, "I think you should let it go. The past is the past."

"Not when you have a child by it," Angelica murmured, starting to scrub again.

"Look," Lou Ann said, "all of us have sinned. Every single one. If you'd look at the inside of my soul, it would be as stained and dirty as this greasy old pan."

"You? No way!"

"You'd be surprised," Lou Ann said. "For one thing, I wasn't always as old and wrinkled as I am now. I had my days of running around. Ask your grandfather sometime."

Angelica laughed. "Gramps already told me you were the belle of the high school ball. In fact, I think he has a crush on you still."

Lou Ann's cheeks turned a pretty shade of pink. "I doubt that. But the point is, we've all done things we're not proud of. I ran around with too many boys in my younger days, and I've also done my share of gossiping and coveting. Not to mention that I don't love my neighbor as well as I should."

When Angelica tried to protest, Lou Ann held out a hand. "Point is, we're all like that. We've all sinned and fallen short, that one—" she pointed the scrubber toward the den where Troy was "—included. So don't go thinking your sins, whatever they are, make you worse than anyone else. Without Jesus, we'd all be on the same sinking ship."

"I guess," Angelica said doubtfully. She knew that was doctrine, and in her head she pretty much believed it. In her heart, though, where it mattered, she felt worse than other people.

"I think you need to sit down and talk to the man," Lou Ann said. "The two of you spend all your time with Xavier, and you don't ever get any couple time to grow your relationship and get to know each other."

"But our connection...well, you've pretty much guessed that it's mainly about Xavier."

"But it shouldn't be," Lou Ann said firmly. "You two should build your own bond first, like putting on your oxygen mask in a plane before you help your kid. If Mom and Dad aren't happy, the kids won't be happy. Xavier needs to see that you two have a stable, committed relationship. That's what will help him."

Angelica sighed. "You're probably right." She'd been thinking about it a lot: the fact that their pretend engagement had grown out of their control and was now of a size to need some tending. Half the town knew they were engaged, and more important, her own feelings had grown beyond pretend to real. She didn't want to think about ending the engagement, partly because of what it would do to Xavier, but also because of what it would do to her.

"You need to get to know him as he is now, not just

the way he was seven years ago. Things have changed. He writes articles in veterinary journals now, and other vets come to consult with him. He's way too busy. And on the home front, his dad's not getting any younger, and Troy needs to make his peace with him. You're the one with the big, immediate issues in the form of that special boy in there, but Troy has his own problems to solve. You need to figure out if you can help him do that."

"Sit down. Take a break." Angelica nudged Lou Ann aside and reached for the scrubber, attacking the worst of the pots and pans. "I've been selfish, haven't I?"

"Not at all. You're preoccupied, and that makes sense. But promise you'll talk to him soon. Maybe even tell him some of that history that's got you feeling so down on yourself."

Angelica sighed. The thought of bringing up their engagement, of having that difficult talk, seemed overwhelming, but she could tell Lou Ann wasn't going to let it go. "All right," she said. "I'll try."

Ten

Angelica strolled toward the field beside the barn, more relaxed than she had felt in a week.

She'd tried to work up the courage to talk to Troy about their relationship, even to tell him the truth about why she'd left him, but it hadn't happened. Finally this morning, she'd turned the whole thing over to God. If He wanted her to talk to Troy, He had to open up the opportunity, because she couldn't do it on her own strength.

Red-winged blackbirds trilled and wild roses added a sweet note to the usual farm fragrances of hay and the neighboring cattle. Beyond the barn, she could hear boys shouting and dogs barking as Troy's Kennel Kids tossed balls for the dogs.

Today—praise the Lord—she'd gotten word that Xavier was accepted into the clinical trial. He'd go for his treatment in a couple of days, and Dr. Ravi was reassuring about everything. The treatment wouldn't be difficult, and he was optimistic that the trial would work, told stories of patients' numbers improving and "positive preliminary findings."

Impulsively she lifted her hands to the sky, feeling the breeze kiss her arms. *Lord, thank You, thank You.*

She rounded the corner of the barn and froze.

One of the Kennel Kids, older and at least twice Xavier's size, loomed over him, fist raised threateningly.

"Hey!" Poised to run to her son, she felt a restraining hand on her shoulder.

"Let him try to handle it himself," Troy said.

She yanked away. "He can't fight that kid! Look at the size difference!"

"Just watch." Troy's voice was still mild, but there was a note of command that halted her. "Wendell always pulls his punches, so don't worry."

Clenching her fist, still primed to run to her son, she paused.

Xavier smiled up guilelessly at the other boy. "Hey, I'm sorry my ball hit you. My pitching stinks."

"Leave him alone, Wendell. He's just a kid." One of the other boys put an arm around Xavier.

The bigger boy drew in a breath, and then his fisted hand dropped. "Yeah, well, don't hit me again. Or else."

One of the puppies jumped into the mix, and as if no threat had ever existed, the group broke into a kaleidoscope of colorful balls and yipping puppies and running boys.

As her adrenaline slowly dissipated, Angelica leaned against the wall of the barn and sank down to a sitting position.

"I want to go give Wendell some positive feedback. He's getting better about controlling his anger."

"I'm still working on that myself," she snapped at him, but halfheartedly. She knew it was good for Xavier to socialize with other kids, but these rough-around-the-edges boys scared her.

She watched Troy walk over and speak briefly with Wendell and then clap him on the back. Xavier, completely unmoved by his near brush with getting the tar kicked out of him, was rolling with one of the puppies.

Taking deep breaths, she willed herself to calm down. She hated the way Troy was high-handed with her, but after all, he was right, wasn't he? Xavier had handled the situation himself just fine and was fitting in nicely with the other boys. If she'd run in to save him, that might not be the case.

A few minutes later, Troy came back and sat down beside her. "You mad at me?"

"Yes and no." She watched as one of the other boys threw a ball back and forth with Xavier. The other boy was older; in fact, most of the boys were, but Xavier was holding his own. It reminded her of what a good athlete he could be.

If he got the chance.

And that was where Troy had been incredibly, incredibly helpful. "Listen," she said. "I don't necessarily like being told how to mother my kid, but there are times when you're right." She smiled up at him. "Dr. Ravi called today."

Troy's head jerked toward her, his face lighting up. "And?"

"And Xavier gets into the trial."

"That's fantastic!" He threw his arms around her.

No, no, no. She couldn't breathe, couldn't survive, couldn't stand it. She pushed hard at his brawny chest.

"Hey, fine, sorry!" He dropped his arms immediately and scooted backward, his eyebrows shooting up.

She gulped air. "It's fine. I'm sorry. I just…" Blinking rapidly, she came back from remembered darkness—something she'd had years of practice at doing—and offered Troy a shaky smile. "I'm so grateful that you made us see Dr. Ravi. He's wonderful. And I like that he's going forward aggressively with the treatment. I really, really want Xavier to have it. This could make all the difference."

"I'm glad." Troy continued to look a little puzzled. "But you're still mad at me?"

Mad wasn't the word. She knew she should launch into the talk she'd promised Lou Ann she'd have with Troy. She looked out across the fields and breathed deeply of the farm-scented air.

And changed the subject. "Look, I know I'm overprotective. It kind of comes with the territory of parenting a seriously ill child."

"Of course."

"And I was worried about that bigger kid hitting him. Xavier tends to bruise and bleed easily, or he did when he was in active disease. I try to make sure he doesn't fall a lot and all that."

"Should I have stopped them? I struggle with how much to intervene and how much to let them work it out themselves so they can build better social skills." He studied his hands, clasped between his upraised knees. "Thing is, a lot of these boys are out on their own much of the time. I spend such a small fraction of their lives with them. So I feel like they need to practice solving some of their conflicts themselves. We usually talk it over in group, after they've gotten some of their energy out." He shrugged. "I'm just a vet with a heart to help kids. I don't know sometimes if I'm doing it right."

"You do a great job," she said warmly.

"Thanks." And then he was looking at her again, and she spoke nervously to make the moment pass. "Parenting is like that for me. I never know if there's something I should do differently. Xavier's going to go to school, and he'll have to learn to handle the playground himself. I won't be there to intervene for him, so I guess that's something I'd better get used to."

"We can help each other out. We're a good partnership." He reached out and squeezed her shoulder.

She cringed away instinctively. And when she saw the hurt look on his face, she felt awful.

She opened her mouth to apologize and then closed it again. What was she going to say? How could she explain?

Nervously she pulled a bandanna out of her pocket and wiped off her suddenly sweaty neck and face. The thing was, she didn't know if she was going to get over this, ever. Being touched was hard for her. Oh, she could hug Xavier, did that all the time, and his childish affection was a balm to her spirit. When she stayed with Aunt Dot right after being assaulted, and indeed for years afterward until that wonderful woman had died a year ago, they'd shared hugs galore. And her girlfriends were always hugging on her and plenty of nurses had let her weep in their arms.

Female nurses.

It was only when a man hugged her that she freaked out.

Troy was regarding her seriously. His blue eyes showed hurt and some anger, too. "Look, I'm sorry," he said. "I guess I didn't realize how much you... Well, how much you don't want me near you. That's a problem. How are we…" He broke off, got awkwardly to his feet, favoring his hurt leg. "I better go check on the boys."

He limped off and she wanted to call him back, to apologize, to say she'd work on it, really she would. But the thing was, it had been seven years and she still wasn't over the assault.

She hadn't been motivated to get over it before because she hadn't dated anyone and she hadn't wanted a man around.

But Troy was doing so much for them. Moreover, when he touched her, she felt something uncurl within her, and that as much as anything made her shy away.

There'd been plenty of chemistry between them when they were engaged. Now, though, everything felt different.

She stared absently out at cornfields with tassels almost head high. Above her, the sky shone deep blue with puffy clouds.

She'd seen a counselor right along with her obstetrician, at her aunt's insistence, and the woman had been wonderful and had helped her a lot. But Angelica hadn't wanted to date. Hadn't wanted to open herself up to love—and the accompanying dangers and risks—again.

Still didn't, if the truth be told. She'd rather stay in her safe, comfortable little shell. But Troy was so good with Xavier, and Xavier needed a dad. Holding back like this was selfish of her. She had to fix this.

If she wanted to love again, a part of loving was hugging and kissing and all the intimate physicality created by the same God who'd made the corn and the sky and the sweaty little boys and jumping, bounding dogs in front of her.

She let her head drop into her hands. *Lord, I can't do this myself. Please help me heal. Help me learn to love.*

Slowly, as she listened for God's voice, as she breathed in the wonders of His creation, she felt herself relaxing. She didn't know if it would work for her. She certainly didn't want to tell Troy the reasons for her pain, because she knew he would judge her.

But maybe God would give her a pass on that. Maybe He'd let her have this relationship and let Xavier have a dad—a dad who could do amazing things with his connections, who could actually help Xavier heal—and she wouldn't have to tell Troy the sordid side of her past. Wouldn't have to tell him about her own culpability in what had happened to her.

Because no matter what her therapist had said, Angelica knew the truth. She'd gotten drunk and silly and flirty, and she'd been mad at Troy for not coming out to celebrate her birthday, and she'd been flattered when a handsome older man wanted to walk her home.

It wasn't pretty and it wasn't nice, and she'd regret it for the rest of her life.

God in His amazing excellence had turned it to good. God had brought her Xavier and he was the purpose of her life now, the thing that gave it meaning. And she, flawed as she was, loved him as fiercely as any mother could love any child, despite his bad beginning. God had done that much for them, overlooking her sins.

She could only hope and pray that He'd heal her enough to let her go forward with the marriage to Troy.

Troy strode away from Angelica and out toward the driveway. He just needed a minute to himself.

Apparently, though, he wasn't going to get it, because heading toward him was a police cruiser. Like any red-blooded American male who'd occasionally driven faster than he should, he tensed...until he realized that Dion was at the wheel.

Even seeing his friend didn't make him smile as he walked up to the driver's-side window.

"What's wrong with you, old man?"

Troy shrugged. He'd talk to Dion about almost anything, they were those kinds of friends, but there was a time and a place. "What brings you out my way? You're working nights. You should be home catching Zs."

"Yeah, had an issue." Dion jerked his head toward the backseat and lowered the rear window.

There, on a towel, was the saddest-looking white pit bull Troy had ever seen. Ears down, cringing against the backseat, quivering, skin and bones.

Troy's heart twisted.

"Found her chained to an abandoned house. You got your work cut out for you with this one."

Troy opened the rear car door and wasn't really surprised when the dog shrank against the back of the seat and bared her teeth. "Problem is, I've got the Kennel Kids here today."

"I know you do. I'm gonna help out for a bit while you take care of this little mama. Those boys could use an hour with a cop who's not out to arrest them."

Troy focused in on the word *mama*. "She's pregnant?"

"Oh yeah. It rains, it pours."

Troy drew in a breath and let it out in a sigh. "Okay. Lemme run get a crate and—"

Shaking his head, Dion turned off the engine and got out. "Can't crate her, man. She freaks."

"How'd you get her into the cruiser?" As always, when there was a hurting animal nearby, Troy went into superfocus, forgetting everything else, trying to figure out how to help it. He braced his hands on the car roof and leaned in, studying the dog.

Dion gave his trademark low chuckle. "One of the guys had a sandwich left over from lunch."

"Gotcha. Be right back."

Minutes later, with the help of a piece of chicken, the dog was out of the cruiser and in one of the runs right beside where the boys were playing.

"See what you can do, my man," Dion said, then strode over to the group of boys in the field, who went silent at the sight of the tall, dark-skinned man in full uniform.

Troy watched for a minute. Angelica was with them, and he saw her greet Dion. The two of them spoke, and then Dion squatted down to pet one of the dogs.

A couple of the boys came closer. Dion greeted them and apparently made some kind of a joke, because the boys laughed.

So that would be okay. Dion was great with kids; in fact, some of these boys probably knew him pretty well already, though not for as innocent a reason as his visit here today.

Using treats, Troy tried to get the dog to relax and come to him, but she cowered as far away as possible. From this distance, he could see her distended belly and swollen teats. She'd probably give birth in a week or two.

Xavier, for one, would be excited. He loved the puppies best, and though he was having a blast with the ones already here, watching them grow and playing with them, new babies would thrill him beyond belief. For that reason, Troy was glad they had a mama dog, though he had to wonder about this one's story.

Right on schedule, his sister pulled into the driveway. She helped with the Kennel Kids whenever she could.

"C'mere, Lily." On an impulse he named the dog for her white coat, even if she was more gray than white at the moment. He threw a treat to within a few inches of her nose, and she made several moves toward it, then jerked back. Finally she dove far enough forward to grab the dog biscuit and retreat, and he praised her lavishly. Still when he moved toward her, she backed away, growling.

He settled in, back against the fence, watching the boys, Dion, Angelica and his sister.

Dion said something to Angelica and she laughed, and Troy felt a burning in his chest. Would Angelica go for his best friend?

A year older than Troy, Dion had been a little more suave with the ladies when they played football together in high school. But Troy had never felt jealous of the man...until this moment.

He tried to stifle the feeling, but that just made his heart rate go up, made him madder. Yeah, he was possessive, especially where Angelica was concerned. Nothing to be proud of, but the truth.

He watched Angelica and noticed that, while she was friendly to Dion, she kept a good few feet between them. Not like his sister, who often put an affectionate hand on Dion's arm or fist-bumped him after a joke.

Relief trickled in. Looked as though Angelica wasn't attracted.

He tossed another treat to the dog, and this time she

dove for it and ate it immediately. He scooted a couple of feet closer, still staying low so he didn't look big and threatening to her. She let out a low growl but didn't attack.

He tossed another treat halfway between them, and the dog considered a moment, then crept forward to grab it.

He reached out toward the dog with a piece of food in his hand. This was a risk, as he might get bitten, but he figured it wasn't likely. He had a sense about this one. She wanted help.

A moment later, his instinct was rewarded when she accepted food out of his hand.

He fed her several more pieces and then reached toward her. She backed away, a low growl vibrating in her chest.

Righteous anger rose in him. He'd like to strangle the person who'd mistreated this sweet dog. Maybe ruined her for a home with a family. Fear did awful things to an animal.

Or a person.

It hit him like a two-by-four to the brain.

The dog was reacting the way Angelica reacted.

It was pretty obvious why, in the dog's case: people had treated her badly, and she'd learned to be afraid.

So who'd been mean to Angelica? What had they done? And when?

He jumped up, moved toward the dog and she lunged at him, teeth bared. He backed away immediately. He should know better than to approach a scared dog when he was feeling this agitated; she could sense it.

Had Angelica been abused or attacked?

No, not possible. He spun around and marched over to the kennels, grabbed a water bowl for the dog, filled it.

He had no idea what had gone on in Angelica's life in the years they'd been apart. She could very well have gotten into a bad relationship. And given that she'd apparently been poor, she could have lived in bad areas where risks were high and safety wasn't guaranteed.

He needed to talk to his social-worker sister. He took the water bowl back to the new dog's run and set it down, keeping a good distance from her. Then he beckoned to Daisy.

She came right over. "Hey, bro, what's happening with Xavier and Angelica? Did you find out about the cancer trial?"

"Xavier got in. We're pretty happy."

Hands on hips, she studied him. "Then what's eating you?"

"You know me too well. And you understand women, and I don't."

She raised her eyebrows. "What's up?"

He looked out at the cornfields. "If a woman was... abused, say, or attacked...how would she react? Wouldn't she tell people what happened?"

Daisy cocked her head to one side. "Probably, but maybe not. Why?"

"Why wouldn't she tell?"

"Well..."

He could see her social work training kick in as she thought about it.

"Sometimes women are ashamed. Sometimes their attacker threatens them. Sometimes they're in denial, or they just want to bury it."

He nodded. "Okay, it makes sense that they might

not want to report it, to have it be common knowledge. But if they have close family or friends who would help them…"

"Are you talking about a rape?"

The word slammed into him. And the doors of his mind slammed shut. That couldn't have happened. Not to Angelica. *Please, God, no.*

Daisy crossed her arms over her chest and narrowed her eyes at him. "Whatever you're thinking, you need to talk to that person about it. Not to me."

He nodded, because he couldn't speak.

"So go do it."

He drew in a breath, sighed it out. "Cone of silence?"

"Of course."

Slowly he walked over to where Dion leaned against a fence, talking to a rapt group of boys. Angelica knelt a short distance away beside the pen they'd made to keep Bull safe from too much activity but still included in the fun. She was rubbing the old dog's belly, praising him for how his leg was healing, telling him he'd feel better soon. She looked pensive and beautiful and she didn't hear him coming.

Deliberately he touched her shoulder, and just as he now expected, she jumped and frowned toward him.

He hated being right. "We have to talk," he said to her. "Soon."

Eleven

The next Saturday night, Angelica listened to the closing notes of the praise band and wished she felt the love the musicians had been singing about.

Sometime during the past month, coming to Saturday night services with Lou Ann, Troy and Xavier had become the highlight of her week. The focus on God's love, the sense of being part of a community of believers and the growing hope of a future here—all of it made church wonderful. But tonight, she'd been too jittery to enjoy it.

She felt Troy's gaze on her—again—and scooted toward the edge of the padded pew. "I've got to go get Xavier."

"No, that's okay." Lou Ann sidled past her and out of the pew. "I'll do it."

Oh. Rats.

Troy turned to greet the family next to them, and, hoping he hadn't heard her exchange with Lou Ann, she started edging out of the pew. Grabbing her purse, she stood and took a sideways step, then another.

Suddenly some kind of hook caught her wrist, and

...own to see the crook of a wooden cane
...her.

...spun back toward him. "Troy! What are you
...?"

"I knew this thing was good for something," he said,
holding up the cane he'd borrowed from Lou Ann and
offering her a repentant grin. Then he scanned the
room. "The place is emptying out. We can have some
privacy. Do you mind staying a minute?"

Yes, I mind! She bit her lip, shook her head and sank
back down onto the pew. It was probably better to stay
here in the sanctuary than to go off somewhere by themselves. Somewhere she might feel that strange sense in
her stomach again, that sense of...

Being attracted.

Yeah, that.

She hadn't felt it for years—in fact, she hadn't felt
it since she was engaged to Troy—and it was making
her crazy.

"We've got to talk about why you jump every time
I touch you."

"Don't open that can of worms, Troy," she said
quickly. Of all their possible topics of conversation,
that was the one she most wanted to avoid.

He cocked his head to one side, studying her face.
"Actually we've got to talk about a few things," he said
finally. "One of which is this marriage. People are asking more and more about it. We can't put them off forever with some vague engagement plans in the future."

Early-evening sunshine slanted through stained-
glass windows, and the breeze through the church's
open back door felt cool against Angelica's neck. "I

know. It's Xavier, too. He wants to know when the wedding will be."

"Is there going to be a wedding?" He watched her, his face impassive.

Her heart skipped a beat. "Do you want to back out?"

"Noooooo," he said. "But I'm seeing some implications I wasn't thinking about before." Deliberately he reached out and took her hand.

It felt as if every nerve, every sensation in her body was concentrated in her hand. Concentrated to notice how his hand was bigger, more calloused than hers. To notice the warmth and protection of being completely wrapped in him. Waves of what felt like electricity crackled through her veins.

He was watching her. It seemed he was always watching her. "You feel it?"

Heat rose to her cheeks as she nodded.

"So…we're going to have to figure out what to do with that."

Somehow even admitting she felt something for him—something like physical attraction—made her feel panicky and ashamed. She looked away from him, focusing on the polished light wooden pews, on the simple altar at the front of the church. Her hand still burned, enclosed by his larger one, and she pulled it away, hiding it in the folds of her dress.

"It's not wrong, you know. It's a mutual thing, a gift from God, and He blesses it in the context of marriage." Troy's voice, though quiet, was sure.

Angelica wanted that quiet certainty so much. She wanted Troy's leadership in this area. Wanted to feel okay about her body and wanted to find the beauty in physical intimacy sanctioned by God. It had been

she felt anything but sadness and regret
ysical side of life. Here, in God's house, she
hope. But did she dare? Was change possible
these years? Could God bless her that much?

Xavier and Lou Ann came hurrying in through the side front door of the sanctuary. *Whew, relief.*

"Hey, you two." Lou Ann reached them right behind Xavier and leaned on the pew in front of them. "Some of the kids and parents are walking over to the Meadows for ice cream. Is it okay if I take Xavier along?"

"Please, Mom?" Xavier chimed in.

Angelica grabbed her purse. "I can take him," she said to Lou Ann.

"That's okay. I could use a rocky road ice-cream cone myself." Lou Ann reached over and put a hand on her shoulder, effectively holding her in the pew. She leaned down and whispered, "Besides, you need to talk to him."

"Do I have to?"

"Yes, you have to!" Lou Ann patted her arm. "I'll be praying for you."

"Thanks a lot!" She bit her lip and watched Lou Ann guide Xavier off, trying to remember what was most important: God was with her, always, and God forgave her, and God would help her get through this whole thing.

She drew in a breath, and the peace she'd been seeking during the service came rushing in. *Pneuma.* Holy Spirit. God.

She turned back to Troy and he took her hand again, and immediately that uncurling inside started. That opening; that vulnerability. She tried to pull away a little, but he held on. Not too tight, not forcing her, but letting her know he wanted to keep touching her.

Angelica let him do it, her eyes closed tight. She didn't want to like his touch. Didn't want to need him. It would be so much easier and safer not to open up.

He tightened his grip on her hand, ever so slightly. "I want you to tell me why you pull away all the time."

"I'm not sure—"

"Hey, hey, the engaged couple!" Pastor Ricky came over and clapped Troy on the shoulder, leaned down to hug Angelica, overwhelming her. She shrank back, right into Troy. *Aack.*

"Have you two set a date yet? Are you wanting to get married here? You'd better reserve it now if you're planning to do it any time soon. We're a busy place."

"We were just talking about that," Troy said.

"Make an appointment with me to start some premarital counseling, too." He made a few more minutes of small talk and then turned to another pair of parishioners and walked away with them.

"He's right," Troy said. "We've got to decide."

"I know." But inside, turmoil reigned.

Xavier needed a dad in the worst way, and Troy was the perfect man for the job. The three of them were already close.

Xavier needed it, needed Troy, but she herself was terrified.

Lord, help me. Her heart rate accelerated to the pace of a hummingbird. She could barely breathe. She looked up at Troy, panicky.

"You can talk to me." He slid an arm along the back of the pew behind her, letting it rest ever so lightly around her shoulders. "What is it you need to tell me?"

She took deep, slow, breaths. The fact that she was shaking had to be obvious to Troy.

What part could she tell him? What part did she need to keep private? What part would come back to bite her?

Tell him the worst right away.

Like yanking off a Band-Aid. She moved to the edge of the pew, away from his arm, and pulled her hand from his. Clenching her fists, she turned her head toward him, looking right at his handsome face. "I was... I was raped."

"Raped? What? When?"

It was the first time she'd ever said that word, even to herself. Her vision seemed to blur around the edges, bringing her focus to just his mouth, his eyes. She had to grip the edge of the pew, waiting for the expression of disgust and horror to cross his face.

His mouth twisted.

There it was, the anger she'd expected. She looked away from his face and down at his hands. His enormous hands. They clenched into fists.

She shrank away. Was he going to hit her right here and now? Frantically she looked around for help.

"Tell me." He sounded as though he was gritting his teeth. But his voice was quiet, and when she looked at his hands, they'd relaxed a little. He wasn't moving any closer, either.

"Troy, I'm sorry... I was drinking. I should have been more careful."

"Man, I'd like to kill the jerk who did that to you. When did it happen?" His voice was still angry, and she couldn't blame him. At least it was a controlled anger, so she wasn't at immediate risk.

Even though it would destroy their relationship, she'd

started down this path and she had to keep going. *God, help me.* "It was…after my twenty-first birthday celebration. Remember I went out to that bar?" She heard the urgent sound in her voice. Couldn't seem to calm down.

His expression changed. "I remember that night. I had to work and couldn't go." He pounded a fist lightly against the pew. "I should have been there to take care of you."

"I was drinking."

He took her hand in his. "It's not your fault. Man, I wish I'd been there." He shook his head slowly back and forth, his eyes far away, as if he were reliving that time.

Not her fault? She looked away, bit her lip. That was what her therapist and her aunt had said, but she'd never really believed it. Could Troy?

"Look," he said, "as far as any physical connection between us is concerned, you can have all the time you need. I'll be patient. I understand."

Tears filled her eyes. Was it possible that, even knowing this, Troy could still want her?

"So…wait. That's when Xavier was conceived?"

She nodded, staring down at her lap, kneading her skirt between her hands. He was being kinder than she had any right to expect. She blinked and drew in shuddery breaths as tension released from her body.

Telling him the truth was something she'd barely considered at the time because she was terrified of what his reaction would be. She'd had some vague image of yelling and rage and judgment, and the notion of Troy, her beloved fiancé, doing that had pushed her right out of town. Better to leave than to face that pain.

He didn't seem to be blaming her. She could hardly

believe in it, couldn't imagine that his kindness would stay, but even the edge of it warmed her heart.

"Who did it, Angelica?" Troy's voice grew low, urgent. "Was it someone you knew? Someone we knew?"

And there it was, the part she didn't dare tell him.

"Did we know him?" Troy repeated.

Still looking down at her lap, she shook her head.

Did it count as a lie if she didn't say it out loud?

Troy looked at Angelica with his heart aching for all the pain she'd been through and his fists clenching with anger at the jerk who'd done this to her. He tried to ignore the tiny suspicion that she wasn't telling the whole truth.

His mother had constantly lied to his father. He didn't want to believe it of Angelica, but her body language, her voice, her facial expressions—all of it suggested she was keeping something from him. "We were engaged. You should have told me."

"I blamed myself," she said in a quiet voice. "And I knew how much my chastity meant to you."

Her words hit him like a physical blow. "You think that would be more important than taking care of you? I would've helped you."

"Out of obligation," she said, glancing up at him and then away. "But you wouldn't have liked it."

"Was I that kind of a jerk?" He didn't think so, but look how he was feeling right now. Compassion, sure, but with the slightest shred of doubt in his heart.

He grabbed the Bible from the rack in front of them and held it. For something to do with his hands, but also to remind himself to take the high road and think the best. "I can't believe this happened to you," he said, turning the Good Book over and over in his hands, thinking out loud. "It was a crime committed against you. It's not your fault, and you shouldn't blame yourself." He put the Bible down beside him. "And if you didn't report the crime then…" He searched her face, saw her shake her head, looking at her lap again. "If you didn't say anything already, you should now. The man should be brought to justice. I'll talk to Dion. He knows everything about the law."

"No!" She scooted away from him, an expression of horror on her face. "I don't want to dig into it again. And anyway, it's not…it's not necessary."

"We gotta get the guy! Don't you want justice?"

She shook her head. "No. I don't want anything to do with the police."

"Are you protecting someone?"

"I just don't want to get the police involved. For all kinds of reasons."

Why wouldn't she tell him who did it? Was she telling the truth, that she didn't know the person?

And if she was lying, then how much did she really care for him?

He looked at her face and was shocked by the disappointment he saw there. Immediately he felt awful. She needed support, she needed help. She needed a dad for Xavier, and speaking of that sweet kid…wow, he was the product of an assault. And she'd mothered him despite that, wonderfully.

Whatever mistakes she'd made in the past, he was going to provide what he could for her. He reached out to put his arm around her. Felt her stiffen, but remain still, letting him do it.

There was none of the tender promise of before,

though. There was more of a cringe. He reached out involuntarily to stroke her shiny hair.

She pulled away and stood. "I'm going to leave you to think about this. It's a lot to take in, I know."

"Angelica—"

"We'll talk later, okay?" Her lips twisted and she hurried off toward the back of the sanctuary.

Leaving him to his dark thoughts and guilt and anger, a mixture that didn't seem to belong in this holy place.

Twelve

"I'm terrified," Angelica admitted to Lou Ann as they dug carrots from the garden. "They hated me before and they'll hate me even more now."

The older woman shifted her gardening stool to the next row. "Troy's family isn't that bad."

Hot sun warmed Angelica's head and bare arms, and the garden smells of dirt and tomato vines and marigolds tickled her nose. Around them, rows of green were starting to reveal the fruit of the season: red tomatoes, yellow squash, purple eggplant.

Later today, she and Troy and Xavier were going to join his family at the small country club's Labor Day picnic. Just the words *country club* made Angelica shudder.

Not only that, but her relationship with Troy had felt strained ever since last Saturday, when she'd revealed the truth about how Xavier was conceived. Although he'd responded better than she'd expected, she still felt questions in his eyes every time he looked at her. It made her want to avoid him, but they'd had the plan to go to the Labor Day picnic for weeks.

And she had to see whether she could stand it and whether his family could accept Xavier. Had to see whether to go forward with the marriage or run as fast as she could in the opposite direction.

The older woman sat back on her gardening stool. "You put way too much stock in what those people think."

"What they think about me isn't that important," Angelica said, "but I don't want them to reject Xavier."

Lou Ann used the back of her hand to push gray curls out of her eyes. "I've yet to meet a person who could dislike that child. What God didn't give him in health, He gave him double in charm."

"Which he knows how to use," Angelica said wryly. "But what he doesn't know is which fork to pick up at what time. I don't, either. We've neither of us ever been to a country club."

"He never took you when you were engaged?" Lou Ann asked, and when Angelica shook her head, the other woman waved a dismissive hand. "Honey, this isn't some ritzy East Coast place. This is a picnic in small-town Ohio. I've been to the country club dozens of times. It's just a golf course with a pool and some tennis courts. Ordinary people go there."

"People like me? I don't think so." She remembered the girls from high school who spent their summers at the club. They wore their perfect tans and tennis whites around town as status symbols. Angelica could only pretend not to see their sneers as she scooped their ice cream or rang up their snack purchases, working summers at the local Shop Star Market.

"You've got the wrong idea," Lou Ann said. "Rescue River's country club has always been a welcoming place. Never had a color barrier, never dug into your marital status, never turned away families based on their religion. They're open to anybody who can pay the fee, which isn't all that much these days. I've thought about joining just to have a nice place to swim."

Angelica tugged at a stubborn weed. "You may be right, but Troy's family can't stand me. Not only did I dump their son, but my grandfather threw a wrench in their plans to dominate the county with their giant farm. We've been feuding from way back."

"Isn't it time that ended?" Lou Ann pulled radishes while she spoke. "The Lord wants us to be forces of reconciliation. I know Troy believes in that. You should, too."

Angelica sat back in the grass, listening to crickets chirping as a breeze rustled the leaves of an oak tree nearby. God's peace. She smiled at Lou Ann. "You're my hero, you know that? I want to be you when I grow up."

"Oh, go on." Lou Ann's flush of pleasure belied her dismissive words.

"But I'm still scared."

"You know what Pastor Ricky would say. God doesn't give us a spirit of fear, but of power and love and self-control."

"Yeah." Angelica tried to feel it. Sometimes, more and more often these days, she felt God's strength and peace inside her.

But this Labor Day picnic had put her into a tailspin. Steaks and burgers weren't the only thing likely to be grilled; she would be, too.

"Here's a little tip," Lou Ann said. "Pretend like they're people from another country, another culture.

You're a representative of your culture, bringing your own special gifts. You're not expecting to be the same as them, just to visit. Like you're an ambassador to a foreign land."

Angelica cocked her head to one side, her fingers stilling in the warm, loose dirt. Slowly a smile came to her face. "That's a nice idea. If I'm an ambassador, I'm not under pressure to be just like them."

"Right. You just have to think, that's interesting, that's not how we do it in my culture, but that's okay."

"Yes! And in my culture, we'd bring a gift." Angelica reached for a sugar snap pea and popped it into her mouth, savoring the vegetable's sweet crunch.

Lou Ann smiled. "Atta girl. What would you bring?"

"Food, probably. But that's the last thing they need, especially at a country club bash."

Lou Ann tugged at a recalcitrant carrot and then held it up triumphantly. "Anyone would welcome fresh vegetables from a garden."

Angelica flashed forward to imagine herself and Xavier walking onto the country club grounds. The image improved when she threw in a basket of zucchini, tomatoes and carrots. She threw her arms around the older woman. "You're a genius!"

Troy pulled up to the bunkhouse and, on an impulse, tooted the horn in the same pattern he used when he'd dated Angelica years ago. It was a joke, because he'd always insisted on coming to the door even though she urged him not to. It used to be something of a race, with him hustling to get out of his car and up to the door before she could grab her things and burst outside.

He couldn't beat her now, though. By the time he'd

grabbed his stupid cane and edged gingerly out of the truck—man, his leg ached today—Angelica had emerged from the bunkhouse. Her rolled-up jeans fit her like a dream, and her tanned, toned arms rocked the basket she was carrying, and Troy wanted to wrap his arms around her, she looked so cute.

"What do you have there?" Troy asked. He was proud of her, proud of bringing her to meet his family. Remeet them, actually; they'd all known each other forever. But Angelica was a different person now, and they all had a different relationship.

"Just a little something for your dad."

"For Dad, huh?" Troy tried to smile, but he wondered how that would be received. His father was notoriously difficult, and Troy had already warned Angelica that his dad's moodiness had gotten worse. None of them could go a whole evening without causing him to yell or cuss or storm out of the house.

Lou Ann came out bringing Xavier, fresh-scrubbed and grinning.

Troy gave him a high five. "You ready for some fun, buddy? They have a blow-up bounce house and a ball pit and face painting."

"Face painting is for girls," Xavier said scornfully.

"I just now saw your outfit," Lou Ann said to Angelica, then turned to Troy. "Have they changed their rules about denim?"

Angelica's face fell. "Aren't you supposed to wear jeans?"

"It's no problem," Troy said. "They did away with that rule a couple of years ago."

"I didn't even think of it," Angelica said uneasily.

He put a protective arm around her shoulder. "You'll

be fine. You look great!" But the truth was, he was on edge himself. It wasn't just his dad's bad moods; his older brother wasn't much better. Dad and Samuel, the two wealthiest men in the community, could be an intimidating pair.

"It'll be fine," he repeated. And hoped it was true.

When they got to the club, they were greeted with the smell of steaks and burgers grilling and the sound of a brass quartet playing patriotic songs. The whole place was set up like a carnival, with music and clowns and inflatables, and kids ran in small packs from one attraction to the next.

"This is so cool, Mom!" Xavier's eyes were wide, as if he'd never seen anything like this before. And knowing how poor they'd been, maybe he hadn't.

"It really is." She was a little wide-eyed herself.

He took Xavier by one hand and Angelica by the other and urged them forward. "We'll find you someone fun to play with," he told Xavier. "Samuel's girl, Mindy."

"A girl?"

"Girls can be fun!" He squeezed Angelica's hand, trying to help her relax, and looked around for his brother's daughter. Truthfully he worried about the girl. With an overprotective, suspicious father who tended to stay isolated, she often seemed lonely. "Hey, Sam!" He waved to his brother, gestured him over.

Sam walked toward them, frowning, holding Mindy's hand.

"Hey," Troy greeted his brother, glaring to remind him to be polite. "You remember Angelica, right?"

Sam gave him a quick nod and turned to Angelica. "Angelica. It's been a long time."

"And this is Xavier, Angelica's son."

"Say hello," she prompted gently.

But Xavier was staring at Mindy. "What happened to your other hand?"

"Xavier!" Angelica sounded mortified.

"I was born without it," Mindy said matter-of-factly. "What happened to your hair?"

"Leukemia, but it's gonna be gone soon and then I'll have hair."

Mindy nodded. "Want to go see the ball pit? It's cool."

"Sure!" And they were off.

"I'm so sorry he said that," Angelica said to his brother. "He should know better."

"No problem," Sam said, but to Troy's experienced ear, the irritation in his brother's voice was evident. He hated for anyone to comment on his daughter's disability. Plus, the man was frazzled; since his wife's death, he'd had his hands full trying to run his business empire and care for his daughter.

"Kids will be kids," Troy said as a general reminder to everybody, especially his brother.

"That's true," Sam said. "I'm sorry Mindy commented on your son's hair. Are things going okay with his treatment?"

"I'm hopeful," Angelica said quietly. "Lots of people are praying for him."

They strolled behind the two running children. Troy kept putting his arm around Angelica while trying not to actually touch her. He was being an idiot, but there'd been awkwardness between them ever since their botched conversation the other night, when she told him about her attack. He wished he hadn't pushed her to reveal her assailant, but he wanted to know because the guy deserved punishment. He also needed to be off the street.

Xavier and Mindy were chattering away as they zig-zagged from craft table to ball toss. The adults, on the other hand, were too quiet. "Angelica brought some vegetables for Dad," Troy told Sam, trying to keep this reunion from being a total fail.

His brother nodded. "Too bad Dad hates vegetables."

"Oh." Angelica's face fell. "They're fresh from the garden back at Troy's house. I've been helping Lou Ann take care of it. Does he even hate fresh tomatoes?"

"Pretty much. But," Sam added grudgingly, "his doctor told him he needs to eat better, so maybe this will help."

"We made some zucchini bread, too. Maybe he'll like that, at least."

"I'm sure he will," Troy said firmly.

Sam didn't answer, and after a raised-eyebrow glance at him, Angelica shrugged and got very busy with examining the Popsicle-stick crafts at the kids' stand and checking out the tissue-paper flowers some of the older girls were making. The brass quintet started playing old-fashioned songs, of the "Camptown Races" sort, and the smell of grilled sausage and onions grew stronger, making Troy's mouth water.

"Where's Dad?" he asked to kill the awkward silence.

"I'll get him," Sam said. "Watch Mindy, would you?"

"Sure."

As Sam left, Angelica looked up at Troy. "He hates me. I can tell."

"Well, he doesn't *hate* you. He doesn't hate anyone.

He's a good guy underneath. But he's had people take advantage of him a lot, and his wife's death was really traumatic. So bear with him. He's protective of his family, and he thinks you hurt me."

"I did hurt you," she said softly. After a minute's hesitation, she reached out and lightly grasped his forearm, and the touch seemed to travel straight to his heart. "I never apologized about that. I shouldn't have left like I did, Troy. I should have trusted you more, and it was wrong of me to leave without any explanation. You can maybe understand how desperate I was, but still, I realize now that it was a mistake."

"Thanks for saying that." Seven years later, he found that the apology still mattered. His throat tightened. "I appreciate hearing those words from you. But I'm sorry, too."

"For what?" She looked up at him through her long lashes, and she was so pretty he just wanted to grab her into his arms. But you didn't do that with Angelica.

"For being the type of person who'd judge a woman for something that wasn't her fault." He saw Mindy stumble, watched Xavier reach out a hand to steady her. "Life's taught me not to be so rigid about everything."

"Isn't that the truth?" She laughed a little, looking off toward the cornfields in the distance. "We all learn as we get older."

"Well, most of us." He nudged her and nodded toward his father, who was being urged out of his seat by Sam and Daisy. "Some are a little more thickheaded and it takes longer."

"Here we go," she said, obviously trying to be funny, but he could hear the dread in her voice.

"Just don't let anything he says get to you. I've got your back."

"Thanks." She tightened her grip on his arm and then let go. Today was the first time Angelica had initiated touching him since they met again, and he had to hope that it meant there was some promise for them together.

Xavier and Mindy shouted for them, and they turned to watch the two kids skim down the inflatable slide together. Around them, people were starting to gather at tables covered by checkered tablecloths. Parents were trying to get their kids to come to supper, helped along by the smell of hot dogs and cotton candy.

The warm sun and music and patriotic decorations brought back memories of his parents in happier days, of playing baseball and Frisbee with his brother and sister here at the club, of eating and laughing together before everything had started to go wrong in his family.

Behind them, he heard his father's grousing voice. "I don't want to walk all the way over there. I just got comfortable sitting down and—"

"Come on, Dad." It was Daisy, and when he turned to look he saw that she was urging their father along by herself; Sam had apparently bailed on supervising this meeting. "Troy's fiancée is here," Daisy continued determinedly, "and you need to welcome her. Hi, Angelica!"

Angelica offered a big smile. "It's good to see you, Daisy. Hi, Mr. Hinton."

"Hello." His father didn't say anything rude, thankfully; that probably meant he hadn't had much to drink yet. But he looked Angelica up and down with a frown.

"Dad, Angelica brought you some vegetables from the garden."

She rolled her eyes at him, subtly, and he realized he was trying too hard.

"Humph." His father looked at the basket dismissively. "Green stuff."

Troy opened his mouth to smooth things over, but Angelica took a step in front of him, effectively nudging him out of her way. "Sam said you don't like vegetables, but there's some zucchini bread I made from Lou Ann Miller's recipe. I hope you like it." She held out the basket.

"Thank you." His father took it begrudgingly. "That woman always won the prize at picnics when we were teenagers. Even back then, she was a good cook."

Angelica smiled. "She still is. Maybe you could come visit sometime."

Troy gritted his teeth. He avoided inviting his dad over because the man was so difficult. He didn't like what Troy was doing with his life—being a vet, especially doing rescue. The Hinton sons should be making money hand over fist in the world of agricultural high finance, according to his dad.

"So you've taken to being a hostess at Troy's house, have you?" his father asked.

"Dad!" Daisy scolded before Troy could intervene. "Angelica has every right. She's marrying Troy."

As Angelica followed the group toward the long dining tables, Daisy's words rang in her ears like chimes foretelling her fate. *"She's marrying Troy."*

"Hi, Angelica!" A blonde in spike-heeled sandals approached, with mirror-image blond girls holding each hand. Ugh. She'd wanted a distraction, but not necessarily in the form of Nora Templeton—one of the country-club girls who'd been meanest when they were in high school together. Was her voice really prissy? Or was Angelica just defensive?

"Hi, Nora," she said, holding out a hand.

"Let Mommy shake hands, Stella," Nora said, pulling loose from one of her daughters to hold out a perfectly manicured hand.

Which made Angelica wonder if she'd gotten all the dirt out from under her own nails since her marathon gardening session that morning.

"Run along and play a minute." Nora shooed her daughters away. "How are you? I heard you were back in town."

"Yes." As Nora's daughters high-fived each other and ran off toward the dessert table, Angelica debated how much to tell. "My son and I wanted to spend more time with my grandpa."

"That's sweet. I see your grandpa sometimes at the Towers when I visit my aunt." She leaned closer. "Your son looks a lot like his daddy."

Angelica's world blurred as she stared at the other woman. Did Nora know Jeremy, her assailant, then? Who else did?

"He's got that same dark hair and sweet smile."

Around them, people stood in clusters or found seats at family-sized tables. Troy's friend Dion was sitting down with an older couple, and he saw her and gave a friendly wave.

Angelica fought to stay in the present and analyze Nora's words. Did she mean Jeremy? Had Jeremy talked about what had happened, then, after threatening her with a worse assault if she ever said a word?

Nora's eyes grew round. "Did I say something wrong? I just assumed Troy's your son's father."

Angelica's breath whooshed out. Troy. Nora thought Troy was Xavier's dad.

"If it's supposed to be a secret, I won't say anything to anyone. But I think it's just so sweet that you two are finally getting married."

Angelica stared at the other woman blankly while her mind raced. Should she just let this happen, let the misperception remain? Was that fair to Troy? To Xavier?

"Mom! Stella rubbed cake in my face and we didn't even eat dinner yet!"

"Girls! Stop that!" Nora looked apologetically at Angelica. "They're not always such brats. See you around!" She rushed off, leaving Angelica in a haze of self-doubt.

Oh, she'd been stupid, thinking she could bring Xavier here to live without putting this small, close-knit community on alert. Everyone had to be doing the math in their heads, figuring out that Xavier was of an age to have been conceived during her former engagement to Troy.

"Come on, Angelica." Daisy's voice brought her back from the brink. "They're about ready to serve dinner, and Dad likes to be first in line."

"Make me sound like a cad," her father grumbled.

The savory tang of barbecue sauce and the slightly burned scent of kettle corn filled the air as they straggled toward long tables heaped with potato salad, watermelon and enormous silver chafing dishes of baked beans.

Lou Ann had been right: the crowd included all skin colors, just like the town. There was even a man wearing a turban at one table and a group of women in brightly colored saris at another. Cooks and servers in pristine white aprons and chefs' hats shouted instructions to one another, punctuated by the laughter of family groups and the shouts of children.

Angelica ran a hand over Xavier's bald head and felt the tiniest hint of stubble. A bubble of joy rose in her chest, reminding her of what was really important.

As Angelica helped Xavier load his plate for dinner, Troy's father stood next to her in line. "I told my son not to get together with you," he said in what was apparently supposed to be a whisper, but was probably audible to everyone up and down the long serving buffet.

"Oh?" Ignoring the stares and nudges around them, she scooped some baked ziti onto Xavier's plate. "Why's that?"

"Because you dumped him before," Mr. Hinton said. "Fool me once, shame on you, fool me twice, shame on me."

Heat rose to her cheeks, but she just nodded. What could she say? She had left Troy, it was true.

"What's that man talking about, Mom?" Xavier asked in a stage whisper.

"Ancient history," she said.

"Actually history about the same age as you are."

The server behind the grill was openly staring. "Shrimp or steak, ma'am?"

"Xavier," she said, "take this plate over where Mindy's sitting. I'll be right there."

As soon as Xavier left, she turned to Mr. Hinton, hands on hips. "Any issues you have with me, you're welcome to tell me. But don't involve my son. None of this is his fault, and he has a lot to deal with right now."

Mr. Hinton narrowed his eyes at her. "Your son is part of the issue. Is he related to me?"

She cocked her head to one side.

"I mean, is my son his father?"

Light dawned. "No, of course not! Troy would never..." She trailed off. Mr. Hinton believed that, too? She'd known on some level that acquaintances like Nora might think Xavier was Troy's son. But she was shocked to realize that his own father suspected it.

Keeping Xavier's parentage a secret was hurting Troy. But revealing it would hurt Xavier.

Lou Ann's words came back to her. As a Christian, she was supposed to be all about reconciliation.

She turned to Mr. Hinton, gently took his plate and put it down on the buffet table and nudged him off to the side, ignoring the raised eyebrows of family members and bystanders around them. She pulled him by the hand to a bench out of earshot of the crowd and sat down, patting the seat beside her.

He gave her a grouchy look and then sat.

Aware that she didn't have long before he left in a hissy fit, she talked fast. "Look, I can understand why you're upset with me. And I can understand why you want to know whether Xavier is a blood relative. The answer is no. He's not."

Mr. Hinton crossed his arms and glared at her. "All the more reason for me to be angry, then. Isn't that right? Isn't my son opening himself up to a lying, cheating woman by getting back together with you?"

His voice had risen and people were staring; conversations in the area had died down. She'd *thought* this area was secluded enough to keep their conversation private, but apparently, with the volume of Mr. Hinton's hard-of-hearing voice, it wasn't.

It was her worst nightmare come true: she was a spectacle at the country club, looked down on by the other guests.

What's the right thing to do, Lord? The prayer shot straight up through the tears that she couldn't keep from forming in her eyes.

An arm came around her shoulder, and Troy sat beside her, pulling her to his side. His strength held her up where she felt like collapsing.

"Dad," Daisy said as she hurried over to clutch her father's shoulder, leaning over him from the other side. "Why are you making a scene? You know this isn't right."

"No." Angelica straightened her spine, pulled away from Troy, and stood. "He's not doing anything but protecting his son. That's totally understandable."

"Thank you!" Mr. Hinton's exasperated words almost made her smile.

"But, Mr. Hinton," she said, reaching out to clasp his arm. "That's what I need to do, too. Xavier's story is his own to tell, and he's too young to understand it and share it yet. So I'm just going to have to ask you to take it on faith that, when the time is right, you'll know the right amount about his parentage."

"That's about as convoluted as a story can get," Mr. Hinton complained, but his voice wasn't as loud and angry as it had been before.

"Dad. I know enough to understand what happened," Troy said. "None of it is Angelica's fault, and I'd just ask you to accept Xavier without any questions right now. That's what I'm planning to do."

"And that's what this family is about," Daisy said firmly. "We accept kids. All kids."

Angelica took deep breaths and shot up a prayer of thanks. Troy had supported her. And it looked as though Daisy was coming around to her side, too.

Mr. Hinton was a tougher case, but he was just trying to protect his child and his family. That was something she could understand.

"Come on," she said, and took the risk of clasping his hand. "Let's go get back in line before the food's all gone."

He cleared his throat. "Finally somebody said something that makes sense." As they walked together to the line, he leaned down to mutter in her ear, "You tell Lou Ann that nothing on the dessert table here holds a candle to her zucchini bread."

"Wait. You've been sampling dessert already?"

"Life's short. Eat dessert first. Right?"

"I think I'm going to follow that philosophy," Angelica said, grabbing a big piece of chocolate cake.

"You're not my favorite person in the world," Mr. Hinton said to her. "But I reckon I can back off of hassling you. Xavier's not accountable for your problems. And come to think of it, you're not accountable for your grandfather's."

Angelica gave the old man a sidearm hug and then sidled away before he could either embrace her or reject her.

"Humph." He glared at her and bustled off.

It wasn't a warm welcome, but Angelica felt that progress had been made. And she shot up a prayer of thanks and wonder to God, who was clearly the author of the peace and reconciliation she'd just felt.

Thirteen

After dinner, they all moved over to sit near the band. Xavier was fighting tiredness, but losing the battle, so Angelica talked him into lying down for a little rest on the blanket beside her. He resisted, but in minutes, he was asleep.

The gentle music prompted a few older couples onto the makeshift dance floor, where moonlight illuminated them in a soft glow. Most of the younger kids were quieting down or already asleep, while the teenagers paired off at the edges of the crowd. Nearby, most of the Hintons were spreading blankets and settling in to listen to the music.

She wanted this for Xavier. She wanted the community and the family and the security represented by life here.

She'd never thought she could have it. When she left seven years ago, running scared, she'd thought her connection with this community was severed. Now she had a chance to regain it, stronger than when she was young, to regain it as part of a connected, loving family.

She wanted it so badly, but was she just setting herself up for disappointment?

"Aw, he's so sweet," Daisy said, coming over to settle in the grass beside her. "He got along really well with everyone, didn't he?"

"I was pleased. But he's a great kid that way. He's always had an ease and charm with people that I can only envy."

Daisy cocked her head to one side, studying Xavier. "I wonder where he gets that."

The comment echoed in Angelica's head. Where did Xavier get his charm and people skills?

The thought pushed her toward his genetics, toward Jeremy and his superficial charm, but she shoved that idea away. "My aunt helped out with him so much when he was small. She was an amazing woman, and I'm sure he picked up some of her better traits."

"I'm sure he's picked up some of your great traits," Daisy said, patting her knee. "I really admire what you've done, raising him even though…" She stopped.

"Even thought what?"

"Look," Daisy said, "I'm guessing Xavier is the product of some kind of an assault. Remember, I'm a social worker. I see stuff like this all the time. I can tell you're wary of men in a way that suggests you've been treated badly, and I know you didn't use to be like that, so…" She spread her hands expressively.

Angelica stared at the woman, feeling defeated. Daisy had guessed most of the story of her past. As much as Angelica wanted to hide it, it was written and apparent in the existence of Xavier.

"I'm sorry." Daisy patted Angelica's arm. "There

I go blurting stuff out again. I should learn to put a sock in it."

Angelica let out a rueful sigh. "For sure, I don't want to talk about my past troubles. But am I going to be able to escape it? Is it wrong for me to want to keep it all private?"

"From me, it's okay," Daisy said. "I have no right to your private information. But I would think that Troy would want to know whatever information is available about Xavier's father."

"That's what I'm afraid of." Troy was the last person she wanted to tell. The trust developing between them was a beautiful thing, but fragile. Revealing the name of her attacker might downright destroy it. After all, Troy had looked up to Jeremy. Would he believe that a guy he admired, a guy who'd mentored him, who'd been a town athletic star, had done something so awful to Angelica?

Or would he turn on her instead?

"But maybe not," Daisy went on, lying back to stare up at the emerging stars. "Maybe he won't need to know. Troy is a rescuer at heart. He's taken in animals since he was a little kid, and in those cases you don't know what happened. But you deal with the results."

"Gee, thanks, Daisy." She whacked the woman on the calf, welcoming the distraction from her own uneasy thoughts. "Did you just compare me to a rescue dog?"

Daisy grinned. "If the shoe fits…"

"If the dog coat fits…" Angelica played along. She was glad that she and Daisy could joke. But what the woman had said bothered her. Why did Troy want to be with her, anyway? Why was he willing to put up with not knowing Xavier's background?

Was it because he saw her, not as an equal human being, but as a creature to be rescued?

"Today's the day, buddy!" Troy turned in the passenger seat to give Xavier a high five. "I get my cast off, and you get to start playing soccer on the team."

"Just to try it," Angelica warned as she swung the truck around the corner. "Remember, when we go to your checkup on Thursday, Dr. Ravi is going to let us know if soccer is the right thing for you to do."

Xavier's jaw jutted out, and Troy could almost see his decision to ignore his mom. He looked down, grabbed the soccer ball from the seat beside him and clutched it to his chest. "Hey, Mr. Troy, do you think you could be one of the coaches?"

"I don't know much about soccer, buddy." But the idea tickled his fancy. What a great way that would be to connect with Xavier. And to help kids. Coaches had been a huge part of his own childhood, giving him the encouragement his dad hadn't.

Xavier was bouncing up and down in the car seat. "You played football before. You could learn about soccer. Please?"

"We'll see, buddy. I have to get the okay from my doctor. Just like you."

"Really?" Xavier's eyes went round as quarters. "I didn't think grown-ups had any rules."

Troy and Angelica exchanged amused glances, and Troy reached back to pat Xavier's shoulder. "We have more rules than you know. And if we're smart, we follow the rules. We listen to doctors."

Xavier frowned and nodded, obviously thinking over this new concept.

Angelica flashed Troy a grateful smile as she pulled up to the door of the hospital. *Thanks*, she mouthed.

Looking at her made his heart catch fire. She was everything to him, and once he got this wretched cast off, he'd feel whole again and as if he could take control. She wouldn't have to drive him and he would be able to be a full partner to her and Xavier. They'd be able to set a wedding date and move forward with their lives, with a real marriage.

"Let me know if you need a ride when you're done."

"This should be pretty quick. Afterward, I'll just stroll over to the park and you guys should still be doing practice."

He gave in to a sudden urge, leaned over and dropped a kiss on her cheek. Her hair's fruity scent and the sound of her breathy little sigh made him want to linger, and only his awareness of Xavier in the backseat held him to propriety.

Especially when she didn't pull back.

He felt ten feet tall. They were making real progress as a couple. What a great day.

"What was that for?" she asked while Xavier giggled from the backseat.

"Just feeling good about everything."

He walked into the hospital easily, barely using his cane. After checking in and waiting impatiently in a roomful of people, the nurse put him in a room to wait for X-rays.

The technician came in and told Troy to hop up on the exam table. "First I'll cut the cast off and then we'll x-ray everything." He was bent over an electronic tablet, recording and filling things in. Finally he looked up. "Hey, I know you."

Troy studied the bearded man, who looked a little younger than Troy. "You do look a little familiar." Then it clicked into place: this was the man they'd seen outside the Senior Towers, that day they'd done the weeding. The one Angelica hadn't liked. His friend's younger brother.

"I'm Logan Filmore." He held out his name tag as if to prove it. "I was a couple years behind you in school, but I watched you play football with my brother."

"Right, right!" Troy reached out, shook the man's hand. "I'm sorry for your loss." Logan's brother had died in a car accident about five years ago. "The whole town came out for Jeremy's funeral. What a loss."

"Yeah." Logan frowned as he positioned Troy on the x-ray table. "I keep hearing that from everyone now that I've moved back permanently."

They made small talk as Logan took pictures of Troy's leg in every position. When the ordeal seemed to be almost over, Logan looked at Troy with a serious expression. "I hate to bring this up, but I heard that you're pretty intense with Angelica Camden. Is that true?"

"Yeah." Troy smiled to remember their exchange in the car. "In fact, we're getting married pretty soon."

"That's great." Logan moved the X-ray machine to another position. "Now, lie still for this one. It's a full 360 and takes a few minutes to get warmed up." He made a tiny adjustment to Troy's leg. "So, you feel okay about everything that happened before?"

Something in the man's tone made Troy's stomach clench. "What do you mean?"

"I mean, about her leaving town pregnant, staying away. You…" He shook his head. "I don't know if I could do that, raise another man's child."

Heat rose inside Troy but he tamped it down. "That's between me and Angelica. And anyway, a kid's a kid."

Logan took a step back, palms out like stop signs. "For sure. Didn't mean anything by it."

"No problem." He'd have to learn to deal with nosy people. It came with the territory of marrying a woman with a kid and a bit of mystery in her past.

"Anyway, I'm glad to see my nephew get a good home. After Jeremy passed, I always thought I should do something, but since Jeremy said she didn't want it…"

His *nephew*? Icy shock froze Troy's body. "Want what?"

"Well, any help with the baby. I guess she felt like, since it was just a one-night stand, he didn't owe her anything."

"Just a one-night stand." Troy repeated the words parrotlike, feeling about as dumb as an animal. "What do you mean? Are you saying Xavier is Jeremy's son?"

"Yeah. Oh man, didn't you know?" Logan's eyebrows shot up. "I thought sure she would've told you. Or you would've asked." He slapped the heel of his hand to his forehead. "Man, I feel like a fool. I'm sorry. What a way to find out."

Troy just lay there on his back under a giant machine, his heart pounding like sledgehammer blows, sweat dripping from his face into his ears. *He* was the one who felt like a fool.

"Okay, ready? Lie still now."

Troy forced himself to obey while the machine moved its slow path up and down his leg. Inside, anger licked slow flames through his body. It took massive self-control not to jump up and slug Logan, though none of this was his fault.

It wasn't Troy's fault, either, nor Xavier's.

It was Angelica's fault. Angelica, and the guy Troy had always looked up to, the guy who'd stayed after practice to help him when he was a scrawny freshman, the guy who'd argued his case when the coach thought Troy was too focused on his studies to play first string.

Troy's mind reeled. Angelica had called it a rape, and he'd 99 percent believed her. So why did Logan think Jeremy was Xavier's dad?

And why did he have details about Angelica not wanting Jeremy's help? Wouldn't she have wanted it?

Well, but if it had been a one-night stand…

Because Jeremy wouldn't rape anyone. Would he?

He felt as if a million little dwarves were hammering at his brain. He wanted out of this conversation. This room. This whole wretched situation.

"Why do you think Xavier is Jeremy's child?" he ground out after the infernal machine had done its work and Logan was back in the room, a sheaf of X-rays in hand.

"Because he told me." Logan crossed his arms over his chest, looking off into space. "Man, that was one of the last times I saw my brother, right before I went overseas. We were out drinking one night and got to talking. He told me they'd hooked up." Logan's gaze flickered down, and he must have seen the turmoil on Troy's face. "Oh man, I'm sorry to break that news. Especially to a guy who's having this kind of trouble with his leg."

"What?" What did his leg have to do with anything? Who cared about his leg now?

"Here, sit up. Take a look." Logan pinned Troy's X-rays up on a light board and pointed. "That didn't heal worth nothing, man. It's all wrong. I don't know if they'll rebreak it or just leave it." He studied the light board, cocking his head to one side. "I don't think I ever saw a break heal that bad before, dude. My sympathy." He went to the door. "Sit tight. Doc will be in any minute. And hey, sorry to be the bearer of bad news."

Angelica sat on the grass watching Xavier joyously joining in the soccer practice. She still felt a little out of place with the other parents, all of whom seemed to have known each other for years. People were friendly, but Angelica knew she was still an outsider. Had always been an outsider, even when she was a kid.

"Good kick, Xavier!" one of the other children yelled.

Coach Linda, Becka's mom, waved to her. "Your son's a natural! Hope he can stay on the team!"

She watched as her son, completely new to soccer, raced to the ball and took it down the field in short, perfect kicks. Or whatever you'd call it…dribbling, maybe? She was way short on soccer terminology.

She so wanted for Xavier to fit in, and truthfully she wanted to fit in with the community, too. During her early years with Xavier, scrambling with work and day care, sometimes struggling to find a place to live before she'd settled in with her aunt, she'd looked enviously at families watching their kids play sports, kids with not only parents but grandparents and aunts and uncles to cheer them on. Families that could afford the right uniforms, could get their kids private lessons or coaching. She'd never even had the chance to dream of such a thing for her and Xavier, but now, hesitantly, she was starting to hope it could happen. They could be a part of things. They could have love, and a community, and a future.

When Nora, the woman from the country club, came up to her with a clipboard, Angelica smiled at her, determined to keep her walls down, to make a fresh start. "Hi," she said, extending her hand. "Are your girls on the team? I'm hoping Xavier can join."

"I heard. He seems really good." The woman settled down on the bench beside Angelica. "I'm head of the parents' organization. We do fund-raising and plan the end-of-season banquet for the kids, so I wanted to get you involved."

Pleasure surged inside Angelica. "Great. I'm pretty new to all this, but I'm glad to help however I can."

"Let me get your contact information." Nora pulled out her iPhone.

As she punched in Angelica's address, she smiled. "So you're living with Troy already, are you?"

Angelica swallowed. *She doesn't mean anything by it. Don't take it personally.* "No, we're not living together exactly. Xavier and I live on the farm, in the guesthouse."

"Oh, I'm sorry! I just assumed, since you have the same address... Great job, Nora, foot in mouth as usual. Never mind."

"It's okay. I work at the kennels," Angelica said, hearing the stiffness in her own voice. "That's why we live there."

"Oh! I misunderstood." The woman leaned in confidingly. "You know, ever since I got divorced, people have been trying to match me up with Troy."

Angelica looked sideways at the woman's perfect haircut and designer shorts. She was tall with an hour-glass figure. What had Troy thought of her? Had they gone out?

Nora waved her hand airily. "It didn't work out. He's a great guy, though."

"Yes, he is," Angelica said guardedly. Why hadn't it ever occurred to her that Troy had other options he was closing off by being involved with her? That he could date, or even marry, someone like Nora, the gorgeous, well-off, country-club-bred head of the parents' group?

"So, I notice Xavier doesn't have a uniform yet," the woman continued. "They cost fifty dollars. And we ask that parents make a donation of fifty dollars to the group, for parties and snacks and special events."

Angelica swallowed. "Um, okay. I might need to do one thing per paycheck, if that's okay. Money's a little tight."

The woman laughed. "You're kidding, right? Troy has all the money in the world."

I want to fit in, God, but do I have to be nice to this busybody? "Like I said, we'll take it one thing at a time. I'd like to get him the uniform first, but if you need the parents' fee right away—"

"Oh no, it's fine." The woman shrugged, palms up. "You pay when you're ready. Or when you tie the knot! I know Troy's good for it."

That rankled, and then another truth dawned as Angelica realized how her engagement to Troy must look to much of the town. Here she was, in her ancient cut-offs, and Xavier in his mismatched holey T-shirt and thrift-store gym shorts, and apparently Troy was known as one of the richest men in town. Just like when they'd been engaged before. They were two people from opposite sides of the tracks. They didn't fit.

Did everyone think she was marrying Troy for his money?

Angelica's phone buzzed, and when she saw Dr. Ravi's office number on the caller ID, she wrinkled her nose apologetically at Nora. "Sorry, I have to take this." When the woman didn't get up to move, Angelica stood and walked out of earshot. "Hello?"

"Angelica, it's Dr. Ravi. I got your message about Xavier playing soccer, and I wanted to tell you I think it's wonderful."

"Really? He's cleared to play?"

"Not only that, but all the signs about the treatment are very, very positive. Of course, definitive cures aren't part of the language of cancer doctors, but we are looking at very, very good numbers."

"Oh, Dr. Ravi, thank you! That's wonderful!"

"I agree." In his voice, she could hear his sincere happiness. "One never likes to make promises, but if I were you, I would be planning a long, healthy future for that young man."

Angelica half walked, half skipped back to the bench and sat down, vaguely conscious that there were a couple of other moms there with Nora now. She couldn't even remember why she'd felt upset with Nora.

What an incredible gift from God. She looked up at the sky, grinning her gratitude. Wow, just wow. She felt like shouting.

"Could you give me your email and cell phone information for our parents' directory?" Nora was looking at her, eyebrows raised.

"Um, yes, I… You know what, can we do this later? I

just got some really, really good medical news. Xavier! Hey, Zavey!"

Xavier came trotting over. "Mom, did you see me score a goal?"

She reached out widespread arms and caught him in them, holding him so tight that he started to struggle. Reluctantly she let him go but held his shoulders to look into his eyes. "Guess what?"

"Mom, can I go back and play more?"

Her smile felt so broad that her cheeks hurt. "You sure can. In fact, Dr. Ravi says you're cleared to play, and that the treatment seems to be working."

His eyes and his mouth both went wide and round. "You mean I'm getting well?"

"Looks like it, kiddo."

"And I can be on the team? And have my own shirt?"

"Absolutely. Just as soon as I get my next paycheck, you'll have a uniform, buddy."

He took off his hat and threw it high in the air, and the other moms seemed to draw in a collective sigh at the sight of his cancer-bald head.

"You know," Nora said, "I'm sure that, between us, we can get him a uniform right away. Can't we, ladies?"

The others nodded, and one of them, an acquaintance from years ago, reached out to give Angelica an impulsive hug. "We're so glad you moved back. It'll be great to get to know you again."

"Yes, and with Xavier playing, maybe our team will win a game every once in a while," chimed in one of the other moms, and they all laughed.

"Hey, there's Dad!" Xavier pointed down the street. "Can I go tell him, Mom? Can I?"

She was so happy that it didn't even bother her that

Xavier had called Troy "Dad" in front of all these mothers, who, no matter how nice, were likely to gossip about it. She looked in the direction Xavier was pointing and saw Troy walking toward them, along the sidewalk. A part of her wanted to tell Troy the great news about Xavier herself, but she couldn't deny Xavier the delight of telling. After all, it was his news. "Go for it, honey. Just don't knock him down. He looks a little bit tired."

Angelica watched Xavier running toward Troy, soccer ball under one arm, and happiness flooded her heart. It almost seemed in slow motion, like a dream: she was surrounded by other moms who seemed, suddenly, like supportive friends. The warm, late-afternoon air kissed her cheeks, tinged with the scent of just-mown grass. Giant trees shaded them all, testimony to how long this park had been here, how deeply the community was grounded in history.

She wanted this, especially for Xavier, so much she could taste it. And here it was within their grasp.

Xavier got to Troy, shouting, "Mr. Troy! Dad! Guess what!"

Troy kept walking. Limping, actually, and he still had his cane.

Angelica's heart faltered.

"Mr. Troy, hey! Don't you hear me?" Xavier grabbed Troy's leg.

Troy stumbled a little.

Angelica sprang from the bench and strode toward them, ignoring the concerned exclamations of the other mothers.

"Hey, Mr. Troy, guess what!"

Finally Troy stopped and turned to Xavier. "What?" His voice was oddly flat.

"I can play soccer! And I'm gonna get all better!"

Knowing Troy so well, Angelica could see him pull his mind from whatever faraway place it had been. He turned and bent down awkwardly, slowly. "That's great news, buddy." He was clearly trying to show enthusiasm. Trying, and failing.

To which her excited son was oblivious. "So that means you can be my coach, right? Can you, Dad? Can you?"

"We could use a few extra coaches, Troy," Coach Linda called from among the group of mothers. "Hint, hint."

Troy looked toward them, forehead wrinkled, frowning. "No," he said. "No, I can't do that."

"Whaddya mean you can't, Dad? You gotta coach me! You said you would."

Angelica reached the pair then and, breathless, knelt down beside Xavier. "Give Mr. Troy a minute here, buddy." She studied Troy's face.

He was looking from her to Xavier with the strangest expression she'd ever seen. Eyes hooded, corners of his mouth turned down. She couldn't read it and for some reason, it scared her.

"What's wrong?" she asked, putting a protective arm around Xavier.

"Mr. Troy, watch what I learned already!" Xavier threw the soccer ball he'd been carrying up into the air and bounced it off his head. Then he dribbled it in a circle, then kicked it up into his hands again.

His ability to handle the ball took Angelica's breath away. He was well, or pretty close, and he was going to be able to develop this amazing talent. She clasped her hands to her chest, almost as if she could hold the joy inside.

"Don't you want to coach me now?"

Troy looked at the two of them for a minute more. Then, without another word, he turned and started limping toward the truck.

She felt Xavier's shoulders slump.

"Troy!" she said. "Come back here and tell us what's going on."

He didn't answer, didn't look at her, just kept walking. And now she could see that he had a pronounced limp from some new, big kind of bandage around his leg, beneath his long pants.

"Troy!" When he didn't answer, she put her hands on her son's shoulders. "Remember how tired and cranky you can get from going to the doctor?"

Xavier nodded. But his lower lip was wobbling. He was so vulnerable, and she could have kicked Troy right in his bad leg for hurting her son's feelings. "Well, I think that's how Mr. Troy is feeling now."

"Did he have a treatment?" Xavier asked. "Does he have cancer, like me?"

"He doesn't have cancer, but I think he must have had a treatment that hurt or something. So we'll talk to him later. Right now I think your team needs you." Gently, she turned him back toward the playing field. She waved to Coach Linda, ignoring the curious stares of the other mothers. "Hey, Coach, Xavier's coming back in to play some, okay?"

"We can use him," Linda called, and as Xavier ran toward her, she reached out an arm to put around his shoulders.

Angelica watched long enough to see the pair head

back toward the field. Both of them glanced back a couple of times, Xavier still looking a little crestfallen.

She marched after Troy.

"Hey, what's going on?"

He didn't stop, but she caught up with him easily.

"Troy! What happened at the doctor's? Did you get bad news?"

He got to the truck and looked at it. Shut his eyes as though he was in physical pain. Then walked to the passenger door and opened it.

"Troy! I thought you... What happened?"

He closed the door and sat in the truck, staring straight ahead.

She reached out and pulled the door open before he could lock her out. "Look, I get that you've had some bad news, but let me in, okay? Tell me what's going on. We're a team, remember? We're engaged! We're getting married!"

"No, we're not."

The three words, spoken in that same flat tone he'd used with Xavier, pricked a hole in her anger. She felt her energy start to flow out of her, like a tire with a slow leak. "What do you mean? Talk to me."

He didn't.

"What happened? Why aren't we getting married now? Troy, no matter what happened to you, which I'd appreciate being told about, you can't just shut me out. And I don't like your ignoring Xavier that way. You really hurt his feelings."

"And of course I wouldn't want to hurt the feelings of Jeremy's son."

Jeremy's son.

A core of ice formed inside her. He knew. Troy knew the truth.

Jeremy's son.

She never thought of Xavier that way. Xavier was her son. God's son. Soon, she'd thought, he would be Troy's son.

Though Jeremy Filmore had had a role in his conception, a role she'd spent a lot of years blocking out, it had ended there.

Hearing Troy say that name made her feel like throwing up. She staggered and leaned against the side of the truck. It was hot, but somehow the sun's warmth didn't penetrate the icy cold she felt inside.

Her worst nightmare. Troy had found out her assailant, who wasn't some stranger he could hate from a distance, but his own good friend, someone they'd both known. "What did you hear?" she asked in a dull voice.

"Well, for one thing, I heard that my leg is permanently screwed up. That I'll have to wear this boot for six months and I won't be able to drive or exercise. After that, I have to have some surgery that might or might not allow me to walk without a cane."

She didn't answer, couldn't. She could barely focus on what he was saying, only realizing that it had something to do with his leg not healing.

That awful name kept echoing through her head. *Jeremy. Jeremy. Jeremy.*

It whirled her back to a night she'd spent years trying to forget. To a very handsome and charming older guy who'd flattered her at her birthday celebration, walked her partway home, then dragged her into his apartment and spent what seemed like hours hurting her in ways she'd had no idea a man could hurt a woman.

Her screams had been ineffectual; the other apartments had been empty. Her pleas had fallen on deaf ears, even made him laugh.

What he'd done to her physically was horrible enough. But his name-calling, his degradation of her as a woman, his comments about her past, her unworthiness, her asking for it... All of those words had stuck to her like poison glue, growing inside her right along with the baby growing in her womb. The ugly descriptions of herself had expanded until they were all she could see, all she could feel.

Only the tireless nurturing of her aunt, and intensive sessions with a skilled therapist, had been able to pull her out of the deep depression she'd sunk into.

"You cheated on me," Troy said now. "And you lied to me."

Cheater. Liar. Even though the words Jeremy had uttered had been much stronger and more degrading, the echo in the voice of her beloved Troy made her double over, the hurt was so sudden and so strong.

She knelt in the dirt beside the truck, holding her stomach.

"Don't even try to defend yourself. I won't believe a word you say."

His flat, angry, judgmental certainty slammed into her. It was just the way she'd figured he would react; it was the reason she'd thrown clothes into a bag and left town the day she learned she was pregnant.

Now, though, her automatic reaction was different. To her own surprise, she didn't feel like running. She felt her shoulders go back as she glared at him. "Did you just tell me not to say anything?"

"Yeah," he said, leaning out of the truck, breathing hard. "That's exactly what I told you."

Gravel dug into her knees. What was she doing on her knees? Holding on to the side of the truck for support, she climbed to her feet. "Don't you ever tell me I can't say what's on my mind. I spent a lot of years keeping silent, and I'm tired of it. I don't deserve what happened to me, and I don't deserve for you to blame me for what someone else did to me."

He looked at her with huge sags under his eyes, as if he'd aged ten years. "You wanted to be with him. Right?"

Whoa! Just like Jeremy! Her hands went to her hips as heat flushed through her body. "You can stop right now with telling me what I did and didn't want. No woman would want what happened to me, and any man who says otherwise is messed up." She walked closer to him, her heart pounding in her ears. "You hear me? Totally. Messed. Up." With each word, she jabbed a pointing finger at him. "If that's what you're thinking, you can get out of my life."

He swung his legs down with a painful wince. "I'm going, just as soon as I can get a ride. And you can get out of mine. I want your bags packed and you…" He trailed off, swallowed hard. "You and Xavier…off my property. By tomorrow."

Fourteen

Troy watched the woman he'd thought he loved draw in a rasping breath, then clench her jaw. "I'll drive you home," she said. "Let me get Xavier."

She turned before he could answer and marched down toward the playing field. Her back was straight, shoulders squared.

He stared after her, then squeezed his eyes shut and looked away. His heart rebelled against the sudden change he was asking of it: stop loving her, start hating her. Stop believing in her, realize that she'd been lying this whole time.

She *had* been lying, right? Because she'd said she hadn't known her assailant, but when he'd confronted her with Jeremy's name, she'd tacitly acknowledged him as Xavier's father.

But why would she have lied about it being Jeremy?

The answer had to be that she'd gone with him willingly. Just as Jeremy's brother had said.

Sliding out of the truck, he landed painfully on his bad leg, and the metal cane the doctor had lent him—

the old man's cane with four little feet on the end—crashed to the ground.

A teenage girl on a skateboard swooped down, picked it up, then skidded in a circle to hand it back to him.

He wasn't even man enough to pick up his wretched cane for himself.

Angelica came back, pulling an obviously reluctant and angry Xavier by the hand. "Mom!" he was whining, almost crying. "I don't want to go."

"Get in the truck," she ordered.

"But—"

"Now." Her voice was harsh.

Tears spilled from Xavier's eyes, and his lower lip pouted out, but he climbed into the truck.

"Mr. Troy!" Xavier said as soon as they were all in. "Mama says we have to move away. But that's not true, is it?"

Troy looked over at Angelica and saw a muscle twitch in her cheek. Her jaw was set and obviously she wasn't about to answer.

Troy was already regretting his hasty order that they leave. He turned back to Xavier, looked at his hopeful face.

Looked into Jeremy's eyes. How had he not noticed that before? "I'm sorry, but yes. You do have to leave."

"Why?" Xavier's face screwed up. "I love it here. I hate moving."

Troy looked over at Angelica and saw a single tear trickle down her cheek.

Well, sure, she was upset. Her game was up.

"Mom, you promised we wouldn't have to move again!"

Angelica cleared her throat. "I'm sorry, honey. I made a promise I couldn't keep."

"Seems you make a habit of that," Troy muttered.

Angelica's body gave the slightest little jerk, as if she'd been hit.

The truth hurt. He tried to work up some more righteous anger about that, but he was finding it hard to do.

What she'd done was wrong, but it had happened a long time ago.

But she's been lying to you just in the past few weeks.

But she'd seemed to genuinely care about him. Hadn't she? "Look," he said, "maybe I've overreacted. I... I need to take a breath, think about this. I don't want to throw the two of you out on the street..."

"We've been there before." She spun the truck around a corner too fast, making the tires squeal. "We'll manage."

"I don't want you to just manage. I need to pray about this, get right with God, figure things out. I was blindsided, but we all make mistakes. I...maybe I can work through it and learn to forgive you."

"Don't strain yourself." She pulled the truck into the long driveway and squealed to a jerky stop in front of his house. "Here you go."

There were a couple of unfamiliar cars parked in front of the house, and he couldn't deal with strangers. Didn't want to talk to anyone but Angelica. "I... Look. Let's talk before you go."

"I think you've said all you need to say. I know what you think about me. I know how much respect you have for me. All I want now is to pack my things and be gone."

"Mom! You should listen to Mr. Troy! Maybe we won't have to leave."

"Are you getting out?" she asked him through clenched teeth.

"No. Angelica—"

She pulled out fast enough to make the wheels spit gravel, drove past the kennels and down to the bunkhouse. She skidded to a halt and slammed the truck into park. "C'mon, Xavier. Out." As soon as the sobbing boy had obeyed, she faced Troy. "By tonight, we'll be gone." She slammed the truck's door and walked into the bunkhouse, back stiff, one arm around Xavier.

Troy sat in the truck, his legs and arms too heavy to move. He stared out at the cornfields and wondered what he could do now.

His life had been snatched out from under him. Instead of being active, doing everything himself, he'd need help. With the kennels. With his practice. Even with driving, for pity's sake. Instead of getting married to the woman he loved, instead of becoming dad to the child he'd come to care deeply for, he'd be alone.

Alone, with a big empty space in his heart.

He knew he shouldn't be sitting here feeling sorry for himself, but he couldn't seem to make himself move. He didn't know what to do next.

Well, he did know: he should pray, put it in God's hands.

He let his face fall forward into his hands. *God...* He didn't know how to ask or what to say. Even looking at the bunkhouse and knowing that Xavier and Angelica were inside packing made his throat tighten up and his heart ache.

Help, he prayed.

The word echoed in his mind, as if God was saying it back to him.

There was nothing to do but try to help them. He'd help them load their stuff into the truck, as much as a crippled guy could. Find someone to drive them to the station. He'd pay for tickets wherever they wanted to go.

Where would they go, though?

And what about follow-ups to Xavier's treatments? What would Angelica do for a job? She'd worried that this would happen, that the "us" wouldn't work out and that she'd be alone, unable to afford the rest of the cost of treatment. He'd waved her concern aside.

Had she suspected he'd find out the truth about her?

What *was* the truth about her? He pounded the seat beside him. Why had she cheated on him? Why had she given herself to Jeremy?

"Mr. Troy! Mr. Troy! Come in here!"

At first he thought he was imagining the sound, but no; it was Xavier pounding on the truck's door. He lowered the window and looked out. "You okay, kiddo?"

"I am, but Lily's not! She's having her puppies! And Mom says she's in trouble!"

Troy grabbed the bag he always kept in the backseat and swung out of the vehicle.

"Come on! Mom said you wouldn't still be here, but I knew you would!"

They hurried into the bunkhouse together and there in a dark corner of the living room was Angelica, leaning over Lily.

Her dark hair was pulled back with a rubber band and she was doing something with a towel.

"What's going on?"

"She's having trouble with this last one." The anger

was gone from her voice, replaced by worry. "She can't get it out. I've been trying to help her, but I'm afraid of hurting the puppy."

"Let me see." He squatted down and saw the puppy's hindquarters protruding from Lily, who was whimpering and bending, trying to lick at the new puppy while three other pups pushed at her teats.

"Get a couple towels," he told Xavier, and to Angelica, "Get the surgical scissors out of my bag while I try to ease the pup out."

It took several minutes, and when the puppy was finally born he saw why: it was half again as big as the other puppies. Lily sank back, too exhausted for the usual maternal duties, so Troy carefully removed the sac and cut the cord and rubbed the puppy vigorously in a clean towel until he was sure it was breathing on its own.

"Poor thing," Angelica cooed, stroking Lily's ears and head. "You did a good job."

The pup was breathing well, so Troy tucked it against Lily's tummy, where it rooted blindly until it found a teat to latch on to.

Lily lifted her head feebly and licked the new puppy a couple of times, then dropped her head back to the floor.

"You can rest now," Angelica said to the tired dog. "We'll help you."

A small hand tugged at his shoulder as Xavier peered past him to look at Lily. "Is she gonna die? Why's she bleeding?"

He'd half forgotten that Xavier was there. "She's doing great. There's always a little blood when a dog gives birth, but she should be just fine."

"The puppies look…yucky."

Troy glanced over at Angelica, not sure how much detail she wanted her son to know. She shrugged, so he gave Xavier a barebones account of placentas and amniotic fluid and umbilical cords.

Fortunately the boy took it in stride. "Is she gonna have more?"

"I feel one more little bump, so she'll probably have one more." He smiled at Xavier. "It'll be okay. Just takes a while."

"Can I watch?"

Troy looked over at Angelica, eyebrows raised.

"Sure, I guess." She stood up, stretched with her hands on her lower back, then walked over to the small bookcase. And started putting books in boxes.

Troy's heart dove down to his boots. For a minute there, he'd forgotten their conflict, forgotten that he'd kicked her out, forgotten they weren't a couple anymore. He opened his mouth to say something and then shut it again.

Should he take back his request that she leave? Beg her to stay? If she stayed, what would they do? Because the fact remained, she'd betrayed him.

Lily whimpered, and he looked down at her and petted and soothed her.

And then it hit him. Again. His revelation about how Angelica had cringed and held back from the physical.

If she'd consented to the relationship with Jeremy, then why did she act like an abused animal when a man tried to touch her?

Her phone buzzed just then, and he watched her as she answered it, wondering what to believe. Saw her frown and look despairingly at the half-filled box of books. "Are you sure you can't manage it? I'm kind of busy here."

She listened again.

"Okay. No, of course I can help." She clicked off the phone and sighed. "Lou Ann needs me to help her with something up at the house. Says she needs a woman, that you won't do. Can you…"

"I'll stay with Lily. And Xavier can stay with me." He felt so good being able to do something for her. Lord help him, he wanted to take care of her. Still.

"All right. I'll be as quick as possible. I still want to get going by nightfall."

"Angelica—"

"No time to talk." And she was out the door.

Angelica stalked into the house with her fists clenched and teeth gritted tight against the tears that wanted to pour out of her. "Lou Ann!" she called past the lump in her throat.

"Out here," came a voice from the backyard.

She walked through the kitchen, trying not to look at the table where she and Xavier had shared so many meals with Troy. The counter where they'd leaned together, talking. The window through which she'd watched him playing ball with her son.

The whole place was soaked in memories, and if she and Xavier weren't going to have Troy, if this wasn't going to work, then it was best for them to get out of here now.

She walked through the back door.

"Surprise!"

The sounds of female laughter, the pretty white tablecloth over a round table decorated with flowers, the banner congratulating her and Troy...all of it was totally overwhelming.

She looked around at Lou Ann; Daisy; Xavier's teacher, Susan Hayashi; Miss Minnie Falcon from the Senior Towers; and her two best friends from Boston, Imani and Ruth. She burst into tears.

Immediately the women surrounded her. "It's a surprise shower!"

"We're so happy for you!"

"Aw, she's so emotional!"

"Wait a minute." Lou Ann broke through the squealing circle of women to step right in front of Angelica and look at her face. "Honey, what's wrong?"

Something in her voice made the rest of the women quiet down. Angelica looked into Lou Ann's calm brown eyes and bit her lip. "It's not going to work. Xavier and I are leaving."

"What?" The older woman looked shocked, and around her, gasps and words of dismay echoed in Angelica's ears.

"Come on, sit down and tell us about it," her friend Imani said.

"I think I'll head over to see Troy." The deep voice belonged to Dion, and he waved a hand and headed for the front of the house.

"Go on, we'll catch up with you later," Lou Ann said. "He was helping us set up the canopy," she explained to Angelica.

"What did you mean, you're leaving?" Daisy asked.

So, haltingly, hesitatingly, Angelica explained what had driven her and Troy apart. What was the point in hiding it all now? And they'd be gone, so if any gossip came from this good group of women—which she doubted—it wouldn't hurt Xavier.

"But God's good," she finished, choking out the words. "It looks like Xavier's going to get well."

Hugs and tears and murmurs of support surrounded her.

"Men can be such idiots." Daisy pulled her chair closer to Angelica and squeezed her hand. "My brother most of all."

"That jerk Jeremy most of all," her friend Ruth said.

"So I don't *need* to marry Troy anymore, to help Xavier," Angelica explained, her voice still scratchy. "I mean, of course, he still wants a dad. But he's got time now, and he's got his health. And I can't be with someone who doesn't trust me."

"But what do you *want*?" Imani took her hand. "If Xavier weren't in the equation, would you love Troy? Do you want to be married to him?"

Angelica shut her eyes, and a slide show of memories played through her head.

The first time he'd asked her out, when she'd thought he must be joking, that no one as handsome and rich and popular as Troy could possibly want someone like her.

Riding horses together. Going to her first superfancy restaurant. Looking up to see his marriage proposal in skywriting, in front of the whole town.

Back then, she'd been in love in a naive way. Impressed with him, infatuated with him. And down on herself, seeing no alternatives.

Now things were different. She'd gotten through the past six years by relying on God's strength. With His help, she'd mothered Xavier through the worst moments a child could have and come out stronger. She'd built friendships like those with Ruth and Imani, who'd come all the way from Boston to celebrate a milestone. Now she could add Daisy and Lou Ann to that circle of lifetime friends.

Now she didn't *need* Troy. But the thought of life without him was colorless, plain, lonely.

Now her images of him were different. She thought of him not only helping her get rid of a drunken Buck but also giving her cola and comfort and a shoulder to cry on afterward. She thought of him bent over Bull in the road, caring for the wounded animal and still remembering her son's feelings. Thought of him admitting he'd been wrong to accuse her of still dating Buck, apologizing, going on to find Dr. Ravi for Xavier.

"If he could accept my past without thinking less of me, then yeah." She looked around at the circle of concerned, supportive faces. "Yeah. I still love him."

"All right," Lou Ann said. "Then we've got to find a way to make this right."

A sharp rap on the door made Troy's heart thump in double time: *Angelica*. Maybe she'd decided not to go. Maybe she wanted to talk to him.

He didn't know why he was so eager for that when she'd betrayed him with Jeremy. *If* she'd betrayed him. Because now that his initial anger was fading, he was having a hard time believing that of her.

"I know you're in there, my man," came Dion's deep voice.

"Come on in." Although he was glad to see his friend, needed a friend, Troy couldn't hide his disappointment.

Dion walked in looking anything but friendly. "Angelica's a mess. What did you do to her?"

Troy gave a tiny headshake, nodding toward Xavier. "We're watching Lily. She just had her last pup, and we're making sure she's okay."

"I'm helping," Xavier chimed in, bumping his shoulder against Troy. "Right, Mr. Troy?"

"Yep." Troy could barely choke out the word. How was he going to let this kid go?

Dion narrowed his eyes at Troy and flipped on the television to an old Western, complete with flaming arrows, bareback-riding Navajos and gun-toting cowboys. "Take a look, Xavier. You ever seen a cowboy show before?"

"Angelica wouldn't let..." Troy broke off. A little old-fashioned violence wouldn't hurt the kid. Xavier was immediately engrossed, leaving Dion and Troy free to move to an out-of-earshot spot at the kitchen table.

"What happened?" Dion glared at him.

Troy sighed, laced his hands together. "I found out who Xavier's dad is."

Dion looked at him expectantly.

"Jeremy Filmore."

Dion reared back and stared. "No kidding?"

Troy nodded. "No wonder she didn't want me to know, right? She could hardly claim assault with Jeremy." As he spoke, his anger came bubbling back.

"What do you mean? Does she say he attacked her?"

Troy nodded impatiently. "That's what she says, but I knew Jeremy. He wouldn't have done that."

Dion drummed his fingers on the table, frowning. "You sure about that, man?"

"You're not?"

"He had a pretty bad drinking problem." Dion studied the ceiling. "And he wasn't above clashing with the law. I broke up a few bar fights he started."

"True." And Troy had heard a few rumors, come to think of it, about how awful Jeremy had been to his wife.

"Not only that," Dion said, "but I was on duty for the car crash he died in. He was dead drunk. We didn't publicize that, and it was never in the paper—what would have been the point, when he was the only one involved, except to make his kids feel bad? But I can tell you it's so. I have the police reports to prove it."

"Wow." Jeremy, who'd had such potential, been a powerhouse of a football player, had died drunk. "So, what are you saying?"

"I'm saying that if Jeremy was drinking, he turned into an idiot. One who didn't have the ability to control himself."

"Even to the point of forcing himself on a woman?" The thought of Jeremy doing that to Angelica tapped in to a primal kind of outrage, but Troy fought to stay calm, to think. "Would he go that far, just because he wanted her?"

Dion shook his head. "It's about rage, not desire. They drill that into us at the police academy."

"But why would he be mad at Angelica? It just doesn't compute." Slowly he shook his head. "But it doesn't compute that she's lying, either."

"He was mad at women, period. Remember the so-called jokes he used to tell?"

"Yeah." Troy turned his cane over and over in his hand. "I guess I didn't spend much time with him once we were done with school."

"There could be another reason he kept his distance."

The sound of televised gunshots and war whoops punctuated Dion's words. "He could have felt guilty about what he'd done."

"Getting her pregnant?"

"By force."

Troy pounded his fist on his knee.

"You have some apologizing to do."

Troy heaved out a sigh. "I screwed everything up."

"You might have, but pray Father God forgive you, and He will. Might even help you to make things right."

Troy nodded, staring down at the floor.

"And pray fast," Dion said. "Because there's a lot of estrogen coming our way."

Troy looked out the window Dion was looking out of. Marching in a line toward them, arms linked, were seven or eight women, his sister, Daisy, included. Angelica was at the center, and she looked shell-shocked. The rest of the ladies just looked angry and determined.

Man, was he in for it! But at least Angelica was still here.

Just before the women got within earshot, Angelica pulled away. The other women gathered around her and seemed to be urging her forward, but she shook her head vehemently. Then she broke away from the women and climbed into his truck.

Daisy marched over and yanked open the truck door. She and Angelica exchanged words, and then Angelica slid over to the passenger seat.

Daisy climbed into the driver's seat and they drove away, leaving clouds of dust behind them.

It was a mark of how upset Troy was that he didn't even care that his reckless sister was driving his vehicle.

He just wanted to be in there with Angelica.

The women watched her go and then headed toward the bunkhouse, looking more serious and less angry now.

"You better go out there and face them," Dion advised.

Xavier pushed in between them to look out the window. "Those ladies look mad."

"I know. But they're not mad at you, buddy." He spoke the reassuring words automatically, but his mind wasn't on Xavier. Mostly he wanted to know where Angelica had gone.

As the women reached the bunkhouse, he went out the front door and stood on the porch, arms crossed.

"You stay in here with me, Little Bit," he heard Dion say behind him.

The women stood in a line in front of Troy. "Come down here," said a dark-skinned woman he'd never seen before.

Troy used his cane to make his way halfway down the front steps.

"You've hurt that girl something terrible," Lou Ann said.

The dark-skinned woman added, "You accused her of stuff she didn't do."

"She'd never have cheated on you."

"I...yeah." Troy sat down on the edge of the porch and let his head sink into his hands. He was only now realizing the enormity of what he'd done. He'd made a terrible mistake, maybe lost the best part of his life—Xavier and Angelica. He looked up. "Where'd Angelica go?"

The women consulted and murmured among themselves for a couple of minutes. "We think she went out Highway 93," Lou Ann said finally.

Dion came out behind him, clapped a hand on his shoulder. "If you want to follow her, I can drive you. But not if you're going to make a fool of yourself again."

"No promises. I've already been an idiot. But I want to tell her how sorry I am."

That seemed to make the women happy; there were a couple of approving nods. "Take him out there, Dion," Lou Ann said, "but keep an eye on him."

Angelica knelt at the white roadside cross. *Jeremy Filmore* was painted on the horizontal board; *In loving memory* on the vertical one.

It wasn't his grave, but this was where he'd had his fatal accident. Somehow it had seemed to make more sense to come here, to this place she'd driven by dozens of times, getting mad and hating him with each pass. Never before had she stopped, gotten out of the car and studied it.

Now she saw the plastic flowers, the kids' football, the baby shoe and picture that decorated the cross, all looking surprisingly new, given that he'd died almost five years ago.

It reminded her that Jeremy had had a life, kids, people who loved him enough to keep up a memorial.

How could he be loved when he'd done something so awful?

Her legs went weak and she sank to her knees as regret overcame her. If only she hadn't been drunk that night. If only he hadn't. If only a friend had walked home with them. If only Troy had come out with her.

She'd never understand the why of it, no way. Why had God let it happen, something so awful?

She sat back and hugged her knees to her chest, aching as she remembered the years of hating herself, all the loose, ugly clothes she'd taken to wearing, scared of provoking unwanted male attention. Afraid of being the tramp Jeremy had accused her of being.

"I wasted the best years of my life hating you!" she cried out, pounding the ground, as if Jeremy lay beneath the memorial, as if he could still feel pain. She wanted to hurt him as he'd hurt her. Wanted to make him feel ashamed and awful. Wanted him to lose the love of his life, the way she'd lost Troy, twice now.

"Hey," Daisy said, getting out of the truck. "You okay?"

Angelica kept her eyes closed, her whole body tense as a coiled spring. "I hate him," she said. "I can't make myself stop hating him. I can't forgive him. I thought I could, but I can't."

Daisy knelt and put an arm around her. "He was awful. A complete jerk. No one deserves to be treated the way you were treated."

"I hate him, hate him, hate him! I want him to suffer like I did. I want him to lose everything."

"Can't blame you there. Stinks that he lived in the community like a good person, and meanwhile, you felt like you had to leave."

"Yeah."

A breeze kicked up, and a few leaves fell around them. Fall was coming. Maybe it was already here.

Something was tugging at her. She thought about the years since the assault. "I hurt a lot in the past seven years."

"I know you must have."

"But I also had Xavier and got closer to God and... and grew up. Where Jeremy...he must have always had this in the back of his mind, what he did."

"Nah." Daisy let out a snort. "Guys like that are jerks. He didn't suffer."

"I think he did suffer. I think that's one reason he drank so much."

"Don't try to humanize him. It's okay to hate the guy who assaulted you!"

Angelica hugged Daisy; half laughing through her tears. "You're wonderful. But I don't actually think that it *is* okay to hate."

Daisy rolled her eyes. "Don't go all holy on me."

"I'm not very holy at all." Angelica shifted from her knees to a more comfortable sitting position. "I've always felt guilty myself, because I..." Tears rose to her eyes again. "Because I dressed up pretty and flirted with all the guys at the bar. Including Jeremy." She could barely squeeze the words out past the lump in her throat.

"Oh, give me a break. Men flirt every day and no woman commits assault on them. It wasn't fair, what happened to you." Daisy squeezed her shoulder. "And you totally didn't deserve it."

"You don't think so?"

"No! You'd probably make different decisions today, and you'd probably see more red flags with Jeremy." Daisy's voice went into social-worker mode. "Our brains keep developing and learn from experience. But no way—no *way*—did you deserve to be raped. Whether you flirt or dress up or get drunk, no means no." She squeezed Angelica's shoulder. "And you have to forgive yourself for being a silly twenty-one-year-old."

Daisy's words washed over her like a balm.

If she could forgive herself—the way God forgave her—then maybe she could forgive Jeremy. And get on with her life.

But it wasn't easy. "I'm still mad at myself. And even though I'm figuring it out, I still feel pretty hostile toward Jeremy."

Daisy was weaving a handful of clovers into a long chain. "I have a terrible temper," she said. "Pastor Ricky always tells me that forgiveness is a decision, not a feeling."

Forgiveness is a decision, not a feeling. The words echoed in her mind with the ring of truth.

Behind them, a truck lumbered by, adding a whiff of diesel to the air.

Forgiveness is a decision, not a feeling.

Angelica reached out a finger to the baby shoe that hung on the crossbar. "I know, I've known all along, that God worked it for good by giving me Xavier." She drew in a breath. "Okay. I forgive you, Jeremy."

"And yourself?" Daisy prompted.

"I forgive… I forgive myself, too."

No fireworks exploded, and no church bells rang. But a tiny flower of peace took seed in Angelica's heart. For now, it was enough.

"Now, don't go ballistic," Dion warned Troy. "I think I see Angelica and Daisy up there."

"Why are they out of the car on the highway?"

"They're by a roadside memorial." Dion paused, then added, "For Jeremy Filmore."

Troy's hands balled into fists as Dion slowed the truck to a crawl and drove slowly past Daisy and Angelica. "If this doesn't show she's got feelings for him—"

"I'm sure she does have feelings." Dion pulled the truck off the road and turned off the ignition. "Wouldn't you hate the guy that did what he did?"

"That's not what I—" And Troy stopped. He was doing it again, being a jerk. He had to stop jumping to conclusions about Angelica, about how she felt and what she was doing. It wasn't fair to her or to him or to Xavier.

He sat there and watched while Daisy and Angelica held hands and prayed together. Man, his sister was a good person.

And so was Angelica. Talking with Dion had confirmed what his heart had already suspected: No way would she cheat on him.

He was a fool.

Troy dropped his head into his hands. If Angelica was praying, he should do that, too. She was amazing, always plunging forward and trying to do the right thing, to make a change, to live the way she was supposed to despite the horrible circumstances life always seemed to be throwing at her.

And he, what did he do?

He got his feelings hurt and suffered a minor disability and he fell apart.

He'd tried to fix her life and Xavier's on his own, giving her a job, letting them live on his place, getting medical help, even the marriage proposal. Looking back, it seemed as if he'd been waving his arms around uselessly, acting like some comic-book hero, trying to fix problems way too big for him.

For the first time in his life, he saw—just dimly—that there might be another way. The way that gave Dion his uncanny peacefulness. The way that made Angelica able to kneel by that jerk Jeremy's memorial and pray, after all she'd suffered.

He wanted, needed, that ability to let God in, to trust Him. Most of all, to ask Him for help. To recognize that he himself wasn't God and that God could do better than he could on his own poor human strength.

I'm sorry, God. Help me do better.

It was a simple prayer, but when he lifted his head, he felt some kind of peace. And when he looked over at Dion, he saw his friend smile. "What do you say I take Daisy home so you and Angelica can have some time?" he asked.

"That's a good idea."

Troy got out of the truck then and limped over to the two women. When he got there, Daisy stood and studied his face. Then, nodding as if satisfied, she walked back toward Dion's truck.

Leaving Troy to kneel beside Angelica.

She finished her prayer, turned and looked at him. Eyes full of wisdom but guarded against the pain he might inflict.

He reached out hesitantly and touched her dark hair.

She didn't flinch away. Just studied his face.

A car whizzed by behind them. Another. The sound faded away into the horizon, and quiet fell.

He looked down at the cross for Jeremy. A man who'd done something so horrendous to the woman he loved. Reflexively his fist clenched. "I could kill him."

Angelica reached out and put her hand over his. "He's gone. Leave it to God." Her voice shook a little, and when he looked away from Jeremy's cross and into her eyes, he saw that they were shiny with tears.

One overflowed, rolled down her cheek. "You kicked us out. You didn't believe me."

"I'm so sorry." He relaxed his fist and reached out slowly to thumb the tears away. "I love you. I never stopped loving you. Can you forgive me?"

There was a moment's silence. Long enough for him to feel the cooling breeze against his back and smell the sweet, pungent zing of ozone. It was going to rain.

"I don't know." She knelt there, her face still wet with tears, and studied him seriously. As though she was trying to read him. "I love you, too, Troy. But I can't live with being distrusted, and I can't live with someone who thinks I'm a bad person inside."

"You're the best person I know!" The words burst out of him and he realized they were the exact truth. She'd gone through so much, and with such faith, and there was humility and wisdom and dignity in every move she made, every word she spoke. "Look, I screwed up, and I screwed up bad. I want to spend the rest of my life making it up to you. Even that won't be enough, but I want to try."

"Really?"

"Yeah, really." He touched her hand, tentatively, carefully. "I can't guarantee I'll never make another mistake, but I can guarantee it won't be about who you are inside."

She didn't look convinced.

He blundered on. "Like, I tend to be jealous."

She lifted an eyebrow. "No kidding. Right?"

"It's just, I know how incredible you are, and I see other men seeing it, and it makes me crazy."

Her lips tightened. "I'm not flattered by that, Troy. It's not a good thing."

"I know. I'm willing to do whatever I need to do to fix this. Read self-help books. Get counseling. Join Dion's men's group at church."

"That," she said instantly. "That's what you need. Other men to rein you in when you go all macho."

"I'll call him tomorrow." He took both of her hands in his. "Look, Angelica, I'm nowhere near as good of a person as you are. But I need you to know that I'll do everything in my power to protect you and Xavier. I'll take care of you and love you for the rest of my days. And I will never, ever tell you to leave again."

She looked steadily into his eyes as if she was reading him, judging him. And she had the right. She had to protect her son.

Finally her face broke into a smile. "I'm not a better person than you are. I've made plenty of mistakes and I'm sure I'll make more."

"Does this mean..." He trailed off, hardly daring to hope.

To his shock, she laughed, a pure, joyous sound. "You caught me on the right day," she said. "I'm on a forgiveness roll."

He took her face in his hands and was blown away by the sheer goodness of who she was. "I don't deserve you. You're...you're amazing, inside and out. I..." He ran out of words. *Way to go, Hinton. Smooth with the ladies, as always.*

She lifted her eyebrows, a tiny smile quirking the corner of her mouth. "Does this mean... What does this mean?"

She looked at peace about whether he wanted to

marry her or not, whether they had a future or not. She had that glow of faith. She'd always had it, but it glowed brighter now.

He had so much to learn from her. And what could he, with his gimpy leg and his ignorant rages and his general guy immaturity, offer her?

Little enough, but if he could ease her parenting burdens and listen to her problems and protect her from anyone—anyone!—who so much as looked sideways at her, he wanted to do it. Would devote his life to doing it.

"It means," he said, "that I want you to marry me. For real. Forever. I want to help you and support you and be Xavier's dad. And I want it for the rest of our lives, through thickheadedness and illness and whatever else life throws at us. If you'll have me."

She looked at him with love glowing in her eyes. "Of course I will."

And as they embraced, the sky opened up and a warm, gentle rain started to fall, offering God's blessing on their new beginning.

Fifteen

"That was awesome, Mom!"

Angelica turned toward her son's excited voice, only slightly slowed down by her wedding dress. Pure white. Traditional. What she'd always wanted.

"What was awesome, honey? The wedding?"

"No, the ride in a Hummer!"

Of course, her healthy, normal son had loved their unorthodox ride back from the church more than fidgeting through the wedding ceremony and receiving line.

Now they were back at the farm for the reception, which Lou Ann had insisted on orchestrating. There were two canopies set up, in case the warm October sunshine turned to rain, and Angelica could smell the good hearty dinner that was on buffet tables for the guests.

A small wedding, but meaningful. Just what she'd hoped for...and for many years hadn't dreamed possible for herself.

Since forgiving Jeremy that day by the side of the

road, since feeling the sincerity of Troy's love and belief in her, she'd felt light enough to fly.

Gramps hustled over to give her a hug. "Did I tell you how beautiful you look?"

"About a dozen times, but it's okay." She kissed his grizzled cheek. "Thank you for walking me down the aisle. You've been wonderful today. I'm so grateful."

"Not sure about the rest of those Hintons, but Troy is all right." Troy had tried to talk Gramps into moving out of the Senior Towers and into the bunkhouse. When Gramps had refused, insisting on staying with his friends, Troy had helped him move into a bigger apartment at the Towers, paying the difference in rent secretly to save the old man's pride.

That was part of what she loved about Troy: he was willing to change, to break from the long-held Hinton animosity toward Gramps, to embrace her family with all its flaws.

Lou Ann had ridden from the church with Troy's father. As she emerged, radiant in a maroon dress and hat, from Mr. Hinton's vintage Cadillac, Gramps sniffed. "I'm gonna go over there and make sure he's not bothering Lou Ann. He always did have a crush on her."

People were all arriving now, and Angelica watched Lou Ann rush away from both men with an eye roll, hurrying on to direct the caterers and welcome guests. Angelica hadn't wanted a big fancy reception, but thanks to Lou Ann, everything was simple and perfect, from the centerpieces—a pretty mix of sunflowers, orange dahlias and autumn leaves—to the bluegrass band strumming lively music.

"Hey, Mom, look!" Xavier came out of the kennels, his suit knees dusty. "I have a 'prise for you!"

"You'll want to watch this," Troy said, coming up behind her. He wrapped his arms around her middle and she swayed back against him. He made her dizzy...in a good way. A very good way.

"Mom, pay attention!" Xavier stood frowning, hands on hips.

Troy chuckled into her ear, and Angelica laughed with self-conscious delight. It amazed her that she could feel so attracted to Troy, that it was easy and good to be close to him. No more cringing, no more fear. She trusted him completely.

She was getting back the girl she'd been, with God's help. He truly did make all things new.

She eased herself over to Troy's side, where she could breathe a little more easily. "What's the surprise, sweetie?" she called to her son.

"Lily's dressed up for the wedding!" Xavier yelled, so loud that everyone turned to see.

The rescued pit bull, her collar decorated with yellow roses, emerged from the barn with a line of puppies behind her. Amid the happy murmur of the guests, Xavier's voice rang out again. "Look what else!"

He whistled, and Bull came running full tilt from the barn.

Angelica did a double take. How was Bull moving so fast?

And then she realized that his back legs were supported by a doggie wheelchair, also decorated with yellow and white flowers. As he zigzagged after Xavier, Angelica pressed her hands to her mouth, amazed.

"We've been practicing with him for a couple of weeks," Troy said. "Xavier was determined that Bull could come to the wedding and play."

And trust Troy to make it happen, to take the time to work with Xavier and the dog and to keep the surprise for her.

"Come and get it, everyone!" Lou Ann called, and people flowed toward the tables to eat, stopping to greet them on the way. And there were hugs. So many hugs.

As she and Troy stood there arm in arm, welcoming their guests, Angelica lifted her face to the afternoon sunshine and thanked God for all He'd done for them.

Xavier barreled up toward them, and at the same time, both Troy and Angelica reached out to hold him. "Our whole family," Angelica said, rubbing her son's head, roughened by newly sprouted hair. Joy bubbled up inside her, rich and full and satisfying.

"Well…" Troy said, sounding guilty.

"Mom? There's one other thing. Dad and I have been talking about it."

"What?" She stepped out of Troy's embrace to frown in mock exasperation at her two men. "Are you guys conspiring against me?"

"What's 'spiring?"

"Hatching a secret plan, buddy. And…kinda. Tell her, Zavey."

Her son reached out and took one of her hands and one of Troy's. "I want a little sister."

"Oh, Zavey Davey…" She looked up at Troy as her mind flashed back to a family she'd seen in the park. Mom, Dad and two children, one an adorable little girl.

She hadn't thought it was possible God could be so good to her, but now she knew He could.

The last of her old doubts about the future faded away at the sight of Troy's smile. "What do you think?"

"I think it's a distinct possibility." He gave her a quick wink and reached out to pull her back into his arms.

* * * * *